To Tiac

15⁹⁵ N

cry of the banshee

MW00759922

Be prepared to be scared!

history & hauntings of west virginia and the ohio valley

by susan sheppard
with additional stories by richard southall

Susan Sheppard

- A Whitechapel Productions Press Publication -

10 / 15 / 2005

We dedicate this book to the memory of William Brett "Bo" Kitchens, a special soul who appeared to us for a few, brief hours, yet one we will always remember..

Original Cover Artwork Designed by
Michael Schwab, M & S Graphics & Troy Taylor
Visit M & S Graphics at www.msgrfx.com

THIS BOOK IS PUBLISHED BY

- Whitechapel Productions Press -
A Division of the History & Hauntings Book Co.
515 East Third Street - Alton, Illinois -62002
(618) 465-1086 / 1-888-GHOSTLY
Visit us on the Internet at www.historyandhauntings.com

First Edition - April 2004
ISBN: 1-892523-36-1

Printed in the United States of America

Probably my earliest memories are of times when the power would go out and we would have to get down the kerosene lamps. My grandmother used these times to the best advantage by telling ghost stories --- or "booger" tales. I don't remember the tales as such, but I can remember the lamp that lighted only her face as she recalled the choicest horrors of her childhood --- That the people of this region should have a rich supply of "haint" tales is not at all surprising. They had conquered the land but only in a small area outside their doors. No matter how friendly the woods seemed in daylight, there were noises and mysterious lights out there at night that were hard to ignore if you were out there alone!

david wilson ⋍⋍ foxfire books

Ghosts are creatures of twilight. Apparitions emerge from the sunless hollows of the mind, glide from the corner of the eye, flit about in the dusky half-light of a forgotten structure or in the damp shade of a brier-tangled thicket. The sun disappears below the horizon and murky half-shadows appear. Even the sophisticated citizen becomes apprehensive at the approach of an all-encompassing darkness that cannot be controlled and that still holds unknown terrors.

charles edwin price ⋍⋍ haints, witches & boogers

From the most ancient days, men have not merely believed in ghosts; they claim to have seen them, heard them and even to have touched them --- and the mystery remains unsolved. As far as science goes, there has never been a satisfactory answer – none of the natural sciences has ever determined whether or not there are any rips in the impalpable curtain that divides the natural world or our experience from all the tremendous mystery that lies beyond.
Many attempts however have been made.

from great tales of terror & the supernatural

Remember me as you pass by
As you are now, so once was I
As I am now, so you must be
Prepare for death & Follow me
early american epitaph

table of contents

cry of the banshee

introduction

In Appalachia, the word "haint" isn't necessarily a crude misuse of the English language. In old-timey terms, a 'haint' is merely a haunt – a meddlesome ghost or spirit, a mysterious force that that is somehow visited upon you, your neighbor or your kin.

Haints are the lost souls that haunt crumbling houses, spirits who vex you at the Crossroads, wraiths who doom you in dark hollows or ghosts that chase your sorry self through old, abandoned railroad tunnels. They are the nightmares that ride you and startle you awake at night. Haints can be regrets or feelings of dread that somehow find ways into your consciousness... just to devil you, so they say.

In this book, haints become death-shrouded Banshees that keen along isolated riverbeds while washing out the bloody clothes of the dead. They are women-in-white that linger along the shorelines of the Ohio River's mystifying islands. Haints are the apparitions of John Brown and his men, abolitionists who lost their fight in the streets of Harpers Ferry. Haints are wisps that wait along long ago Indian mounds. They are the souls of the unquiet dead who don't have their business settled yet – ones that stalk us in the indigo darkness of West Virginia's foreboding hills.

The Allegheny and Appalachian mountain region of the United States is steeped in the history of ghosts, weird creatures and restless spirits and has been from the beginning. After all, Native American Indians steered clear of what is now West Virginia, because they viewed it as a troublesome place, plagued by angry ghosts and even more menacing monsters. Perhaps the terrain itself (once you make it down one hill it is already the time to climb up another one) simply wasn't a convenient place for the Seneca, Delaware, Cherokee, Mingo and Shawnee peoples to settle. They were superstitious about the lands that fell between the Potomac and Ohio rivers and pretty well stuck to the waterways, claiming their prizes of flint, fish and game along the way.

The earliest European settlers, the Irish-Scottish, the English and the Germans, brought their own views about ghosts and other incredible beings or creatures. Later came other ideas through the African-Native-European tri-racial isolates called Guineas (West Virginia's version of a Creole) and even Gypsy/Rom beliefs in the supernatural through its mysterious Black Dutch, then the Black Irish population, a group that is probably Pictish, as well as the barely northern Pennsylvania Dutch.

The Celtic/Pictish peoples brought to the Allegheny Mountain and Ohio Valley regions a belief in banshees, witches, haints, and Will O' the Wisps. In fact, from the word 'Pict" (a diminutive early people of the British Isles) was created the word "pixie." Through the early German/ Pennsylvania Dutch came the poltergeists, doppelgangers, hexing and hexens (witches). Africans and Guineas added devils, boogers and spooks while the Black Dutch included the concept of the Crossroads as a place of spiritual danger, combining Rom/Gypsy/Pennsylvania Dutch Powwow magic with ghosts, and graveyard ghouls who had masqueraded earlier in Eastern Europe as vampires.

While these groups intermixed, they were still remote to such a degree that words that were an archaic form of the Queen's English were still being spoken in the foothills and valleys as late as the 1960s. This isolation created a unique blend of ideas when it came to ghosts, spirits, boogers and things that go bump in the night. After all, there was plenty of time to think about and more than enough time to tell and re-tell such tales.

In the mid 20th Century, Appalachian haints assumed a modern persona through a surprising number of UFO and creature sightings in West Virginia and the Ohio Valley. None more famous than the West Virginia Mothman, the Flatwoods monster and the UFO contactee tale of Woodrow Derenberger and the alien Indrid Cold that occurred near Mineral Wells in November of 1966. Many such strange stories parallel ancient European fairy tales where the unsuspecting are abducted by fairies, spirited away at night into alternate realms of awareness and experience.

That explains the folklore, but what about the science of ghosts? If anything, ghosts and their related folklore don't just belong to the past. They also belong to the here and now where hauntings – such as those at the Blennerhassett Hotel in downtown Parkersburg and sightings of John Brown at Harpers Ferry – are ongoing and ever evolving. Reports of ghosts are now being studied with tools of the 21st Century, such as digital cameras, electronic voice phenomena, electromagnetic detectors, camcorders, infra-red photography, heat monitors and numerous other kinds of equipment that now belong to the over one-hundred-year-old science of ghosts that evolved from the 19th Century Spiritualism.

It is getting more difficult for skeptics to disprove that "something isn't out there," things of a more spiritual nature that we are yet to truly understand. In this book, *Cry Of The Banshee*, we look at the various related phenomena considered to be our haints, ghosts, apparitions, contactees, mothmen, banshees and other unexplained occurrences that can only fall under the category of the paranormal.

Through our study of ghosts, we are reminded, time and time again, of the classic movie 'The Wizard of Oz," of a scene in the haunted forest that takes place at the crossroads. It is here Dorothy, Tin Man, Scarecrow and the Cowardly Lion re-consider their quest for the witch's broom. The first sign points up a winding road that reads: This Way To The Witch's Castle while the second sign says: I'd Turn Back If I Were You!

Are the perils of chasing ghosts worth the trouble? Yes. Every human being has a right to explore the mysterious – even against risk or ridicule.

Over the past years of a great adventure, our midnights were spent in two-hundred-year-old graveyards. In summer afternoons, we crawled through foul rooms of abandoned buildings—possessed by angry ghosts. We have sat in darkened places waiting for spirits to come. We scrutinized dozens of mysterious photographs sent by enthusiasts who visited the ghost tour. We followed up on ghostly leads and attended séances.

We embraced the light. And we embraced the gloom.

It is through such connections in spirit that we tunneled our way out of our fears and allowed those fears to see the light of day.

Near the end, we are once again reminded of the movie "The Wizard of Oz" when Scarecrow, Tin Man and the Cowardly Lion all receive their badges and degrees of honor. After the ceremony, the Wizard reminds the Cowardly Lion that he was really courageous all along. His answer is much like ours:

"Hain't it da truth! Hain't it da truth!"

--Susan Sheppard
Parkersburg, West Virginia
October 31, 2003

1. tales of appalachian banshees

Double, Double toil and trouble;
Fire burn and cauldron bubble.
Cool It with a baboon's blood.
Then the charm is firm and good.
O, well done, I commend your pains.
And now about the cauldron sing
Like elves and fairies in a ring.
By the pricking of my thumbs,
Something wicked this way comes

from 'macbeth' by william shakespeare

Not all fairy tales have happy endings. Not all fairies bring goodness and light. Among the Irish and Scottish people there is a supernatural creature they call "the Banshee."

The Banshee is an attendant death fairy, one that brings an omen of doom to Irish or Scottish clans. It is the Banshee that announces the death of a family member, usually over bodies of water with her keening, or *caoine*, a shrill crying for the dead.

But the Banshee doesn't just stay near bodies of water washing out the grave clothes of the dead as it is told. She also travels to the homes of those about to die, sometimes mounted on a pale steed or riding a black funeral coach with two, pale headless horses leading the way.

There are various descriptions of the Banshee. The Irish Banshee is called Bean Sidhe in an older tongue. Depending upon what source you use, "Bean" means woman and "Sidhe" means fairy. But other sources say that Bean Sidhe is translated as "woman of the hills." Some ancient lore says the Banshee can even be the ghost of a young woman who has died in childbirth, especially if she was not given the last rites of confession.

The Irish Banshee is described as a beautiful young woman with streaming auburn hair. She is said to wear a green woolen dress with gray cloak clasped about her shoulders. The Irish Banshee hangs out at rivers and waterfalls. The only hint that this beautiful Banshee is a messenger of doom comes from the fact that her eyes are blood red from crying for her dead.

The Scottish Banshee, the "Bean Nighe," is more menacing. The Scottish Banshee dresses in moldering grave clothes, her face covered by a tattered veil. Often, she rides a white dancing steed. Her age and features are difficult to make out but she appears to be an old crone. And yet, the Banshee's movements are lithe and she rides her pale horse sometimes with a black hearse following behind her. Rarely, the shroud of the Scottish Banshee is crimson, reddened by the gore of blood.

The Mid-Ohio Valley as well as West Virginia was settled predominantly of people of Irish and Scottish ancestry. Along with the Welsh and French, they shard ancient Celtic ties and are descended from clans. The Celts believed in unique forms of mysticism, such as sorcerers, witches, leprechauns and fairies, and not the least of them – the Banshee.

Stories of Banshee spirits went underground as Irish and Scottish immigrants moved into the green hills of the Ohio Valley and West Virginia. But the legend of the Banshee is not entirely forgotten, as you will see by reading the following pages.

Let us travel back to the shores of Scotland on a blustery winter day in the year 1590. A group of women, known later as the Berwick Witches, summoned their powers at the ocean's edge. Over the icy waters of the North Sea, King James VI and his new bride Anne of Denmark made their way back to Scotland when their boat nearly capsized. Later, rumors circulated that King James was in great danger from a plot or a curse put upon him by the witches of North Berwick.

This quickly caught King James's attention, since he had always been fascinated by witchcraft. It wasn't long until the supposed witches were captured and put on trial.

One young woman, called Gilly Duncan, confessed under torture that she and other witches cursed the King, and were intent upon murdering him by chanting spells and evil curses. She also claimed that she and other witches were in cahoots with the Earl of Boswell, first in line to the throne after King James's death, and they wished him dead.

King James's morbid fascination with witchcraft only fed his paranoid delusions about the mysterious powers of woman. It was during James's translation of the King James Bible that he changed the Hebrew word for "poisoner" into the

English word for "witch," two terms that are hardly interchangeable. The word stuck however, and the rest is history.

King James had earlier written a treatise against witchcraft. Wild claims about the Devil being intent upon murdering King James were made and rumors flew. It was reported back to King James that a group of Scottish witches had gathered at night near a castle in Edinburgh where they fashioned a waxen image, or witch's poppet (a European version of a voodoo doll) of the King. In front of a raging bonfire, the witches passed the wax doll amongst themselves, chanting in unison: "This is King James the VI, ordained to be consumed at the instance of a nobleman, Francis Hepburn, Earl of Bothwell." The witches' poppet was tossed into the flames and it melted away instantly.

Did this event happen as it was told? This is highly doubtful.

But the story fit in perfectly with what the King already believed, making him even more determined to hunt down the witches who were "persecuting" him. More "witches" were brought forth and the King himself interrogated them. It was alleged that 200 witches met at a Church in North Berwick on All Hallows Eve to curse King James again. It was then told that the Devil himself presided over the meeting wearing a black mask, preaching obedience to him and bringing great evil against the King. Unable to stay quiet a moment longer, King James interjected and called the witches present liars.

For some inexplicable reason, one of the witches gestured for the King to come closer. She whispered words King James had spoken to his wife on their wedding night. No one knew why the woman would do such a thing. It sealed their doom.

The witches were later executed at Edinburgh's Castle Hill. But it did not end there. In later years, Scottish witches were "brought to justice" at MacBeth's Hill near the town of Nairn. Witchcraft had a strong hold in Scotland. Scottish rule executed 4,400 alleged witches. Only a handful of witches were executed in England and Ireland. Next to Germany, Scotland murdered more people during their witch trials than any other country.

In light of our tale, if the names of "Duncan" and "MacBeth" sound familiar, there is a reason for it. It has long been thought that King James held great influence over William Shakespeare and was even responsible for Shakespeare's unflattering portrayal of Scottish witches in his play "Macbeth." James supported the works of Shakespeare, whose famous plays came about later.

King James was certainly one of the most literate of all British Kings and Shakespeare's *Macbeth* was written only seventeen years after initial royal paranoia about the Berwick witches, a long enough time for the imagination to fodder and take certain liberties with the actual story.

Most of the scenes for *MacBeth* took place at Glamis Castle, allegedly the most haunted castle in Scotland. This was even acknowledged in the day of Shakespeare.

But Scotland's influence on public thought having to do with witches and witchcraft did not end there. Many trials and executions were to follow later.

And yet the powers of witchcraft still lurked in Scotland's remote forests, in those rolling, mystic mountains of gloom.

North of Aberdeen, there is a haunted place called the "Forest of Marr." It is believed this is the area where some of the Scottish witches escaped. As they went underground, the witches' occult powers grew. It is told that the ghosts of the executed witches eventually became Banshee spirits and continued to roam the countryside bringing death to the Scottish Clans who backed King James or were responsible for their persecution.

From that area of Scotland to Wood County, came a family named "Marr." Some might say their lives were marred by tragedy. And now we begin our first tale – moving from the dark reaches of Scotland into the even darker reaches of West Virginia...

the banshee of marrtown

On certain lonely, moonless nights in the Mid-Ohio Valley, under a sky littered with stars, riding over the hills of Marrtown, there appears a shrouded figure on a white horse— one that is known as "the Banshee of Marrtown."

Marrtown was once a small farming community southeast of the city of Parkersburg. The family of Scottish immigrant Thomas Marr settled Marrtown in 1836. Thomas later married a local woman named Mary Disosche. The Marr family brought to America many of the ancient beliefs and superstitions from their native land of Scotland, in a mysterious region called Marr, where a belief in banshees, witches and ghosts remained strong.

The daughter of a widow, Mary Marr was an autumn bride, considered to be an ill omen by the Scottish people. In years to come, Mary would lose six of the eight children that she bore. Only two would carry on the Marr name.

Times were hard for Thomas and Mary Marr but they did not lose their dream of a better life, pouring their energies into a simple tract of land that is now Marrtown.

Soon, a picturesque white farmhouse stood against shadowy woods thick with sumac, milkweed and blackberry brambles, framed by a sweeping green valley. To the west of the Marr homestead was a steep hill that ran directly into the Ohio River. To the north was Fort Boreman Hill, where Union troops camped during the Civil War, and where a Pest House housed locals and soldiers who had contracted typhoid fever and small pox.

The years of the Civil War, as for most, were not happy ones for the Marr Family. They lost two of their children to typhoid fever. From their front window Thomas and Mary witnessed small clashes that turned into bloody battles between Yankee and Confederate soldiers. There were public hangings on nearby Fort Boreman Hill. As the Civil War drew to a close, marauding soldiers from both sides stole freely from the Marrs, making off with what food and stock the family had put away for themselves.

Shortly after the Civil War, the Marr family's Scottish brew of bad luck appeared to come to an end. Thomas landed a job as night watchman at the toll bridge that crossed over the Little Kanawha River from lower Parkersburg to the road leading into Marrtown. Mary would stay home to tend the farm and children. Still, there were ominous hints of what was about to unfold.

On several occasions as Thomas traveled to and from his work, he mentioned to Mary about seeing a robed figure riding a white horse. Thomas said that he came upon this rider nearly every night in the identical spot not far from his farmhouse. It was as if their paths were fated to meet. Mr. Marr said he was not able to determine the gender of the person on the horse. The face remained covered by a tattered hood. Whenever Thomas tried to approach the shrouded figure, the white mare reared. Horse and rider then disappeared into the mists of morning. Some sense told Thomas that the person was a woman but he couldn't be sure.

On a cold February night in the year 1876, Mary sat by the front window awaiting Thomas to come home from his job. Earlier, Mary had awakened suddenly and was eager to see her husband. The middle-aged woman heard footsteps coming up the road. She stood up to peer out the window. But instead of Thomas, a white horse walked up to the front gate of the house and then stopped. Sitting atop the horse was a rider whose face was covered by a ragged veil. It looked to be a woman. Alarmed, Mary moved from her chair and walked outside into the frigid night air. The rider, dressed in the tattered clothes of a beggar, remained silent.

As bitter winds gusted, Mary pulled her woolen shawl close. Mary asked the rider what she wanted. There was no answer. Plumes of icy air billowed from the nostrils of the white horse. As Mary repeated her question, rider and horse inched closer. The decrepit woman sat stiffly in her saddle. Underneath the gauzy veil, Mary saw that the woman's eyes radiated an eerie red glow.

After a few moments, the woman on the horse spoke. "I am here to tell you, Mary Marr, that Thomas Marr has just died. Say your prayers, Lady. I bid you well. " Rider and horse turned abruptly and galloped away.

Mary collapsed onto the front stoop. Through tears, she watched the shrouded woman and her horse vanish entirely just as they reached the bend in the road. Within the hour, a man who worked with Thomas came to deliver the dreaded news.

No one knows for sure what happened to Thomas Marr that fated winter evening. Some say that while working at the toll bridge Thomas was shot by an assailant's bullet then fell and drowned in the Little Kanawha River. Others claim that it was the cry of the Banshee that startled Thomas into meeting his end in the river below. Other reports have him found dead along the B&O railroad tracks only a few yards away from the turbulent waters. After all, it is known that the keening of the Banshee is most often heard over bodies of water. The truth is, Thomas Marr did die on February 5th, 1878 when the Marrtown Banshee was to have made her visit, and she had to cross water to do so.

In years to come, the Banshee did not abandon her Marr clan just yet. The ghostly rider continued to make other visits to the family.

Mary Marr lived to be ninety years old. Such advanced years were an exception for the time. As Mary lay as a corpse in the parlor of her home many years after her husband's death, family members heard the rattling of chains in the attic. Others claimed to hear the shrieks of a woman near the house around the same time.

A few years after Mary died, one of the Marr children had his hand cut off in a tragic accident. As family members sat up with the boy, they heard snarling and growling sounds on the porch. When the women went outside to see what is was, the stoop where Mary met her Banshee was covered with blood as if a terrible struggle had taken place.

What has become of the Banshee of Marrtown? It is said she still rides, giving dreaded omens to those of Scottish Blood. Not Scottish or Irish, you say? You would still be wise to avoid Marrtown on certain still, dark and moonless nights...

the banshee of center point

Banshees aside, if you have ever had the opportunity to fly over West Virginia and the Mid-Ohio Valley in a small plane, you may have noticed the foliage below appears as dense and electric-green as that of a rainforest, an excellent place for harboring fugitives but terrible for your sinuses!

In a time where most of the wilderness in the U.S. is vanishing, West Virginia is still "wild and wonderful," as the slogan says. But what kind of "wildness" may mean something other than what the travel ads claim. Native American tribes were afraid of these lands. Generally, the Indians did not settle what is now West

Virginia, thinking it cursed by ghosts and strange beasts. The Shawnee Indians were especially spooked by the lands east of the Ohio River and avoided it as much as possible.

There is a community in a remote part of Doddridge County called Center Point, a place that is now a virtual ghost town. Center Point is typical of small mountain communities reclaimed by the woods. The village used to have a post office and the Ross Country Store, but that is all but gone. A craggy, brown creek courses through lush foliage with leaves as big as mud flaps. Modest white houses cling to the sides of hills, with sloping yards made muddy by children at play.

In Center Point, there isn't much for children to do other than chase each other with sticks or head for the creek in search of the little brown clots with pinchers known so familiar to West Virginians as "crawdads."

Unless you're crazy about pleasant green scenery, country areas, like Center Point, can be pretty dull. That is, until the summer of 1918, when the Black Flu hit. That was the year when the people of Center Point thought the entire world was coming to an end. The rest of the world did, too. Millions had already died.

Unless you were a seven-year-old girl named Pearl White who loved to play in the woods then dreamed of flapping her arms and flying away like a bird, a place like Center Point left one with little to do. But there was plenty for Pearl to do. She had drive and imagination. She wasn't worried about the Black Flu. Sickness happened to people older than she was and Pearl was invincible. Why, she almost knew how to fly already!

It was near dusk in late summer. Pearl was staying with her Grandmother at Center Point on the farm while relatives traveled to Pennsboro to help those already stricken by Black Flu. Like so many of the flu victims, Pearl's young, unmarried uncle had taken sick but appeared to be doing fine. His flu wasn't much worse than a chest cold. It did seem odd how the Black Flu preyed upon those in the full bloom of life. Many victims that succumbed to the Black Flu were young, only in their twenties and thirties. But Pearls' uncle was in good spirits, sitting up and talking as the day wore on.

Evening drew in. The indigo of twilight was soon upon them. The night was clear. There was not one cloud among the stars. Flickering lights studded the evening sky. Pearl counted them as the Big Dipper, the belt of Orion, the North Star and dreamed of flying to all of them. Center Point was small, but the world was still hers.

Pearl's grandmother was in the process of taking her granddaughter to the outhouse one more time. Before it was the time to go to bed when they heard the clip-clop sound of horses' hooves coming up the road.

The trot was slow and measured. Whoever it was didn't seem to be in a hurry. They looked around to see a rider on a horse. Grandmother thought, perhaps it was the mailman paying a late visit. After all, the Black Flu had taken its toll on

Center Point. Many people had died. Mail could arrive at just about anytime of day or evening.

Pearl and her grandmother paused to watch the rider and horse make their way toward the farmhouse. Crickets sang in the shadows.

It seemed strange how the figure sat erect on the horse and was enshrouded in pale, fluttering rags, almost like a mummy. The horse itself was also pale like a ghost. The gender of the rider could not be made out either although something told them it was a woman.

Pearl felt an urge to draw near the figure. She was curious and ran toward the front porch, where the horse and rider seemed to be intent upon stopping. Her grandmother followed Pearl. Now they could see that the rider looked more like an old woman and still, the little girl was not sure. The rider's face was covered by what was a torn, ragged veil. Garnet red eyes glittered beneath the gauzy fabric. The hands looked old and waxen, too, like those that had been sealed tight within a coffin.

Pearl's grandmother recoiled but still the little girl ran to meet the figure on the horse anyway. They sauntered up the front walk. The sun was entirely gone, the world left in shadows. The rider tugged on the bridle and the horse stopped. In later years, Pearl would say that she was so close to that Banshee's horse that she could feel it's hot breath on her face.

Yes, those of Celtic blood called this creature a Banshee. Pearl and her relatives were of Scottish descent and this is a classic way that the Scottish Banshee appears, always as a shrouded figure.

And yet, on that fated night in Center Point the Banshee spirit issued a warning. She pointed a bony finger at Pearl's Grandmother and proclaimed in a rasping voice, "One of yours is to die this very night!" A keening cry split the evening's stillness. The Banshee and her horse instantly vanished.

Shaken and left in shadows, Pearl and her grandmother hugged each other. But there was no time to think about the terrible thing that had just happened. Already sounds were coming from the house, sounds of someone struggling for air.

It was Pearl's uncle. The two ran inside just in time to realize that the young man's lungs were filling with fluid. Blood foamed from his nose and mouth. This was the usual way people died when they had the Black Flu. Grandmother knew it. There was no saving him. Within moments, Pearl's uncle had drowned in his own blood. After the death rattle, all became still, except for the sound of horses' hooves galloping away. It was then something squalled like a wildcat.

Despite the evening when she witnessed her uncle's terrible death from the Black Flu, Pearl White grew up and she did learn to fly. She became a pioneer in the field of aviation and was the first woman to parachute out of a plane. Pearl was a member of the "Barnstormers," a name given to pilots who performed dangerous stunts.

Pearl performed her stunts all the way from the Pennsboro Fair in 1935 to the movies in Hollywood, California. If you have ever watched the movie "Sunset Boulevard," her name is mentioned in that movie.

In her life, Pearl White feared very little. In fact, as a young woman she loved danger. When she was just at the age of sixteen, men would strap Pearl's body to the belly of a plane, go up and then swoop down so she could pick up small objects off the ground. She broke her back one time, and that was at Ravenswood, West Virginia in 1935.

But in later years, Pearl was often afraid to sit outside on her front porch at her modest home on upper Juliana Street. There was something that disturbed her... the coming on of night.

Pearl was not afraid to be strapped to a plane and fly through the air. She was not afraid to jump out of one as a teenager. After meeting up with the Center Point Banshee as a small child the only thing Pearl White was ever afraid of – was the dark.

the coach-a-bower of mineral wells

The Banshee has a power that she shares with witches, and that is the power of glamoury. Glamoury is a Gaelic word that simply means to 'shape shift' to alter ones self at will. To some, glamoury is an illusion. To others glamoury is real.

Witches are said to master glamoury by turning into birds, animals or even a more attractive or younger person. But in Ireland, Scotland and West Virginia the Banshee sometimes takes on another form, one that is neither animal nor human.

Along Route 14, between the small communities of Mineral Wells and Elizabeth, the Banshee assumes the disquieting form of a death omen. In Gaelic it is called the Coiste-Bodhar, or the 'Coach-A-Bower,' a black hearse with a coffin strapped to the top and lead by two white headless horses. In Ireland and Scotland, the Coach-A-Bower often precedes the visit of the Banshee. And since the Banshee appears at households to announce a death, you would best do well not to open the door when you hear the rumbling of a carriage outside for it is then the darker side of the Banshee's fairy powers of the Coach-A-Bower become evident. Those who are unwise enough to open the door are met with a basin of blood tossed into their faces.

However, even in the quiet meadows and mossy woods of West Virginia, the Coach-A-Bower is updated. It is a phantom black hearse that winds its way along Route 14 between Mineral Wells and Elizabeth. And yet, the hearse is not entirely modern. It appears to be one from the time of the 1950s, perhaps even earlier.

A spiritualist group meets in Mineral Wells once a month upon every Full Moon. They have done so for a few years, and many evenings are spent communicating with spirits from other realms. No one had given a thought to the idea of a Banshee appearing!

In the spring of 1998, one séance lasted well past midnight. As one of the participants got into her car to go home, she noticed that the air had grown quite chilly and the full moon, that now looked to be the size of a pearl, had slipped behind veils of black clouds. As the woman proceeded with her drive on Route 14 toward Parkersburg from Mineral Wells, she soon noticed that she was trailing a black hearse.

As the hearse ambled through the hills, it looked shiny but dangerous, like a loaded gun. In the mist and fog, it's taillights blinked like a pulse. The woman thought that it was odd that a hearse would be out at such a late hour. What was more strange, was the fact that the hearse, with pulled velvet curtains, appeared to be from a different era like a relic put in antique car shows, or those dusted off for community parades as curiosities from the past.

The woman followed closely, it would seem rude or disrespectful to pass a hearse. Within moments the hearse had vanished. Curious, the woman sped up a bit to see if she could catch another glimpse of the black, snaking vehicle. By the time she got the to interchange that would take her back to Parkersburg there was no sign of the hearse.

But seeing the old-fashioned hearse was so unusual the woman did not forget it and later asked the others if they had seen the hearse on the way home? No one else had.

Within the month, one of the members of the spiritual group experienced a wrenching family tragedy so terrible that it would be sacrilege to reveal in a format like this that is meant to entertain. The woman often talked of visiting Scotland and was proud of having Scottish blood. She dreamed of a time when she could see first-hand ancient Scotland where a belief in psychic powers and omens remained strong. Was it the Banshee's Coach-A-Bower or just a strange mix of circumstances that foreshadowed the tragic event?

As with many mysteries, we will never know.

And yet, it is important to remember that every Scottish and Irish clan has it's own Banshee. According to the Irish poet Yeats, important people often have an entire chorus of Banshees to sing upon their demise.

Luckily, I've not met my Banshee yet.

Let us hope you won't meet yours any time too soon.

2. otherworldly tales

woodrow derenberger, indrid cold & the men in black

The date is November 2nd, 1966. The time is 7:25 p.m. You are driving down a lonely stretch of highway, somewhere between the valleys and sloping hills of western West Virginia. Your car radio is tuned in to a ballad sung by the late Patsy Cline or maybe a Willie Nelson tune…before he grew his hair out and got famous. Over your right shoulder, the sky is tinged a faint pink. The hills are inky black. As a light rain falls, you turn on the windshield wipers but you barely need them, so you switch on your wipers every minute or so. Rainfall is minimal and it's less distracting that way.

A few passing cars catch you in their beams. Your trip home is relaxing traveling through the slanting landscape. The world inside your truck is so comforting and insulated that you struggle to keep your eyelids open. Perhaps you dream of your wife's famous homemade vegetable soup and putting your soaking feet up by the fire and making small talk with your better half about what happened at work today. Business was slow, but should pick up shortly as many homemakers would be expecting a new Singer sewing machine on Christmas morning – because that's what you sell at your store in Marietta, Ohio – brand new Singer sewing machines.

Almost dreaming, in a place between wakefulness and sleep, something enormous and dark rushes up behind you. The force makes your entire vehicle rattle and shake – just like a Jerry Lee Lewis song. The thing is huge and dark and menacing … A tractor-trailer truck veering out of control? Can't be… there aren't any lights. Hey, what kind of a crazy sonofabitch would drive without his lights on anyway?

Now, the thing pushes you off the highway. It's barreling down. Cripes! You struggle with your steering wheel and try to bring your vehicle under control. After a few tense moments, you get your truck to the side of the road. The 'craft' (as you will learn to call it later) swerves slightly then rolls over you. Just like a ball of fire. And yet, there is no light to see by. As you clutch your steering wheel, with beaded sweat on your brow, you notice a door opening in the craft. It's some kind of hatch. You see warm light and a man pass through it. A human arm helps him out the door. A tall stranger steps from the craft and walks toward you in an unhurried manner. As he gets closer to your car, the dark gray craft shoots seventy feet straight up and hovers suspended in space.

You hear the man's words over and over: "Do not be afraid. I mean you no harm..." words that will eventually sear into your brain like a brand. And yet his lips do not move.

Your name is Woodrow Derenberger and your life will never be the same...

ᕼᕼᕼᕼᕼᕼᕼᕼᕼᕼᕼᕼᕼᕼᕼᕼᕼᕼᕼᕼᕼᕼᕼᕼᕼᕼᕼᕼᕼᕼᕼᕼ

To most people in the 21st Century, the name Woodrow Derenberger may no longer be significant. But to a select number of UFO enthusiasts and residents of West Virginia and the Ohio Valley, the name "Derenberger" holds a great deal of meaning. After all, Mr. Derenberger was at the center of one of the most fascinating UFO cases in U.S. history – one that would spawn a Hollywood movie thirty-five years later.

Woodrow Derenberger was a man of modest means. He worked as a salesman, commuting from his farm in Mineral Wells, West Virginia to his job in Marietta, Ohio, a distance of about twenty miles. Up until November 2nd, 1966, Woody Derenberger could only be described as your average Joe, serving as Deacon at his local church, going about his routine as husband and father of two small children at the time.

However, life for Woodrow Derenberger would change after that date, in ways that he could not imagine. Depending upon whom you ask, opinions of Derenberger vary greatly. Some consider Mr. Derenberger to be the first person to go on record by reporting his 'close encounter" to the authorities. Others believe the stresses of every day life may have been too much for Derenberger and he fashioned a story of an alien encounter for the attention or some other complex, emotional reason.

No matter what we believe, something extraordinary occurred to Woodrow Derenberger on that early November night, whether real or imagined, as he drove south on I-77 home to his farm in Mineral Wells. Derenberger's claims were so mind-boggling service men from West Virginia and the Ohio Valley listened to reports of the Derenberger's close encounter over the radio while serving in the jungles of Viet Nam. This fantastic tale of a brush with a UFO proved so compelling that media from Australia and Japan descended upon the small West Virginia City called Parkersburg.

Derenberger's meeting up with the UFO took place sometime after 7:00 p.m. A slight rain misted. The highway was completely dark except for the headlights of the occasional cars that he met along the way toward home. Derenberger was nearing his turn off at State Route 47 exit when his panel truck rocked with the force of something pretty large coming up behind him at a high rate of speed. As he glanced into the rearview mirror, he could see a dark object on his tail. But at that point the object did not touch the ground. The UFO then rolled over the top of Derenberger's vehicle forcing him to the side of the road.

Derenberger later described the craft as being similar to "the shape of a glass chimney of an old-fashioned kerosene lamp lying on its side, with a dome-like top." Derenberger also stated the UFO was charcoal gray in color and until its hatch opened, he never saw any lights. One peculiar aspect of the craft was that it did not touch the ground, but rather floated about a foot off the ground.

Within minutes Derenberger glimpsed a harsh yellow light as a hatch opened in the side of the craft and a tall man wearing what looked to be dark trench coat climbed out. Derenberger later described the individual as – "Like any man you would see on the street" and added "there was really nothing exceptional about his appearance."

As the stranger walked toward Derenberger's vehicle, the alien craft shot vertically into the air to a height of approximately 75 feet and that is where it stayed for the entire duration of the conversation.

Mr. Derenberger saw that the craft's occupant appeared between 35 and 40 years old, was close to six feet tall and weighed about 185 pounds. The man had a tan complexion and dark brown hair, which was slicked back. The man's clothing described as gray and shimmering, was covered partially by an overcoat of sorts.

As rain fell lightly the stranger talked to Mr. Derenberger in a friendly, soothing way. Derenberger thought it strange he understood what the man was saying so easily because his car window was rolled up. The stranger again reassured Woodrow: "Do not be afraid," the dark-haired man repeated, "I mean you no harm. I only want to ask you a few questions."

But the Marietta businessman was alarmed because while the man talked, his lips did not move at all. He apparently communicated with the salesman through mental telepathy.

The tall man introduced himself as first as "Cold" and pointed toward the city lights of Parkersburg that glimmered in the distance. He asked, "What do you call that?"

Mr. Derenberger answered, "That's Parkersburg. I call that a city."

Indrid Cold then said, "Where I come from, we call it 'a gathering." The alien being would later tell Woodrow Derenberger in other visits that he was from "a place called 'Lanulos' a country less powerful than yours."

This struck Derenberger as curious since Cold claimed to have traveled to Mineral Wells from another galaxy, a feat technologically impossible on earth.

Even so, Cold held a 10-15 minute conversation with Derenberger, discussing topics such as cities and towns, the climate, population, and oddly, the farming of livestock in the area. Throughout the conversation Indrid Cold kept a beaming smile and had his arms crossed over his chest, with his hands under his armpits. This was distracting at first, but no more so than conducting a conversation with someone whose lips did not move while he spoke.

During their talk, Derenberger couldn't recall ever seeing Cold's hands. At times there seemed to be an echo to his words. In fact, Cold's voice at times seemed to be nothing more than echoes reverberating in Woody's head.

There was another eerie feature to this strange tale. Derenberger claimed that as he talked to the alien visitor, other cars passed under the craft, unbeknownst to what was suspended above. The Mineral Wells resident saw no lights.

Once the conversation ended and Indrid Cold gave his farewell, the alien walked back toward the craft, which by this time had once again settled to its former position. As the Cold entered the ship, Derenberger reported that a second arm appeared from the doorway to help him inside. After the hatch shut behind the stranger, the space ship shot into the air and flew away at a high rate of speed.

Derenberger sat in the darkness of his car wondering what to do next. As soon as the UFO was out of sight, the Mineral Wells resident turned on his ignition and drove to his house in a daze. His wife met him at the door and was startled by his paleness and trembling. "What has happened to you?" she asked as she helped him inside. After explaining his frightening encounter to his wife, she promptly called the West Virginia State Police.

A media storm in the Mid-Ohio Valley followed the initial telling of Derenberger's story. A press conference was called the next day with local media and law enforcement as well as officials from the Wood County Airport. Once again, Woody Derenberger told his strange tale the afternoon of November 3, 1966. Derenberger was to give a live interview on WTAP-TV, the local NBC affiliate, when interviewed by veteran reporter Glenn Wilson and Wood County Sheriff Ed Plumb. It was in that format that Derenberger chose to enlighten the world of his encounter with Indrid Cold the visitor who came from a "country less powerful than yours" that still holds sway over our imaginations.

The tale of alien visitors told by Woodrow Derenberger is not a simple one. Yet the middle-aged sewing machine salesman never deviated from his original story. No amount of criticism or ridicule caused him to recant his original tale of alien visitors and Indrid Cold – at least not in the beginning...

Television/Government Interviews

While conducting research for the Haunted Parkersburg tour in 1996, we happened upon one of the more fascinating elements of the story: the actual reel-to-reel audio tapes of Woodrow Derenberger's live press conference in November of 1966.

The tapes were in the possession of veteran newsman Glenn Wilson who interviewed Derenberger at least twice for more than an hour. Wilson decided to donate these rare tapes to the Haunted Parkersburg team for historical value and safekeeping. Until they were transferred to cassette, the tapes had not been listened for over thirty years. The interview runs over two hours. At times Derenberger is flustered and repeats himself, or tries to clarify what he has previously stated. As the tapes progress, so does the sincerity of Mr. Derenberger's words—a man who is clearly still frightened.

Tape #1

The first tape is the initial interview with Derenberger, Glenn Wilson (WTAP Anchor), and Ronald Maines (WTAP General Manager). The running time of tape #1 is approximately 27 minutes. It simply covers the story of Derenberger's experience on I-77 of the previous evening.

At one point in the interview a reporter was asked of Mr. Derenberger if he drank alcohol or had stopped at a bar on his way home. As a deacon of a Christian Church on Parkersburg's South Side, Derenberger emphatically stated that he did not drink alcohol, nor was he drinking at the time of his encounter.

Wood County Sheriff Ed Plumb mentions to Derenberger that there had been a story similar to his written up in newspapers and magazines weeks before. Plumb asked Mr. Derenberger if he had previously read that reported tale of a UFO?

Woodrow Derenberger states, that no, he did not, because up until his encounter with Indrid Cold he did not believe in UFOs, therefore, he had no interest in the subject and he would not have read such an article.

Tape 2#

On this tape Derenberger relates as to how the UFO forced him to the side of the road, how long it took him to stop and how close he was to Cold's craft. The reporters questioned him about the distance between his car, the spacecraft and the highway. Other questions had to do with what time it started raining, when the rain stopped and how Derenberger was able to talk with the alien visitor since his window was rolled up?

After describing Indrid Cold and his clothing it was asked how Derenberger was able to see such detail since it was dark and also rainy? Mr. Derenberger stuck to his guns and said that throughout his conversation with Indrid Cold other cars passed under the suspended craft, and shone light on both of them enabling him to see what Cold looked like easily. Derenberger's said Cold's face was not one he would likely forget.

Tape 3#

It is mentioned on Tape 3# that officials were en route from Wright-Patterson Airforce Base in Dayton, Ohio to question Woodrow Derenberger further and to this Derenberger he had no objections. The middle-aged man commented that he had nothing to hide since he was telling the truth and he did not care who questioned him. (What happened during this interview is not known because no other officials seemed to be present for it.)

This is when the conversation turned more personal and Derenberger began to be questioned about his private life. He declined to give out any information about his family, saying that except for his wife, they knew nothing of his story.

Sometime during the interview, one asked, "Mr. Derenberger, if this Indrid Cold told you to 'be not afraid,' and did not threaten you in any way, why are you frightened? Would you be happy ... to see him again?"

"I would be happy to, but..." Then Woodrow Derenberger contradicted his earlier words, "Cold said 'we will see you again,' and I'm afraid... I'm afraid he will and I don't want him to."

When saying this Mr. Derenberger's voice fades out...

The MIB Visitations

After the initial press conference, Woodrow Derenberger's life careened out of control, turning into a surreal circus.

First, there was the issue of public ridicule where some locals scoffed at Derenberger's "flying saucer" and his "Martians." Reporters from Japan and France began to call on Mr. Derenberger at all hours of the day and night. Local citizens would stop him on street, occasionally to offer support, but just as often to mock him. Finally, Derenberger began to look over his shoulder and tried to avoid as many people as possible. What Derenberger had thought would be a marginal tale with a simple truth had turned into a fiasco. Woodrow Derenberger's simple life had changed, and he was more alone in this bizarre experience than any everyday person could ever be.

And then there were the visitations—No, not Indrid Cold exactly. (That would come later, if not in a physical way, then telepathically.) Derenberger began to be visited by the "Men in Black". Just when he thought things couldn't get worse, three visitors dressed entirely in black and driving a black Cadillac came rolling up his driveway. Thinking they were government officials, Derenberger invited the men into his home. The men were odd in their mannerisms, almost robotic and they had a quick, mechanical way of speaking. The Men in Black questioned Woodrow about his early November encounter with the spacecraft and Indrid Cold.

At first they acted interested in Mr. Derenberger's story. But intermingled with the questions were vague threats for Derenberger to keep quiet in the future or something 'unfortunate' may happen to him and his family. At the time, he believed the Men in Black to be members of the Mafia.

For a while, fearing he was being threatened by the Mafia or the United States Government, Mr. Derenberger backed off and tried to return to a normal family life. That's when he began to receive the messages. At first it started with buzzing and clicking sounds in his head and the familiar words: Do not be afraid. I mean you no harm...

It was Cold again. Through mental telepathy, or some other form of mind control, the alien said he was coming back and Woody was supposed to prepare a place for Cold's ship to land, on top of a ridge beyond Mineral Wells, at an area called Bogle Run. At various times, Mr. Derenberger and several others went up on the ridge to await Cold's spacecraft but the alien ship never materialized.

What really happened to Derenberger after Cold's visit is open to speculation. Some say that Woodrow Derenberger went about his life as normally as possible, ignoring both public's sympathies and insults. He became more active in his church. Yet, he claimed to remain in contact with the space aliens, and said that he was visited by Cold in the flesh on several other occasions. There are claims that after a few years of stress and confusion, Mr. Derenberger recanted his original story of Indrid Cold. But many believe this was after a particularly frightening visit by the Men in Black at his Mineral Wells farm.

What did the Wood County resident really encounter on November 2, 1966 as a mid-autumn rain misted around his modest panel truck on I-77 during that chilly, damp night?

Were Derenberger's words at the TV news conference the day following his encounter the ravings of a lunatic or the boasting of a sad, lonely man craving attention? Was 'Woody' (as his friends called him) simply a pawn in the secrets our government continues to keep? Or was he a prophet for the enlightenment of a new age?

In some published correspondences, writer John Keel said he was not convinced over Woodrow Derenberger's account of his meeting with Indrid Cold. Keel wrote, "I thought he may have (Derenberger) made it up." And yet, how did Derenberger know that less than two weeks later, another spectacular sighting would occur – an event that frightened residents throughout West Virginia and that had little to do with Indrid Cold. Those were reports of a red-eyed, winged creature that came to be known as the Mothman.

How did he know what was about to unfold? When the Mineral Wells man reported his encounter to the West Virginia State police, the state had not yet experienced such a spectacular event since the Flatwoods monster in the mid-1950s. Was Derenberger a prophet, a victim trapped by insane circumstances or a misguided hoaxer?

There is no clear answer. For this reason, the mystery of Woodrow Derenberger's astonishing encounter will most likely never be solved.

The Plot Thickens

Before you dismiss the stories that Derenberger shared with the world, what if we were to tell you about a second man who lived in Ohio who had an independent encounter with Indrid Cold that was just as amazing?

After having the account of Woodrow Derenberger's uncanny visit with Indrid Cold appeared in the June 2001 issue of Fate magazine, I (Richard Southall) received a rather unusual phone call one evening. The call came from a quiet man who told me that he had more information on Indrid Cold if I wanted to hear about it. He even claimed that he knew Woodrow Derenberger. In fact, the man got to know Woody well after the initial Indrid Cold visitation. Intrigued, I listened to his amazing tale for the next two hours.

Apparently, Indrid Cold did not single out Mr. Derenberger to visit. The alien's next appearance happened before Christmas in December of 1967, one year and one month after Cold's brief visit with Derenberger. A man named Jonathan Maheran was walking along the shore of a lake on his property in Ohio when he noticed a large charcoal gray object silently appear from out of nowhere.

The object acted in much the same way that Derenberger described it to officials following his own encounter. However, Maheran certainly did no know this and claims to have never heard of a Woodrow Derenberger before his own visitation from aliens. Maheran went on to say the object hovered between six and eight inches from the surface of the water. (Derenberger claimed that Cold's spacecraft hovered 8-10 inches above the ground then shot 75 feet into the air.) Maheran noticed that although the object was so close to the water's surface, it did not disturb the water at all. If it had been propelled like a helicopter or plane, there would have been an impressive rippling effect.

Maheran said that he was crystal clear about what happened next. After what seemed like an eternity of hovering silently above the water, the globe-shaped craft noiselessly glided to the nearby shore in front of Maheran.

A doorway opened and out stepped a normal looking man. He wore a shimmering overcoat, had thick dark hair that was combed straight back. His smile stretched from ear to ear. As soon as the stranger placed his feet firmly on the ground, the craft immediately shot straight up to a height of about thirty feet. The stranger approached Maheran, offered his hand and said, "Do not fear. I am not here to hurt you."

Indrid Cold was back – but this time in northern Ohio.

Cold asked the same type of questions of Maheran that he had asked of Derenberger. Maheran felt no apprehension or fear as he answered Cold about local government, society, family, and the area's weather patterns. But like Derenberger, Maheran noticed that throughout the entire conversation, Indrid Cold's lips did not move and his arms were folded neatly under his sleeves.

But this is where the tale that Maheran spins begins to differ from Derenberger's. When Cold was finished asking questions, Maheran began to interview the alien. Indrid Cold gladly answered anything that Maheran asked. The being appeared to be pleased that he was the one being interrogated. If possible, Cold's smile became even broader while Maheran interviewed him.

The information that Maheran received was an amazing story. Cold again said that he was from a country 'less powerful than the United States.' When Maheran asked what that meant, Cold explained that technologically his home planet of Lanulos was more advanced, but that the United States devoted a great time and resources to the development of weapons that Cold's world did not need. One day he was certain that Earth would evolve to a point where we lost interest in wars and could concentrate our efforts on peaceful endeavors.

Cold explained that he was sent to observe what people in our world believed and to gather information for a very important mission. He would slowly introduce the people of Earth to future visitation from other beings that would occur at a 'correct and proper time.' Cold wanted the earth people he contacted to be the messengers to the masses, telling them of the existence of aliens and that the earth has been visited for thousands of years by a number of different races from neighboring solar systems.

Cold told Maheran that his system of government was similar to our House of Representatives, where a person from each part of Lanulos represented the masses. There was a council of nine planets and that they worked very effectively and fairly. Earth was on the verge of exploding technologically and was being considered as a tenth member of this council provided a few changes took place. First, we needed to evolve a bit spiritually and become more open minded regarding our view of our place in the universe. We needed to look at ourselves globally instead of as separate countries. Second, we needed to be more conscientious of our ecosystems and learn to use many of the energy resources that are not destructive to our planet. Only then would human beings be considered for inclusion into this planetary council.

Maheran was understandably overwhelmed by this information, but soon began to accept it. Cold said that he needed to leave but that he would return soon. After Cold returned to his craft and disappeared, Maheran sat by the lakeshore and thought about his amazing encounter for a few hours before walking home.

Two days later, Maheran was walking by his lakeshore when Cold's vehicle appeared again. The craft leveled to just a few inches from the ground and Cold stepped out. After exchanging greetings telepathically, Cold asked Maheran more questions.

Cold volunteered more information about his own life as well. Lanulos was a small planet not far from Earth and that only a few people have known of its existence. The topography and climate were very similar to Earth, which was something that intrigued Maheran greatly.

Cold also explained to Maheran what a "gathering" was in much more detail than he did to Derenberger. A gathering was a series of single-level houses concentrated in a small area. Single families stayed in these buildings, but the entire gathering was more of a communal setting. Everybody looked out for one another and nobody was in need of anything. Cold explained that it had been like this for as far back as he could remember and that the idea of capitalism was foreign to him.

Because of the advances in medicine and changes in diet, people from Lanulos had an average life span of between 130 and 150 years. Some people even lived to be as old as 190 years of age. Cold explained that physiologically, there was very little difference between people from Lanulos and Earth and that eventually we would reach a similar life span if we allowed ourselves to.

Cold continued to explain some of the more domestic qualities of life on Lanulos. Most of the people from his home were vegetarian and did not eat any form of meat at all. There were two types of bread that were popular with Cold's kind. One was 'a-pancake-like' bread that was quite healthy to eat. The second type was like Biscotti bread that could be kept for months.

The visitor from Lanulos also described some of their pets to Maheran. Cold claimed to have a pet dog-like creature that resembled an armadillo. This creature was intelligent and could communicate with their owners on a basic level. They were docile creatures and very dedicated to the family that they were with.

Over the course of the next few months, Cold visited Maheran on at least three more occasions. Maheran invited Cold to his home and prepared a meal for him.

One day Cold explained to Maheran that he was given another assignment and that this would be his last visit. But before he left, Cold gave Maheran two gifts to remember him by. (Developing a friendship with an extraterrestrial would be forgotten?)

The first gift was a lump of a dark gray metal, similar in appearance to polished hematite. When Maheran put the metal in his hand, it was heavy at first but suddenly grew lighter. Cold explained the metal was used to create the spacecraft that he and others of his kind used. It was a heavy alloy – until touched by any living individual. Then the metal lightened to one-tenth of its original weight. The alloy was made up of metals that were common throughout the galaxy and could be found on Earth. According to Cold, humans had not discovered the correct combination. The second gift was a silver necklace with an obsidian-like amulet. The amulet vibrated whenever touched.

Maheran thanked Cold. They talked longer until it was time for Cold to leave. As the alien started to step inside his craft, he turned and said there were others that he had visited on his assignment and that Maheran should look them up. One contactee lived not too far from Maheran and there was a man by the name of 'Derenberger,' said Indrid Cold. The being then entered his ship and flew away, never to be seen by Maheran again.

With only a name to go on, Jonathan searched for anyone that might have the name of Derenberger or something close to it. The first few times yielded nothing. He wasn't certain how the name was spelled. It was then Maheran mouthed the name to himself until he hit upon the proper spelling: D-E-R-E-N-B-E-R-G-E-R.

It didn't take Maheran long to find newspaper reports about Derenberger's account. The man with the soft voice claimed to have contacted Derenberger shortly thereafter, but there is no way to prove or disprove this. Derenberger had passed away years ago and late in his life he had stopped talking about Cold entirely.

This may have been the case since the two contactees wanted to keep their meetings secret for fear of ridicule until it came to a time both felt comfortable revealing their almost identical tales. That time never came for Woodrow Deremberger. He died with many of the general public disbelieving him.

But before we close the pages on the Indrid Cold visitations, there is one more bit of information to share.

On the same night Woodrow Derenberger had his visitation near the turn off at route 47 near Parkersburg, an elderly gentleman was driving home toward Point Pleasant (fifty-some miles down river from Parkersburg) who claimed to have had a similar encounter but without seeing a UFO. The older man reported that a tall man had stopped him along the edge of the highway only to ask him a bunch of pointless questions like if he knew what the weather was going to be or of anyone who had livestock? Fearing he was about to be robbed, the senior citizen didn't stick around for the entire interview. He never rolled down his window entirely. He then spun away quickly, leaving the man standing by the side of the road.

Instead of calling the police, the older man dropped in at a local newspaper the next morning to see if anyone else had witnessed or reported the same experience. (The Derenberger story had not yet hit the newspapers or the evening news.)

Around this time period handfuls of people from around the world claimed to experience similar visitations from benevolent beings from other worlds. Although only Derenberger and Maheran said the craft came from a planet called Lanulos, the particular method of operation were from contactee to contactee was the same. The visitors would scout out a solitary person, approach them, and then ask questions that sometimes had no relevance at all. The beings always appeared humanoid, attractive, and had an open smile upon their face.

Often, the messages took on a more serious tone, claiming Earth was on the verge of a major evolutionary leap and that their mission was to choose selected people to help prepare for the day when first official contact would be made. The warnings were the same as well: the people of Earth needed to start thinking globally and stop concentrating on fighting one another and the people of Earth needed to find forms of renewable resources before we destroy the 'Ecosphere.'

Perhaps the most famous visitation of this type other than Woodrow Derenberger's was of George Adamski, a quiet man that lived in Europe. His visitation matched Mahern's and Derenberger's visit nearly to the letter, down to Cold's description of gatherings and the peaceful vegetarian lifestyle. Adamski claimed that the visitor he had referred to his kind as the "Space Brothers". The description of the Space Brother was identical to Cold with the exception that Adamski's visitor had long flowing sandy hair, where Cold's hair was dark and combed straight back.

After thirty-five years since the initial visit with Indrid Cold to the Ohio Valley several unanswered questions remain. Was Indrid Cold a Space Brother flying down from a place called Lanulos to warn us all? Are these made-up tales, by very imaginative individuals? Or could these Indrid Cold visitations be based on reality – a reality the rest of us are blind to?

No matter what the tried and true facts are, the accounts of Indrid Cold reach much farther than a visit with a tired sewing machine salesman on a cold, rainy November night on a lonely stretch of road in rural West Virginia.

Another, Perhaps, Related Sighting

This letter appeared as a posted message on a UFO sighting report on the Internet:

"I want to relate a sighting that another witness and I had in 1997. I was training a new driver for a produce delivery route that I had in West Virginia. We were about 10 miles or so south of Marietta, Ohio. This was about six miles north of Mineral Wells.

"As I was proceeding down the highway (I-77), my partner yelled, "Look at that!" He startled me so bad that I almost lost control of the truck. Anyway, I looked out my window, and to my total amazement, I witnessed a large, black triangle, heading eastward just above the hills.'

" I gathered my senses and pulled the truck to the side of the road. We both got out of the truck to look at it. As I held my arm straight up and made a fist. It was about twice the size of my fist. If I had a rock, I could have hit it! I could see plainly, that is had a non-reflective, kind of like flat-black, surface. On the bottom of this craft were four lights. They looked as if they were on dim. That is to say, they did not shine brightly, but were definitely visible.'

"The one thing that caught my attention was that the craft appeared to make no sound what-so-ever! It just seemed to float. It was moving so slowly that I could have out-raced it on foot. We watched it for at least 10 minutes, then it moved over the hills, and we lost sight of it. We got back into the truck and went south a few miles and I pulled over to see if I could see it again. We didn't see anything again that night."

gray barker: prankster, media genius or flying saucer boogie man?

One can hardly discuss UFOs in West Virginia, the Mothman, Men in Black or the Flatwoods monster without bringing up the name of a man from Clarksburg named Gray Barker.

As some have written of the West Virginia Mothman, Gray Barker was without a doubt a "strange bird." For a number of years, Barker managed a local bijou in his hometown of Clarksburg promoting Saturday matinee horror films, while writing and publishing on the side. In the 1957, Barker published his famous book *They Knew Too Much About Saucers*, introducing to the general public stories about the conspiracies involving UFOs and strange tales concerning "the Men in Black," an idea introduced to Barker by his friend UFO investigator Albert Bender in Connecticut. (Bender formed the UFO investigation group he called The International Flying Saucer Bureau and had encouraged Barker to form a West Virginia chapter.)

The Men in Black have become a much talked about enigma. Dressed entirely in black, they were said to threaten witnesses to UFO's into silence. It was noted and written about by Albert Bender (and later by Gray Barker) that when some individuals report sightings of UFOs, or claimed encounters with aliens, they are soon visited by bizarre, rather menacing men who arrive in vintage 1950s Cadillac's. These men uniformed in black are said to threaten witnesses into not talking anymore about "saucers" or to retract their stories. Usually with tanned or pasty pale complexions, almond- shaped eyes and a strange mechanical way of speaking, the Men in Black (MIBs) were theorized to be government agents or even the aliens themselves.

Probably the strangest fact about the Men in Black is they usually come across as intellectually slow or just plain stupid. It is hard to believe such cretins could frighten anyone, yet apparently they do. (So much so, that writer John Keel discourages children or young people from getting too involved in interests dealing with UFO sightings, especially the Men in Black. Albert Bender had to retire from investigating UFOs because of chronic migraine headaches. Bender felt this was a type of "extraterrestrial interference.")

It is hard to apply the word "danger" to the Men in Black, because to anyone who has ever met one can clearly see their ineptitude. For instance, in Point Pleasant during the Mothman scare, one of the Men in Black was witnessed swaying back and forth on a street corner chirping with the birds in the trees. Others were reported trying to drink their bowls of Jello in local restaurants. One MIB showed up to question and threaten a witness while wearing bright orange lipstick. (And not applied very well, at that!)

Other than making ridiculous demands on UFO contactees to keep quiet about their saucer sightings, the Men in Black come across as pretty dumb. Still there is a sense of menacing to the black-clad automatons and many they contacted grew frightened of them.

Stories about the MIBs were quickly noted and written about in UFO circles shortly after Bender released his details. It was Gray Barker, Albert Bender and later John Keel who enabled the tales of the Men in Black to become a fixture among American pop culture. It was only after Gray Barker died in the 1980s that his ideas about saucers, government conspiracies and Men in Black came under fire. Some couldn't help but notice that Gray Barker appeared to be "a little too close" to these strange unfoldings of UFOs, MIBs and the Mothman in the Mountain State.

Associates of Gray Barker pointed out that the Clarksburg writer always showed up when anything of a paranormal nature surfaced in West Virginia – this included the Flatwoods monster in the 1950s, and even Derenberger's Indrid Cold in the 1960s. Some of Barker's "friends" claimed that he was quite the hoaxer and could have fabricated any or all of the above stories, sightings, events and would have done so to make a buck. That even meant dressing up like the Mothman or posing as one of the Men in Black.

So, was this mischievous merry maker of Harrison County really our Mothman? Did Gray Barker dress up in a Halloween suit then appear in Point Pleasant to later sell his paranormal books? Frankly, Gray Barker hoaxing the Mothman OR Indrid Cold is even more unlikely than the appearance of this winged beast chasing people away from an isolated TNT plant in the remote countryside. How could he and why would he? Along with being an oddball UFO guy, Gray would have had to have premonitions of the bizarre events ready to unfold.

Many of Barker's detractors obviously don't know much about the geography and highways of West Virginia, especially during the 1950s and 1960s. For one thing, the road to Point Pleasant, located along the Ohio River, (where most of the Mothman sightings occurred) was a twisting and turning, grueling three-hour drive over two-lane road from Clarksburg. To claim that Gray Barker dressed up in a

Mothman suit (and some have alleged this,) so he could drive three hours or more in order to scare people whom he did not know, nor ever met, is ludicrous.

To our knowledge, Woodrow Derenberger did not know of nor did her ever come face to face with Gray Barker. Most of the UFO and Mothman sightings occurred in lonely, isolated spots during late hours, far away from the humble abode of Gray Barker in Clarksburg.

No doubt writer Gray Barker did help fan the flames of these now famous, still controversial tales. He may have stirred things up a bit, but Gray Barker did not start the fires that would later put spooky, brooding West Virginia as a key spot on the United States' paranormal map.

men in black on shannon's knob

In the months following Derenberger's encounter with Ingrid Cold, several other unexplained events began to materialize in surrounding areas.

In March of 1967, two small girls played on a hillside overlooking the picturesque town of West Union. The hill was called Shannon's Knob.

At the top of Shannon's Knob was a power area that provided most of the electricity for the town. As the girls chased each other and hid behind trees, they noticed two darkly garbed men walking along a level spot below the power lines. They were dressed in dark clothes. One looked to be wearing a black uniform, with a black shirt and pants, while the other wore a dark gray trench coat. One man appeared to have lightened his hair to somewhat the color and texture of straw. He also had almond shaped eyes and the yellow complexion of an Asian person.

There seemed to be something false about the blond-haired man. His skin tone didn't match his hair at all. It appeared as if he was dressed for some "effect."

As an adult, one of the women who witnessed the MIBs wrote this: "Do you know how you go to a high school play and you a see young person portray an elderly person? You see the hair is sprayed white, the wrinkles penciled in – but you still know it is a young person. The posture is too good. The bones are too straight. Well, it was the same for the Men in Black. At first they looked normal. But as you watched them – there was something deceptive about the men's appearance. I think that is why we were scared and hid in the weeds."

As the girls watched from the bushes, they noticed the men in black said little to one another as they surveyed the area. A feeling told the girls not to get too close, as there was something menacing about the men. They reminded the girls of black-suited spies that were so popular on TV shows in the 1960s. This only gave the girls another reason to be frightened. Finally, the men wearing black disappeared over the knob. What was particularly fascinating was that the men had barely talked to each other the entire time. It was as if everything was understood and there was no need for verbal communication.

The girls ran home and quickly forgot about the men wearing black. But a few days later, another group of school children came upon the same site and found a circular area where weeds were mashed and the ground singed. The circle was around 25 feet in diameter.

In the Mid 1960s, West Virginia had a plethora of UFO sightings as well as other bizarre happenings. One such sighting was of a creature that superseded the appearances and hoopla surrounding Bigfoot in the Pacific Northwest. West Virginia's creature had enormous wings that unfolded like the wings of a bat, a terrible countenance that stopped the heart almost cold, and glowing red eyes that electrified witnesses with a sense of dread. This creature spawned a cult-classic book and a major motion picture. He was uniquely West Virginia spawned – his name was "Mothman!"

3. west virginia mothman

strange forces, strange beasts

The place is Doddridge County, West Virginia. The date is November 14th, 1966. It is 10:30 at night as Newell Partridge watches television with his young son. The rest of the Partridge children and Newell's wife have turned in for the evening. Suddenly, the TV set goes blank. Interference causes the picture screen to develop a herringbone pattern.

The TV set blanking out was not unusual when one lived in rural West Virginia in the 1960s. This was well before cable channels and satellite dishes. Most TV reception in farm areas came pretty much as the crows fly. Picking up favorite shows depended upon how deft you were at turning your roof top television antennae to stations in Clarksburg, Wheeling and Pittsburgh. Consider yourself lucky if you got all three.

For the most part, it was an ordinary night. But what happened to Newell Partridge next was very much out-of-the-ordinary. His television set whined…loudly, like a generator winding up. At this point, Bandit, the Partridges' pet dog howled eerily. As Partridge peered outside, he saw that his German Shepherd faced the hay barn -- about the length of a football field away from the house. The family dog barked at the dark doorway of the barn extremely agitated.

Newell Partridge grabbed his flashlight and went outside. Bandit had disappeared although Partridge heard the dog wailing in the area of the barn. As he shined his light in the direction of Bandit, it caught two red circles or eyes that looked like bicycle reflectors. Newell was later to describe the red eyes in an interview with writer John Keel, "I certainly know what animal eyes look like… These were much larger…still those eyes showed up as huge even for that distance."

In an attempt to describe how he felt, Partridge added, "It was an eerie feeling … like the sort I've not felt before…It was as if you knew something was really wrong but couldn't place just what it was."

A snarling Bandit came into focus. He bolted toward the barn. A cold chill swept over Newell Partridge. He hurried inside the house. He would sleep little that night keeping his shotgun beside his bed. The next day, he and his six-year-old searched for their pet. They went to where the dog was last seen. The barn had a dirt floor. Partridge found the dog's tracks, but not Bandit. "Those tracks were going around in a circle" as if the dog had been chasing its tail, "But Bandit never did that," added Partridge.

And then there were no more tracks as if the dog had been lifted up and carried away by something much larger and much stronger.

Bandit, the family pet, was never seen again.

The period of November 1966 leading into 1967 marked a peculiar time for West Virginians. During these days, the state was swept up by numerous sightings of a pale, gray, flying creature that was reported by witnesses as close to seven feet tall. Motorists told stories of driving along country roads late at night and hearing a whooshing sound above their vehicle. As the drivers slowed down to look, they saw a large gray creature with glowing, red eyes and a wingspan of about ten feet. Even more strangely the creature seemed to want to race people's cars by flying parallel to the vehicle. Other witnesses who encountered the Mothman claimed that if you made the awful mistake of locking eyes with the creature, you would become paralyzed for seconds or even minutes.

Reports of the Mothman, alone, were bizarre enough to make state and national news. However, during the time of Mothman sightings, there were also hundreds of eyewitness accounts of UFOs and Men In Black throughout the state and the Ohio Valley region. (Woodrow Derenberger's close encounter with Indrid Cold and his spacecraft at Mineral Wells on November 2nd preceded the Mothman sightings by about 12 days.) Such bizarre events ended with the tragic collapse of the Silver Bridge in Point Pleasant that snuffed out the lives of 47 people who plunged in the icy waters of the Ohio River below.

And yet, what did these seemingly incredible events have to do with one another? What did the Mothman have to do with UFOs, missing pets in Doddridge County, the TNT plant and the Silver Bridge collapse in Point Pleasant?

Many believe it all began with a Shawnee Indian curse…

chief cornstalk's curse

The area surrounding the Point Pleasant, West Virginia is considered one of the most beautiful spots along the Ohio River. Where the Ohio meets the Kanawha

Rivers is a rich and fertile ground to grow crops and live off the fat of the land. Fish and game are plentiful. Nomadic tribes often used what is now Point Pleasant as a rest area before continuing to their destination. And yet, Native Americans inhabitants were afraid of the lands now known as West Virginia, considering the Alleghenies, wedged between the Ohio and Potomac Rivers to be plagued by evil ghosts and terrifying night creatures.

When the first white men visited the area in the mid-1700s, they saw great potential for farmlands along the calming Ohio River and the gentle sloping hills. In 1765, Major George Crogham of Pennsylvania was one of the first officials to explore and admire the area. Five years later, on October 31, 1770, George Washington made a trip to the area and decided that he found one of the most beautiful stretches of land ever. Some people in his party nicknamed the Point Pleasant delta El Dorado, after the fabled city of gold in the Central Americas. A settlement was constructed and the first settlers began to build permanent homes, much to the chagrin of the Native Americans in the area.

Chief Cornstalk, a Shawnee chieftain, thought making peace with the Europeans would be the best way to preserve some of the Native American way of life. He realized that an overt act of hostility against the white men would prove devastating for his tribe because the settlers possessed firearms while his group did not.

However, subordinate chiefs from his group attacked the settlement of Fort Randolph, which led to one of the most intense battles of the area. Cornstalk commanded nearly 12,000 troops, which matched Captain Matthew Arbuckle's army, and he defended his land when it was attacked. The battle of Point Pleasant took place in October 1774 and is considered by many historians to be the first true battle of the Revolutionary War.

Three years later, on November 8, 1777 (a particularly bloody year for natives and settlers both), Cornstalk led a party of Shawnee to Fort Randolph to pay the settlers a visit to see how they were faring along the Ohio lands. During his visit, the chief came with his son Elenipsico and a trusted friend, Red Hawk. When the Shawnee arrived to the Fort, found themselves surrounded by a group of Virginia Militiamen, already angry because one of their trackers was ambushed earlier by a group of renegades. (Why this violence occurred can be understood when one realizes that most of the renegades who made war on whites were young men, many not even out of their teens. The actions of these unruly youngsters often to led to violence when the more clear-headed adults did not want to fight or make war because they were tired of it.)

Since Cornstalk and his party came to the Fort a few hours later, it was convenient for the whites to seek vengeance on Chief Cornstalk and his son.

Arbuckle attempted to stop the settlers from attacking Cornstalk and Elenipsico, but he was overpowered. Cornstalk and his son were pushed to the front where the white men opened fire. The son fell mortally wounded. Chief Cornstalk stood and showed no sign of fear or pain as the musket balls ripped his flesh.

After the first volley of shots was fired, Cornstalk remained, much to the surprise of his attackers. The Indian raised his right hand, indicating that he wanted to speak. The awestruck militiamen were silenced. The words that came from the Chief's mouth have haunted the people of the Ohio Valley for over 200 years.

"I was the friend of the bordermen. Many a time I have saved him and his people from harm. I never warred with you save to protect our wigwams and our lands. I refused to join your pale-faced enemy. I came to your house as a friend, and you murdered me. You have murdered by my side, my son, the young Chief Elinipsico."

The Militiamen soon realized that they made a terrible, fatal mistake, but it was too late. Witnesses later said that Cornstalk seemed to grow stronger for an instant. His slanted dark eyes burned with vengeance. He then uttered these unforgettable words:

"For this may the curse of the Great Spirit rest upon this spot; favored as it is by nature, may it ever be blighted in its hopes, its growth dwarfed, its enterprises blasted, and the energies of its people paralyzed by the stain of our blood."

As Cornstalk ceased, he fell to the ground. Within moments, he was dead. His lifeless eyes stared and his body slumped next to the battered remains of his son Elinipsico and his Red Hawk.

By sunset of the same day, the Militiamen led by Arbuckle dug a grave for the three slain Shawnee Indians right outside of the wall of Fort Randolph. Not a word was said among the men as they shoveled into the frozen ground to put the remains of the men they had mistakenly killed in a fit of anger.

After the fort was demolished and the village of Point Pleasant grew, Cornstalk's bones were exhumed and moved to the Mason County Courthouse Lawn. Years after that, his bones were moved once again and buried at the Tu Endi Wei Park by the Ohio River. A granite monument marks the remains of the chief. The stone depicts the battle of Point Pleasant. As you will learn later, removing the remains from a grave is considerably dangerous in terms of curses.

Following his death, Cornstalk's curse became legend among the people of the Ohio Valley. The story was passed down from generation to generation. Parents often warned unruly children about the curse and most of the time, the children behaved upon hearing it. A few residents still avoid the area where Cornstalk's remains are buried for fear of stirring up the curse. People in Point Pleasant with native blood offer homage and leave tokens of appreciation at his gravesite out of respect and in hopes of ending the curse.

There is some validity to the Cornstalk curse. You don't kill someone and then move his bones around. Spirits don't like that. This is especially true among natives who believe they cannot enter the afterlife unless all of their remains are intact. What might happen after an Indian curse?

At least two major events took that within a month of the anniversary of Cornstalk's death. The first event was a series of sightings of the Mothman in and around the TNT area in the fall of 1966 and 1967. The second event was the tragic Silver Bridge Collapse in 1967 that took the lives of 47 people. In 1977, in Pleasants County, upriver from Point Pleasant, close to one hundred men died during a scaffolding collapse at the Willow Island Plant. Some claim there are too many eerie connections between Cornstalk, the Silver Bridge, Willow Island, the TNT area, the UFO sightings, and Mothman to put aside as mere coincidence. What is definite is that some strange forces have been at work in the Ohio Valley area since the massacre of Chief Cornstalk.

the point pleasant tnt area

A place where the "Mothman" was said to take refuge was the TNT plant near the city limits of Point Pleasant. The monster's red, disc eyes were glimpsed by locals. (Some residents of Point Pleasant will still not go near the place.)

The TNT area was once a military complex that manufactured explosives during the World Wars. After World War II, the 9000-acre complex was closed down and abandoned. Empty shells where left where the igloos that held the explosives were created. The roads that were once used by hundreds of military vehicles daily are now unused and the weeds have taken over. This abandoned complex was the perfect place for teenagers to pass countless summer nights. By 1950, the TNT area had become the most popular place in the area for teens and young adults to congregate on the weekend.

One thing that the teenagers couldn't predict was that the TNT area would soon became the site of one of the most widely publicized events ever to occur in the annuals of parapsychology.

The strangeness began simply enough. Soon after it closed down, shortly after World War II, mysterious events began to take place. Lights were seen flying above the TNT area day and night. As strange as the lights were though, spectral lights alone would not become the reason that people from all over the country and around the world would swoop down upon the now very quiet town of Point Pleasant. The TNT area was the location where some of the first documented sighting of the Mothman took place. People came out of the wild and abandoned area very frightened, after once being inside, and refused to tell others of their experiences.

Soon it began to have the reputation of being haunted—but by what?

descriptions of the mothman

Witnesses to the Mothman agree on these essential facts: The creature was six to seven feet tall, with a wingspan of seven to ten feet. Glowing red eyes, almost two inches in diameter and about six or eight inches apart, radiated from the Mothman's head. The being was gray and emitted a shrill noise as it passed over cars. The flying creature was apparently afraid of the lights of Point Pleasant for the strange being immediately cut off its pursuit of more than one car on the outskirts of town.

Over 100 sightings of the creature were reported throughout West Virginia and parts of southern Ohio between 1966 and 1967. According to one author, "and probably at least as many others were afraid to give their names".

After the collapse of the Silver Bridge, the West Virginia Mothman was not reported in the area again – at least not in the same way.

But were these his last sightings?

first sighting of mothman in pt. pleasant

An unusually tall figure stood in the middle of the road ahead of a woman who drove her father along Route 2 in the Chief Cornstalk Hunting Grounds of Point Pleasant in 1960 or 1961. As they got closer, the driver slowed the car. The two apprehensive witnesses saw a fleshy gray creature with a human body but much taller than any man. The woman later reported what happened next:

"A pair of wings unfolded from its back and they practically filled the whole road. It almost looked like a small airplane. Then it took off straight up...disappearing out of sight in seconds. We were both terrified. I stepped on the gas and raced out of there. We talked it over and decided not to tell anybody about it. Who would believe us anyway?"

scarberry sightings of the mothman

The first four people to see the Mothman and report him were newlyweds Roger and Linda Scarberry along with friends Steve and Mary Mallette. The sightings that occurred have since became famous and have been exhaustively recounted, eventually leading to a reporter dubbing the described beast as "Mothman", a character from the popular "Batman" television show.

After this initial Mothman sighting, armed deputies who visited the deserted power plant, found oval-shaped footprints measuring about 4 ½ inches across and fresh animal droppings that none of the men in the party could identify.

other mothman/ufo sightings

During the one-year reign of terror that followed the late 1966 sightings, Mothman held the citizens of Point Pleasant under siege. A total of over one hundred sightings of the Mothman were reported. These ranged as claims coming from Point Pleasant businessmen to a gravedigger as well as the local military. One West Virginian (otherwise nameless) experienced a couple of Mothman sightings. This stimulated poltergeist activity in his home as a child and the man told authors Sheppard and Southall, "I can't explain in a logical way what went on in 1966 and 1967 all over the state. All I can say is there was weird stuff going on all the time that year."

In keeping with this, Kenneth Duncan and some other men were digging his brother-in-laws grave on a Saturday morning when something that "looked like a brownish-human being" buzzed past. "It was gliding through the trees and was in sight for about a minute." Duncan was shocked but the other men didn't see it.

Dave Peyton wrote later: "The number of Mothman sightings couldn't hold a candle to the number of other unidentified flying objects sighted over the skies eastern Cabell, Mason, and parts of Putnam counties during the same period of time. Eventually there were so many UFO sightings at the *Herald Dispatch* that they could no longer be ignored. Eventually the calls became so numerous that we had to set up a special "UFO desk" to take all of them. The story of Mothman was big, but the continuing stories of UFO sightings took up more newspaper space"

However, at 11:30 p.m. on the night of Tuesday November 15, 1966, two young Point Pleasant couples drove through the grounds of the abandoned West Virginia Ordinance Works six miles north of town. Looking for friends, the foursome drove around on twisting back roads past igloos designed to store munitions for the WWII effort. In the woods they saw two reflective red eyes. As they sped away, the creature chased them several miles down the road making unnatural chirping noises. After several tense moments, the birdman vanished as suddenly as it had appeared.

From Gray Barker's book, *The Silver Bridge*. On November 16, 1966, the Mothman visited the Ralph Thomas home in Point Pleasant. Katherine Wamsley and Marcella Bennett stopped to visit Mrs. Thomas. As Mrs. Bennett and Mrs.Wamsley were leaving they came upon the Mothman outside the door. One of the women was so frightened she dropped her newborn baby.

Not only did civilians see the Mothman and UFOs in Mason County, local law enforcement had their sightings as well. Firemen, police, and National Guardsmen were among those who claimed encounters with the Mothman and Flying Saucers. These included Capt. Paul Yoder and Ben Enochs, Point Pleasant police officer Harold Harmon, Robert Spears and Charles Fry of the National Guard, plus George

Carson and J.A. Wilson of Civil Defense were among those who had encounters with West Virginia's bizarre appearances of 1966-1967.

In Wood County, north of Point Pleasant, residents that lived on Quincy Hill in Parkersburg reported what sounded like human footsteps walking on their roofs at night during the Mothman terrors. One of the higher points in Parkersburg's downtown area, Quincy Hill overlooks the business district, the railroad and Blennerhassett Island. A number of schoolchildren in the area still refer to a small cave near the bottom of Quincy Hill as "the Mothman's lair."

Former Haunted Parkersburg tour guide Doni Enoch once shared a hospital room with a woman from the Point Pleasant area. The woman told Doni that the winter following the initial Mothman sightings she and her husband happened to be around the area of the TNT plant on other business. A light snow powdered the ground. The couple soon noticed large tracks in the snow. The woman claimed that "The prints looked just like turkey tracks... except for the fact that they were huge and about six feet apart! I would never go to that place (TNT plant) alone... not even to this very day."

Back in Point Pleasant, Thomas Ury, a shoe store manager at the time, saw the creature from about 500 yards away as he was passing the Kirkland Memorial Gardens, ten days after the first sighting. It chased his car, which had reached speeds up to 90 mph, before it broke pursuit. This was the first reported sighting during the day. Ury thinks it was a huge bird with 10 to 12 foot-wing-span and an oversized body too big for its wings.

Billy Burdette, 16, Darrell Love, 18, Johnny Love, 14, and John Morrow, 14 informed the local authorities they spotted disc-shaped red eyes and a creature taking off at a fast rate of speed when they got close to it. They saw the winged beast again at 3:00 a.m. on Camp Conley Road close to a mile from the highway.

Back in Doddridge County between West Union and Salem, Newell Partridge felt the red-eyed flying man had something to do with the disappearance of his purebred German Shepherd dog, Bandit, who was worth $350 in 1966. Partridge said he sighted the 'thing' in a barn, a football field away from his house in Doddridge County about 90 minutes before one of the Pt. Pleasant sightings. Partridge claimed that his television set "began acting like a generator" and that Bandit "started carrying on something terrible." When Newell Partridge shined a flashlight into the field, he saw something that had eyes like red reflectors. The dog's hair stood straight up and he snarled, heading for the Partridge's barn. There was no trace of Bandit in the morning.

Later in November 1966, a crop circle was discovered outside Gallipolis, Ohio, a small city directly across the Ohio River from the town of Point Pleasant, which was experiencing the plethora of Mothman sightings at the time.

Five pilots in the Gallipolis area, Eddie Atkins (WJEH Radio DJ) Everett Wedge, Henry Upton, Leon Edwards, and Ernie Thompson reported seeing a large bird apparently following the Ohio River and traveling at a speed at approximately 70 mph. The men claimed the creature was 300 feet above the shore and had a neck nearly four feet long and a body the size of a small man. Some feel this sighting was the end of the Mothman.

But was it really?

No species of bird in West Virginia, to our knowledge, seeks out human blood. In 2002, John Keel, author of *The Mothman Prophecies*, said in a television interview the Mothman seemed to be drawn to women during their menstrual cycles. This attraction to blood might have put this bizarre creature under the category of a ghoul rather than any space alien. Other reports had the Mothman chasing a Red Cross bloodmobile in 1967.

theories of about the mothman

There were nearly as many theories pertaining to the West Virginia Mothman in 1966 and 1967 as there were witnesses who claimed to see the winged creature. Most speculators were of two or three schools of thought and then some. A few theorized the creature was actually an exotic bird that had flown off course.

Others speculated that the Mothman was a type of inter-dimensional able to fade in and out of our own dimension at will. (That means he was able to slip through a tear in our three dimensions.) Others link the Mothman to UFOs since he was sighted near areas that were already in a frenzy of UFO sightings. Because of the red eyes, some thought the Mothman was some kind of a devil, come to curse the people of the Ohio Valley.

West Virginia writer and folklorist Greg Leatherman points out that the Mothman has similarities to mythological creatures throughout antiquity, "The Egyptian Seth is identified in the late Graeco-Egyptian pantheon with a headless demon whose red-eyes are placed in his shoulders, just like the mid-20th Century reports of the Mothman. In that pantheon, he is called Akephelos. It is no surprise that in another Grimoire, 'The Testament of Solomon,' this headless demon is said to carry out things at Crossroads."

Leatherman also added, "The Ohio Valley region has more species of moths than any other spot in Northern Hemisphere. Ghosts reside in cemeteries. The Virgin Mary appears in Catholic matriarchal societies, and the Abominable Snowman is so in tune with his environment, he's practically camouflaged. It seems fitting that we'd have our own Mothman." Leatherman lent another twist to the Mothman tale as a different take on the Rip Van Winkle story. (See Senator Peter Godwin Van Winkle in Chapter 8) Legend has it that a man fell asleep along the banks of the Ohio River on a chilly night. Moths, attracted to his warmth, landed on him and formed a fuzzy blanket. When he woke, his body was crawling with moths, and as the first sunrays hit him, he turned into a 'moth-man.' "This is far-fetched, of course," added Leatherman, "but it's fun to consider in terms of the folkloric aspect."

Except for the disappearance of Bandit, the Partridge's German Shepherd the Mothman never harmed anyone. He seemed to be curious about the world he slipped into, and just as fascinated with us as we were about him. But this does not explain why the Mothman came to West Virginia and why he disappeared.

was the mothman a hoax?

Jimmy Joe Wedge thinks that it was all a big joke that got out of hand. "Someone dressed up and was scaring people in their cars." Wedge says that he knows names, but won't reveal them because the people involved are no longer alive and he doesn't want to embarrass their relatives. "I had friends who were crazy-acting, fun-loving people. I knew some of the people who supposedly dressed up the Mothman. They just had some fun chasing people."

Dick Thomas claims that he was in the general area that the Scarberry's were that night and saw nothing out of the ordinary. "I was in the basic area of the old powerhouse that first night. I could see everything and I never saw anything out of the ordinary. I think those people ought to change their brand of liquor."

W. Joseph Wyatt, associate professor of psychology at Marshall University, thinks that people are afraid to talk about it now to this day for fear of ridicule. After all, human beings can talk themselves into and out of anything once they realize their thoughts are out of step with more normal people, or their peers.

And, of course, there was Clarksburg writer Gray Barker who many thought a hoaxer.

There were much later sightings of a winged creature in rural West Virginia however, by Parkersburg resident and Haunted Parkersburg guide Lea Wilson. She had a scare in the mid-1980s when she was staying with relatives in Calhoun County. Not yet in her teens, Wilson said she was with her uncle when she heard a strange scream coming from outside the house. Wilson said the screech reminded her most of the "lost time movies" that had animation of dinosaurs and other prehistoric creatures. "Honest to God, it sounded like a pre-historic bird …or what movies made those Pterodactyl animations sound like. When we ran outside, this large winged thing flew right over us, blocking out the sky. What I remember most was that it was huge."

theories of birds

Sheriff Johnson said that if the thing was a migratory crane, local monster hunters had better not shoot it. The sheriff explained that migratory birds were protected by federal and state law. He also said he would arrest anybody caught with a loaded gun in the TNT area after dark. There were earlier reports of armed people in the area. Some believe the Mothman was nothing more than a snow-owl, or a sand-hill-crane.

One local by the name of George Johnson believed that the Mothman was simply a "freak Shitepoke," or shag, a large bird from the heron family. Yet those who witnessed the West Virginia Mothman were certain that he was no bird.

Dr. Robert Smith of WVU, informed Mason County sheriff department that the Mothman was probably a sand hill crane (this was before it was given the name 'Mothman'). Sand hill cranes are found in Florida, Georgia and the Mississippi Valley but are not common as far north as the Mid to Upper Ohio Valley region. The sand hill crane doesn't really have big red eyes, but has red feathers around its eyes, has an 80-inch wingspan, and does stand six feet or better. It would not attack humans unless provoked. It is mainly a vegetarian. It does have a large bill, and could potentially kill a dog but would not eat it.

the silver bridge

The collapse of the Silver Bridge between Point Pleasant and Gallipolis, Ohio was the event that most feel brought an end to the Mothman sightings – or perhaps it merely turned attention elsewhere, so that a flying beast no longer seemed as important as it once had. The bridge had been built in 1928 and earned its name when it became the first in the area to be painted with aluminum shortly after it was erected.

During rush hour, on December 15, 1967, the Silver Bridge buckled and writhed like a giant serpent. By 5:00 p.m. the bridge had completely collapsed into the frigid waters of the Ohio River below. At the time it fell, 67 people were on the collapsed portion of the bridge in 31 vehicles. The bridge was packed to its full capacity with mostly Christmas shoppers. In the end, 46 of those people were killed, including two people that were never found. Five were killed on the Ohio shoreline. Later, 23 of the lost vehicles were recovered from the river and to this day, eight of them have never been discovered.

One man later reported that he started to drive up onto the bridge, but then reversed his truck back down because he wanted to call his wife to see if she wanted him to pick anything up at a nearby grocery store. The man became one of the Silver Bridge survivors.

In the year leading up to the disaster, the people of Point Pleasant experienced sightings of a Mothman, UFOs and had their community rattled by the deaths of many of its residents after a bridge fell for no apparent reason.

But one cannot find clarity in insanity.

mothmania

Over the years, many books and articles have been written about Mothman, including two by John Keel, *The Mothman Prophecies* (about Mothman sightings and other paranormal events in WV, including Derenberger) and *The Eighth Tower* (This one concentrates on psychic phenomena rather than UFOs or the Mothman.) Others have included his *Strange Mutants: From Mothmen To Demon Dogs and Phantom Cats* and *Disneyland of the Gods.* (A number of John Keel's books are a smorgasbord of speculation meant to tantalize with his unique vision and dry wit.)

Other books have included *The Silver Bridge* by Gray Barker, about the paranormal events that led to the Silver Bridge disaster in 1967, *Mothman: The Facts Behind the Legend* by local residents Donnie Sergent Jr. & Jeff Wamsley, *Mothman & Other Curious Encounters* by strange phenomena expert Loren Coleman and many others.

Television shows and documentaries have been based on the Mothman and the Newell Partridge Mothman sighting was covered partly on an "X-Files" episode. There have also been two films made about the case, including a limited release called "Mothman" in 2000 and the popular "The Mothman Prophecies," a movie based on John Keel's classic book, released on January 25th, 2002. Interestingly, its star, actor Richard Gere, appeared in the movie "Runaway Bride" with Parkersburg native Paul Dooley who played Julia Robert's father.

In the previous year, Richard Gere sent representatives of his friend the Dalai Lama to Parkersburg to bless and nourish the Ohio River and its people. They did this by building a multi-colored sand Mandela at the Parkersburg Art Center. Later, they marched to the Ohio River and poured the colored sands and cow's milk into the water. We suspect Richard Gere may have somewhat believed in the Mothman, Indrid Cold and Cornstalk's curse, perhaps not wanting another Silver Bridge to occur.

The contactee character 'Gordon' in "The Mothman Prophecies" movie is loosely based on former Mineral Wells resident Woodrow Derenberger who was the first to encounter the entity Indrid Cold along highway I-77 a few miles south of Parkersburg, not Point Pleasant as is portrayed in the movie. (See previous chapter.)

Since that time, The West Virginia Mothman has been the inspiration for songs, band names, bumper stickers, T-shirts and even a Beanie Baby Mothman. It seems the Mothman is one legend that is not about to go away.

strangely ~~~ mothman not unique

Winged, red-eyed creatures have been spotted all over the world. If the Mothman was unique to the Point Pleasant area, it could be dismissed simply as mass hysteria or the misidentification of a bird, just as many non-believers claim. However, there is a universal flavor to all of these 'birdman' sightings – only the names and places are different.

One of the most famous accounts of a large winged creature comes from across the ocean nearly ten years after the rash of Mothman sightings in Point Pleasant. The "Owlman" was seen by a number of people between April 1976 and July 1978 just outside of Cornwall, England. Just as the Mothman sightings were limited to an area of the TNT area, the Owlman sightings were restricted to an area around the Mawnan Church on the outskirts of Cornwall.

The first sighting of the Cornish Owlman, as the creature became to be known, was by three young girls on the afternoon of April 17, 1976. Twelve-year old June Melling and her younger sister, nine-year old Vicky, were out playing near the Church when they noticed a very large winged creature flying near the church tower. After the girls reported this to authorities, June was asked to draw and to describe exactly what she saw. June drew a humanoid shape with large eyes and outstretched wings that were attached to its shoulders. The girl said that she was close enough to notice that it had dark gray feathers and glowing red eyes.

Not many people believed that the girls had actually seen anything, so the entire story was dismissed as the wild yarn of a young and imaginative mind. Perhaps she had witnessed a large bird, but it certainly could not have been the size of a man. Soon, another report came in. Perhaps the authorities were mistaken...

The second sighting of the Owlman took place three months after June Mellings' episode. This was another appearance of the Owlman spotted by two young girls. Sally Chapman and Barbara Perry, both fourteen years old, were camping in the woods near the church. About 10:00 p.m., they started to hear a strange hissing noise that reminded them of a large snake. The hissing continued and they left their tent to investigate the sound, not knowing what they would encounter. Sally later told authorities what she saw that night:

"It was like a big owl with pointed ears, as big as a man. The eyes were red and glowing. At first, I thought it was someone dressed up, playing a joke, trying to scare us. I laughed at it – We both did. Then it went up in the air and we screamed for our lives. When it went up, you could see its feet were like pincers!"

After a second, independent report of a creature in the same area, the authorities took notice. There had been no public report or newspaper article of the Owlman and the girls did not know one another. The sightings had been independent and the descriptions were almost identical. Apparently, this was only the beginning....

The very next day Jane Greenwood and her sister claimed to have seen the Owlman while in the area the next day. In this case, the Greenwoods went to the newspaper, where Jane described the creature in very minute detail.

"It was Sunday morning and the place was in the trees near Mawnan Church, above the rocky beach. It was in the trees standing like a full-grown man, but the legs bent backwards like a bird's. It saw us and quickly jumped up and rose straight up through the trees. My sister and I saw it very clearly before it rose up. It had red slanting eyes and a very large mouth. The feathers are slightly gray and so are his body and legs. The feet are like big, black crab's legs. We were frightened at the time. It was so strange, like something in a horror film. After the thing went up, there was crackling sounds in the tree tops for ages."

Once the account of the creature was published in the local newspaper, people began to take notice. Worried parents started to make the church and the surrounding land off limits to their children. Clearly, something was happening out by the old Mawnan Church, and the people of Cornwall did not want to find out what it was.

People from all over decided to come to the church to find this elusive Owlman. Over the course of the next year, nearly thirty people claimed to have seen the Owlman. The sightings eventually moved to an area away from the old church. Some believe that since so many people went there to find the Owlman, it disturbed his habitat and he apparently migrated to an area right outside of Cornwall, for the sightings continued.

The sightings of the Cornwall Owlman ceased as suddenly as they began. The last sighting was in the summer of 1978 by a couple of farmers a few miles from the Mawhan Church. It is interesting the note that the Owlman and the Mothman have similarities to a frightening creature in old British-Celtic fairy lore, called the "Phouka." The Phouka was actually the inspiration for Shakespeare's Puck fairy character in his play *A Mid-Summer Night's Dream*. Puck, like Phouka, was really an Irish-Scottish Fairy as is our Marrtown Banshee mentioned earlier in the book.

The Phouka is said to be a night creature and claimed to be extremely terrifying to anyone who chances to meet him. Some say the Phouka closely resembles an ugly horse (related to the dreaded "nightmare") a goat-like creature or even a large white dog. The Phouka sneaks into the homes where he kidnaps unsuspecting people to give them "the ride of their lives," flying and dragging their victims' exhausted bodies across the countryside all night long. But like the alien visitors of the 20th and 21st Centuries, the Phouka always tucks his victims safely into their beds the following morning. Maybe not too terrifying, after all.

But did one of these Phouka visit Parkersburg?

In the early days of the 19th Century, three farmers were planting gardens down by what is now Parkersburg's Point Park early one morning, in the exact area where the Ohio and Kanawha Rivers meet. One farmer looked up to see a massive white beast whipping its way through the clouds, seemingly oblivious to all. The beast resembled a cross between a horse and a goat, but it had wings. The men watched in amazement as the animal passed over them and continued south. This Phouka-like creature was never, to our knowledge, reported again.

tales of a black dog

West Virginia has a few other supernatural creature sightings.

As mentioned earlier in the book, stories are told of a black dog digging around Riverview Cemetery in Parkersburg even though a dog that size could never squeeze under the surrounding fence. As an animal from English folklore, Black Dog appearances are associated with death and tragedy. Numerous accounts report sightings of a black dog in areas where a person has been killed in an automobile accident. Black dogs protect the graves of those who die in some unfortunate manner.

It is suggested the Black Dog appears shortly before a person dies, much in the way the Banshee does, to howl or cry or bring a message about someone's inevitable demise.

So, do such legends of the Black Dog belong in books of folklore or to some superstitious ancient past? Read on and learn about a modern appearance of a Black Dog in the Parkersburg area. The email we received reads:

"Many years ago I was working as a nurse in a local hospital. This day, a friend of my mother's had had a catastrophic stroke, and I was sure she would die that day. However, the day wore on and nothing untoward happened. When it was time for me to go off duty, I checked her one last time and left, certain that she was stabilized.

"I walked to the parking lot and just as I came close to my car, a large black dog appeared beside me. I had not noticed a dog in the area before, and the parking lot was a huge expanse of concrete with only a few cars left and I thought I surely would have noticed a big dog coming near.

"I glanced around but the dog stayed beside me. I finally spoke to the dog, saying, "Where did you come from?" The black dog looked up at me. Much to my shock the dog's face had completely transformed into my patient's face! This was quite startling. Despite my shock the thought struck me that the woman had just died, even as I told myself this experience was impossible.

"The dog then walked to the front of my car and disappeared.

"I got down on my knees, looking under the few cars that were left in the lot. I saw no trace of any dog whatsoever. Just then, someone called my name and asked me what in the world I was looking for under the cars...a friend of mine was crossing the parking lot behind me. She saw me looking around in puzzlement. I asked her if she didn't see a dog near me moments earlier and if she did where had it gone? My friend told me I was crazy...that she'd been behind me for several minutes and she didn't see a black dog...only me crouching down, looking under cars. I glimpsed at my watch and it was 4:10 p.m. The next day when I went back to work, I found that my patient had died at exactly 4:10 p.m.

"I never forgot this and some time later, I heard about the "Black Dog," an animal spirit that is associated with death or the passing onto the next realm. I was certain the folklore about, but very real, Black Dog is what I truly encountered that day ... Not just any old stray dog wandering around parking lots. Nothing will convince me otherwise... What do you think? Thanks for reading this...As you can imagine, I have told very few people."

For a few years I (Susan Sheppard) wrote monthly horoscopes for a local Internet company. One of my readers wrote to me with this unusual tale about a creature she and her husband spotted near Belleville in south Wood County late one night:

"My husband is a Capricorn so you know he doesn't usually believe in this kind of stuff but he was with me when this incident actually happened. We were driving home late in the evening when an animal that was about four-feet tall and completely white ran in front of our car lights. At first I thought it might be an albino fox or raccoon until the animal suddenly stood up on two legs and tottered across the road, almost like a monkey that wasn't used to standing upright. I mean, it ran on two legs! What wildlife in this area is capable of doing that? I can't imagine what it might have been and neither can my husband. No circuses were in the area and no shop with exotic pets was within miles of the place. If you have any idea of what this creature might have been, please let us know. We are baffled by it."

the flatwoods monster

It turns out the Mothman isn't the only elusive monster to terrorize the hills and valleys of West Virginia during the autumn months in the middle of the 20th Century. There was an equally, if not more, horrible encounter with a monstrous creature near the small community of Flatwoods in Braxton County.

It all began on September 12, 1952 when the Braxton County Sheriff Robert Carr and Deputy Burnell Long witnessed something burning and bright fall out of the sky. Thinking it was a downed aircraft the two went to investigate but found nothing amiss.

That same evening, four boys playing football at the Flatwoods School ball field saw another illuminating object hit the earth on the top of the hill of the Bailey Fisher property. Ever curious and thinking it was an airplane, the boys decided to investigate. However, they became frightened as they made their way up the hill. Something smelled bad. The youths stopped at the home of Kathleen May. She and her two sons who joined the boys to find out what it was had dropped to earth.

The early September evening was a misty one. Cicadas whirred in the grass like wind-up toys. Where the object fell, there was a strange smell in the air.

Mrs. May later reported there was a distinct metallic odor but she could not pinpoint exactly what it was. "It burned our eyes and noses." The boys and woman soon came upon a glowing object that seemed to hiss on the object were two lights approximately one foot apart.

One of the boys held a flashlight. As he swept the area with his light, the group was shocked to see what the light revealed: a massive creature nearly ten feet tall, in bright green clothing, with a fiery, red face and a head shaped like the ace of spades in a deck of cards. The thing's clothing, from the waist down, hung in long folds. The woman and boys could see no feet beneath the folds, and rather than walking or running, the creature floated toward them. The group ran back to the May home at a break-neck speed and called Sheriff Carr. When he came to interview them, the boys were so frightened they could barely speak.

Later, when a reporter went back to the hilltop site, he saw nothing unusual but it was now quite dark. An investigation the next morning, however, revealed odd skid marks. Sheriff Carr concluded the whole incident was nothing more than a meteor that inspired the group's wild imaginings after seeing the meteor's descent to earth. Carr did admit later that went he went on the hill later that night, he did see odd reflective eyes in a tree such as those belonging to an owl, cat or raccoon.

Other residents of Braxton County later confessed they had seen the plummeting lights and the monster but were afraid to come forward because of the ridicule they and their families might suffer. Some even claimed to have seen a spherical object resembling a classic spacecraft.

Such conical UFOs were popular props in Hollywood movies of the 1950s so it is possible those who saw such movies might have interpreted strange lights or objects in this way. Still, no one has ever been able to explain away the green-suited monster, with fiery crimson face and a head like the ace of spades. As Kathleen May later described, "What I saw looked worse than Frankenstein. It could not have been human."

Thus, the mystery of the Flatwoods monster that appeared only one time on a hilltop of West Virginia - precisely September 12, 1952 - remains just that - a incredible tale filled with many eccentricities, and like the Mothman, never solved.

and the stories continue ...

West Virginia and the Ohio Valley continue to be visited by uncanny creatures - many great and small - some physical and maybe others that are not so physical. One day we will have this all figured out perhaps. But don't count on us to unravel these mysteries of strange forces and even stranger beasts anytime too soon.

As Einstein once wrote, "The most beautiful thing we experience in life is the mysterious." Perhaps tales about the Mothman, the Irish Phouka and the Flatwoods monster are not supposed to be solved. Such enigmas of the material realm and the non-material realm are the most fascinating things we encounter in life. A mystery explained may end up rather dull. But a mystery left unexplained is another story – after all.

4. haunted rails

the ghost of silver run
& the east end ghoul

Early in the 20th Century, in an area remote to everyone but B & O Railroad workers and engineers is a place called Silver Run. Imagine a time nearing midnight. A full moon hangs in indistinct, drowsy gases directly over the Silver Run railroad tunnel.

Everyone calls you O' Flannery and you work as an engineer for the B & O railroad. Like your Ulster Irish ancestors, you have worked for the railroad most of your life and can hardly imagine a job anywhere else. You are hardened and pragmatic because that is the way the world has been toward you.

For the most part, your route, between Clarksburg and Parkersburg, is a ninety-mile stretch of curving, monotonous railroad. You see or encounter very little along the rails - except for an occasional dairy cow that breaks through a fence and loses her way.

As your engine makes the bend heading toward Silver Run tunnel you glimpse something pale and fluttering in dead center of the railroad tracks. As you draw closer you clearly see it is a young woman with pitch-black hair and white, bloodless skin. She wears a pale gown. She does not look at you at all. In fact, you wonder if she is a sleepwalker from one of the surrounding houses that has wandered out on the tracks.

You find that you are not able to move. Your hands freeze on the engine full-throttle. Suddenly, you glimpse the ethereal woman who turns toward you with eyes cold and foreboding. She makes no effort to move. Instead, she flies up into the air like a great white bat and is spirited away into the night. Shaken, you remember the stories about the Ghost of Silver Run you heard from other engineers and you taunted them. You said you didn't believe in ghosts and anyone who did was a damned fool. Only now you believe...

The idea of phantom travelers is in every culture. The belief is that ghosts will haunt travel routes, trains, highways and even airports that they have some emotional connection to, such as having their destinations interrupted through death or injury. The spirits will continue to appear where the traumatic event happened in effort to resolve it.

Traumatic events, such as sudden death and even murder, can leave a residual energy of the deceased that somehow exists outside of our human conception of time. In this way, the actual apparition or ghost has no consciousness, and is more like a hologram or recording getting played over and over again. This type of ghostly appearance is like terrible scream that is heard but continues to resonate. Because of the shock or trauma it never loses the emotional power behind the event.

The following tales, such as the Ghost of Silver Run, are similar to many phantom traveler and ghostly hitchhiker stories reported over the last fifty years, all a part of urban legends of the 20th and 21st Centuries. Ghostly hitchhikers began to be recorded after the availability of automobiles in the U.S. However, stories of phantom travelers have been told throughout the world for hundreds, if not thousands of years. Some of these tales trace back to a belief in the Crossroads, a place where ghosts and devils lurk.

The appearance of phantom travelers in trains, planes, cars, buses and even motorcycles are very recent, of course, but they do hint at a parallel realm that we, as frail humans, cannot fully understand. The explanation may be as simple as the phantoms contacting the living in ways the living can understand. Yet somehow the realm of the phantom traveler does exists outside our mortal ability to comprehend matters of a more spiritual nature. It seems the spirits of the dead are more than happy to remind us time and again of their existence by their unexpected visits and ghostly calling cards.

the ghost of silver run

Not far from Parkersburg, in an isolated patch of Ritchie County is the small community of Silver Run, a lonely place where tales of a ghostly traveler still causes flesh to crawl. Accounts tell of a raven-haired apparition with skin as white as moon light, one that haunts the old railroad tracks. Dressed in a long gown, the ghost always appears at the mouth of the Silver Run Tunnel.

Anyone familiar with the history of northern West Virginia knows of the pivotal role the B & O railroad played in developing the north central part of the state. While the southern region of the state had its coal wars and family feuds, the history of north central West Virginia is calmer, more subdued, a bit more civilized perhaps…

…That is, unless you believe in ghosts.

Today Silver Run is (no pun intended) a ghost town, where flowers with names like Tiger Lily, Snowballs and Black-Eyed-Susan's strain under the dusty talc of Ritchie County's backcountry roads. If you drive down Silver Run road today, you can still see the old tunnel and abandoned houses reclaimed by the weeds, as well as the remains of a once-thriving marble factory, a place that made marbles with names like "cat eyes." Even still, one can imagine the inside of the factory lit up by the bright orange, molten lava of liquid glass. Such glass plants, so typical of northern West Virginia, even in their hey-day, looked like tin-sheeted, thrown-together, squatter's shacks.

However, the little town of Silver Run did exist once, as did its very own ghost. And so, this is her story, "the Ghost of Silver Run."

Over100-years-ago, when the B & O railroad was a considerable force in West Virginia, and trains rolling through Silver Run was almost an hourly occurrence, an event happened so strange, it is still fresh in the minds of some older residents of Wood and Ritchie counties.

Nearing midnight one late August night, as mid-summer fog hung in thick, wet veils across the rails, an engineer making his way toward the Silver Run Tunnel spotted a young woman standing in dead center of the tracks.

This, by itself, was out of the ordinary. Mostly drunks wandered out on the rails at night, usually ending up scattered in pieces over the tracks, never knowing what hit them. But the young woman's face appeared blank, stricken, as if she had lost her way, perhaps after having an argument. After all, the young woman did appear to be upset or confused since she made no effort to move away from the railroad tracks.

As the engineer turned on his whistle to warn of the oncoming train, the woman turned and stared at him but seemed frozen in time. Although the lady was visible only for a matter of seconds, the engineer saw that she was thinly dressed in a filmy dress. But what was most striking was her black hair and white skin. At the moment the startled engineer thought that his train was about to slam into the woman, he watched her fly up into the air only to disappear into the night.

As he tried to control his train, the engineer's heart nearly lunged out of his chest. Striking down any person was bad enough, but hitting a beautiful young woman took on the shades of a nightmare. He could only imagine the horror of maroon blood spattered against that pearly, white skin…

After several frantic moments, the engineer brought his engine to a stop. He was sure he'd find her dead body (or parts of one) along the tracks. With his engine fireman beside him, the engineer embarked on a short search for the woman. Neither man was anxious to see the destruction that a train would do to a human body, but leaving it there until the light of the day would be a disgrace. This was someone's child, it made no difference how lost she was.

After searching the tracks for a while the men concluded there was no body. It so happened that this mesmerizing, dark-haired woman was indeed a ghost.

Convinced he'd had too much coffee and too little sleep, the engineer pushed this unsettling occurrence out of his mind and continued with his duties over the time. But the ghost of the young woman had a message to convey at the Silver Run Tunnel, and made several more appearances at the tunnel over the following weeks. Each week a train came to a stop and each time the figure flew upward and disappeared into the darkness of the night.

After sharing his unsettling experience with other engineers at the 6th Street station in Parkersburg, the engineer was surprised to learn that the apparition had appeared to other railroad men nearing Silver Run Tunnel over the years and nearly all were familiar with the scene as he had encountered it. Some noted the ghostly appearances coincided with the moon phases, the spirit appearing most commonly during a full moon. August appeared to be the most active month for the apparition to reveal herself to the railroad workers. No one knew exactly why.

It so happened that one engineer by the name of O'Flannery hadn't yet run into the Ghost of Silver Run. In fact, he had never seen any ghost at all and made no bones of the fact that he didn't believe in ghosts, and anyone that did (according to O'Flannery) was a fool or at least a liar. After a pensive silence, one engineer challenged O'Flannery, saying to the effect that all engineers who had passed through Silver Run Tunnel saw the ghost, and up until then, they never believed in ghosts either.

O'Flannery wouldn't have any of it. He laughed with bitter sarcasm and vowed that no ghost was going to stop his train— he'd run her down first.

Of course, those schooled in the science of spirits and apparitions understand that one does not challenge a ghost. Ridicule tends to cause spirits to step up their ghostly activity.

About two weeks later it was O'Flannery who was nearing the Silver Run Tunnel. The time was near midnight. An incandescent moon glowed inside the charcoal-colored clouds. A rich darkness surrounded the traveling train.

As he came upon the Silver Run Tunnel, O'Flannery noticed a flutter of pale movement along the railroad tracks. Much to his surprise, he saw that it was a young woman standing there. She made no effort to move. And, as described by other railroad men earlier, it appeared the raven-haired apparition flew into the air and was spirited away into the darkness, to be seen no more.

By this time, O'Flannery was, in fact, unnerved. Sweat poured from his brow. He felt tremendously relieved to get his train through the Silver Run Tunnel.

Even so, O'Flannery was still a boastful type who looked forward to bragging about how he ran the Ghost of Silver Run down to the other engineers. Later, as the

Irishman pulled into the 6th Street train station in Parkersburg, O'Flannery noticed the place was in a bit of a panic bordering on bedlam. As he walked through the door, he asked another engineer, "Hey—what's all the commotion about?"

The engineer answered, "Man, don't you know? You hit a woman at the Silver Run Tunnel and she rode all the way into Parkersburg on your cow-catcher!"

O'Flannery was left uncharacteristically speechless. After all, the spirit had made a mockery of the man as she would many doubters to come.

Apparently, earlier in the evening, calls flooded the 6th Street train station in Parkersburg from smaller stations along the rails that reported a thinly dressed woman was riding the cowcatcher of O'Flannery's engine as it passed by! As soon as the engine made its appearance at the 6th Street Station, the woman vanished.

An 1897 Photograph of the 6th Street B &O Railroad Station in Parkersburg in the same general area where the Ghost of Silver Run was said to disappear.

Many of the B & O railroad engineers claimed to see or encounter the Ghost of Silver Run after the turn of the last century well into the 1940s. The reason for her ghostly appearances, however, remains a mystery.

There are two possible explanations that can neither be proved nor disproved. One story goes that a richly dressed young woman was riding into Parkersburg to meet her betrothed and never arrived. After an exhaustive search, the woman's body was never found. No one knew what happened to the young bride.

There is another old tale whispered by grandmothers to grandchildren in Ritchie County on mid-summer nights, especially in homes not far from the Silver Run Tunnel. Legend has it that when an abandoned house was torn down at Silver Run, the skeleton of a woman was found walled up in the chimney. The workers knew it was the skeleton of a woman because the skeleton wore a white bridal gown. Although the few remains were never claimed or identified, the skeleton was given a proper burial in an old cemetery not far from the Silver Run Tunnel. After funeral rites had ended, the Ghost of Silver Run was not seen again. Or was she?

Does the Ghost of Silver Run still haunt the old tunnel? Only those who still live there might know. Many say they still hear the whistle of a train coming up near the Silver Run Tunnel at night. Others claim they see the form of a thinly dressed woman floating eerily along the railroad tracks.

But for the rest of us who have never seen her are left to contemplate her mystery – the one they still call the Ghost of Silver Run...

The Silver Run Tunnel Today
(Photo by Kristall Chambers)

the eaton tunnel

Another B & O railroad tunnel in Ritchie County with tales of haunts is the Eaton Tunnel, where two workers were buried alive in 1982 as they were lowering the bottom of the tunnel so that diesel engines could pass through. As the men worked, the sides of the tunnel caved in trapping them alive with their bulldozer, truck and backhoe. Herculean efforts tried to save them, but to no avail. The men probably suffocated. Their remains were never rescued. A marker was set on the old tunnel. This was the best they could do for a burial for the men.

To this day, the tunnel holds a hollow, resonating energy (one area rock group even recorded an album in the tunnel) and high-pitched moans are often heard throughout the night, mostly on the anniversary of the worker's deaths. Photographs taken here typically reveal ghostly orbs of light, as well as what appear to be phantasms of hooded figures bending over the curve of the tunnel as if in mourning.

moonville's haunted tunnel
vinton, county, ohio

It now must seem that many areas along the old B & O railroad route in West Virginia have haunted tunnels, and this naturally carries over into southeastern Ohio, in another remote spot bedded in the hills of Ohio's Appalachia. The Moonville Tunnel is located in Vinton County, not far from the college town of Athens. Over the years there have been tales of a ghostly apparition that swings a light or a lantern through the tunnel after dark. Some stories claim than an inebriated conductor or brakeman fell to his death during a card game when he should have been watching the tracks in early 1859.

Another spirit that is said to haunt the tunnel is similar to the Ghost of Silver Run. It is the vision of a young woman at night in a flowing blue nightgown. Many claim the ghost pulls at her hair and runs through the railroad tunnel screaming bloody-murder.

There are no recorded sources to support the idea of a ghost of a young woman haunting the tracks, however, since the only female listed killed on the railroad tracks near the tunnel was an eighty-year-old woman.

Southeastern Ohio's Moonville Tunnel
(Photo by Troy Taylor)

There is one recorded source that refers to the haunting of the Moonville Tunnel. It ran in the *Chillicothe Gazette* on February 17, 1895:

"The ghost of Moonville, after an absence of one year, has returned and is again at its old pranks, haunting the B & O Southwest Freight trains and their crews. It appeared Monday night in front of a fast freight. Number 99 west bound, just east of the cut which is one half mile the other side of Moonville at the point where Engineer Lawhead lost his life and Engineer Walters was injured.

"The ghost, attired in a pure white robe, carried a lantern. It had a long flowing white beard, its eyes glistened like balls of fire and surrounding it was a halo of twinkling stars. When the train stopped the ghost stepped off the track and disappeared into the rocks nearby."

Ghost hunters who have investigated the Moonville Tunnel have witnessed the appearance of a strange light bobbing through the tunnel as if someone carries the lantern or holds it up. Before the light reaches the end of the tunnel, it disappears as if snuffed out.

the east end ghoul

If ghosts frighten you, you might not want to consider the thought of being chased by a ghoul. So what is a ghoul, you ask? A ghoul is a hideous, graveyard creature that preys upon the bodies and souls of the dead. The word ghoul comes from the Arabic language meaning to "grab quick" or "take a hold of." Ghouls are universally malevolent spirit entities. They are like ghosts but are more visceral – you can smell the ghoul's foul breath and touch his rotting skin. Ghouls come on as physical and not so much of a fleeting apparition.

Ghouls are here to do evil and are more closely related to graveyard demons or vampires than ghosts or lost souls of the dead. Ancient lore says ghouls will feast upon the flesh of road worn travelers or corpses stolen out of graves at night. This is why ghouls often hang around cemeteries or at the ever-menacing Crossroads.

Most ghouls are content to terrify. Their purpose is to scare the living so bad they wish to the hell that they were dead.

The dreaded ghoul has a gruesome face but devoid of features. They typically moan, groan and rattle their chains. These midnight demons are said to even inhabit old ruins, cemeteries, abandoned houses and other lonely, isolated places.

In European folklore, ghouls are most strongly attracted to travelers. The reason for this is not really known except for the fact that travelers seem to be vulnerable. In older Dracula movies, you may remember how the movie often opens with a scene of weary travelers, after delayed by thunderstorms or losing their way, eventually find them selves at Castle Dracula. Therefore it is no surprise that in Eastern European lore, a vampire and a ghoul are pretty much the same thing. Both are re-animated corpses with evil spirits inside. But only in the cases of extreme evil do human beings ever become ghouls.

Perhaps ghouls are attracted to travelers because travelers are vulnerable, easy to prey upon and confuse. After people in route somewhere are not immediately missed by family members. That is, if something "unexpected" happens to them.

This is where our tale unfolds, at the Crossroads, a place where the malevolent energies of the supernatural are at their most powerful. The exact place is the East End B & O railroad yard in Parkersburg, and at the Rowland Boarding House where weary sojourners working the rails chose to rest their heads at night as they dreamed of the safety of home and family, back in the Appalachian foothills.

The year is 1886. It is the last week of June, twenty years after the Civil War has ended. The 6th Street train trestle and bridge has been completed – jobs are plentiful and West Virginia coal is being shipped out west.

The exact place of the haunting is the coal chutes of the B & O Railroad yard in the East End of the city. The time closes in on midnight, 'the witching hour,' a tenuous moment when supernatural forces are the strongest and most unpredictable. Tired rail workers were leaving their late evening shifts when they encountered a mysterious being that both startled and terrified them. More than six feet and moving at a "funereal pace," the apparition was completely enshrouded in white from head-to-toe.

Although ghostly in appearance, the being was more horrible than any ghost was; far more menacing than ethereal phantasms spotted on nearby Blennerhassett Island. What the men encountered was an actual ghoul, the 'East End Ghoul,' to be precise.

The B & O railroad workers were made aware of the ghoul when they first heard "a clanking of chains." As the men looked in the direction of the sounds came from, they saw something large and white floating along the railroad tracks. Its feet never touched the ground even though the men heard echoing footsteps. The face was mostly covered, but absent of any human features. As this incredible apparition swayed down the tracks, it emitted an unearthly groan that could be heard for several yards.

The workers that didn't scatter immediately took refuge behind some barrels to watch the bizarre event unfold. The ghoul drifted along, moaning all the way, seemingly unaware of the men's presence. The ghoul then came upon the Rowland Boarding House where railroad men and travelers stayed. The hulking phantom hesitated for a few moments as if pondering whether to go in or not. The sounds of the chains were fainter. The thing seemed to have lost its direction. But without missing a beat, the ghoul sped up and coursed down the tracks, past the cemetery, where it came upon an alleyway and vanished into a gray smoke.

This appearance of the ghoul might be easily explained as a hoax except for the fact that it appeared every night for a week in late June and was witnessed by dozens of people. And as such, it was written up in local newspapers as the story unfolded during mid-summer on 1886.

As with many haunted tales, a skeptic enters the scene to challenge the validity of such frightening and puzzling appearances. In this story, the skeptic is one Mr. Crolley, (accounts of a first name were not mentioned in the 1886 news article) who did not work for the B & O Railroad but was employed by the Camden Consolidated Oil Company.

Crolley happened to be at the railroad-yard one late June night handling a business transaction, and perhaps also to spin a yarn with the B & O workers around quitting time. This was shortly before the towering ghoul appeared once more.

As Mr. Crolley left for home, he heard a god-awful groaning near the railroad yard. When he glanced around, he spotted a shrouded phantom exactly as the other men had reported on earlier in the week. The apparition drifted up and down the tracks in the area of the coal chutes, approximately one hundred yards from the Rowland Boarding House.

Too shocked to breathe, Crolley receded quietly into the shadows. The ghoul paused in the area of the Rowland Boarding House as if something inside interested it. Gaslights fluttered at the glass. Songs of drunken men poured out of the second story windows, oblivious to the unearthly thing that was now focused on them.

Of indeterminate sex, the ghoul glided down the tracks. A sweet stench of decay filled the air – it was the kind of smell that reminded Crolley of a back alley behind a funeral parlor. With caution, he inched closer to the ghoul only to realize that he was completely drained, taken over by an overwhelming tiredness. As Crolley fought his fatigue, the ghoul stopped at an alleyway and stared, still not noticing him. The strange being then vanished just as it did before.

Crolley was not a man who was easily frightened or frustrated by spooky things. He promised himself that he would investigate the ghoulish appearance the very next night.

Mr. Crolley was not disappointed.

It was now after eleven o' clock on a Thursday night, a time when many of the railroad workers ended their shifts. As Crolley waited, strange echoing footsteps sounded. This was certainly odd, because the ghoul, in fact, did not appear to have any feet at all as it floated above the railroad tracks. And yet, footsteps echoed!

As with the previous night, the ghoul moved in the direction of the Rowland House, where it stopped for a few brief moments, then diverted its attention toward the alleyway. Only this time, Crolley started to run after the ghoul. He wasn't about to let this mystery get away from him! What happened next was utterly unexpected.

With a supernatural force, the East End Ghoul wheeled around and approached the terrified man at a high rate of speed. Not knowing what else to do, Crolley leapt behind a tree where he hid for several seconds. As soon as the man regained his courage, he peered out from behind the tree to see where the ghoul was now. What he witnessed there startled him.

The East End Ghoul was joined at the tracks by another one, an exact replica! But this particular ghoul was dark, its face and clothes completely blackened as if by the sulphurous fires of Hell.

Twin-like, the ghouls moved at a lingering, slow pace, echoing the same movements. Later it was said they were resembled photograph negatives of the identical image. The ghouls were alike, but in contrasting tones of white and black. Even so, both ghoulish manifestations seemed to be intent on one Mr. Crolley, who now ran away, feet barely touching the brick-street, glancing over his shoulder all the while. It wasn't long before the ghouls halted. It seemed they had lost interest in the frightened, bedraggled man.

The "Ghouls of East End" turned and floated back toward Rowland Boarding House where they paused for another few moments as if straining to hear the lively sounds of happy men inside. The figures then peered down the alley and in a phantomlike silence they both disappeared. Perhaps, as ghouls are concerned, Crolley wasn't much of a catch anyway. More fun seemed to be had by those spending the night in the Rowland Boarding House.

Nevertheless, the East End haunts were quite the sensation for the rest of the summer based upon the puzzling events of the last week of June in 1886. However, the East End Ghoul and his black-enshrouded partner were never seen in Parkersburg again.

What happened to Crolley, is pure speculation. It appears his name also faded from the newspapers' pages. One thing that is for certain about Mr. Crolley though – only a fool would chase a ghoul!

portraits of more ghosts in black and white

Reports of the black and white apparitions near the coal chutes in the East End of Parkersburg might stand alone on account of their utter strangeness except for similar ghost sightings in August of 1888. These sightings involved the apparition of a little girl who was said to play in the streets near dusk.

An article that appeared in *The State Journal* on August 13, 1888 states "The citizens of some parts of the East End are scared out of their wits over an alleged ghost. The children especially are all torn up over the mysterious visitor.

"The "ghost" presents the appearance of a young girl in a perfectly white dress, and has been seen on Latrobe Street and other East End streets. A girl in a white dress on the streets is not a strange or unusual sight, but the actions of this particular individual seem peculiar to the citizens of that neighborhood.

"Last week this "ghost" wore a black dress and was seen on Seventh Street— The police will probably have him or her in the coop before long if he or she does not quit his or her monkey business."

A more recent sighting of another ghostly figure in the East End was disclosed as recently as the summer of 2000. Shortly after dusk, a resident of the area glimpsed the figure of what looked to be a woman in a white shroud gliding up one of the side streets.

Since the features on this apparition were quite unspecific, this reported spirit appears to be similar to ones sighted in the 19th Century near the railroad yards. It is possible that such creatures of the night still haunt the shadowy rails and alleys of East End.

5. ghosts that grieve

eva zona shue, delsie harris & margaret blennerhassett

Margaret, Margaret,
Why are you grieving?
Over Goldengrove unleaving?
Leaves, like the things of man, you
With your fresh thoughts care for, can you?
Ah! As the heart grows even older
It will come to such sights colder..
Nor mouth had, no, nor mind expressed
What heart had heard of or ghost had guessed:
It is the blight man was born for.
It is Margaret you mourn for..

from 'spring and fall'
by gerard manley hopkins

Grieving ghosts, or "women in white" apparitions, are a universal phenomenon. They are thought to be ghosts of women with unsettled issues and are linked to tragedies such as suicide, murder, betrayal or even the death of a child. Why some spirits hold on, while others do not, is not clearly known, but in such cases they carry a sense of regret or sadness over unfair treatment in life.

We have all experienced sad or disappointing circumstances that tend to haunt us over a period of time. But eventually we come to terms with the grief or disappointment, and move on. "Women in white," or grieving ghosts, are not able to do this – they are unable to let go of the same sad circumstances that haunted them in life.

There is urgency to their haunting – appearing again and again until they find justice, resolution – or they appear just long enough for their pleading messages to be conveyed and understood by the living – that they have wrongly suffered.

West Virginia has three famous tales of grieving ghosts – all women. Why these spirits continue to haunt, you will learn in the following pages.

the ghost of greenbrier county

When twenty-four year old Zona Shue died suddenly in her home on January 23, 1897 few people were suspicious. After all, wherever Zona went, trouble and mishap followed. She had already embarrassed her religious family by giving birth to an illegitimate child in 1895. Everyone thought the girl was easily led astray and lacked "good horse sense." Zona's accidental death only seemed to prove that she didn't have brains enough to watch out for herself.

But 1896 began on a happier note for Eva Zona Heaster – at least so she hoped. She met a charming middle-aged man by the name of Edward (Erasmus) Stribbling Trout Shue who had traveled to Greenbrier County, West Virginia to work as a blacksmith.

Shue was a thickly built man, with oily black hair and fists as big as smokehouse hams. Zona needed someone strong to take care of her and Edward Shue appeared to be the one. At first, she didn't mind the fact that Shue drank, and was mean and crude at times. In fact, his roughness attracted her. She figured he was big enough and mean enough to keep her fully protected.

Mary Jane Heaster, Zona's mother, however, was not convinced that Erasmus Shue was a suitable husband for her naïve daughter. She saw that Shue was sneaky and he never looked her directly in the eye. When Mary Jane visited her daughter in her new home, Shue got up from the table and left the room. Erasmus was edgy whenever Zona's mother came around.

On January 27, 1897 Zona Shue's body was discovered by a neighborhood boy. The boy was on his way to the store and stopped to see if Zona wanted anything. Zona's body lay on the floor with her head turned to the side and one hand placed on her stomach. Although the body was mostly stiff from rigor mortis Zona's head remained loose.

Local coroner Dr. George Knapp was called in but it took him over an hour to get to the Shue farmhouse. The Doctor found that Zona Shue was already carried upstairs by her husband and placed on the bed in an odd arranged way. She was not dressed in her usual housedress but in a high-necked dress, the type reserved for special occasions for a young woman in West Virginia. The Doctor had difficulty examining the body because each time he got up to the neck and head of the corpse, Edward Shue fell over the body, wept inconsolably, and cradled his wife's head. Although Doc Knapp noticed some bruising around the corpses' neck and was skeptical, he was buffaloed by Shue and ruled the cause of Zona's death as "everlasting faint." After more pleading words from the bull-necked man, the Doctor reconsidered and wrote down "childbirth" indicating a sudden, fatal miscarriage. Knapp was just glad to get out of the house—Shue now sweated like a sausage in his clothes. His eyes grew strange and wild.

The viewing for Zona's wake only added to the suspicion of her friends, family and residents of Greenbrier. Even before the viewing at the wake, Shue had placed a pillow against Zona's head "so she can rest easier." A colorful scarf was tied around her throat. Shue mentioned it was Zona's "favorite" even though no one remembered ever seeing Zona wear scarves. As family tried to get closer to Zona's body lying in the casket, Shue hovered, not allowing anyone near. Whenever her mother stared down at her child, Shue pushed Mrs. Heaster away then fell over sobbing and caressed Zona's soft brown hair.

Hushed whispers filled the wake. Those who attended the funeral agreed that "all was not right" when it came to Zona's untimely death – but none as much as Zona's mother who suspected Shue from the very instant she learned her daughter had died.

For four weeks after the funeral, Zona Shue's ghost appeared to her mother at the foot of the old woman's bed to reveal the true facts of her demise. Not surprisingly, Zona's ghost affirmed that she had been murdered and Shue was the one who did it. For four more days, Zona's ghost returned to add more specifics and details to the case.

Throughout her short marriage to Erasmus Shue, she had been violated, beaten and abused. One night, when supper was not waiting for Shue on the table at the time he thought it should be, so he flew into a fit of rage and killed his wife. With his huge, rough hands, he choked her into unconsciousness. In doing so, he crushed her windpipe and snapped her neck. After seeing what he had done, Erasmus fled the house and only returned later when authorities notified him that his young wife had died.

After learning of the details of her daughter's death from her anguished ghost, Mary Jane Heaster contacted the Greenbrier prosecutor John Alfred Preston and described in minute detail the circumstances surrounding what she called "murder." Mrs. Heaster informed the prosecutor of the appearance, and testimony of her daughter's ghost – whom she said had appeared numerous times at the foot of her bed.

Whether Preston believed Mrs. Heaster's account or not, one thing was for certain – he was already very suspicious over the odd behavior of Erasmus Shue following his wife's funeral. Heaster ordered Zona Shue's body exhumed on February 22nd. The autopsy revealed Zona, indeed, was strangled, her windpipe crushed and her neck broken exactly in the way her ghost said it happened.

Although the information about Zona's spirit visiting her mother was deemed inadmissible, Erasmus Shue was tried for murdering his wife on very thin evidence. At one point, the defense lawyer brought in information about the ghost, implying that Mary Jane Heaster was a nutcase on a vendetta against her former son-in-law. But the testimony of Zona's ghost at the foot of her mother's bed never entered the courtroom.

Shue was found guilty anyway.

Still, such tales of dastardly deeds do get around – especially in small, mountain communities like those in Greenbrier County. Erasmus Shue was sent to the state prison in Moundsville to live out the rest of his days. He died there on March of 1900. His restless ghost, unlike that of his poor, young wife, has never been seen.

soul on fire at burnt house

Burnt House, a tiny village in Ritchie County, was once made up by a few roughly hewn log cabins. But it was still a heavily traveled crossroads for from Staunton, Virginia to Parkersburg before and after the Civil War.

One of its earliest settlers was Jack Harris, a large, burly man who came up from Randolph County in the south to set down roots at what is now Burnt House around 1843. Because of the turnpike, (any number of travelers passed through the area each day) Jack decided to build a two-story log house and turn it into a tavern.

The Harris tavern was an instant success. It became a major stopping point for the stagecoach with its weary travelers. In 1855, a medicine show arrived. Medicine shows were a popular diversion for locals since they offered various elixirs that promised to heal the sick and also female dancers to entertain those who were, perhaps, not so sick.

When the medicine show brought a sienna-skinned dancer named Deloris, the crowds were awed. Although this bewitching young woman was rumored to be a slave, she had no trouble commanding attention and was called by the nickname "Delsie."

Delsie was an exotic, mixed-race woman. Some stories claimed that she was, in fact, a captured Cherokee woman while others told she was a striking mulatto dressed in swirling, colorful skirts and the bangles of a Gypsy. Since mixed-race people of black, red and white bloodlines were not unusual in the backwoods of West Virginia at the time, Delsie may well have been all three. Her reddish skin, gold-flecked eyes and raven-hair contrasted mysteriously with the many bright baubles and colorful silks that the young woman adorned her beautiful body with.

No matter what her true heritage was, Jack Harris's son William fell head over heels in love with Delsie. William begged his father to buy her. Knowing Delsie would be quite an attraction for his tavern, Harris did purchase the young slave woman and immediately put her to work to act as bar maid and singer.

Business was brisk. The mainstay for Harris's tavern was now the many salesmen and peddlers traveling to Parkersburg to sell their wares. Delsie worked well into the late hours. One night, two jewelry peddlers staying at the tavern vanished without a trace.

Soon Delsie turned up wearing jewelry valuable beyond anything she or William could easily buy. Locals and tavern customers talked. How could a mixed-raced girl end up wearing such expensive baubles? The kind only fine white women could afford? An investigator from Richmond was called in by a man, related to a judge in Parkersburg and had stayed at the tavern the night of the disappearance.

During his investigation the detective found out that a stable boy had witnessed William Harris behead of one of the salesman as he peeked through the window of the tavern unobserved. The boy also said he saw Delsie carrying what looked to be a burlap sack that oozed a maroon substance and contained something the size of a human head.

Jack Harris and his son (whether guilty or not) were privy to the rumors and, knowing what a lynch mob could do, fled Burnt House. Like the true cowards they turned out to be – they left the petite woman behind to face the music …or the rope.

But locals went soft on Delsie. After all, she was gorgeous, and some local men hoped she'd be "kind" to them now that she realized that they had saved her neck. Thus, they left Delsie to wile away the weeks and months, pining over the loss of the lover who jilted her, many in anticipation that the slave girl in her loneliness might share their beds. But it wasn't long until another owner came in and hired Delsie to continue working there. She already knew all of the "ropes" of tavern life and most of the customers.

Yet Delsie's depression over her lost love failed to subside. One Sunday evening, the singer and dancer brought her Bohemian clothes out of storage and put them on… yards of a scarlet skirt, her apple green vest, the coin necklace and the tinkling ankle bracelets. Gold hoops shone red by firelight through Delsie's ringlets of black hair. She stole into the loft of the tavern and lit a fire. The slave girl, now carrying a torch, danced with that flame. She whirled like a dervish throughout the second story as raging fires spread.

A group from a nearby church gathered. They watched Delsie spin while fire licked her arms and face. The second floor of the tavern collapsed into a hellish inferno. The slave girl's screamed interrupted stillness of the valley.

Once the morning came, all that was left of the tavern was in ruins. Delsie's physical remains were forever lost in smoking debris.

After Delsie's death, the sheriff made a search of the hollow not far from what was once the Harris tavern and discovered two human skeletons left on an overhang – one of the skeletons was lacking a head. Everyone assumed it was the missing salesmen, but no one ever knew for sure. After that the hollow was given the name "Dead Man's Hollow" as it is still called today. Many are still afraid to go there after nightfall.

But did not take long for Delsie's ghost to return to the lonely, foreboding stop at Burnt House. By dark of night, many describe the apparition of Delsie rising up from the grounds where the tavern once stood. Her ghost appears as dancing fire that assumes the shape of a curvaceous woman. The ghostly form then takes on the energy of a funnel cloud, picks up speed, and disappears into the black woods. With each disappearance, the ghost screams in self-banishment, writhing in pain over separation from the very place she is doomed to haunt.

In 1883, crashing thunder and lightning storms wrenched trees from their roots at Burnt House. After that terrible storm, the slave girl's ghost appeared to find rest. Many claim that this was the very last time Delsie's ghost was ever seen – careening just like a hellish fire– for one brief moment, setting the woods or perhaps the setting whole damned world, on fire. But the mounting flames were dampened, soon vanquished by pouring rains. Perhaps the spirit of the bewitching slave girl of Burnt House found peace in that torrential night of rain in 1883… and perhaps she did not. We do know this: Delsie never recovered the love of William Harris, the man who wrecked her life and brought her so much pain.

ghost of margaret blennerhassett

In the following pages we will explore the history of hauntings on Blennerhassett Island, a lush, scenic, island located slightly south of Parkersburg on the Ohio River.

We would be remiss not to include sightings concerning the lingering apparition of Margaret Blennerhassett on the island. Margaret's ghost fits the classic "woman in white" apparition, which are spirits unable to let go of the emotional complications that held them here in life.

After moving onto Blennerhassett Island in 1801, Irish aristocrats Margaret, with her husband Harmon Blennerhassett, took time, money and effort to turn their remote island into a heaven on earth. After the Mount Vernon Style mansion was finally completed on the island, the couple experienced a series of unfortunate events.

Increasingly, Harmon was seldom home. He had political and business dealings in Philadelphia and New York, leaving Margaret at the mansion with the servants, and the couple's children—both natural and adopted. During their stay on the island, the couple's two year-old-daughter, Baby Margaret, died. The toddler was buried on the island. The loss filled Margaret, who typically sparkled with optimism, with a deep sadness.

Later, political rogue Aaron Burr, arrived on the scene still smarting from his defeat by Thomas Jefferson and hatched a plan with Harmon: They would start a new country west of the Ohio River and lord over its riches, resources and bounty. (By this time, the Blennerhassetts were in need of money.)

Soon, their plan was foiled. It wasn't long before Aaron Burr and Harmon were brought up on charges of treason. (Burr was officially charged on February 19, 1807 and imprisoned.) Margaret Blennerhassett, as well as other residents fled the island never to return. After their abandonment, the mansion caught fire and burned to the ground. The mix-up was left for historians to sort out decades, if not centuries later.

Usually in mid-October, especially on the night of October 16th, although the reason is not clearly understood, the ghost of a woman in white appears on the island. This apparition has also been viewed during the day. Visitors on the island who have had face-to-face encounters with Margaret's ghost say she appears with the high sweet scent of a floral perfume, and sometimes the smell of horses, her favorite animal companions. Margaret is dressed in a pale gown, gazing as if eager for human contact once more. Most of the time, her spirit walks alone, with hand shielding her brow, looking onward as if searching for someone.

Is Margaret's ghost expecting her sojourning husband to come home from his latest business trip? Is she searching for the lost grave of her small child?

Who the lady in white still searches for, we do not know. Whatever her reason might be, the spirit of Margaret Blennerhassett still watches... and she waits.

6. haunted island

the blennerhassetts & why they haunt

How many times have I looked
Out this window?
How many times have I
Waited here?
Glorious was the sunlight
Upon the stream—
Along this green way
There is a path—
Where I escaped into wonderment—
I still remember the way –
But cold was the moonlight
When all was lost—
Yet in praise I return
To the dream this day—

It is difficult to imagine that rustic West Virginia (an area known most for steep hills and majestic mountains) has its very own enchanted island – one with a love story attached – a place so lush and pristine that it was once christened "Eden on the River."

It may seem just as unlikely that a handsome couple of noble, European breeding would move to an area that was little more than a howling wilderness, at their own peril, in order to create a paradise on earth. And yet, this is precisely so.

But what if tragedy and bitter disappointment befell this promising couple? What if the husband was tried for treason then felt the shame of being imprisoned?

Imagine if during this unhappiness, the couple's two-year-old daughter succumbs to a terrible, sudden illness. What if the remains or resting place of the baby were lost and never again located?

What if the couple was eventually forced to leave their island home with very little notice? What if the mother's ghost still wanders, always searching? And if so, what is her ghost searching for?

Harman and Margaret Blennerhassett arrived in the Mid-Ohio Valley in the last years of the 18th Century. The couple decided to move to the United States where few knew they were, in fact, of the same blood. Harman, the dashing, thirty-year old husband of the finely featured young woman still in her teens, was in fact Margaret's uncle.

The Blennerhassetts booked passage on a ship bound for the New World in the spring of 1796. The Irish couple brought with them some of their favorite pieces of furniture, a wardrobe of stylish clothing, jewelry, and Harman's inheritance. They arrived with their belongings on American soil on August 1st, 1796.

The large merchant ship took seventy-three days to travel from England to New York City. During that time, one peculiar event took place that foreshadowed things to come for Margaret and Harman. During the voyage, the ship's captain died very quickly. He fell gravely ill en route to New York. Poison was suspected but they had no obvious suspects. (Of course, food poisoning would have the same symptoms.) Thus, the reason behind such a sudden death was never solved. Later, other eerie and unfortunate events seemed to nip at the heels of the Blennerhassetts.

After traveling from Philadelphia to Pittsburgh, Harman and Margaret moved south toward the small towns of Marietta and Belle Prairie, Ohio, and what would become Parkersburg, West Virginia across the Ohio River. Soon, the Blennerhassetts purchased a small island on the Ohio River south of the villages of what are now Belpre and Parkersburg. The Irish couple cleared a section of land to build a Palladian mansion so splendid in its grandeur that it is still talked about to this day.

This was perfect retreat for European aristocrats, even dubbed "Little Eden" by others, forming a destiny that held the Blennerhassetts on the island for less than five years. The mansion took two and a half years to complete from natural hardwoods and other supplies imported from Pennsylvania and Europe. Soon Blennerhassett Island became the most magnificent sight along the Ohio River at the birth of the 19th Century.

The Blennerhassetts had three children, Harman junior, Dominic (a French boy they adopted), and baby Margaret, the youngest child. Unfortunately, the toddler Margaret died when she was only two years old. A small, unmarked grave behind the mansion is where is where the remains of baby are thought to be. The children that survived were given the finest of education and upbringings.

But Margaret's spirit was so attached to the island that she wrote poetry in her unmistakable, fluent handwriting about her 'paradise.' Some of her verse praised the natural beauty of the island with yearnings about how she never wanted to leave it. Little did Margaret know she would be forced to abandon her island home, and would never again return – at least not in her lifetime.

Before the downfall of the Blennerhassetts, they met up with a brilliant, troubled man by the name of Aaron Burr, former Vice President of the United

States. Burr had come up with the idea to purchase a vast amount of lands that are now Louisiana, Florida, and Mexico in order to form a separate country – apart from the laws of the U.S. government. This made sense to Harmon since he had worked for Irish Independence from England earlier in an underground movement of wealthy Irish aristocrats.

An old engraving of Blennerhassett Island

Burr was also in need of a supporter with a large amount of money to invest in the plan, and remembered his friend Harman Blennerhassett. By this time, the Blennerhassetts were feeling the effects of their lavish living. Harman's finances were stretched, so he eagerly accepted Burr's proposal in the hopes of replenishing his fortune.

Alexander Hamilton, now the President of the United States and Burr's old foe, got wind of the scheme and sent Federal troops to the island. Blennerhassett and Burr fled the island, leaving Margaret and the children behind. After being imprisoned for treason over a short time, Harman and Margaret were reunited. Later the couple attempted to start plantations in Canada and Mississippi but those were losses as well. Margaret regretted each day that she could not return to the island, but the fiasco with Burr slandered the noble name of Blennerhassett. She realized it would never be the same on the island.

After being abandoned, the mansion soon fell into disrepair. Expensive belongings were taken earlier from the mansion by some that Harmon owed money to. Glass windows were shattered. Weeds reclaimed the grounds of formerly groomed and cut shrubbery. The mansion dwindled to a shell. After the Blennerhassetts left, the mansion was used to store hay and hemp from nearby farms.

One night, thieves stormed the mansion. They aimed to steal whatever remaining liquor there was from the wine cellar. A lantern brushed against a bale of hay and caught fire. Within minutes, the mansion was engulfed in flames. In 1811, in only an hour, the Blennerhassett mansion burned to the ground. All was lost. Or was it?

This compelling story did not end when the Blennerhassetts abandoned the island. It did not even end when the Blennerhassetts died. Those who understand the workings of the spirit world know that when issues are not settled ghosts will haunt.

Numerous accounts claim that Margaret's ghost still appears on the island along with other mystifying apparitions. There is a long history of reports of seeing Margaret's pale ghost, as well as others, on the island. Over the years, visitors reported many odd and spectacular sightings that suggest the island is still haunted. Here are just a few of the ghostly tales below.

native american apparition

Long before Harman and Margaret Blennerhassett settled on the land, there were people who had earlier lived on the island. Archaeologists have unearthed human artifacts from dozens of Native American graves that may date back nearly 12,000 years. The remains of what appears to be important American Indians (judged by the type of relics found beside the skeletons) were buried beside rudimentary weapons, tools and rich grave goods. This gives us reason to believe the island may have been a sacred site as well as a burial site for the nomadic groups who traveled through the Mid-Ohio Valley before whites arrived.

As is in the tradition of some Native Indians, if a holy place or a burial site is desecrated, whoever defiles the remains can become cursed until the area is returned to its original condition. Is this what caused of Harman and Margaret's hardships after they built the mansion on the island? We may never know.

However, we do know the Blennerhassetts are not the only former inhabitants to return to island – if only in spirit. Long before the island was turned into an historical state park, people traveled by boat to camp out. A few that ventured into the woods claimed to see a man with long black hair, wearing buckskin clothing, walking between the older trees on the island. It was the specter of an unusually tall Indian.

But no one saw the stranger's face. He appeared viewed from behind. Those that saw the apparition agreed that he was a Native American from long ago. The aboriginal stranger acted preoccupied as if hunting for game... or maybe tracking something else. Whenever approached, the native was said to quicken his pace and disappear deep into the thicket. He became known as "the wild Indian of the island."

This story of a haunting Indian intrigued a local group of college students. They decided to visit the island to find out more about this wild man. Four youths, three men and a woman traveled to the island one early spring night. Fog on the river made finding the island a bit difficult, but eventually the four landed at the island and set up camp.

They soon split up into two parties and searched the island. Armed with a canteen, compass, walkie-talkie, and camera, each party went to a separate part of the isle, hoping to find some sign or evidence of the apparition.

After hours of searching, the parties returned to the camp and considered their adventure a failure. Two members of the group headed for the shoreline at the opposite end of the island. The girl then heard what sounded like a large object break through the brush.

As the two hid behind a fallen sycamore tree, they heard sounds inching closer. About ten feet ahead stood the wild man with his face painted scarlet. The Indian's dark eyes flashed. At over six and a half feet tall, his crow-black hair brushed his shoulders. At his side was a tomahawk that glistened from a fresh kill in the moonlight. The native paused, as if listening. Slowly, he turned toward the hiding couple. The wild man took a few steps closer but disappeared before their very eyes.

Frightened, they ran to their tents, where they found the other party breaking camp. The group returned to the shoreline in silence. Years passed before anyone in the group told others of their experience.

When archaeologists conducted a dig on the island a decade later, not only was the original foundation of the Blennerhassett mansion found, but a number of skeletons of Native Americans that were ceremoniously buried at different places on the island. One set of remains was found on the north side of the island near a fallen sycamore tree.

According to the archaeologists, this particular male must have been a giant among his tribe, standing almost seven-feet-tall. Next to him were the remains of a tomahawk, some shells, mica sheets and other artifacts typical of a Native American hunter. His height and grave goods indicated he was a leader – probably a shaman or a chief.

The remains were studied then returned to the Island. Although the "Wild Indian" story is now more than twenty-five years old, a few visitors to the Island still claim to see an aboriginal man with raven hair and bronze skin hiding within the older trees on Blennerhassett Island.

apparitions of margaret blennerhassett

By far the most famous haunt on Blennerhassett Island is that of Margaret Blennerhassett herself. Her ghost typically appears as a young woman in a white empire-style dress whose vision is often accompanied by the sweet scent of floral perfume and sometimes, even the smell of horses. (Margaret was an equestrian.) Witnesses describe her ghost as in early adulthood, perhaps thirty years of age. When approached, Margaret typically fades away into nothingness before the eyes of surprised onlookers.

Live horses (there are weekend carriage rides on the island) tend to get spooked easily for no apparent reason while on Blennerhassett Island. Horses are just not at ease while visiting there. It is recorded that Micah Phillips, a slave to the Blennerhassetts, was responsible for bringing the horses over the river to the island. Riding in the boat made Mrs. Blennerhassett's horses extremely nervous. Horses who visit the island to this very day seem to suffer from mysterious anxieties and unexplained nervousness.

Visitors to the island also report seeing a willowy woman along the shoreline dressed entirely in white. With hand shading her brow, she gazes as if waiting for someone to return. Like many haunts, she at first materializes as if in the flesh, then fades.

A woman riding on the *Mississippi Queen* down river spied two women dressed in white walking on the shoreline of island. Later, she asked one of the docents on the island if there was a convent or nunnery in Parkersburg?

Thinking the visitor meant the DeSales Heights Convent and Academy that was closed down in 1994, the docent answered that there used to be a convent in Parkersburg but it had shut down. The woman then told the docent of seeing two women cloaked entirely in white walking up and down as the boat approached. She thought, perhaps, they were Catholic sisters visiting the island that day. But no one else mentioned ever having seen the two women on that day.

Margaret waited for her husband hours on end at the edge of the island. She often wore a white gown on her walks. Was this the apparition of Margaret? If so, who was the second woman? Perhaps she was a servant or friend who dressed similarly to Margaret. After all, the Blennerhassetts were very kind to their servants. Most of them were of African descent or mixed-race slaves.

As pointed out previously, Margaret gave birth to a daughter while on the island, also named Margaret, who died at two years of age from a sudden illness. Some believe the small girl was buried behind the mansion – no one is really sure where it is.

After the Blennerhassetts fled the island over the debacle with Aaron Burr, the baby's gravesite fell victim to neglect and the elements. One legend claims two farmers plowed a field on the island near where the mansion once was and unearthed a tiny skeleton. They immediately reburied it in a small, unmarked grave. To this day the gravesite has yet to be found.

Locals visiting the island claim to see Margaret's ghost search the area where the small bones some believed are buried. Startled by the sudden presence of an incandescent woman, two farmers claimed the same apparition walked through their crops. One man recognized Margaret Blennerhassett because of her silky, chestnut hair and old-fashioned clothing. The other recognized her by her rich dress.

Now Margaret's remains and her son's bones have been returned to the island. But like their daughter, what is left of Harman has not been located. His body was interred on an island off of England's coast. Strangely, Mr. Blennerhassett requested to be buried at night. He did not want visitors at his gravesite. Harmon did a good job of hiding himself because no one knows exactly where his final resting spot is. Spirits can sometimes wander unhappily if they do not know where the remains of their loved ones are.

Historian Ray Swick and author Susan Sheppard contacting the spirit of Margaret Blennerhassett on Blennerhassett Island 1998, (Photograph by Doni Enoch)

an untimely visit from aaron burr

When lyricist Joyce Ancrile penned the lyrics for the musical drama "Eden on the River" (a story based upon the romance of the Blennerhassetts while they lived on the island) she decided to lie down and get some shut-eye after a long period of writing. Only moments passed when Ancrile sensed a presence in the room and opened her eyes to see a hawkish-featured man in early 19th century clothing gazing across the room at her. The gentleman was dressed in a rich, blue jacket and was resting on a settee.

Startled, Ms. Ancrile immediately sat up. The man faded. But Ancrile recognized her apparition from the research she had been doing for the play.

There was no doubt. The man was Aaron Burr.

Later Joyce Ancrile said that Aaron Burr's expression conveyed the words to her, "What has taken you so long?" as if he had been pressing her to tell his story.

Sightings of the ghost of Aaron Burr are not the norm for Parkersburg but it is interesting to note that there is a long history behind Aaron Burr ghost sightings in New York City.

Apparently, Burr's specter shows up at various addresses in Greenwich Village. One such place is a restaurant that was Burr's former carriage house. Workers in the "One If By Land, Two If By Sea" restaurant, claim that Burr's ghost returns to smash dishes, swing lamps and scoot chairs noisily.

Also in Greenwich Village, Burr's spirit also visits the area of his former stables, now a café called "Quantum Leap Natural Food." Many believe he is searching for his daughter Theodosia who was lost at sea. When Burr appears, he reveals intense dark eyes, is always dressed in a ruffled shirt but cloaked in a gloom of guilt and sorrow.

It does seem for certain that the spirit of Aaron Burr, even centuries later, has some unsettled business to contend with. His is the case of a sad yet true haunting.

the tale of the wandering reporter

In 1988, a Pittsburgh magazine writer came to the area by boat in order to write an article about all of the sights and sounds along the Ohio River. Blennerhassett Island would be a perfect addition to his article.

It was in October when he stopped at the island and sat up camp. Nearing dawn, the writer was awakened by rustling sounds outside. Strange shadows surged against the side of his tent.

The writer stepped outside and discovered the source of the sounds. Much to his surprise he saw a pale woman in a white, flowing dress. The lady stood staring, never moving. Stunned, he waited for her to speak but the woman said not a word to him.

Since there was a chill in the air, the reporter motioned for her to sit by the fire and offered to make her coffee. She simply gazed upon him then receded into the early morning fog. The writer was unnerved by the appearance of the lady who stared but did not talk.

Not able to figure this visit out, he decided to get a few hours of shut-eye before his trip in the morning. With the reporter was a collection his own writings and other reading materials. He had them inside his knapsack outside the tent. Shortly after drifting off, the writer was awakened by sounds once more.

Someone was going through his knapsack! Papers rattled as they were being shuffled. When the sounds finally halted, the man opened his tent and was amazed at what he saw. Every book was taken from his bag, and neatly stacked beside the smoldering remains of the campfire. Whoever discovered them— read every one, then carefully placed them back into a pile.

The reporter told workers on the island about his uncanny experience the next day. When he described the woman to the small group of people they were not surprised. The writer described Margaret Blennerhassett perfectly even down to the fine brown hair. Some had already encountered the apparition of Margaret – but never so closely!

Margaret Blennerhassett was a bibliophile. The passion she felt for books apparently survived the grave. The writer promised he would return to the island to find out more about Margaret and the hauntings on the island. But unlike Margaret's ghost, the writer has yet to return to the island. It seems he was spooked away by the entire encounter.

other island apparitions

It is common knowledge that Harman and Margaret Blennerhassett had slaves while on the island. However, the slaves they had were treated humanely and as a part of the family. Although Ohio was a free state and freedom lay less than a mile across the Ohio River, not one of the Blennerhassett's slaves, or servants, were known to have even attempted an escape, at least, while Margaret and Harman were still there.

Many slaves remained loyal to Harman and Margaret in later times when the Blennerhassetts began a plantation called La Cashe in the Deep South—until their funds were depleted.

On the island, one slave in particular was close to Harman and Margaret. Some believe he is Ransom Reed. Reed often rode horses alongside Margaret where they admired the beauty of the island and surrounding valley. Like the Blennerhassetts many of the slaves often referred to the island as their true home.

After the Blennerhassett estate was rebuilt as a state park in the 1980s, some who visited the island described seeing a black man wearing clothing common during the 18th and early 19th Centuries, at times circling the perimeter of the mansion.

Most people thought little of a dusky-skinned man who wore period clothing, taking a solitary tour of the island. There are dozens of artisans from the island's craft village and volunteers dressed in period clothing. When workers were asked about the gentleman, they didn't have a clue as to his identity. No one knew of an African American male who worked at the craft village or as a volunteer on the island.

But if one looks back to two-hundred-years ago, an individual is found who fits the description. Ransom Reed was a favored slave of the Blennerhassetts.

Margaret, especially, was a lover of humanity and didn't have the usual prejudices that others in her class might have. Many believe Ransom Reed, as well as other slaves, were Margaret's trusted friends during her years on the island.

Over time, the apparition of the African-American man was reported on less and less to the point that his ghost is rarely seen. The servant's appearances have especially waned after the return of Margaret's remains to the island in the early 1990s. Still, the phantom does occasionally turn up to visitors.

Perhaps, being the dedicated servant that he was, this proud man continues to keep vigilant watch until Harman's remains finally joins Margaret's on the island.

So, is Margaret's ghost an earthbound spirit, doomed to haunt her enchanted island?

No, the spirit of Margaret Blennerhassett is able to move as freely about as any other spirit. Ghosts are not so different than the living. They sometimes like to re-visit places, people and memories from times past and most of all – also, spirits still care about the living and how we carry on with our lives.

Sometimes, when conditions are just right, as it so often is on Blennerhassett Island, we can connect with these wandering spirits and are able to see and experience the dead exactly as they once lived.

7. the crossroads: parkersburg

hauntings at upper juliana, market & thirteenth streets

Does the possibility of vengeful ghosts make you a bit squeamish? What about elemental spirits and graveyard ghouls? Do tales of voodoo make you shudder? Or are you just another one who dreads the dead?

Then you would do best to avoid the Crossroads, a place in every town where roads intersect and form a cross. In ancient lore, the Crossroads is a place where spiritual danger and ghostly powers are said to lurk. This is more so if there is a cemetery near by.

Why the Crossroads? Throughout the world, the Crossroads hold a special significance. After all, it is a place where psychic powers, ghostly powers if you will, are the most focused and strong.

The meeting and parting of ways is associated with the Crossroads. This may explain why ancient peoples were suspicious over paths that intersect – especially lonely, isolated roads where the more sinister elements of the supernatural

Night is a riddle
Hidden within the magician's dark
sleeve.
Consider the vagaries of stars
How they tinkle as tiny bells
On a jester's velvet cap.
Consider a future
Crowded with saints and lunatics.
Consider lying awake all night
To face the funhouse mirror
Where you have only yourself,
And yourself and yourself
Where a blue window slides
away,
Becomes a floating tomb,
Where suicides hang like smoke
What you cannot see
Is a sky wrought with messages
Like an intaglio on the palms.
At the end of the street
Graves have been emptied.
The moon lets go of her stem,
Becomes a ship of bones.

from ' crossroads,'
a poem by susan sheppard

- such as vampires and devils—have long been connected.

All type of unnatural beings hang around the Crossroads like a foul mist, willing and waiting to gobble up your immortal soul. The Devil himself is linked to the Crossroads. This is especially true not only in African American folk tales but also in European lore. Not only is the Devil associated with the Crossroads, fairies are said to frequent there— but not the benevolent kind in children's tales. These are fairies of evil so one should never fall asleep at the Crossroads. All manner of misfortune will find you. You may wake up "bewitched" or "fairy led." You may even wake up in the land of the dead.

Long ago, gallows for the condemned were built at the Crossroads. Suicides and victims of murder were buried at the Crossroads as well. This was done so their restless souls wouldn't wander seeking revenge upon those who harmed them in life. Some believed it was the power of the Christian cross that the Crossroads symbolized, to protect the living from vengeful acts of the unhappy dead.

Contrary to popular opinion menacing ghosts are not always the earthbound souls of the departed. But they can sometimes be an evil component of the personality that survives death. This ghost is usually one that is said to lack authority and direction. It is believed that a malevolent ghost will stand at the Crossroads all night long trying to make up his mind which way to go. Upon morning, the pure rays of sunlight will send the spirit screaming into banishment. Vampires are said to carry their shrouds to the Crossroads in search of fresh victims. In Voodoo rites, tail feathers from a black rooster will help protect you at the Crossroads from devils, ghosts and boogers that usually haunt mountain hollows. A rooster claw works as well.

However, the magic and mayhem of the Crossroads traces further into history than the advent of Christianity. This legend is much older having appeared in Asia, Africa and North America well before the European influences came about. This is one of the mysteries that surround it.

Ancient peoples all over the world believed that magic was at its most powerful at the Crossroads, and a path associated with witchcraft. Hecate, the Greek goddess of the underworld, howling dogs and witchery lurks at the Crossroads where it is said she prowls looking for someone to haunt.

In ancient times, offerings of food and cakes were set out at the Crossroads to appease Hecate and her mysterious forces for good and evil. Such cakes were then called "Hecate cakes," in which a lighted candle was placed in the center so Hecate could find her way to the Crossroads. This was also done to light the way so dark Hecate could find her food after dark. This is where the custom of candles on birthday cakes originates.

Voodoo gives great spiritual influence to the Crossroads. Voodoo spells are often performed at the Crossroads, lending its magical powers to the spell caster. Crossroads dirt, as well as graveyard dirt, is still used as protection from the Evil

Eye and other negative forces. (In this way, the idea is similar to Europeans putting gargoyles on their churches to scare away evil. The worse the gargoyle looks the more successful it is in chasing away evil spirits.)

In Voodoo spells, the Priest or Priestess who casts the spell waits at the Crossroads until an apparition (sometimes the Devil) appears. If this apparition does not make himself known immediately, the spell will be made more difficult to work. But if the devil or ghost arrives just on time, you can be assured the spell will work, but in the most dangerous and diabolical way possible.

How did a belief in the Crossroads make its way to West Virginia and other southeastern states? Mysteriously, a group of small diminutive people called "The Black Dutch" eventually settled in the mountain state. They brought with them a belief in the Crossroads – from their places of earliest origin – India, then Romania and later Germany. The Black Dutch were Chikkener among the PA Dutch – or German Gypsies.

Gypsy tradition says one should not toy with the mysterious witchery of the Crossroads. Uninvited forces of a malevolent nature might enter your life... So whatever you send out comes back to you threefold, and then some. And don't forget: The Crossroads exist everywhere, even in your town....

13th & juliana streets

Whenever you get an impressive row of old houses together, there are bound to be a few ghost stories. The crossroads at 13th & Juliana Streets is no exception. Possibly it is because Riverview Cemetery, the second oldest cemetery in Wood County, is right off the beaten path with its towering hemlocks and pine-littered graves.

Many of the houses surrounding Riverview Cemetery are allegedly haunted. At one time, the graveyard extended to the corner of 13th Street. Some of the houses on 13th and Juliana Streets may exist overtop archaic graves, the first one dating at around 1801.

Normally, there's no problem if a person happens to sleep on a grave. Most spirits don't mind. People do it in Africa, Mexico and Haiti during their holidays every year. That is, of course, unless those graves are located at the Crossroads. And unless your street is numbered Thirteen...

Needless to say there are a number of haunts reported in this area of the Parkersburg.

One modest two-story house has the shadowy form of man who appears at night in a hall and upper room that faces the cemetery. Lights tend to go haywire in the home. No matter what wattage of light bulbs, the light inside the house always seems filmy and dim. Residents of other homes in the area complain of sinkholes, foul odors and a pounding in the walls during the middle of the night. Neighbors noticed phantom smoke, vague apparitions and objects turn up missing only to appear later in unlikely places.

One home on upper Juliana Street seems to house a lighter, friendlier spirit, one who presses her warmth against women visitors. The ghost wears an old-fashioned, sweet-smelling perfume and carries with her a feeling of warmth and openness.

The ghost seldom approaches men. Perhaps she is too shy or perhaps she doesn't care. Still, this lady continues to haunt. After all, she is still there.

haunted buddha

Given the omens and superstitions surrounding the number thirteen, it is no surprise to learn that several houses on 13th Street in Parkersburg are haunted.

Not far from Juliana and Market Streets, there is a modest brick home that has long been plagued by forces of a spiritual nature. But it wasn't until 1979 when area woman Betty Stewart moved in did the stranger and unexplained occurrences take place.

At first, Betty said that the brick ranch had a "warm, welcoming feeling." She loved the house and she had no qualms about moving in immediately. Everything seemed light and airy, plus the house had the extra bonus of being in walking distance to Betty's job at Public Debt, a federal position with great benefits.

It all seemed too perfect. Betty enjoyed looking into store windows and passing by the second hand shops on Market Street as she made her way home in the evenings. One late afternoon, a statue in the window of one of the shops caught her eye.

It was a green statue of a Buddha. Beside it was a coiled cobra with glittering red eyes. The statues looked to be pretty old and were most unusual. Betty was drawn to art with an Oriental theme so she walked inside to inquire about a price.

The statues were a little more expensive than she had in mind, but on a whim, and with the few dollars she had she decided to lay them away. Betty wasn't overly enthused with the cobra. With its red eyes, the statue looked malevolent. It was the green, pot-bellied Buddha that Betty really wanted. But the shopkeeper informed her that the pieces were to be sold together.

The owner suggested the pair should not be separated. Betty agreed.

Every time Betty collected another paycheck she paid a few dollars more on the statues whenever she passed by the store. Within the month, the two ceramic pieces were hers and she took them home.

For the first week, all was well in the house. Life was a routine. Betty placed the Asian statues side by side on an antique table and they looked splendid together. But then Betty had the sensation that someone was always watching her...

Feelings of being watched eventually were so powerful that Betty feared glancing into a mirror afraid of who might be staring back at her. She had never been frightened in quite the same way before. She did not consider herself particularly impressionable and she was never afraid of ghosts. In fact, Betty didn't believe in ghosts at the time.

Still, the house on 13th Street had its bonuses. It was near some of Betty's relatives on Quincy Street. A niece gave Betty a cat for company but the cat always ran away.

One day, a nephew came to spend the afternoon. He reached for a piece a candy in a nearby dish but accidentally hit the Buddha statue, shattering the candy dish into hundreds of pieces. Somehow, this acted as a catalyst for the strange, psychic energies that already had been unleashed in the house.

A stuffed dog that Betty kept on her sofa disappeared and turned up in unexpected places. Betty wondered if a prankster was at work. Muffled and rapping sounds awakened the Stewarts at night. Betty experienced one of the most frightening encounters of spirit infestations and haunting, and that is night paralysis. Unable to scream or move Betty woke up to the feeling of an evil presence in the room.

Doors in the house creaked open only to shut with a bang. One night Betty awakened to what seemed to be an odd, pensive feeling in the room. She looked up to see a young boy, about twelve years old, standing in the doorway to her bedroom, dressed in a plaid shirt and jeans. "He looked absolutely real, not like a ghost in a movie or anything," Betty later reported. "I thought someone's child was lost and had wandered into our house." Several nights later, Betty's husband saw the same little boy.

Convinced that certain forces had been unleashed in the house, the couple called upon their son for help.

"It's those statues," the son replied. "I especially don't like that ugly snake. No matter where I am, its eyes seem to follow me around the room." That was enough to convince other family members that something was amiss. Betty's brother took the two statues and placed them in a box in the basement. The house quieted down for a time.

Circumstances in Betty's life caused her to change jobs and move to another area. Later, Betty was told that about fifteen years before she had moved into the house on 13th Street, a young boy had gotten lost in the neighborhood and died looking for his mother. Years later, in the 1980s, a young couple moved into the home and decided to throw a party. One of the women who attended the party turned up missing. It wasn't long before odors seeped up from the basement. A party guest fell down the stairs and broke her neck. She died instantly. The woman's body lay there for several days before it was discovered at the bottom of the stairs.

Is the house still occupied? It is.

Who knows what now lurks in the basements of the homes on 13th Street?

What happened to the statues of the green Buddha and wicked-eyed cobra? Betty put them in a garage sale priced for $2.00 — far less than what she had originally paid for them. They sold right away. Are the spirit-possessed statues still in Parkersburg? No one, not even Betty knows for sure.

ghost of runaway slave on market street

It seems as if every small town along the B&O railroad route has the story of a ghost of a slave that haunts a tunnel. Usually, the slave has lost his head and carries it under his arm. Usually the fugitive slave is said to moan and groan and rattle his shackles.

Before the Civil War, central West Virginia and southern Ohio became major routes along the Underground Railroad. Several ghost stories from the region involve the misfortunes of runaway slaves who ventured through.

The problem with such stories is the B&O railroad was not really in use (in what was to later become West Virginia) before the Civil War times, so it's unlikely a slave would be jumping a train in order to escape into freedom before then. Yet, areas of travel, such as railroads and crossroads, remain important in African American folklore. They became places where the two worlds met – the world of the living and also the unquiet dead.

Not far from 13th Street, on Market Street, a neglected house welcomed a young woman to move in after her diligent search for generous old home with "lots of character." Part of the house had been broken up into apartments but her area of the house had a family feeling since it had an upstairs bedroom and a downstairs living room with kitchen. The apartment had not been updated for a while but was nicely carpeted of the plush, new variety, definitely a "plus" for the times – the late 1980s.

Shortly after moving in, the woman heard noises downstairs while trying to sleep. She thought it was, perhaps, the settling of boards in the old home and was surprised when in the morning she found a man's bare footprints in the freshly vacuumed carpet. At other times, the woman's radio switched on or changed channels during the night. Later as she listened to footsteps in her downstairs, she heard identical sounds in the attic, especially in the area where there was a small attic window.

Feeling vulnerable and unsure over who or what was making the mysterious sounds, the woman moved out but not before telling her friend about the apartment being vacated. The friend liked the woman's apartment so decided to move in and take over the rent. After all, she considered herself brave a person and was not particularly worried.

It didn't take long for the footsteps in the attic to start up as well as bare footprints appearing downstairs in the carpet. One night, the second woman listened to noises leading from her bedroom into the living room. The woman got up and grabbed a flashlight that she kept on her inn table. As she ventured forward and flashed a beam of light down the stairs, she caught the apparition of a young black man in rags. His hands were chained. The man held up his chained wrists and pleaded with sad, dark eyes.

In a split second, the runaway slave had vanished into a wisp.

Days later so did the young woman –At least from the house on Market Street.

Where did she go? Like the other woman, she found a much less haunted place to stay. But not before learning that the old house on Market Street had been built upon a site that was along a well-traveled route of the Underground Railroad.

the haunted convent
ghosts & legends of desales heights

If old buildings could scream, the DeSales Heights Convent and Academy was one that might have. By most accounts, the spirits inside the famous West Virginia landmark were restless if not unhappy. When exploring the cavernous, abandoned building, visitors felt anything but welcome. In fact, the spirits were known to slap, raise welts and even leave bloody scratches on visitors.

So why were the spirits inside DeSales Heights upset? Time was not kind to the old convent. Local youth often vandalized the spacious building. Rumors of the place being haunted attracted the curious and those who dared to risk encountering an angry spirit.

Following the Civil War, a convent was built that eventually became the DeSales Heights Academy. A rambling structure with courtyard and meandering hallways, the one-hundred-year-old Catholic Girls School was closed down in 1994 due to low enrollment and aging residents.

Several elderly nuns were placed in nursing homes while younger sisters went on to serve their church elsewhere. Shortly before the closing of the De Sales, the bodies of seventy-nine nuns were exhumed from their crypts and reburied in Catholic cemeteries. Religious relics and some personal objects were sold at auction.

It seemed that chapter of the school was closed forever – but was it?

Many of the cloistered nuns who lived and died at DeSales ended up in those crypts. That means they made an oath to never leave that place. Some of the nuns, over a span of sixty and even seventy years, never set foot outside the property. Until the nun's bodies were removed and taken somewhere else. By most accounts, spirits do not like this. This would be especially true if the spirits had given their solemn oath to never leave the nunnery – and this is precisely what happened when DeSales Heights finally closed down.

(One interesting fact about hauntings is that it appears personalities do not change their religion after dying. This is why in all ghost investigations, the parties involved should show the utmost respect if the investigation involves a grave, a sacred site, or a cemetery.)

The DeSales Heights Convent after it was closed down
(Photograph by Kristall Chambers)

There have been several reports and perhaps reasons behind the haunting. One story has it years ago one DeSales Height's nun fell down the elevator shaft, but because of her vow of silence after dinner leading into morning, she did not call out for help during the night. By the time the woman was discovered it was too late. Her injuries proved fatal – yet, many believed had she cried out earlier – she could have been saved.

There is another account of a young man who stole a gold cross from the convent and then died suddenly before he had a chance to return it. They say the boy's ghost is one that haunts the place.

When filming a documentary about the convent and school several years back, two cameramen happened upon a cellar beneath the basement area. As they filmed, a cold wind whipped around their legs chilling them to their very bones. Since the room was sealed off at the time, this was impossible. Suddenly the tiny, isolated room became as icy cold as the deepest bottom of the ocean. A mumbling of voices started –barely beyond detection – but definitely creepy. The camera crew ended up bolting.

Two women visiting DeSales Heights discovered the same area beneath the floors. As they took pictures, they caught a few ghost orbs that appeared dingy. The last picture showed a heart-shaped face, almost like a nun's face under her habit. But the face with vacant eyes and leering grin looked more like that of a skull.

While working on a school project, a mother, daughter and a few of their friends went inside DeSales Height in 2002 by stealth of night in order to videotape the inside of the building. Within the enclosing shadows, one of the girls grew afraid. To break the tension, the mother cracked a joke to ease the young girl's fears. Once they returned safely at home and viewed the videotape, they detected a woman's voice over top that of the mothers.' The rasping female voice hissed the command, "Get out!"

The convent once created an ominous presence with wind-weathered cross on the highest peak. Lonely hallways were carpeted with broken glass. Stained glass windows were removed and the windows nailed over with inexpensive board. That altar remained after the school was closed, but odd things happened whenever a picture was taken there.

Unwanted visitors caught hundreds of ghost orbs in and outside DeSales Heights. One picture showed a dark red funnel shape coming out of the top of the building.

On July 15, 2002 DeSales Heights was torn down after vandals set a fire in the rectory of the building. A candlelight vigil was held a few days later. Not surprisingly photographs snapped revealed a number of orbs in motion.

Dark rumors still abound. But we will leave them where they belong, left in a dark place unable to be examined. Just like the souls once inside … waiting…waiting… and praying for peace.

(DeSales Heights' creepy reputation made it to Hollywood when the 2001-2002 TV show "Scariest Places on Earth" asked to tape a segment before it was torn down. The request was denied and the old convent was leveled a few months later.)

houdini plays parkersburg

Many find it surprising that master magician Harry Houdini once played Parkersburg in January of 1920 at the Old Camden Theater that took up most of the block between 8th and 7th Streets on Market Street. Those who know much about Houdini's life are aware of the fact that, after his mother's death, this sleight-of-hand escape artist became increasingly interested in proving (and also disproving) the existence of an afterlife. Most of Houdini's investigations into psychic mediums proved to be disappointing though, as he (often in a disguise) exposed frauds time and time again.

As he was to his mother, Houdini was extremely devoted to his wife Beatrice. He made a pact with his wife that should he precede her in death, he would come back to her in a séance with a special coded message that would prove the existence of life beyond the grave. But if an afterlife did not exist, no medium would be able to break the code.

Harry Houdini

Harry Houdini, in fact, did die before his wife on Halloween night, October 31, 1926 of peritonitis two years before the Camden Theater in Parkersburg burned to the ground.

Although many faithful to the religion of Spiritualism believed famed medium Arthur Ford broke the Houdini's code, others claimed Ford had previous knowledge and thus, the validity of his psychic impressions could never be proven. Even unto the current day, séances are held each Halloween night to entice back the ghost of Harry Houdini.

So far, Houdini's charismatic figure has not appeared, unless of course, he has something to do with the ghost, sometimes referred to as "the Warlock," that haunts many of the businesses of the block that once held the old Camden Theater.

Here is a related story contributed by Parkersburg native Kevin Morehead:

power country ghost

"My name is Kevin Morehead and I worked at Power Country 99 and WADC AM 1050 from 1995-98. I was told by a friend of mine you were inquiring about the "ghost of Power Country 99 in the old theatre at 703 Market Street here in Parkersburg. I was Music Director and Assistant Engineer and Program Manager with a radio show on WHCM, "The Top Ten at Ten," a request call-in show for the listeners.

"It started back when I was hired in 1995. I was learning the ropes so to speak with the late Mark Eveland who at the time was our Music Director and Program Director/Manager.

"Less than a week of working at the radio station I was on the air running Pittsburgh Pirate Baseball on WADC when the manager came over to my studio and told me about smelling hot, buttered popcorn. I, at the time thought I was working with a real cuckoo until about fifteen minutes after being told that, I too smelled popcorn! The manager mentioned about the station being haunted and said a person had hung himself in the projector room on the top floor. I never confirmed whether that was true but working there at nights I sure seen and heard my share of 'What was THAT?'

"There would be many nights as I worked as the 'Six p.m. to Midnight Jock' where I witnessed and heard many strange occurrences that I am still chilled by and unable to explain. For instance, our production room was right across from our break room and loading the computer up at night I would always see something that would catch the corner of my eye but nothing would be there when I looked straight on! My youngest brother worked with me around until when our boss sold out to Results Radio in 98.

"I would say the most terrifying time for me was when myself, one of our sales guys, and our afternoon girl and my brother was there. The afternoon girl thought it would be fun to hold a little ritual with candles and other things she brought in. She put lit candles in our old WADC studio were it was always cold and could never get it heated up enough to work in even in a six hour shift. The girl said this is the room where the spirits were concentrated.

"Not believing a word of this I went along what she was doing, of course, thinking the whole time she was trying to scare us since everyone considered the place haunted. All of our studios had sliding glass doors on them so we could be on the air in private and not to pick up background noise from the programming room. She put the candles on the counter by the door and closed the studio door. Immediately the candles flickered and leapt around as she said something about how I could find out more about this in the movie The Warlock! I laughed, not really believing what I was seeing or hearing as I darted back in forth from my studio for I was on the air that night on Power Country.

"After about 20 minutes of this I, being the man thinking there is explanation for everything, made the comment that it was the air conditioner in the studio blowing on the candles that made them dance like that. I investigated further to find the air conditioner was not running and even checked myself to see if the unit was on. It was not.

"The girl went on for about two more minutes and I had about enough of this or so I thought. I went over to her and told her: 'I don't believe in this junk, so please stop this or get out!'

"Well, to say after I got that out, and it was right after let me tell you the door that held our satellite switcher bounced wide open with a bang! The door was above my head and I had to reach up to open it. Strong magnets held it in place and sometimes you had to really pull on the darn thing. Besides that, there was no one near it! Nevertheless, this made me an instant believer.

"But wait, this is not the end of my story! It seemed like the spirit harassed me the rest of the evening with the ceiling tiles falling down in my studio. My cart rack that held all the commercials or spots as we say in radio twisted and toppled to the floor. The cart weighed over 200 pounds and no one touched it.

"Afterwards we had many unexplained things happen to us before the building was sold. We all saw things out of the corners of our eyes, and that popcorn, still to this day I bet people working in that area of the block still smell it now! The radio station had 2 basements one a little scary than the other. A couple of us Jocks would go down to the one closest to Market Street— it was dark but very spacious. The other basement near the back of the building was the weirdest. My brother and I explored it and it has a large room sealed off from the alley behind the building. Most of the theater is still intact if you pry a ceiling tile up in the hallway, you can see the entire theater, where the old screen is, (it's still up!) and the projector room holes where the projector lens would be. There are many more things to tell about working there. Let me just end by saying, to this die-hard skeptic, it was just downright eerie."

An old postcard showing the Camden Theater

During the fall 2002 Haunted Parkersburg Ghost Tour, the guides paused at the location of the Camden Theater to briefly tell of Houdini's visit to Parkersburg. That night I (Susan Sheppard) mentioned that although Houdini was intrigued by the possibility of an afterlife, he was never able to prove it and as far as we know, has not returned to his earthly realm.

The minute I said that Houdini never came back or proved life after death, an empty car on the street blared as its burglar alarm suddenly went off. No one came out to check the car and no one stood near it at all.

Despite the noisy distraction, I continued with my story, concluding, perhaps, medium Arthur Ford did break Houdini's code, translating this sentimental message "Rosabelle, Believe" from the grave. I then acknowledged to the crowd,

"Maybe there was an afterlife for Houdini, after all." At that exact moment the car alarm abruptly quieted, my story ended and the confused ghost walkers continued their journey down Market Street

tales of black cats

It didn't take long, after Parkersburg's ghost tours began, to notice the walk acted as like a psychic magnet for black cats. We had black cats – here, there and everywhere – inkblots with green, fiery eyes and tails floating over sidewalks to greet us just as we began to tell our stories of local haunts. We could not have planned it any better – how good can it get? Black cats turning up on practically all of our ghost tours.

Except for the fact that we hadn't planned it that way. And the cats were real.

Yet there is one tale of a black cat that is truly mystifying. You might even call this story a "Tale of A Tail." The apparition of a black cat appears in one of the homes – but only its hindquarters and back legs.

One might ask why the distressed cat is sawed in half? This particular home was built around the time of 1900. Streetcars were used well into the 1940s in Parkersburg and ran directly in front of some of the homes. One could just imagine what might happen if a family pet wandered out onto the streetcar tracks...

More black cats, the flesh and blood kind, continue to inhabit homes in the Upper Julian Square District. It may be such a haunted street is in dire need of black cats.

On 13th Street, a palatial home has a snoring ghost. This particular home stayed in the same family for a number of years. The original owner was a robust man at one time, but in later years he became extremely disabled. His sick bed was put in the kitchen. Sometimes, current residents can still hear the old man snore in the kitchen late at night.

Then there are the other houses along the route. One of the haunted homes near is a residence behind a local funeral parlor where a poltergeist throws plates whenever a dog is brought inside. (The wife of the previous owner would not allow a dog in her house.) The activity abruptly stops as soon as the animal is taken outside again.

Of course, Riverview Cemetery, with its sinkholes and its reports of haunting, is only a few blocks away.

And what would the Crossroads at 13th and Juliana Streets be without black cats and snoring ghosts?

What would Parkersburg be without its famous haunts?

8. riverview cemetery

the lady walks at midnight

This is the light of the mind, cold and planetary.
The trees of the mind are black. The light is blue.
The grasses unload their grief on my feet as if I am
a god,
Prickling my ankles and murmuring their humility.
Fumy, spiritous mists inhabit this place.

from "the moon and the yew tree"
by sylvia plath

Sometimes at dusk, as the veil between worlds begin to part, as diminishing sunlight cast shadows long and deep, the faces of those buried in Riverview Cemetery come alive in the dark and light that mingle on tombstones.

To people uninitiated into the world of spirits, Riverview invites dreams. Mossy grounds become a carpet of green. Pine needles scatter the paved walkway. Hemlock trees embrace each one that passes through its gates.

The array of ancient graves include Irish crosses, headstones with cryptic Masonic symbols, marble angels, one lonely grave of a young Chinese woman, the plot of a well-loved slave marked "occupied" and three impressive statues. The historical figures entombed at Riverview Cemetery include two West Virginia governors, the French wife of artist Joseph H. Diss Debar, two West Virginia senators, a New England sea captain and the famed Jackson family for which there are numerous graves in Riverview.

Even to those who do not know of the history, Riverview Cemetery is a place where dreams float and fly— where statues are said to stand up and walk. It is within the graveyard that the living energies of those thought gone still remain curiously alive.

Go to Riverview Cemetery at dusk on a summer evening. Wait patiently, watch and listen. Don't be surprised to see shadows dance on gravestones or spectral lights flying by.

Rumors abound about the mysterious forces inside the cemetery gates. For years, there has been talk in the neighborhood of peculiar sounds coming from the graveyard. Dry sticks snap, brittle as old bones. Leaves shuffle along the paved path. Late into the evening hours there is a shifting of weight and stony pauses, the clicking of heels and mysterious footsteps – perhaps the rustling of a long silk skirt echoes over the stones.

Might it be the Weeping Woman statue rising up?

Schoolchildren swear all of the statues in Riverview stand up and walk. If only in the mind's eye, who says they don't?

A look at the history and personalities of early Parkersburg might explain what is behind these mysterious happenings. The rest, as in keeping with most paranormal activity, might never be explained. Such fascination lies within its mystery and is why we are drawn to the unknown realities of what most of us call 'ghosts.'

history of riverview cemetery

The first grave in Riverview Cemetery was that of B. W. Jackson, who died in 1801 at the age of the thirty-four. There are a number of prominent people buried in the graveyard as well, including cousins of General Thomas "Stonewall" Jackson and notable historical figures. Sometimes called 'the Cook' Cemetery, the Cooks, the Dils, the Jacksons and the Van Winkles are just a few of the historical people buried inside.

With the exception of the Revolutionary and Gulf wars, veterans of every American war are represented at Riverview Cemetery including the Seminole War and the War of 1812. Some of the graves have confederate flags, unusual for a northern West Virginia cemetery.

Legend says George Washington was the first white man to own the land that is now the cemetery, which he sold to the Jackson family in the 1700s. A number of colorful personalities, including a sea captain and a Chinese laundress, were laid to rest in Riverview Cemetery. It should come as no surprise that many of these spirits are still interested in maintaining communications with the living.

the captain's grave

Witnesses claim to see the vision of a man in a black coat leaning over this 150-year-old headstone that has the carving of a ship on it. The spirit is seen as often by the light of day as he is at night. Perhaps this historical grave has a tragedy surrounding it... enough of a tragedy to cause someone to return to the grave site time and time again, even if the black-coated visitor is a ghost.

Captain George Deming was a master mariner from New Haven, Connecticut who moved to what was then Virginia in the 1850s. A successful businessman, Captain Deming was proud enough to mention he was a direct descendent of Miles Standish, the founder of the early Plymouth colony, on his tombstone. He also included the carving of a ship.

George Deming traveled to the Ohio Valley to seek his fame and fortune in the oil and gas business barely beginning. After acquiring a small fortune, the Captain set out to build a quaint home on the corner of 11th and Juliana streets. The Captain's House (also called the Markey House) is easy to spot in the district since it is the only house on street that does not have much of a yard. In the style of a New England street house, the interior of the home, with high wooden beams and narrow halls, resembles the inside of a ship.

Off of 13th and Juliana Streets near the chain length fence in Riverview Cemetery, the grave of Captain Deming is three-minute walk from his former home. Completed in 1860 one short year before the Captain's death, the house is alleged to have a number haunts. Orange-colored embers from the Captain's pipe are still seen glowing in the bay window that faces Juliana Street. But, there are other reasons for the Captain's apparition to materialize.

When looking at spirit disturbances and other hauntings, there seems to be one event that surpasses all other in tragedy -- the death of a beloved child. As workers were updating the Captain's home in the 1990s and handling the repairs, they noticed a child's bare footprints in the dust that had settled in the attic. After the footprints were brushed away, they came back as soon as the dust settled. Each time the child's footprints were swept up, they always returned. This happened countless times. History shows that Parkersburg had Typhoid Fever epidemics that swept through the area in the 1860s and 1870s. Perhaps the Captain and his child were victims. They are the only two Deming burials in the graveyard.

As we were researching this book, we were told of this story of a child's ghost in the attic but didn't know what to make of it until we discovered that the Captain's young son had died shortly after he did in 1861 at the age of fifty-five. This is according to cemetery records.

Directly beside of the Captain's grave, the one with the unique carving of a sailing ship on it is the small weathered tombstone that belongs to his child. This tells us that the black-coated specter is probably not mourning himself – it is the dead child that the Captain still mourns for.

sink holes and unmarked graves of slaves

At one point in its history, Riverview Cemetery was said to extend all the way to where Thirteenth Street is now. It is speculated some of the graves in this section of the graveyard were unmarked burials of escaped slaves.

One legend has it that some runaway slaves who didn't make it across the Ohio River when escaping via the Underground Railroad, were hastily buried on the edge of Riverview. One resident of the area claims to have found a boat hook by which the slaves were fished out of the river. The jury is still out as to whether this was true or not. There is one grave of a former slave that is marked "occupied" since slaves were not allowed to have their names written on a tombstone in a white only cemetery.

Residents of surrounding houses near the graveyard have their share of strange tales to tell. Several describe impressions of sinkholes in their yards while others report erratic poltergeist activity.

One haunted house near Riverview is alongside the southern edge of the cemetery. The two-story pleasant home with window boxes continues to have a number of occurrences of a true haunting. The dining room and kitchen area maintains a shadowy or 'overcast' quality that very haunted rooms tend to have.

When the couple's children were smaller, they often complained of the lumbering form of a man who stood in the doorway to their bedroom or waking up and seeing a dark shape standing at the foot of their beds. Later, the mother walked into a room and was surprised to see a white-bearded elderly man race across the floor. (The woman later commented that the ghost looked so old she was surprised over how fast he ran!)

Startled, the owner of the house came to realize this was a former resident of the home. A clairvoyant who visited the home did not entirely agree and thought she recognized the ghost of the man with a shock of white hair as a caretaker of the cemetery. This same woman later ran across a dated picture in the *Parkersburg News* in a story that appeared about Riverview Cemetery in 1950. In an article by reporter Marie Wood, the clairvoyant recognized the man in her vision. No name was given but he was listed as a 'kindly old caretaker of Riverview Cemetery.' The psychic recognized the man as the one she saw earlier in the home.

jfk visits riverview cemetery

During the 1960 presidential campaign, John F. Kennedy and his brother Teddy stopped in Parkersburg on their campaign. (West Virginia was a major factor in deciding the outcome of the presidential election.) The Kennedy's spent part of the day at a house on Ann Street, two blocks south of the graveyard. Legend has it John Fitzgerald Kennedy actually walked through Riverview Cemetery. There are Kennedy graves in Riverview but this is not who JFK came to see during his visit to the cemetery.

People who remember say that John Kennedy did visit Riverview Cemetery, but he came to see the grave of West Virginia Senator Peter Godwin Van Winkle (1808-1872). The reason this grave was significant to Kennedy is that Van Winkle was one of ten who men who cast the deciding vote against the impeachment of President Andrew Johnson on May 30, 1868. If it had not been for Senator Van Winkle's and others deciding vote of 'not guilty' Andrew Johnson would have been the first American President to be brought up on impeachment charges.

Senator Van Winkle (a relative of Rip Van Winkle, who was an actual person) rests beneath some shady trees in the graveyard. Echoing footsteps continue to be reported at the otherwise peaceful grave. His mansion, known as "the Castle," is just a short block away. In the Senator's former grand and palatial home, exceptionally bright ghost orbs have been photographed in the attic and at the bottom of the stairs on the first floor. In the house, there is a long history of ghost sightings.

one lonely chinese laundress

Other than the burial sites of small children in the graveyard, perhaps the saddest grave is one belonging to a young Chinese woman who died far away from her native country, in a land she probably had little connection to. This grave, imprinted with symbols from the Chinese alphabet, is located near the chain-link fence that parallels the alley behind the houses. Her tombstone slants in a melancholy way.

Apparently some of the young woman's relatives ran a laundry business on Ann Street and she moved to United States work for them. When the woman died suddenly, she was buried hastily in Riverview Cemetery. Over the years, family members moved elsewhere or returned to China.

But the Chinese have a belief that the spirit can not rest well being buried so far away from one's ancestral home and so, a young Chinese man came to collect the girl's remains, which he placed in a metal suitcase and carried home to their native land.

It is the only gravestone in Riverview Cemetery that does not have a body. It is also the grave that has the least spirit activity.

henry logan's indiscretion

Henry Logan generously gave of himself to the city of Parkersburg as well as the Ohio Valley when he opened up the Henry Logan's Children's Home, a badly needed orphanage for cast-off youngsters in the 1800s. He also offered help and moral support to black churches and schools in the area. Riverview Cemetery is the final resting-place for this giving man and a statue of his likeness wearing a long breech coat is one of three impressive statues that graces the cemetery.

There wasn't any thing unusual or out of place with the Henry Logan statue until the 1990s when mud wasps began to build their nests all over Henry Logan. But most of the wasp activity was focused on a most delicate spot on the statue. No one knows why.

Once the nest was torn down, it wasn't long until the wasps built it back up just as before. Recently, though, it seems the wasp nests have left old Henry Logan alone. Why the wasps were attracted to this statue we do not know. It is a widely accepted fact that insect infestations can be a sign of a significantly haunted place.

angel of night

There is only one angel in the cemetery, beautifully carved from marble. Imported from Europe, the melancholy angel holds a bouquet of limp flowers that appear to wither in her hands. The angel, with heavy-lidded eyes and pale lunar forehead, represents a time when early death was not a surprise. Instead, early death was a tragic romance, inviting ghosts.

One legend surrounding the angel says that her image cannot be captured. Something always goes wrong with the film or picture afterwards. A few photographs taken show a puzzling mist or spectral lights at the base of the statue or surrounding the angel. Odd, serpentine shapes also show around the angel in pictures. The voices of small children are heard singing and playing in the vicinity of the angel. Perhaps this has something to do with the mild look and the peaceful energies she exudes.

One evening in Riverview in early October, one woman noticed a green light flickering behind the angel. She thought the light came from one of those glow-in-the dark flashlights kids use for trick-or-treating. Thinking, perhaps, a child was playing a trick, the woman walked down to investigate but found no one at all. Perhaps it was her imagination or light reflected on a tombstone.

She filed the thought away. Photographs taken later during the ghost tour that same night revealed mysterious green lights all around the cemetery, but most often behind the marble angel statue.

ghostly photographs

Why ghosts tend to turn up in pictures taken in graveyards may seem obvious... Most ghosts return to sulk in their lonely tombs, don't they? What an afterlife! Let's face it. This makes no sense. Perhaps where the human remains are is simply where the ghosts are. Or are they?

What are the real reasons ghosts are so often sighted and photographed around burials of the dead? One reason may be that graveyards, like hospitals and battlegrounds, are areas of high emotion. Such high emotions transcend space and time and can be tapped into when the conditions are just right for the haunting to occur. Often these images, or "imprints" get played back. If you're real lucky, you may catch or see one.

Graveyards tend to hold on to such tragic feelings, more so from the mourners than from those buried therein. Perhaps such intensity of emotions attracts sympathetic spirits who come to the rescue of the mourners. Cemeteries usually have less noise and human activity, making it an ideal spot for ghosts to haunt.

Another theory might be that spirits go back to where they once lived or are buried to gain their bearings, perhaps in hopes of finding relatives or anyone else open to them, especially if they have a message or point they want to bring across.

So how are such ghosts photographed and are the pictures real? There are numerous ways ghosts materialize in photographs. And with the new sensitivity in cameras, ghosts are caught easier than ever before.

So what is this interest in ghost hunting in graveyards all about? Why are we so hooked on ghosts as a culture?

Spiritualism was a major religious movement in the Victorian Age. Psychic Mediums often faked photographs of ghosts to drum up customers. However, this opened the door for ghost photography and also the hopes that existence of spirits could eventually be proven by science. Even so the reality of the spirit world is hard to prove so ghost evidence began to be faked – this included pictures.

Bogus ghost pictures are easy to spot because, in general, spirits don't photograph as looking like people at all. Rare pictures do show some ghosts as they appeared in life, as fully realized apparitions. But more common spirit manifestations are Ghost Orbs, Vortexes and Mists in pictures. Ghost orbs are the most common way spirits turn up in photographs and videos. Many speculate the reason spirits come across as "orbs" is that circles are the easiest way for energies to assume a physical shape. Let us look at the various ways ghosts can appear in pictures:

Orbs: First of all, orbs are difficult to see by the naked eye, although the authors of this book have, on occasion, glimpsed them. Ghost orbs tend to dart and dance about, somewhat like a bug, often changing its direction – not like a dust mote floating down. In picture, orbs appear as globes something like the one Glinda rode in on to meet Dorothy of Oz, but less opaque.

Orbs are seldom so large though. Orbs appear smaller on video cameras than they do in still pictures. True ghost orbs resemble dense balls of smoke, of any color. There are red orbs, white orbs, green orbs, blue orbs and purple orbs. Most orbs are pale grayish or almost tan in color. Some orbs have interesting details, such as what looks to be human faces – at times resembling infants, at other times appearing grinning skulls.

Of course, much controversy surrounds ghost orbs. Some claim they are weather related such as the appearance of raindrops on the lens, dust motes or snowflakes. (No ghost-hunter worth his or her salt would go out in anything but clear weather.)

Others explain the appearance of the orbs are the result of faults in the film, pixels, or are created in the developing process if the developer touches the negative with moist hands. Of course, in cases of digital cameras, there is no film involved.

In the case of extremely haunted areas, ghost orbs can be visible to the naked eye. One West Virginia couple visited a cemetery in Scotland that was 900 years old that has more than 300,00 graves. The minute the couple took a picture and the camera's flash went off, they glimpsed thousands of orbs scatter like moths. The pictures they captured show hundreds of orbs layering back. Scotland is moist, but it wasn't raining.

The truth is, no one understands clearly what these orbs are. True Ghost Orbs show up no matter what kind of camera a person uses. They have a dense quality that dust fragments fail to show. One can use anywhere from expensive digital cameras to cheap disposable ones.

Ghost Orbs tend to turn up mostly in graveyards but it is not clearly understood why. They appear other places as well. They may simply be projections of energies by those taking the pictures. Then again, we believe, they may be spirits or living souls.

Are all orbs human? Perhaps. Then again, perhaps not.

No matter how you feel about ghost orbs, they are still an area worthy study. However, it is easy to kick up some dust and create orbs. I've done this myself, but I can tell you dust orbs do not look like the ones I usually get in the graveyard with my camera.

Mists: Well now, mists or are mysterious forms that we already associate with the supernatural, aren't they? We see them in scary movies such as "Dracula" darkly cloaked in castle mists or the creature from the Black Lagoon lumbering through some swampy fog. Ghost mists, or Ecto Mists, are different though. Like orbs, Ghost mists are not normally seen by the naked eye. They just turn up in pictures in areas that are alleged haunted. As the picture is being taken, the photographer often doesn't see anything. Ghost mists are sometimes erroneously explained away as cigarette smoke or humidity in the atmosphere.

Ghost or Ecto Mist has a quality of streaking and oftentimes resemble whitish fog with appendages. While some mists look simply foggy others have amorphous shapes that are wispy – like wafting smoke. Most mists are white, but red, green, blue, and violet mists can occur.

Vortexes: Vortexes, or vortices, resemble coils of light, waves or long tubes, or can be crescent shaped areas that appear in photographs of haunted areas. While no vortexes have been photographed in Riverview Cemetery so far only time will tell when this type of anomaly turns up. What appears to be vortexes are sometimes orbs traveling at a higher rate of speed than the camera is able to photograph. The reason many of these spirit appearances are not visible to the naked eye but are captured by cameras is the spectrum of light in the camera is wider and more sensitive than what the human eye is capable of detecting. It is generally accepted that spirits vibrate on a much faster level than anything in the physical realm is able to do. So for ghosts to appear on film, they must slow down a great deal.

What is interesting, if you slow down your film speed on a 35 millimeter camera, you have the better chance of catching ghost mists, vortexes and especially apparitions.

the weeping woman statue

If Riverview Cemetery has a point of legend, it is the "Weeping Woman" statue. Known also as the "Gray Lady," this impressive feature at Riverview acts as a watcher over the graves of a local family of note – the Jacksons. A number of Jackson graves in the cemetery are cousins to General Stonewall Jackson, the famed confederate strategist from the Civil War. The statue of the Weeping Woman was made in Evanston, Illinois, but the exact is date unknown.

Many tell that at midnight, when the moon is full or high in the sky, when psychic energies are the most pristine, "the Lady" will stand up from her spot and walk through the cemetery wringing her hands and crying over all of the souls lost in the Civil War.

Did we believe this much-told tale of statues walking?

Statues can't stand up and walk, can they? Granite isn't able to move on its own! This was just a local legend that caused the imaginations of impressionable people to stir, or so we thought...

If the story is folklore, there is something true about it to begin with, but real truth gets lost as the story becomes more and more embellished over the years of people telling it. Yet, area schoolchildren swear the statuary in Riverview have all learned to walk!

To understand the history behind the statue of the Weeping Woman, one must understand some local history. The Jackson's were a prominent family with great ambition. Among them were artists, poets, judges, mayors, governors and Civil War generals.

These include the graves of Lily Irene Jackson (1848-1928) and her father Judge John Jay Jackson (1824-1907.) Governor

Jacob Beeson Jackson rests in an adjoining plot. The graves of the Neal and Van Winkle families are situated nearby. Also near by the Weeping Woman statue is Clara Diss Debar, the French wife of Joseph H. Diss Debar, who designed West Virginia's state seal. Most resting near the Weeping Woman statue must joined in eternity by their high aspirations. All with their own ideas and purposes, none were more unique than Lily Irene, a talented artist with a national reputation.

But does any of this explain a strolling statue or a walking ghost?

After the first couple of years of telling the Weeping Woman tale on the local ghost tour, guides were worried that crowds would be disappointed if the lady did not stand up and walk one Halloween night. After all, Halloween was the night schoolchildren said it happened.

One of the guides offered to dress up as the Weeping Woman. She planned to wear a veil and hold a candle so tour goers could spot her in front of the statue pacing back and forth, quite forlornly. This night for certain the Lady would stand up and walk!

Earlier in the afternoon, the guide placed a candle, a veil and a box of matches near the base of the statue. She was to later join the tour but would leave the tour early so she could get up to the cemetery to put on her ghost act.

The evening turned out to be unlike the others. Excitement mounted as people congregated at the cemetery early in the evening. Fearing damage to the graves and tombstones, a guard was posted at the cemetery gate to keep crowds away until the tour group arrived.

All went according to plan. When the tour guide left the group to sneak into the cemetery and play the Weeping Woman, she was surprised to find her candle already lit and placed atop the statue. She assumed her friend who acted as guard at the gate had gone up and lit the candle earlier so she could find her way through the dark. Mysterious and beautiful against the darkness, the candle fluttered warmly in the late fall night.

The sound of voices at the cemetery gate reminded the tour guide the group was drawing near. She placed the veil on her head, held the candle in front of her and stood in what was now a foreboding dark. Suddenly, the noise of sticks snapping and the pressure of footsteps surrounded the guide. It was the unmistakable sound of a person walking, perhaps a woman's long skirt brushing over fallen leaves. Although the air in the cemetery was cold, the woman felt closed in and hot. The eerie walking continued with its padding footsteps and the rustling of silk. Now covered by a long veil, the guide heard the tour group laugh as they came up the sidewalk. They had spotted her, she thought, and figured out her trick. The ghostly footsteps finally ceased. Peacefulness resumed.

But who was the one who ended up being tricked?

In the end it was the tour guide who was tricked. She never expected to meet anyone, certainly not a spirit near the Weeping Woman statue. Although the guide strongly believed in spirits, she ended up being very unnerved by the presence.

As the ghost tour concluded the early morning hours of November 1st, the tour guide was relieved to call it quits. She thanked the person who acted as guard at the gate and also for lighting the candle so she could see her way through the graveyard in the dark.

With surprise, the guard asked, "What candle? I didn't light a candle. I stood at the gate for hours. Believe me, other than you, there wasn't another living soul inside."

Other ghostly appearances soon occurred. There was one incidence of a woman on the ghost tour who decided to snap a picture of the statue. As soon as she did, the woman said she felt a cool pressure on her stomach. When she glanced down she saw her belt was unbuckled, her pants were undone and her zipper was unzipped. Much to her embarrassment, she stood with her underwear in full view of everyone.

Several people claim they've had cameras freeze up, camcorders break and batteries drain in the area of the Weeping Woman statue. Women also report having their hair tugged on near the Lady, especially in cases when they decide to light up a cigarette!

(Left) A strange photo of author Susan Sheppard and the Weeping Woman in Riverview Cemetery. (Right) A closer look at the unexplained light that appeared in the photo with her.

There is another legend that surrounds the Weeping Woman statue. This one has a positive spin to it. It is claimed that if one has deeply-felt wish, a desire that will also in the end also help others, you can make a wish near the Weeping Woman statue and she will grant it. If the Lady decides the wish is, in fact, deserved, she will endow that person with good luck within a year's time of making it. Many have claimed to have great success when wishing upon 'the Lady' for her help.

But who is the person that the Weeping Woman represents?

If you follow the most intensely shining ghost orbs in the pictures from Riverview Cemetery ghost investigations, there seems to be one grave where the brightest ghost orbs show up – right over the grave of Lily Irene Jackson, an important personality from Parkersburg's gilded age.

Of the politically famous Jackson family, Lily Irene was a woman who knew her own mind. As daughter of John Jay Jackson, she lived from 1848 until 1928. Against criticism of the ladies in the community, Lily Irene, although quite a beauty, never married so she never gave birth to children. Instead, she developed her talents as an artist and chose a life with her pets over a husband.

One young couple came on the ghost tour in 2000. As the legend of the Lady granting wishes was being told the young woman suddenly remembered her wish that was made the year before. She gasped, "Oh, now I remember what my wish last year was! I have a condition where I was not able to get pregnant. Last season, with all of my heart, wished to deliver a healthy child. My daughter was born in August – only ten months after asking the Weeping Woman to grant my wish!"

In previous years, the guides had not talked about the Jackson graves that surrounded the Weeping Woman statue, including the gravesite of Lily Irene Jackson. We had not told Lily's story of throwing a mock wedding for herself even though she was lacking a groom or any of her other famous Victorian age antics. We didn't know about them then.

Once Lily Irene's name was mentioned, the young woman gasped once more. "We named our daughter Liliana. We call her 'Lily' for short." Since then, there have been three pregnancies associated with the statue. Interesting, all babies are girls.

But that isn't the only uncanny or mysterious event connected to the Weeping Woman statue. Just recently, a woman was driving up 13th Street in Parkersburg past the old Nash School (now a dance school) below Riverview Cemetery and noticed a woman standing forlornly in the bend of the road. The somber-looking woman had on a floor-length dress and appeared as if she was dressed up for a costume-party even though the dress was rather drab.

The driver thought, perhaps, there was a special event going on at the dance school across the street. But before she could pass by the woman, the lone figure drifted up gracefully into the air, then glided backwards into the cemetery in close proximity to the Weeping Woman statue!

The woman wondered if this was the spirit that haunts the statue and is the one responsible for much of the hair pulling and clothes undoing!

Some of the Jackson's (and other people buried in Riverview) are cousins to Civil War General Stonewall Jackson. One is a first cousin while others second or third cousins to the Confederate warrior. (Although Jackson was born at Jackson's Mills near Clarksburg, others claim the General may have been born in Parkersburg where his mother stayed with relatives through most of her pregnancy.)

black dog in the graveyard

Tales of Black Dogs appearing as harbingers of death and being connected to the occult originates in the British Isles, but this legend has made its way to the United States. Such dogs as death omens are reported to be solid black, larger than average (but usually not terribly large) and have glowing, red eyes that brim with a hellish fire. Interestingly, the ancient Irish associated the Black Dog with their Banshees, or "Black Fairies."

A large black dog often wanders Riverview. The animal is said to walk among the headstones, stopping to dig and scratch for a few moments then disappear into the trees toward the Weeping Woman statue. At times the dog appears to be followed by three black crows that perch on the tombstones watching over as the animal digs about.

The person who reported seeing such a black dog on a number of occasions wondered how a large dog had gotten inside the graveyard? After all, the gates that surround the cemetery were locked, and the dog was too large to have squeezed underneath the chain length fence on the side.

In Greek mythology, Black Dogs are connected to Hecate, goddess of the Crossroads, the underworld and also witchcraft. It is said when you hear dogs howling in your neighborhood late at night you can be assured that the dark goddess Hecate is roaming about. Hecate also reigned over night terrors and midnight. Black dogs and black goats were sacrificed to honor her in ancient times. Whether the Black Dog in Riverview Cemetery is a real one or one in spirit form, the dog is most often seen wandering through the graveyard in late winter or early spring.

A few years ago a man and a woman were visiting the cemetery. The husband took a picture of his wife walking among ancient tombstones. When the picture was developed, it showed the bust of a bearded man behind her. He appeared to have only one arm. The other sleeve was pinned to the man's shoulder. Stonewall Jackson was wounded in battle at Chancellorsville by one of his own men. Jackson's arm was amputated before his death. The man in the picture eerily resembled busts portraying Stonewall Jackson.

evergreen cemetery ⤳ route 64 north

There is a more recent cemetery sighting at a graveyard located north of the city along Route 64. It is called Evergreen North. An older couple that had recently married stepped inside the cemetery at dusk so the man could visit his former wife's grave. The woman was not comfortable going into a graveyard so near dark and expressed the feeling of apprehension to her husband. The man answered, "This is the safest place you could possibly be since no one is alive in here. The dead can't hurt you. Besides," the husband continued, "Look over there. I see another couple sitting together on a bench."

The wife turned and sure enough, a couple sat on a bench several yards away. With heads bowed the silhouetted couple appeared to be whispering to each other. But, as the husband and wife gazed closer, the forms took on a shadowy quality. Black and indistinct, they had no human features. As this fact dawned on the couple, the ghostly figures stood then floated upward into the evergreen trees and vanished entirely.

When interviewed for this book, the man said, "Look at my arms. See the chill bumps rise? I get them every time I remember seeing that ghost couple. I never believed in such things as spirits and haints. But I do now."

9. haunted city

strange goings on at the blennerhassett hotel

There is no clear idea as to why one building is haunted while another one is not. Spirit activity goes on in cycles – a house or room is haunted for a while and oftentimes the activity ceases. Ghost sightings seem to have little to do with the age of the building in which they occur, or even in what shape it is. Even more mysterious is why a haunting will occur over a number of weeks, months or years and suddenly stop.

However, the age and history of a building, not to mention what may have happened there does have a bearing on whether a house will be haunted or not. For instance, a building in which a lot of emotional energy has been invested is ripe for a haunting.

When a place becomes known for its ghostly manifestations, it has generally experienced paranormal activity over a number of years. They tend to be a mixed bag of various anomalies, usually one major haunting with a several minor ones, such as poltergeists (meaning in German "noisy ghosts," or "to rap and to knock"). The haunting might start out with poltergeists, then evolve into spirit recordings, appearances of apparitions, earthbound ghosts, mysterious sounds, smells, and inanimate objects being moved or tossed as if by unseen hands.

Although the reason is not entirely known, renovations, or efforts to bring buildings back to their original state appear to stimulate ghostly activities. Perhaps a sense of "earlier days" attracts spirits who once lived there in the material realm. Perhaps the renovations simply set up the perfect energy and opportunity for residual hauntings to appear as ghosts. But the "why?" of it is not completely understood. Of course, the Blennerhassett Hotel at 4th and Market Streets in Parkersburg is no exception.

This historic downtown hotel first opened its doors in 1889 at the height of the West Virginia's Oil and Gas Boom times. With its 50+ rooms and expansive mirrors in the lobby, the sophisticated air of the Blennerhassett set the tone for West Virginia's Victorian Age.

This could not have been achieved without one man with a singular vision: a man who wanted to make Parkersburg a better place. The man was William N. Chancellor. After the Civil War, Chancellor built not only ornate hotels but also elegant homes in the Parkersburg area. A native of nearby Ritchie County, William Chancellor made most of his money during the oil boom and served as the mayor of Parkersburg twice. But of all of the places that Mr. Chancellor invested his money, time and energy, only two still stand, the current Blennerhassett Hotel and his former abode on Juliana Street.

Both places are believed haunted by unquiet spirits. Apparitions sometimes manifest as fiery, gold lights in the widow's walk of Chancellor's 1878 Federal style home on Juliana Street. We do not know if Mr. Chancellor's apparition appears at his former home. Also called the 'Burwell House,' his relatives still live there and have not reported any haunts. Especially true since the hotel re-opened.

But ghosts with unsettled business, such as Mr. Chancellor, often haunt the very places where they invested the most energy in life. Therefore, it does appear that the Blennerhassett Hotel is the more haunted of the two places yet not in any bad way.

The Chancellor Home on Julian Street – another scene of haunted happenings

Even so, the ingredients are there for a real haunting, creating perfect fodder for apparitions to lurk. Such trappings include the usual "unsettled business," where the apparition or some disembodied personal energy that remains of the deceased person is not able to let go. This usually involves a place where a great deal psychic energy has been invested spent, a place "open to spirits," where they can communicate with the living, to again experience life, (even while dead).

One of the spirits who haunts the Blennerhassett Hotel is so persistent, so determined to communicate with the living, he appears to believers and non-believers alike, often in the same gray suit, with the a melancholy expression that implies his work is not over yet.

the smoking gentleman

A splendid oil painting dating from the late 1890s hangs in the library of the Blennerhassett Hotel. With muted tones and a precision of line, the painting portrays an older gentleman in various shades of blue and gray. If one looks closely at the portrait, it's as if a wreath of smoke surrounds the distinguished looking man in the picture. This may seem to be a trick of the lighting and the eyes, if one had not heard about the strange events that have been reported throughout the Blennerhassett Hotel after reopening its doors as a hotel in 1986. One could even say, the portrait seems have taken on a life of its own.

Unusual balls of lights or "orbs" have been captured in photographs of the portrait, ones that look similar to the burning end of a cigar and perhaps even a pipe. When the smoke does appear, the smell of the cigar is different, as if from another era entirely.

The spicy aroma of cigar smoke is common throughout the hotel, even when there has not been anyone passing through the lobby smoking anything. In fact, smoking is prohibited to smoke in the lobby. It's not unusual for the cigar smoke to turn up just outside the front doors of the hotel as well.

The very first night of the Haunted Parkersburg Tours was rained out so the ghost tour guides decided to tell the ghost tales in the corridor of the hotel near the white Steinway piano. Only few children showed up that night... but so did the cigar smoke. That, for us, was the first time we encountered the ghostly smoke. Since then, not a season goes by that we don't meet up with the cigar smoke numerous times. Sometimes outside the doors of the hotel, in front of Mr. Chancellor's Juliana Street home and even inside the cemetery.

Late into in the 1996 Haunted Parkersburg season, another tour was called off because of rain. We didn't want to dampen the spirits of the fifty-or-so who showed up so once again, so we told our tales of ghosts in the library of the hotel. When we talked of Mr. Chancellor, and how his ghost turns up with the smell of his cigar smoke, we noticed the audience fidgeting and laughing. Puzzled, we asked the people why they were so excited. A few tittered and pointed toward Mr. Chancellor's oil portrait. Sure enough, a spicy aroma had permeated the room and wreathed the picture frame. This peculiar manifestation was captured on videotape by one of our guests.

So, why is there cigar smoke? Could it be that Mr. Chancellor was once fond of expensive cigars? Or might it have been another hotel manager? Read on and learn the evidence so you can decide for your self.

There is an explanation for the cigar smoke smell. One area woman who came on the ghost tour told the story of happening upon quite a treasure at a local yard sale. It was a trunk nearly one-hundred-years old with nicks, buckles, and gritty character. The woman purchased the mysterious trunk for a modest price and took it home. On the trunk there were stickers seemingly collected during travels from various parts of the world. Whoever owned it was wealthy and traveled a lot.

When the woman opened the trunk, she found a name label that said the trunk had belonged to a William N. Chancellor. But she quickly resold it. Why? The woman claimed the trunk smelled bad and reeked of (what else?) cigar smoke.

Is it possible for a ghost to show up as a smell? Yes, this is most definitely. In fact, apparitions commonly show up as smells.

A universal element of many hauntings has to do with the appearance of aromas. These could be referred to as "apparitional smells." Not caused by anything natural in the atmosphere at the time. The scent can be anything, but usually it is some signature aroma that the person or ghost was associated with in life, such as brand of perfume or cologne, coffee perking, flowers, pipes and cigars. One explanation may be that of the five or six senses we have as human beings the one most linked with memory or the past is our sense of smell. Scientists agree that odors stimulate memories in the human brain more than any other sense. Perhaps the smell is evidence, or at least a clue, the spirit is sending to help us to remember that past, most importantly, his or her past.

To begin with our story of the smoking ghost, we should explore the nature of spirits, why they choose to haunt, but more importantly, what events bring about some of the haunting. Since spirits continue to be a subject for much speculation, tangible proof can be evasive. Yet there are traits of hauntings that are profoundly universal.

In the cases of old buildings becoming haunted, there is one activity that appears to stir up apparitions and ghosts more than anything else, and these have to do with renovations. Why renovations tend to stimulate ghostly appearances (that may have remained dormant up until that point) is not readily known.

It seems that whenever property is renovated or restored to its original state, the personalities of those who once invested a great deal of energy or had emotional ties to the place, often come back and make their presence known.

Another reason renovations tend to stir ghosts is they simply don't like or agree with the changes being done to their former living area or business.

We do not know precisely why this is. Perhaps it is nothing more than spirits having trouble giving up something they worked hard for during their earthly lives, such as former residences, businesses and families. It may be that some spirits simply cannot let go of what they owned in life. Some may choose to come back as messengers for friends, family or anyone sensitive enough to see them. Such seems to be the case of the Smoking Gentleman who reportedly haunts the Blennerhassett Hotel.

However, the apparition does not return in a wispy, shapeless form that could just as easily be explained as surging shadows and flickering lights. As a spirit, the

Smoking Gentleman appears as he did in life, looking solid and dressed impeccably in a three-piece gray suit.

The phantom of a Smoking Gentleman appears throughout in the hotel halls, lobby, and elevator as well as in private rooms. Those who report the apparition claim that the man appears as absolutely real but is wearing old-fashioned clothes. Some hotel guests, who have been awakened at night, report witnessing this older man standing at the foot of their beds. Many eyewitnesses claimed the man stares at them in a melancholy way for a few seconds. He will then either disappear or fade entirely.

Generally, the story about the gray-suited man seldom varies, except for one unusual report that happened in broad daylight in a room on the 2nd floor. After showering one morning, a guest stepped from the bathroom back into the bedroom. What he saw caught him off guard. The witness, who had never heard of a ghost in the Blennerhassett Hotel, said that a man who appeared to be "up in years," stood by his bed staring at him. Taken aback, the hotel guest didn't give the older gentleman a chance to speak. (Old men can be ax murderers, too can't they?) It was at this time the completely nude hotel guest fled outside into hallway, leaving his towel behind. Once the frightened man recognized his lack of attire might offend other hotel guests, he sheepishly returned to his hotel room.

By this time, the suited gentleman was gone. Ghosts tend not to hang around for long. This is why they are often described as phantasms and apparitions. It is not because spirits are "see through." Ghosts usually appear as solid as the living do. That's why they are so successful in tricking the rest of us into thinking they are alive.

So, who is the Smoking Gentleman that haunts the Blennerhassett Hotel?

Those who have had a chance encounter with the gray clad gentleman emphatically say that the ghost is the same man pictured in the portrait that hangs in the library. Hotel workers and others who met the reserved ghost in dark of night agree. Depicted in the portrait is Mr. William N. Chancellor, the original builder of the Blennerhassett Hotel.

Always, with the appearance of the Smoking Gentleman, witnesses smell cigar or pipe-smoke. The spicy odor at times wafts out onto the sidewalks surrounding the hotel.

As far as the apparition of Mr. Chancellor is concerned, he seems to hang out in the 2nd Floor hallways most frequently, to check his favorite rooms no doubt. The ghost also enjoys appearing in the elevator to fool with the buttons. It often stops on the wrong floor or not at all. Cigar smoke is encountered in the elevators as well. Often the elevator will stop at the 2nd floor whether the button is pushed for that floor or not.

In the past, the Smoking Gentleman has appeared at late hours in the former area of the front desk. (Where the coffee bar is now.) It is almost as if Mr. William

N. Chancellor is saying, "See me? I am still here. This is my hotel. I'm the one who made this place."

Mr. Chancellor's apparition materialized on October 28th, 2001 around 7:15 p.m to one of the Haunted Parkersburg Tour Guides. As crowds were arriving to take the ghost tour, one of the guides noticed a tall man in gray slacks walking briskly into the library. Since guests usually gather by the door and storytelling begins in the library, the guide followed the man into the library to let him know guests were gathering in

The Blennerhassett Hotel

the lobby. She entered into a room filled with cigar smoke, but found no living soul inside. The guide gestured for another guide to follow her into the library. She asked, "Did you see a tall man walk into the library?" The male guide shook his head "no." At that very moment, the antique typewriter on a nearby desk typed all on it's own. The guides remembered specifically the keys that were struck were "J" and "K."

It was only later they noticed a black & white photograph of JFK meeting and shaking hands with local television reporter Glenn Wilson when he visited Parkersburg during his bid for the presidency. Kennedy and Wilson's picture was placed to the left of the old typewriter. John F. Kennedy also stayed overnight at the Blennerhassett Hotel during his 1960 presidential campaign. None of us who worked on the ghost tour knew this at the time.

i was here first!

In the summer of 2003, the Blennerhassett Hotel underwent even more extensive renovations. A man from another area stayed in one of the newer, refurbished rooms. Looking forward to a restful sleep that night, he switched off the table lamp. As soon as the guest turned off the light, he felt a weight at the foot of the bed as if someone had just sat down. With a start, the man opened his eyes and as they adjusted to the darkness, he saw an older man, sitting at the foot of the bed in his hotel room. The gentleman then turned to the guest and bitterly complained,

"I was here first!" Upon that, the apparition disappeared, and so did the witness – almost!

But Mr. Chancellor isn't the only spirit that shows up along with the aroma of cigar smoke. As it is with most haunted buildings, spirits tend to multiply. Some theorize the hotel has become a portal for more than a few "out of town guests." You know how it is when you throw a really popular party? A few personalities may show up to crash the party that you don't even know. Many times, this is when the fun begins. The Smoking Gentleman isn't the only ghostly act in the Blennerhassett Hotel… There are others.

the four o'clock knocker

It is important to keep in mind that ghostly appearances tend to occur in cycles. Something will "kick in" for a while and then it will change. That is why you really can't go somewhere and "wait" for a ghost to appear.

A home, place or person will experience a great deal of ghostly activity and then the haunts will quiet down for weeks, months or even years. In other words, it is hard to predict when a ghost will appear, or even what form or shape that the ghost will assume. The Blennerhassett Hotel has many such ghosts that may not be a ghost so much as a kinetic energy.

There is a doorway at the side of the former front desk (the area is now a coffee bar) that leads into the office of the hotel. At certain times, especially when a new employee is working the late shift, there will be three sharp knocks at the door. When the doorway is opened, the hallway is empty. That is, except for a powerful cloud of reeking smoke. This particular ghost has come to be known as "The Four O' Clock Knocker."

Recently, there has been a somewhat different appearance of the "Four O'Clock Knocker." On Christmas Eve of 2000, an employee who worked at the front desk was watching a movie in the side office. Beneath the floor she heard a knocking that startled her. This happened numerous times. A young man who worked with the woman went into the basement to check out what was beneath the floor of the office. Down there he found an old cathedral ceiling that could be described as spooky, but really, nothing else was amiss. The front desk employee could not remember the exact time the rapping occurred but she guessed it had happened in the early hours of the morning… perhaps, just perhaps, at exactly 4:00 a.m.

man in the mirror

On the first floor of the hotel and behind the bar in the former Harman's restaurant (now called Spats) and lounge there were some regal antique mirrors.

However, they did not start out as mirrors. The mirrors were actually framed door casings from a Victorian Era apartment building in New York City that had previously been torn down. Upon reaching West Virginia, large mirrors were added. The effect of the framed mirrors behind the bar was quite dramatic. Within the recessive shadows of the room, the overhead lights sparkled mysteriously.

Late at night, as the bar was closing up, a compelling vision appeared in the mirror to those sitting at the bar. Guests reported that when they looked up, they glimpsed an elegant man in a white tuxedo and clutching a black cane, floating through the glass.

But the man in the white tuxedo was not the only ghost who chose to haunt the mirror. During the day, a sea captain in a hat and dark coat was seen standing in the corner of the mirror, the side facing Market Street. Under the lights of the bar the brass buttons on the Captain's coat were said to shine brilliantly.

Such murky figments and phantasms appear in mirrors throughout the hotel. However, it is not known whether the apparitions belong to the Blennerhassett Hotel or to the apartment building that was torn down in New York. But with the appearance of both spirits, there appeared a spicy smoke that continues to linger.

the hotel library

With its old-fashioned woodwork, oil paintings of hunting scenes, sumptuous tables and chairs, and high windows, the library evokes a sense of Parkersburg's gilded past. Just the kind of haunted place ghosts love to hang around in.

A portrait of a smoking gentleman hangs in the room. It was donated to the hotel by the builders' great-granddaughter. The walls of the room are shelved with antique books. There is also a window on the rounded corner of the room that was once a doorway to the First National Bank. The sound of hotel guests checking in at the front desk fills the library as piped-in music drifts softly through the calming atmosphere of the room.

The front of the hotel has always been a busy traffic area. With its high windows, the library is filled with natural light that despite the noise gives a sense of serenity to the room. Still, there is a feeling of suspense that hints at other forces lurking.

For one thing, the antique books don't want to stay on their shelves. A few of the books have this odd habit of flinging themselves across the room. Seldom do those working at the front deck notice until they hear the crash. When someone goes in to investigate, he usually finds that one of the antique books in another corner entirely.

There is one particular, beat-up book that travels around the most. Workers at the Blennerhassett Hotel have taken to putting a potted plant in front of it, and still, on occasion, the red leather bound antique book flies from its shelf.

What is so fascinating about this almost 100-year-old text is that it includes pages with suggestions for after dinner speeches and lectures. When picking up the book for the firs time to examine it, the pages fell open to page 159, to a speech called "The Sorcerer's Response." This speech is on the subject about how men, given the chance and talent, can also be witches. That is a pretty funny spirit, right? Well, many ghosts love to play jokes. Poltergeists (unleashed psychic energies that indicate stress in the atmosphere, however, poltergeists are not considered to be true ghosts) have a prankster type of energy.

Bo Kitchens, a paranormal researcher who visited the area suggested that Mr. Chancellor might well have been a Mason. A mysterious group with mystical rites, the Masons may have been indicated by the poltergeists in the library by pointing out this peculiar dinner speech. Turns out, Kitchens was right on the money. William Chancellor had been, in fact, a devoted Mason. In 1914, the Masonic Temple was built directly behind his Juliana Street home on Market Street.

There are other unexplained peculiarities in the library. Unexplained gold lights circle Mr. Chancellor's portrait. These lights often appear as gold balls and have been captured on film. What looks to be the burning end of a cigar illuminates as a tiny red light in photographs snapped of the portrait.

What is most unnerving is the sound of a woman screaming... Not just in the library but throughout the hotel. It might be a good time to tell her story now.

wailing woman

Earlier in the book, we gave you tales about a type of a spirit, a death fairy actually, called the Banshee by ancient Celtic peoples. This spirit appears in the form of a keening woman who wails upon the moment of a person's death, especially one who is of Irish or Scottish blood. The Blennerhassett Hotel has a similar apparition of a female spirit that wails but unlike the Banshee, this ghost is entirely harmless.

At certain times when the staff at the Blennerhassett Hotel sets up the microphone for an important event in the ballroom, the piercing sound of a woman screams amplifies through those the speakers. This same woman's voice has also been heard over the intercom system throughout the hotel. The staff reports that the scream at times sounds like a woman's surprised shrieks while at other times it is a woman's high-pitched laughter they hear.

Several years ago, a couple from Youngstown, Ohio stayed at the hotel while they searched for a home in the area. In the middle of the night, the wife was startled awake by what sounded like of cats fighting inside her room. It took a few moments for the woman to remember she was sleeping on the second floor of a hotel.

With her husband sleeping beside her, the woman listened intently. She realized the noises sounded more like a woman wailing inside her room. Yet, no one was there. After a moment, the voices ceased. Her husband never woke up through the entire ruckus.

During the local ghost tour, several of the walkers reported that as the group left the building, a woman's cackle was heard at the back of the crowd. Several people were unnerved by this, and rushed to the front of the group. It is not at all unusual for people joining the ghost tour to hear giggling, screams or words spoken by a feminine voice whispered into their ears, inside the hotel as well as outside on the street. So what might be the reason behind the sound of women wailing throughout the hotel? Or maybe it is just one? We were asked this question by two paranormal investigators from the Washington, D.C. area.

For the first few years of the ghost tour, we simply did not know what was behind these apparitions of wailing women. In fact, we couldn't even imagine. To our knowledge, nothing traumatic had happened to a woman during the entire history of the hotel.

We were wrong.

This is what we believed until a local woman came on the ghost tour. As the tour group returned to the hotel, she pointed to the library window that was once a doorway when the hotel was a bank.

The woman said, "Do you see that window? It used to be a doorway when this building was the First National Bank of Parkersburg."

We nodded in agreement, that, yes, we had heard that.

The woman then said, "No, you don't understand. My aunt was killed in that doorway. She was coming inside to make a bank deposit when a tractor-trailer missed a turn and jumped up on the sidewalk. Her body was slammed into the wall and she was crushed."

Might this explain one screaming ghost?

Even so, the woman's ghostly voice is not always a tragic one. Years ago, while some of the staff was setting up the ballroom for a social event, they were all startled by a woman's voice coming across the microphone as "Howdy Fellas!" Needless to say, everyone in the room scrammed.

one maid-a-mopping

Of course, many spirits are less disturbing. These types of ghosts are as harmless as watching an "I Love Lucy" episode. TV viewers can still see Lucy but Lucy can't see us. (At least we don't think she can, but you never know.) This type of spirit, as mentioned earlier, is called a "spirit recording," and is also known as a "residual haunting." There is a pretty good argument that most ghosts are merely "recordings," no more capable of communicating with the living than you having a conversation with your television set. You can try if you want to, but chances are the people on the air won't hear or see you.

In most instances, a spirit recording performs the same task over and over again, without changing the activity. Recordings go through the motions over and over again. You can try and communicate with the ghosts, but good luck. Seemingly pre-occupied with their activity they won't see or hear you. They are recordings.

The Blennerhassett Hotel has several ghosts that are residual hauntings. In fact, most are. One such spirit recording that has been frequently sighted is an old-fashioned maid dressed neatly in a black and white uniform. This maid continues to mop in front of the check-in desk. She never changes her clothes or her methods.

The neatly dressed, dark haired maid busily shines in the hotel lobby. It is interesting to point out that one of the places the maid has been spotted most frequently is nearby the Four O' Clock Knocker's door.

Why in front Four O' Clock Knocker door? No special reason, other than it looks like a door that is just dying to be knocked – especially in the early hours of the morning.

kissing bandit

Women staying at the hotel have reported the pleasant experience of being awakened in the morning by soft, affectionate kisses. As soon as the women open their eyes and are fully awake, the kissing bandit has completely disappeared. Most report the kisses are not frightening, but gentle and lovely. No one knows if the bandit is a male or a woman spirit, but we are willing to bet it is a guy ghost.

the elevators

Elevators can be creepy even when they're not haunted. Most kids can tell you this. However, when you toss a couple of spirits in the mix, well, a ride on an elevator can sometimes be a bit hair-raising especially when you're visiting the Blennerhassett Hotel.

The elevators at the hotel appear to be under the influence of the same supernatural forces as the rest of the building. The doors open repeatedly when the lobby is the most quiet and peaceful, usually past midnight. It's as if when the spirits step in, the door closes and takes the ghosts for a ride. The elevator doors tend to stop at the 2nd floor of the hotel and pause, where the ghost activity appears to be the most intense.

All of this could be taken as sheer coincidence except for the "stories" that surround the elevators. It's no surprise that apparitions are often glimpsed stepping in and out of the elevators.

One of the more interesting ghost sightings took place when a member of the staff was about to carry some laundry a few floors up to the guestrooms in the hotel. The worker spotted an expensively dressed woman hurrying toward the elevator. With arms full of linens, he yelled for the woman to hold the door for him, which apparently she did, since the door was left open. The odd thing was, when he got to the elevator he found no one else inside... only the lingering scent of a woman's floral perfume.

little boy lost

Once a building falls under the bewildering forces of a haunting, other spirits will invariably show up. It seems once the phenomenon starts, others will be attracted the place that has now become a doorway for various spirit entities to come through. It is my belief the conditions have to be right for this to happen, such as individuals with certain receptivity in a place that has the right kind of energy for ghosts to manifest. This does not mean the witness must believe in ghosts. It just means in that moment of time they need to be receptive to the spirit.

You see, not all people who see ghosts are psychic. In fact, most ghost witnesses do not consider themselves psychic in any other way.

One of the more recent and interesting ghostly visitations at the Blennerhassett Hotel happened in the kitchen when the chef was preparing the meals for an important event. As the chef turned to grab a pan, he glimpsed a small boy approximately the age of eight or nine staring up at him dressed in the clothing of a newspaper boy of the 1920s or 30s. Startled, the chef stumbled back. When the man regained his bearings to look in the corner where the boy previously stood, it was empty.

The chef mentioned that he was surprised he was over how physical the boy actually appeared. The chef had children around the same age. It is possible the lost boy was attracted to his openness. The same little boy has been spotted in the basement close to the employees break area.

a little night music

Like many modern hotels, the Blennerhassett Hotel has pleasant, piped in music throughout the building. Of course, this is not at all unusual for any contemporary hotel. That is, unless you consider the fact that the voices of small children (that should not be there) have been heard singing above the music. During the Christmas season one female security guard worked into the late hours of the night reported hearing children singing "Jingle Bells" overtop the piped in music. The guard thought this was just an interesting new feature. She'd never heard actual voices over the piped in music before.

When mentioning hearing children's voices to a maintenance man, he replied, "So you heard it, too, huh? They've been doing that for quite a while. It really messes up the lightning in the hotel whenever the kid's voices come on. I usually have to change the electrical fuses whenever those ghost voices start singing."

The security guard asked, "You mean those children's voices are ghosts!"

The maintenance man replied nonchalantly, "Of course, they're ghosts. Remember where you are. This is the Blennerhassett Hotel."

Also, Big Band music is heard throughout the hotel at night, especially in the various ballrooms.

the second floor

One cannot miss feeling the strong energies on the second floor even if you are not normally sensitive to spiritual things. Many experience a high buzz of energy when walking in the halls. Others report sensing a ghostly presence walking with them or the sensation of carpet rolling under one's feet. After all, it is the second floor where Mr. Chancellor's ghost has been spotted more than once, the pervading cigar smoke. There is also the mysterious sound of running water behind the walls of the rooms on the 2nd floor, but leaks have never been found. Psychics claim some of the hotel rooms seem to be the source or "portals," (places that act as doorways between the spiritual and material realms) for these unexplained, ghostly energies.

Recently, the 3rd Floor has also been an area of unusual happenings. During one evening the electricity for the entire 3rd Floor was completely wiped out for several minutes. Since it was linked to other areas on the hotel, there was no rational reason for the lights to go. They eventually came back on. The staff still hasn't figured it out.

Some have reported the sound of ice being dropped in the sinks or glass shattering. Once it is checked, there is no evidence whatsoever for the breaking noises. When checked, the sinks are dry and empty.

the red room

Something is going on in the Red Room. No one wants to go in there alone.

Everyone at the hotel feels little weird about this room. People give few specifics about the Red Room— such as towering ghosts or ornery poltergeists. It's none of that –it is just a feeling— doors opening, closing but mostly getting stuck, the sound of glasses being rattled when nothing is amiss. The Red Room just has an otherworldly feeling.

We generally don't add stories that are vague, but this short tale about the Red Room on the 2nd Floor is an exception since it points out the continuing saga of the haunting that goes one at the hotel. The Red Room is used for business meetings and other social affairs. It has a large oak table that dominates the center of the room. The floors are carpeted and the walls are wallpapered red.

During one evening, a young man who worked at the hotel was cleaning up the room after a dinner. Within a few minutes, witnesses heard the young man startle and yell. Seconds later, he fled the room. Most of the color was drained from his face.

The young man wouldn't reveal to the other employees why he was afraid, but he vowed never to return to the Red Room. When other workers reminded him that he would have to work in the Red Room, as they all did, the young man turned in his notice.

More recently, a worker at the hotel was asked to unlock the Red Room in order to prepare it for a luncheon. He slipped the key into the lock but it would not budge. As he turned it, the hotel worker said the keyhole felt sluggish as if there were molasses inside. He tried over and over but the door would not unlock. Thinking he had picked up the wrong key, he called for help. Another worker who came to his aid grabbed his keys and the door unlocked instantly.

The second worker gave the first worker what used to be called "the hairy eyeball" and handed the keys back to him. With some embarrassment the employee went to his work of making preparations for the luncheon. After finishing, he proceeded to leave the Red Room and realized that he was now locked in! He pushed against the door with his shoulder. Nothing budged. The worker banged on the door and yelled for help. The young man who opened the door earlier again came to his rescue. Much to the first man's horror the door easily glided open as if it had never been locked at all. Another cause for the old "hairy eyeball" again!

Recent photographs taken in the Red Room reveal strange lights that resemble lightning bugs and typical "plasmoid" orbs with comet-like tails. Is the Red Room still active with ghosts? Most who work there still say yes.

the ballrooms

In the main, first-floor corridor of the hotel is the Charleston Ballroom where special events such as dances, receptions and formal dinners take place. For most events, there is always a need for a microphone. Invariably, after the microphone is turned on, it will switch itself off. If the person setting up the Ballroom is persistent in keeping the microphone on, odd voices will eke out – usually there is cackling or snickering. Sometimes, muffled words are spoken, punctuated by laughs. This, of course, can rattle the nerves of even the calmest of people.

There have been other reports that after the table settings are set up for formal dinners, the worker will come back to the Ballroom to discover that every single piece of silverware put in the exact opposite side where he had earlier placed them.

Although the Blennerhassett Hotel has a number of dimmer lights, the lights throughout the hotel, most especially in the Library and the Ballroom, will brighten and dim entirely on their own.

Earlier, one young woman who worked at the hotel was setting up the ballroom for an event. She glanced up and watched as several heavy glasses exploded before her eyes.

Late at night, when the Ballroom and for the most part the rest of the hotel is closed down for the evening, music can be heard coming from within. Many claim the music sounds like Big Band Music, or lively music from the flapper age. But these aren't the eeriest sounds heard coming out of the Charleston Ballroom. Sometimes, when all is quiet, there will be the sound of scratching and pecking, at the glass, like a bony finger.

fine food and spirits

Contrary to popular opinion, people who study ghosts are not as impressionable as what you might think. Therefore, when we began to tell our ghost stories at the Blennerhassett Hotel in 1996, we were just as surprised as anyone when Mr. Chancellor's inevitable cigar smoke appeared just as everyone claimed it would.

When told this story, we sort of doubted it, thinking people pass through all of the time smoking cigars. And yet later, we smelled it ourselves...during practice sessions for our ghost tour, late, into the dead of night when no one else was around.

There was no denying the aromatic smoke and the special place that it appeared. The smoke would catch up with us just about anywhere. On many occasions, the aroma is smelled by dozens of people. It was also detected in crowds of less than twelve. In 2000, when reporter and photographer Terry Headley of the *West Virginia State Journal* came to Parkersburg to write a feature story on the ghost tour, I (Susan Sheppard) showed him around the Blennerhassett Hotel that led up to the second floor. Just as the two of us stepped off of the elevator, in the vicinity of the Red Room, cigar smoke pretty much floored us as we stepped from the elevator.

It is important to point out, that once you get used to spirit appearances, they cease to be frightening. In fact, it is a privilege to experience such fascinating mysteries. Not everyone gets to.

During the ghost tour, we could not help but notice the smoke seemed the most intense during the times we told the story of Mr. William Chancellor, the original builder of the hotel. Others think it belongs to Mr. Staley, another hotel manager who passed on.

Nonetheless, there is a smoking ghost. We have smelled him too many times.

After leaving the hotel for our ghost walk each year – mysterious occurrences tended to follow us up the street. As we walked past empty cars in parking lots, it wasn't unusual for headlights to suddenly switch on and flash us. Sometimes burglar alarms in the cars went off causing quite a stir.

At other points doors would open and close in vans while no one was inside. Street lamps and other lights behaved strangely while the ghost tour ventured by. Overhead lights of all kinds tended flicker, flash and pulse all the way up to Juliana Street, the residential area of the tour. By the time we get to Riverview Cemetery in the upper historical district, our flashlights are already drained and dim. (Spirits will draw upon power sources in order to make themselves strong enough to appear. You can spend a small fortune on batteries alone while ghost hunting.)

There were also stories from people who came on the tour. One man came back to tell us something quite unusual if not downright scary happened after he returned home after going on the ghost tour. He claimed that when he walked into his house after our ghost tour, he spied a box of old photographs strewn haphazardly across his dining room table. The pictures had been packed away in his basement. He hadn't seen them in years.

On the tour, we witnessed a bright in the sky, mostly over Fort Boreman Hill. When I assured the crowd that the light was most likely the planet Jupiter, the bright light proceeded to move from left to right in a way that no contemporary aircraft could. One woman snapped a picture. Then it simply disappeared.

Perhaps the most unnerving events that happened after the ghost tour ended for the evening. One of the tour guides was driving home about midnight when something large and black flew through the air and hit her car on the right side with a loud thump. It was only two blocks to her house. Still frightened, the woman continued driving, wondering how she was going to explain the huge dent. Later, when she got out of the car, she saw nothing. There was no dent and no hint of the car having been hit.

One employee at the hotel glanced up as he was bringing baggage through the front door of the Blennerhassett Hotel, and saw the apparition of William N. Chancellor standing there, looking very distinguished in his three-piece-suit, holding his cigar and ready to meet each hotel guest. His ghost still appears to those lucky enough to see him.

So the ghostly activity in the Blennerhassett Hotel in downtown Parkersburg continues to this very day.

After all, what would a fine old hotel be without its famous haunts?

10. haunted hills

civil war ghosts, quincy hill, fort boreman hill & droop mountain

Parkersburg is approximately 50 miles south of the Mason-Dixon Line. One can only imagine what the atmosphere was like in this small, river-city during the Civil War where brother fought brother, and the loyalties of neighbors were divided. Despite the fact that Confederate General Stonewall Jackson had relatives in Parkersburg, the city remained a strong hold for the Union. And because the then Virginia town (now West Virginia) is where the Ohio River and B & O Railroad converged, it became a critical area for the Union to defend and maintain.

We cannot dedicate – we cannot consecrate – we cannot hallow – this ground. The brave men, living and dead, who struggled here, have consecrated it, far above our poor power to add or detract. The world will little note, nor long remember what we say here, but it can never forget what they did here. It is for us the living, rather, to be dedicated here to the unfinished work which they who fought here have thus far so nobly advanced.

abraham lincoln
From the Gettysburg Address
November 19, 1863

After the battle of Manassas, Virginia in July 1861, sick and wounded soldiers were brought to Parkersburg via the B & O railroad. The soldiers were actually being shipped to a federal hospital in Ohio but Parkersburg was where their journey ended. The train trestle crossing the Ohio River was not complete. There was no effective way of getting so many men across the river. Five Civil War Hospitals in the city soon sprung up.

The overflow of the battle's wounded were placed in a tent city on Quincy Hill. Although many of the soldiers were wounded, they were not considered to be critical, so they were placed on Quincy Hill to wait for room in other hospitals. Those soldiers who contracted diseases during their enlistment were also sent there. Naturally, because of the crowded conditions (between 500-1000 soldiers were placed in a size a bit smaller than a contemporary city block), disease spread like wildfire. The city experienced an epidemic of illnesses, primarily typhoid fever and small pox, which spread among locals as well.

Infection ran rampant, and wounds that could have easily been taken care of were the cause of many soldiers' deaths. The moans of the sick men on Quincy Hill could be heard at all hours of the day and night. Local women doing shopping on Market Street below heard the soldier's cries of agony and pleas for help. Some soldiers, desperate to find relief, left the tent-city and crawled down the hill, begging to be treated at one of the hospitals located on 7th and Avery Streets.

Of course, with so much death and suffering, there is bound to be a haunting. The psychic pain a person might experience before death, especially where there are unresolved issues, such as a person dying at a young age and away from the loving arms of family members, can create the right atmosphere for these psychic imprints to remain. Tragedy invites ghosts. Haunts often follow.

There has been no greater tragedy in the annals of American history as the Civil War. Nearly 400,000 individuals died during the bloodiest stint in this nation's history. Areas of Civil War happenings have unleashed a host of ghosts. At Gettysburg, Pennsylvania, for instance, troops of ghostly soldiers are sighted at dusk fighting valiantly only to die over and over again. Such haunts fall under the category of "spirit recording" or "residual haunting" – the Civil War alone, has created thousands of those.

One likely place to find a haunting is where a terrible struggle has taken place, or where individuals die under traumatic, unresolved conditions. What tragedy is greater than a young man in the bloom of life to die violently and alone fighting an old man's war for money and power.

If this is the case, Quincy Hill in Parkersburg may be one such place.

Is Quincy Hill haunted or is it not? There are a few tales that creep, crawl and lurk about... so listen well.

the soldier who would not die

As with most reports of serious haunts, the ghostly events that took place on Quincy Hill started innocently enough. It began with doors suddenly slamming, jamming and objects being moved. Loud noises, men's voices, raps, and the sound of footsteps running up the basement stairs began one day in the mid-1970s in one old home not far from the site of the Quincy Hill's tent city.

The young woman who lived there did not think much of the noises. After all, older houses always made strange noises, didn't they? As for the voices, she did have some neighbors, many of who stayed up until the very early morning hours. Other than being slightly annoying, everything else appeared normal enough.

After all, she was a resourceful young woman in her late-twenties and didn't

A haunted house on Quincy Hill

have time to be frightened of things that went bump in the night. She was attending night school, having a full-time career during the day, and was involved with a man she was seriously considering marrying.

However, the routine at her Quincy Hill home was to become a lot more intense in a short amount of time.

One night after working a long shift and taking a test at night school, an odd and frightening event caught her attention. A favorite chair in her parlor was moved into a different spot, facing a window where one could see Avery Street clearly. The young woman kept the chair beside her fireplace so she could warm her feet on chilly nights. The moving of the chair unnerved her somewhat, but she explained it away by thinking that her boyfriend had been sitting there and forgot to put it back. She would have to have a serious talk with him, the woman thought as she placed the chair back in its right place.

The next day when she came in from work, the chair was once again at the window facing Avery Street. Without thinking, she placed it back in its proper location. Over the next few weeks, the chair was moved so often that she got used to it. Although her boyfriend claimed innocence, she couldn't think of any other explanation. Always, with a shrug, she put the chair back where it belonged. She didn't have time to think about why it was moving; finals were coming up and she needed to concentrate on her classes.

After the owner of the home became used to her chair being moved to face Avery Street, the unusual activity became much more pronounced. Objects turned up in unlikely places. The unexplained sounds grew louder and more disturbing.

One night, the woman was awakened by thumps. She opened her eyes to discover that every candle in her house had been gathered and placed on her bedroom dresser. The candles had been assembled from all over the house; the emergency candles in the basement, the dinner candles from the kitchen, the votive and decorative candles from the living and dining rooms. Each candle had been strategically placed on her dresser. Lit candles fluttered eerily in the darkness.

The woman glanced around and sat up. No doubt about it there were creaking sounds below. It couldn't have been her boyfriend. He didn't spend the night and she hadn't seen him all day. When she went to bed two hours before, her dresser had been clear of everything except a comb and a hairbrush. But, now there were footsteps...

Unnerved, the woman walked downstairs. The dining room and living room had been untouched, so it wasn't a burglar. The kitchen was all right, too. As she approached the parlor, she gasped in disbelief. Sitting in the chair, that was once again facing Avery Street below, was a red-haired, bearded man attired in a blue Civil War uniform.

The Union soldier stood up, extended his hand as if to greet her, then vanished. Only the smell of lit matches remained.

By this time, the woman was clearly frightened. She ran from the room. She didn't believe in ghosts but one had just extended his hand to her and a Civil War soldier at that!

As with most 20th Century residents of the valley, the young woman had no prior knowledge of the Quincy Hill's tent city where many of the wounded soldiers died so slowly and horribly. All she knew was that a strange man had been in her house, moved her candles to her bedroom then disappeared in front of her eyes.

Needless to say, as her boyfriend listened to the amazing story of the night before, he wasn't sure he believed her. He thought that his girlfriend must have been dreaming, but since she had been so terrified, he agreed to stay with her for a few weeks until everything settled down. For a few days, life went back to normal. The home was just a home again. There were no longer any sounds, no candles moved to her bedroom, and most importantly, no Union soldiers in her parlor chair looking out the window as if watching for someone on Avery Street.

About a week after the young woman's boyfriend moved in, she was at night class and he was engrossed in reading a book. Around 8:30 that evening, he was interrupted by a loud thud in the basement. The man put his book down and listened more closely. It was as if somebody was dragging a large object up the steps, toward the door that led into the kitchen. Somewhere a door slammed.

Immediately, the boyfriend got up, walked into the kitchen and opened the basement door. He had expected to see an intruder and was prepared to defend himself accordingly. What he saw was not what he expected. Stunned, the boyfriend looked at the same Union soldier that his girlfriend had described to him earlier. But now the red-bearded soldier seemed more interested in a confrontation than a friendly greeting. The ghost looked wild as he waved a pistol and pointed it directly at the man's face.

The boyfriend did not wait for the outcome to this incredible scene. Instead, he escaped from the house and refused to return. When the young woman returned home to see her door wide open and her boyfriend's vehicle not in the driveway, she ran inside, fearing the worst. All appeared well until she started to look throughout the house. The basement door was open. And the parlor had the chair facing Avery Street. The glowing light of a candle caught her attention – one the woman recognized from her bedroom.

By this time the woman had had enough. She went to her neighbor's house and dialed her boyfriend's apartment. He answered the phone, barely able to talk after his experience. After a few minutes he was able to tell her what had happened. She stayed the night at his apartment and they decided to move her things out the next day. Much to her relief, she never saw her ghost again. It so happened the fantastic apparition seemed to be tied to Quincy Hill.

In uncovering some of the history of the house, it was discovered that a Union soldier had once lived there. But there was no record to see if his physical description matched that of the ghost that haunted the young couple. It is more likely that the soldier was, in fact, the ghost of one of the soldiers who died in the make shift hospital, perhaps of small pox or typhoid fever, lingering there all alone.

Contrary to what many believe, a ghost doesn't have to have lived in a house to haunt it. It may be that the ghost of the soldier was mainly attracted to the young woman and considered her boyfriend to be a threat. It may also be that the ghost was one of the men who died miserably in the tent-city and his spirit still wanders looking for an escape for his tormented soul.

The haunted house still stands on Quincy Hill, abandoned now, naturally.

other tales of haunts from quincy & 13th

But that is not where the story ended. Here is another account of haunts along Quincy and 13th Streets: "Your story about the Quincy Hill ghost in the Civil War uniform was chilling!

"I have more to tell about a house on 13th Street to that is now a historical bed and breakfast. My old girlfriend once, lived there as well as her mother and brother and uncle. Apparitions appeared there every night back in 1996! Nurses in uniforms came toward us as soon as we flipped out the light.

"If we switched the light back on, there was nothing there. When we turned the light off, the ghostly nurse would walk back down the hall. I had to get my cousin to see this for he did not believe me when I finally told him what I was experiencing. He too saw the same thing.

"I believe at the time the house to be very haunted. As we came down from up stairs, we often detected a cold chill in the air. It felt like something would go past us or sometimes right through us. I know it does sound crazy but I have people to confirm all this! I don't like to call them "stories" for they happened to me just as I told you. I know about six other people I know who must also be "crazy" since they saw and heard the exact same thing that I did."

A number of tales of Quincy Hill's haunts involve mirrors. One young girl witnessed seeing the apparition of a decrepit old man with straggly gray hair glaring out at her from the bathroom mirror. The old man had a menacing appearance, frightening the girl so much she never looked into that bathroom mirror again. Perhaps he was a rugged old soldier who died up there after giving his life for the Union cause. Either way, a haunted house on Quincy Hill is not an exception.

ghosts of christmas pasts

From the lookout on Quincy Hill, one can easily view the offices and homes of downtown Parkersburg as well as Blennerhassett Island along the Ohio River. This spot was a strategic point for Union troops in the Ohio Valley during the Civil War since Quincy Hill gave easy access to both the Ohio River and the B&O railroad.

Quincy Hill has a number of historical homes but very few, if any, of them date from around the time of the Civil War. Most of the houses are from the Victorian Age while others are 1930s Colonials.

Each year, at Christmastime, the Parkersburg Women's Club hosts an annual Holly Trail to raise money for their club. Owners of stately or historical residences are asked to decorate their houses in festive cheer, and the public is invited in to view the holiday transformations of several old or interesting homes. In 1998, one of the homes featured on the Holly Trail just so happened to be a grand old Victorian located on Quincy Hill.

The woman who owned the house had a number of antiques and old toys. On her mantle she placed several toy trains and cars that had belonged to her father and brother among the pine and holly boughs. The display on the mantle turned out even more charming than the woman had expected so she grabbed her camera and snapped a picture. She took other pictures of decorations around the house as well.

After the photographs were developed, something unusual turned up on the film. One was a picture of the mirror above the mantle. In it appeared to be a crowd of ghostly faces in the glass. The facial features of the men in the mirror were clear. Many could even be seen with beards and moustaches. One was a woman. Some wore hats.

The woman's neighbors knew a local man who was an expert on the Civil War so he was invited over to look at the picture. In the photo, the historian recognized the faces of characters in the area during the Civil War times. Some were soldiers whose faces appeared in the picture were linked to the tent-city. Although the two-story Victorian was not in existence during the time of the Civil War, the house was located not far from the lookout point where the sick men lay, when the view of the Ohio River and Blennerhassett Island from Quincy Hill was still the best seat in town.

another women in white

Apparitions of women in white are generally associated with unhappy hauntings. We have a number of stories about apparitions dressed in white on the Haunted Parkersburg ghost tour. Why there are so many defy explanation, but throughout the remembered history of ghosts, women in white have been associated with tragedies, such as suicide or murder. Or perhaps after dark, on a crowded hilltop like Quincy Hill, a white dress is just easier to see.

A woman in white has been reported to haunt the servant's quarters of one of the older homes atop the hill. During a family illness, this guardian spirit in a white dress stayed close to the old man's sick room until he died. The family said her appearance was a blessing because they always felt someone was watching over him with loving attention. A prominent family built the home and thus, they felt the woman in white must have been an attentive servant to the family. Late at night she is seen carrying a bucket or a basket across the grassy slopes facing Avery Street. Residents in nearby houses say they hear the ghost either whistling or singing.

Although most people would think that this might be where the story of the ghosts of Quincy Hill may end, this is certainly not the case. It was in September of 1996 during the last full lunar eclipse of the 20th century. Two teenage girls were at the lookout on Quincy Hill, surely the best view to watch the eerie transformation of the moon, considering that Quincy was one of the highest hills in the city. As the moon turned a brassy red and disappeared into black, the girls heard something large crawl through the weeds down Quincy Hill toward Avery Street just like the wounded Civil War soldiers had done more than a century ago. When they heard the story of the Union Soldier, they screamed in fright and left the ghost tour early. Others claimed that they heard the soldiers crawling down Quincy Hill pleading help from anyone who will hear or listen.

fort boreman hill

After small pox and typhoid fever spread to the general population of Parkersburg during the Civil War, a pest house was built on Fort Boreman Hill that also overlooked the city and river below, but from a different perspective than Quincy Hill.

Fort Boreman became a critical lookout point for Union soldiers–the hill faced north and it would be easier to monitor the traffic flow on the Ohio River surging south. Many soldiers and local people died up there. Along with the deaths from small pox and typhoid fever, two area men were executed by hanging on Fort Boreman Hill after killing another man in an argument over loyalties divided during the Civil War.

Civil War experts and historians have actually performed archeological digs on Fort Boreman Hill because the Pest House no longer stands. No one is altogether certain as to where the hospital was. The lookout point, on the other hand, is obvious.

Area historians excavating on Fort Boreman digs to uncover evidence of its Civil War history have actually heard the voices of men call out for their mothers and wives as if in great pain. At other times, strange metallic pinging noises are heard, almost like a blacksmith hammering away.

Then seven-year-old Scarlet Sheppard, the daughter of Susan and Roger Sheppard, claimed that when she, her mother and friends went up on Fort Boreman to investigate the many tales of hauntings, she encountered a woman in a pink dress and rouged cheeks who told Scarlet her name was "Mary McCarty." (There were brothels at the bottom of Fort Boreman). It was later someone uncovered pieces of silverware with the name "Margaret Matheny" engraved on them. During one dig, local historians Terry McVey and Brian Kesterson were working together. McVey suddenly looked up and glimpsed the apparition of a Union soldier pointing toward the ground. Later, the men went over the area with a fine-toothed comb and found important Civil War artifacts in that exact spot. Over the years, there have been tales of a white ghost horse haunting the paths along Fort Boreman Hill, but also associated with Marrtown nearby.

Fort Boreman was also an important Native American access trail, and was widely used by Indians who tracked the Ohio River, into the Little Kanawha, and then to the Hughes River in Ritchie County that yielded an important flint site that the natives used to make their implements and tools.

Fort Boreman Hill is soon to become an historical park. Whether the souls of Civil War soldiers will stop their hauntings, only time will tell.

We have learned spirits have a need to stay in touch with the living. For this reason, we speculate a place like Fort Boreman Hill will yield even more tales of Indian apparitions and Civil War ghosts.

But what about the white horse reported there? Is there yet another one?

droop mountain

Located in Pocahontas County, Droop Mountain turns out to be one of the more haunted Civil War battlefields in the state where on November 6, 1863, there were a total of 526 casualties. In the eastern mountains of West Virginia, Droop

Mountain is an area that yields a number of haunted tales. After all, once this battle was over all confederate resistance in West Virginia crumbled.

One report describes a Civil War soldier sitting on a cannon smoking. He is seen most often at dusk, peacefully smoking, as if pondering on his activities passed that day.

Another fascinating ghost sighting comes from Ron Nelson, a Parkersburg Police officer active in Civil War reenactments with the 17th Virginia Calvary for several years.

One year, Nelson and his fellow re-enactors set up camp near Droop Mountain. Ron decided he needed to hit a bathroom before settling in for the night. He glanced over in a clearing and thought he saw a portable toilet, so he grabbed his flashlight and started walking toward it. Before he got there, he realized he was mistaken. It was actually picnic tables turned upon their sides and not a bathroom.

As leaving, the funneled light of his flashlight caught a white horse in its beams. There was something eerie and mysterious about this pure white horse. "A mist floated about the horse and its eye shone just like diamonds," Ron Nelson recalls. "It looked as if it had been ridden pretty hard. It had that sweaty look."

Nelson asked his friend who was standing nearby, "Do you see it?"

The friend answered, "The horse? Yeah, I see it." Later the friend remembered it looked to him like a white blaze on a brown horse. But when he shone his flashlight into the black of night there was a strange, misting gray substance – denser than fog or mist. As soon as the men got ready to leave, the horse was no longer there.

As the two men left the next day, they couldn't help noticing two chestnut horses and one white horse grazing in a field. Nelson's friend said to him, "There's your horse."

"I suppose it is," he answered. But as soon as Ron turned to give the white horse a last look, it was no longer there. Only the chestnut brown horses were grazing. The glowing white horse had vanished. But Ron isn't the only person to encounter Droop Mountain's pale, ghost horse. Others have seen it, too.

Riding away with his friend, Ron Nelson realized the horse he saw belonged to another time. One with a specific date of November 6, 1863 when a terrible battle was fought and where many men and their horses died in that bloody mud on a dreary, autumn day, long ago, in the quiet mountains of West Virginia.

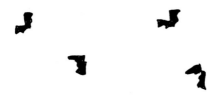

11. haunted houses

the upper historical district of parkersburg

When we hear the word "haunted," the next word that usually springs to mind is "house." Unlike any other space, homes can hold in the energies of anyone who might have lived, died or passed through them. And although any spot of ground can end up haunted, houses are especially prone to spirit recordings, ghost imprints and residual energies left long after the owners have moved on.

This is especially true in cases that involve high emotion that occur within the home, such as a sudden death or emotional shock and even times where the feelings are happy ones, such as those at a party or a celebration.

To explain why some houses are haunted we also have to explain why spirits haunt them. This is not always so easy. We have theories of ghosts, even many sound, scientific explanations of why ghosts are and what they are. No one really knows for sure.

It seems the simplest explanation might be the most accurate one. Perhaps ghosts are simply an essence that is left behind after a person or animal has died. Or, perhaps, some part of the personality that survives death likes to check back in from time to time with the people they knew or where they once lived. There is even some evidence that points out this could even be part of the transition or healing process that follows death. Those who died with unresolved issues are allowed to come back and relive those issues in order to find some resolution or to somehow convey the sadness they feel over not being able to finish something that was important to them in life. This brings up "messenger ghosts" and "unsettled business" but that's another story and another theory.

We all think we know that what a haunted house looks like ... Old, crumbling hag of a house glued together by some distinctly Gothic architecture, full moon blowing behind the widow's walk, shrouds of clouds with a black cat hissing on the front stoop – right?

Don't be so sure. Haunted houses as well as other haunted places don't have any characteristic outside appearance. The same ancient, decrepit homes that scream that word "Ghost!" often end-up hardly haunted at all. It's the ordinary "Beaver Cleaver" houses and the haunted trailer parks that can really catch ghost hunters off guard.

Ghosts appearances are usually quite unexpected in a typical family environment, although there is some bearing on the fact that the older the home is, the more likely events that bring about the haunting have already happened there. The history, itself, makes the home a target for ghosts.

Also, graveyards and ancient burial sites, areas of violence or massacres in the near vicinity of the haunted home does appear to have some bearing or connection to the haunting – but these are of the more dangerous variety in terms of dark entities and menacing ghosts. Such spots should be approached with caution and keen awareness.

So what are you afraid of? Sure ghosts are icy and they tend to sneak up on us when we least expect them. Other than that, experiences with ghosts hardly ever bring on anything bad, as long as you give respect, stand your ground and try not to take them home with you. In many ways, the mysteries of our world are shrinking and ghosts might be one of the last frontiers in human experience.

So – should you call in a priest, a psychic or an Indian shaman?

Not just yet.

Having a ghost is sort of like having a cold – you really don't need to see a doctor. Your cold goes away on it's own. Right?

Likewise, a haunting typically goes away no matter what action you decide to take. But like the common cold, ghosts often do return – to fascinate, bewilder and enthrall. There's no problem unless you get a nasty poltergeist and this is not at all the typical scenario in hauntings no matter how much Hollywood tells us this is so.

This brings up a question. Are haunted houses plagued by of the ghosts who once lived in them a people?

Well, yes-and-No.

Spirits often return to homes they once lived in, as well as checking back on final resting spots. However, some ghosts gravitate to areas where living residents are most receptive to them. If there is a message behind their appearance, they usually do not cease until that message is understood. This is especially true in cases where a young person has died, such as in a war or accident and the family does not know or understood how or when the child or loved one has passed on.

Once a home or area becomes intensely haunted (with some serious ghost business going on) the place does become a portal or 'tear' for other spirits to pour through. The most famous places tend to be areas where lots of witnesses pass through such as hotels, taverns, a theater, castles and homes that have been made into offices. Private homes may be just as intensely haunted. Usually the family is scared off or the haunting is cyclical in nature and peters out leaving the family to question the their own sanity.

When we watch TV shows about ghosts and haunted places we are lead to believe hauntings are both frightening but extremely rare – not likely to happen to us. Well, this assumption is basically untrue. Hauntings are not uncommon. They occur every single day – all around us. But only on occasion are we able to experience ghosts and their activities. Many who do not experience the haunting remain unaware. Perhaps their minds are firmly fixed on the physical world. Most of us do not pick up on the signs until they cannot be denied. Many need a sound "slap" on the head before we will believe.

If you view haunts with a level eye it is really not that scary. After all, spirits entering your home can be no more threatening than a friend walking into your house unannounced. At first there may be surprise or fear. Once we recognize who the person is, there is no threat. The same is true of ghosts.

Like most cities, Parkersburg and the surrounding areas have numerous buildings possessed by spirits – many are local businesses, historical buildings or private homes. Some residents wish to keep their ghosts a secret while others love telling and re-telling the ghostly tales about their properties. What can be more fascinating than having a resident ghost?

There is really no wrong or right way to address your ghosts or haunts. Here are just a few houses where ghosts and apparitions exist, and despite the fact these souls are now quite dead, yet in their own mysterious ways, they are still very much alive.

bickel estates

Witnesses have reported the apparition of a woman cloaked in solid black standing along the road outside the Bickel Estates, a 368-acre estate in the Larkmead section of Marrtown. The figure is seen especially during lightning storms and downpours. As with most spirits, the woman, though pale and distraught, is said to look very much alive but when drivers turn back to see if they can help the stranded woman, she is no longer there. The ghost of a white horse is said to also haunt this section on Wood County.

Many believe a woman dressed in black garb rides the hillsides of nearby Marrtown on a white horse. Both stories appear to have connections to the Marrtown Banshee tale—a Scottish death fairy that people claim still haunts the countryside south of Parkersburg. Another variation on the woman who haunts Bickel Estates appears to share some of the elements of the Marrtown Banshee tale.

"OLD SOUTHSIDE HOUSE IS SAID TO BE HAUNTED"
Built at Marrtown over 70 years ago—
Ghosts said to return to look for Hidden Money!

"Among the few folk tales that still abound in Wood County is the one concerning a house in South Parkersburg, built something over a half century ago that is supposed to be haunted and many still believe it is.

"The house is at Marrtown hill, a gray frame, two-story structure, rambling and falling into disrepair. It was built some 70 or more years ago. Queer tales were told by the owner, who worked on the same side of the river as the house. At nights, he said, often he was followed by a woman all in black who road a white horse. As he was employed on the river, frequently he didn't get home until late and often she was there. He never saw her face and neither did she speak to him.

"Then one night, he stumbled, fell, broke his neck and died. The woman on the white horse was somehow blamed for it. Shortly after that, a brother lost his job. He was known to have quite a bit of money saved up, which isn't nearly so extraneous as it would seem to be. One day the brother went with some garden tools to the Lubeck Mill to have tools ground, and:

"The man's arm got caught in a cog. It was pulled off – all of the blood drained from his body and he died.

"Anyway, before the brother died, he was said to try and talk to his family about the sum of money that was hidden. But his mother told him not to bother about it until he felt better. He didn't; instead he died.

"After that it began in earnest, this ghosting. And nights there were strange noises like the clanking of chains going up and down the old steps heard and the mother knew it was her son's ghost trying to come back to find the hidden money. Too, lights were seen late at night and whenever one went to investigate, there was nothing.

"Then one night, very late an old woman was dying in the house with one neighbor there to watch the flickering of the spirit. It was the granddaughter of this neighbor who has since repeated the story many times that she heard her grandmother detail of the frightening experience; how she sat and awaited the for the promised arrival of a neighbor and a light flickering outside. She heard the gate slam and waited, but nobody ever came. Instead the light went to the back of the house and disappeared. There was nobody there when she went to look. And shortly afterwards, the old woman died and as she died, suddenly there was a great banging as though of wind tearing at the shutters against the house, but there were no shutters. And yet it was still a night without wind. Then the old woman died.

"After that for a long time nobody lived there. Then a family moved in but didn't stay long. For a time the house was without a resident, and one morning those who passed the haunted house saw a great trail of blood from the porch to the roadway, and they could find no end to it. Neither could they find what caused it. Indications a terrific fight had ensued, perhaps over the hidden money. But further than that they found it impossible to go on and again, there was no answer.

"For a long time again, the house was without occupants. Now it is lived in. The householders says they don't believe in ghosts, but elderly neighbors who were children many years ago and heard and saw strange things about this house, know better.

the captain's house

Also called the 'Markey House' this is another example of a perfectly ordinary-looking house being haunted in an atypical way. This Juliana Street home was built in 1860 by New Englander and master mariner George Deming who died in 1861 at the age of fifty-five. Shortly before his death, his small child also died. Legends surround this two-story home such as people who buy the house and live in it eventually are driven mad. Although there is no evidence to support this rumor, the house has other interesting occurrences that could only be considered supernatural. Even so, the house has undergone a series of renovations that have caused workmen to wonder or question the existence of spirits.

Often in the attic there are a child's footprints left imprinted in the settled dust. Thinking a small child had wandered in the workmen continued to sweep away the dust. If the attic is left untouched for a number of months, as soon as the workmen return they see that the child's footprints have re-appeared.

Strange burning fires are said to smolder as orange reflections in the windows. Many claim the fire is simply the reflection of the Captain's pipe. The inside of the house is graced with low ceilings and narrow hallways that resemble the inside of a ship. The Captain's ghost is seen in various places in Parkersburg, most often wearing a black coat. He is buried in Riverview cemetery only two blocks from his home. On the Captain's grave is the carving ship. Beside his gravestone is the small headstone of a child with the undetermined dates of birth and death brushed away by the ravages of weather and time.

There are only two Deming burials in Riverview Cemetery – the Captain and his small child. Several have asked why the Captain's wife isn't buried beside him. When he died, the Captain was in his late fifties and had a small child. This indicates his wife was considerably younger so probably lived on to marry and have another family. Most likely, the Captain and child fell victim to the Typhoid epidemic that swept through the area in the 1860s and 1870s. Still, the Captain's ghost appears not to rest. The apparition of a sea captain has been glimpsed with brass buttons shining softly in the mirrors at the Blennerhassett Hotel.

ghostly hands at the gerwig house

Built by a prominent family of early Parkersburg, this Victorian home located on upper Juliana Street is now a stately law office with stained glass windows that resemble the rich, pastel tones of a Monet painting. The elegant structure has gone through numerous transformations as homes and various businesses.

Since becoming a law office, workers have reported any number of paranormal occurrences in the Gerwig house. These include a woman's disembodied hands floating in the area where files are kept.

A little boy is seen appearing on the stairs that lead from the second floor into the attic. A distinguished gentleman has been spotted on the landing that leads from the first floor into the second story beside one of the stained glass windows. Those brave enough to work into the later evening hours report having heard scratching within the walls ... and then there are ghostly sounds coming from the attic.

Pictures taken outside the Gerwig house during the ghost tour in the evening hours reveal classic ghost orbs. One of the most chilling sightings happened on the ghost tour before the guide filled the audience in on the story about the disembodied hands. Shortly after the story, a woman approached the guide looking pale. She said, "Before you told that last story of the floating hands, the window with the curtain behind you? I saw a woman's hand go around the curtain and pull it back a bit as someone was trying to spy on us. Then the hand suddenly vanished!" Business hours were well over at the time and the building was pitch black. Sporadic psychic disturbances still take place in the Gerwig house and most likely will continue until the ghosts get tired of their own tricks!

camden clark memorial hospital

Also called by locals "City Hospital," Camden Clark got its start as a medical facility when wounded and sick soldiers during the Civil War were taken to the Camden farm as a makeshift hospital (becoming one of five Civil War hospitals in Parkersburg at the time).

Can hospitals be haunted? Because of death, sadness and other unresolved issues, hospitals tend to attract spirits more than any other business – even outdoing funeral homes.

In the older wing of Camden Clark, there is an area that is called "the haunted room." A few young nurses are afraid to go in there. Often when the room is made up for a new patient (yes, it is still being used) within a few minutes of making up the bed, an impression forms of a person's rear end appears near the bottom.

Mineral Wells psychic Millie McNemar worked as a nurse at Camden Clark for a number of years. It was her duty to go in the "haunted room' and remake the beds. Mrs. McNemar said within minutes, the ghostly imprint would form on the bed – but that she was never afraid nor did she sense anything bad in the room. "Just spirits," Millie laughs.

The apparition of a former worker, Miss Ella Blumhart is sighted throughout the hospital. Miss Blumhart not only worked at Camden Clark as a nurse, she taught in what was once a famous nursing school. When the ghost of Miss Blumhart materializes she wears the nursing uniform of the 1940s and 1950s. Former nursing students who have visited Camden Clark years later report that when they see Ella Blumhart walking the halls she looks much as she did in life, only younger than most remember her. When addressed, the vision of Miss Blumhart ignores the person speaking but continues walking until she eventually vanishes through the hospital walls.

blennerhassett museum

The Blennerhassett Museum houses Amerindian artifacts that date back as far as 12,000 years ago, into the splendors of Blennerhassett Island's unique history, throughout the Victorian and Oil and Gas ages in Wood County. Yet such historical items are not the only things the Blennerhassett Museum houses – a number of friendly apparitions like to call the museum their home.

Ghostly figures, such as a little man in straw hat, a seersucker jacket, and full theatrical make-up (many report this ghost appears to belong to the Vaudeville Age) and a rouged woman in a bright scarlet-colored dress, have been glimpsed in the mirrors on the first and second floor. Lights flicker oddly. Wafting throughout the hallways at times flowery fragrance of a woman's perfume.

A row of photographs on the second floor of the museum showcases Parkersburg's most eminent citizens such as 19th Century artist Lily Irene Jackson, Governor Jacob Beeson Jackson and Governor William Erskine Stephenson. (In keeping with the Scottish hauntings in this book, Erskine is an ancient Scottish clan name.)

The second floor area of the museum hums and vibrates with a heavy brand of energy that proves too intense for some children or individuals with special sensitivities. Ghost orbs have also appeared when pictures of the photographic portraits have been snapped. Ray Swick, local historian and head of the Blennerhassett Museum, says that on one occasion after he has left his work in the evening, he looked up to see the lights in his office had been switched back on. It appears that the spirits inside the Blennerhassett Museum don't mind working overtime.

haunts at the elks club

Feelings of apprehension, muffled, phantom noises, boxes that are securely on shelves are falling over, surging shadows and lights where they should not be, loud, spirited meetings that go on in rooms that are later discovered empty and the list goes on. These are just a few of the ghostly happenings that take place in Parkersburg's Elks Club on Juliana Street.

Here is one report of Elks Club paranormal happenings that we received from a former worker about the numerous haunts that continue to occur in the one-hundred year old building:

"I have been meaning to write to you for some time regarding the Elks Club building on Juliana Street. I worked at the club part-time there for about a year and I sincerely believe that building to be the most haunted place I have ever set foot in. I mean, you can literally walk into the building and feel something strange going on.

"For several months while I worked at the Elks, little things happened that I at first attributed to the building just being creaky and old. Lights I turned off suddenly switched back on, boxes that were securely placed flew off their shelves, mysterious sounds that could not be explained.

"Several times I thought there were meetings going on in distant rooms only to find them empty. One night, however, convinced me without a doubt that the building is haunted. My daughter and granddaughter were waiting for me to finish up when the jukebox seemed to come on all by itself (this in itself was not unusual as it was programmed to randomly play different songs). This particular song sounded strange. The tune was very loud and sounded like some type of Big Band music – upbeat but definitely from a different era. My daughter walked over and tried to turn the machine down. She asked me how to turn it down and I (assuming that she didn't know how to operate the jukebox) walked over and turned the volume button. It didn't work so I tried a control button that we had on the wall. It didn't work either. It seemed at that particular moment that my daughter and I both realized that the music wasn't coming from the jukebox. I don't know how to describe it but it seemed to be just kind of floating in the air and one just KNEW that it wasn't "real" music. There was no specific spot that it seemed to originate, it just "was". I reached behind the jukebox and unplugged it but still the music continued.

"We were both terrified and grabbed our things and headed for the door!

"As we passed the kitchen, there was an absolute howl that came from the sink area. It was a straight-out-of-a-horror-movie howl! I have never been so scared in my life.

"We ran out of the building leaving all of the lights on, a mess on the counters and the doors unlocked.

"When I went in the next day to explain why we had left in such a hurry no one seemed real surprised or even skeptical. There were a few members who were amused that I was frightened but most finally agreed that strange things do happen there.

"Some of the members explained that many years ago a young black man who was employed there ended up shot in the bar by an Elks member. It seemed that the man was having an affair with the member's wife. As it was, nothing came of it and the man was never charged. They believe the ghost of the young man still haunts the bar.

"Also, I was told of a member who had drank too much one night and passed out in the library. Sometime in the night he had to go to the restroom and as he walked past the ballroom and found that there was a dance going on. He told other members that the people were dressed in 20's style clothing and the music was from that era.

"As I said, there is a certain feeling in the building. The bar still felt safe to me although I always sensed that I was being watched while I was in there. The kitchen and the back hallways were extremely ominous. I don't know how to explain it other than sometimes the hair would rise on my arms and I would be afraid for no apparent reason.

I apologize for rambling on so. I just thought that you might be interested in investigating the building or at least being aware of this activity."

transallegheny bookstore

People swear this place is haunted. It even has its own black cat that disappears behind the rambling shelves of new and antique books. The stained glass windows give visitors the sense of being inside a chapel. Employees claim that most of the time nothing really out of the ordinary happens at the TransAllegheny Bookstore on Green Street, just an occasional apparition browsing the shelves, turning on lights and floating about.

The building, once the Carnegie Library in Parkersburg, is pretty quiet so to speak... unless you're used to books flying through the air and shadows lurking.

The lights on the second floor flicker quite erratically. Ghost footsteps are heard when the aisles are otherwise empty.

The apparition of a small girl in a white bonnet sits on the third step of the wooden stairway. In the mezzanine part of the bookstore it is not unusual for the overhead lamps to sway and lights flutter eerily. Perhaps it is just antiquated wiring in an older building. Many bookstore visitors claim to see a dapper man in a brown jacket browsing the second floor. The staff assumes it is just one of bookstore's regular ghosts. Perhaps he is the author of one of their books.

the lindsey home on 26th street

Located on the top of a hill overlooking Murdoch Avenue, this pale gray Colonial is haunted by a quick paced, impatient ghost wearing a white shirt. Built in 1950, the apparition of a young man briskly passes the back window leading into the doorway to the house, yet he never comes inside. The ghost is normally seen wearing a white shirt although on one occasion he appeared dressed in an olive green and burgundy-striped sweater. He has also been glimpsed lingering outside at the door that leads into what was once the garage, now an art studio. When the woman of the house works in her studio, it is not unusual for the doorknob to turn followed by the door creaking open. Naturally, there is no one there and not even a wind that might force open the door.

Generally, the spirit of the walking man is witnessed several times per day for a couple of days. His appearances then vanish only to return later. Not wanting to frighten her small daughter, the woman of the house did not mention the jaunty ghost (who most often appears during the afternoon and early evening) but the child later said, "Mommy, I see a boy that walks by the back window." Upon leaving the house once, the owner stepped outside the backdoor and was suddenly hit in the face by something white. ("It didn't hurt," the owner said, "It was just surprising.")

On occasions the television sets act strangely. During one period of time, the TV switched itself on every night at 12:30 a.m. At other times, the TV set turns off or turns to C-Span if anything coarse or unsavory is mentioned on television in front of the woman or little girl living in the house. At other times, the intercom system throughout the two-story house beeps for no apparent reason and the sound of children's voices are heard when no one else is home. The voices never complete a full sentence, but the call button beeps over and over again.

Late into the evening, footsteps and doors opening and closing echo downstairs shortly after the family retires for the night. At other times, the muffled voices of a man and a woman are heard having a heated discussion downstairs.

To the current owners, nothing evil or unhappy ever happened in the house – or they have not been made aware of any such thing. Despite the traffic noise coming from Murdoch Avenue (during Christmas season, the busiest road in West Virginia) it is a peaceful home, warm and calm.

The original builders of the mysterious hilltop Colonial on 26th Street were the Lindsey family, part owners in what was once the Burdette-Lindsay funeral home in downtown Parkersburg. Perhaps once the undertakers moved out, they left some of the residual haunting of former customers behind.

the little girl with the golden heart

Perhaps the saddest ghost stories are the ones that involve the death of a child. On Ann Street there is a home that was built in the 1870s by a prominent dentist by the name of Doctor Bartlett. Along with his wife and other children, Doctor Bartlett had a nine-year-old daughter named Bessie whom he dearly loved.

Unfortunately, yet another Typhoid Epidemic swept through Parkersburg in the 1870s (there had been another one in the 1860s during the Civil War creating a Pest House on Fort Boreman Hill).

Sadly, Bessie Bartlett became one of its victims.

At first, the Doctor Bartlett tried to nurse young Bessie back to health. But because of his dentistry practice (patients would not want to go to a dentist with Typhoid Fever in his family) and because it was the summer, he put Bessie in the basement hoping the coolness might break her fever.

Yet there was no bringing little Bessie back to health. Her fever was too high and she was too 'far gone.' Thus, the basement of the home was where Bessie Bartlett died unexpectedly alone. Over the years, Doctor Bartlett and the rest of his family passed away. Over the span of one-hundred-years people that lived in the home never reported any activity that could be taken as a haunting.

In the 1980s, a family with young daughters would be moving to Parkersburg. The upper historical district appealed to the family. As they drove by the Bartlett home they saw that it was for sale. An odd feeling in the car told them to stop.

The family was surprised that the house was built in the 1870s. From the outside it did not appear to be that old. Once inside, the family could see the house, was indeed, rather aged. They decided if they bought the house, they would like to do some renovations to modernize it. The father grabbed his camera and took pictures throughout the home – this included pictures in the basement.

When pictures from the basement were developed, one featured a striking, but disturbing image of what appeared to be a little girl – yet parts of her were missing. In looking at the picture one could see the part of the hair, perhaps an eye, the side of her face. The child seemed to be wearing a white dress. Her hands were folded together as if waiting for someone – where her heart should have been there was a very bright light.

Only when the family did research on the house did they discover that a young child had died in that basement. At the time, the current owners did not know about the girl's death. The fact that a camera captured the image of the child in the basement suggests Bessie Bartlett is a spirit recording or residual energy type of "imprint" ghost.

Still, the owners claim there have been a number of odd, inexplicable activities in the home, including seeing strange balls of light and energy in the basement, and lights turning themselves off and on – the effects, perhaps, of a ghost imprint.

When the ghost tour passes in front of Bessie's Bartlett's house on Ann Street, and the guides begin to tell her story, the lamp on the front porch typically brightens very sharply, flickers and then dims. It is as if Bessie herself is reminding others to remember her name, and to not forget how she died in that basement cold and alone.

southside k-mart

In the early 1970s, two Parkersburg teenagers set fire to their home, killing their entire family. Some years later, the land where the house stood was purchased to build a new K-Mart store. Things have never been the same since then.

Those who work the midnight shift stocking shelves at the Southside K-Mart report upon a number of ghostly happenings. Sometimes they hear an old-fashioned radio turn on playing a ball game with names from the past. Others report the lights being switched off throughout the entire building as employees work into the night, as well as empty carts coasting through aisles and boxes of merchandise being pushed from their shelves. Some workers at the K-Mart have claimed that after stocking shelves, and going on break, they return a few moments later to discover every single item they have previously stocked, is in the middle of the floor. However, the merchandise is not knocked over in messy pile, as a prankster might do, but neatly stacked in the center of the aisle.

red brick on ann street

Not far from Bessie Bartlett's house is a red brick home that some former owners report to be ridden with spirits of all sorts. It all began when one previous resident to the home woke up in the middle of the night with the feeling of someone pulling the blankets off of her. At other times she would wake up cold with no blankets covering her. In the beginning, she thought, perhaps, she was doing it to herself until she awakened to find herself levitating about five feet off the bed. As soon as the thought, "My God, I'm levitating!" hit her, she dropped and her body slammed into the mattress.

Considering the event freakish, she continued to go about her daily routine. The woman did notice, however, that as she drew a bath for herself, she heard the mumbling of different voices over top the sound of running water. When she turned off the water, the voices always stopped.

The woman soon moved out because she was troubled by too many nightmares that resulted in extreme insomnia. She even felt a demonic rape was forced on her.

Haunted Parkersburg guide Kristall Chambers actually lived in this same home as a small girl, and witnessed a number of puzzling events while staying there.

Kristall writes, "I remember sharp footsteps in the attic, a cold chill in the study on the second floor where I always played. Someone used to touch my feet at night and stand at the foot of my bed. My stepfather started to drink after we moved in and he never drank before. He also shot at "an intruder" in the attic, but then found no one there. The elevator in the house (one of the previous owners was confined to a wheelchair) would switch on all by itself and go up and down at night eerily." It was here Kristall had dramatic encounters with the spirit world, inspiring her life-long interest in ghosts.

The current owners of the red brick home claim no such things have happened to them. This is not surprising. Ghosts like or dislike certain individuals more than others. It could be the current owners are just not sensitive to ghostly things or the woman's ghost attacker left with her and is still tracking her.

12. other tales, other towns

No matter where you go, tales of apparitions and ghosts (likewise stories of UFOs and alien encounters) are not so unique. Our lives are filled with mysteries we do not understand and may never. Whether we chose to tap into these mysteries or not, we live in a world that swims with spirits. It would be far stranger if we lived in a world that was merely matter much in the same way we are the only life in the universe. The odds are against it.

We believe in the existence of the mind even though we can't see it. We speculate that consciousness lies in the brain but we are not entirely sure. We know love exists, but we can't weigh its reality inside the human heart.

Every small town, country community or city seems to have its intriguing claims of spirits. The reason ghost stories continue on is the evidence (although sometimes slippery) still sticks.

When you have a ghost tale, you can be assured there is something behind it. Yes, the story may get embellished over time. But someone making up the whole event is not as common as you might expect. It is human nature to elaborate, and create a better story – this is what separates tales of folklore from ongoing haunts.

Human beings are natural storytellers and have been since we placed bouquets of flowers on our hairy-shouldered dead in Paleolithic caves. Early humans added mystery to give the story a special spin in the telling and re-telling of the tales. Eventually, a belief in ghosts and an afterlife became universal.

No part of America is as rich in tales of the supernatural as the areas south of the Mason-Dixon-line. Perhaps Appalachia's remoteness is the very thing that enables these stories to live on. The following are just a few more West Virginia's and Ohio Valley haunts to prove they are abundant. After all, like most ghosts, our "haints" do get around.

one spirit-filled farmhouse near st. mary's

No longer in existence, there was a haunted farmhouse in rural Pleasants County that was torn down years ago. A former owner offered up this very real tale: "First of all," the man explained to me, "I don't drink. Secondly, I don't think I'm crazy – but after the experience I had at my 135 year-old-farmhouse, I am not so sure. One night, as nature called," he began, "I got up to go to the bathroom down the hall. I was shocked to see a woman standing at the end of the hallway in a long nightgown. She wasn't an old woman at all – and she wasn't bad looking – except for one thing – she didn't have any feet." As the man continued with his story, he nervously rattled the change in his pocket. "Well, maybe she did have feet – her long nightgown probably covered them. She never stared at me or spoke. Instead, she glanced past my shoulder – eerily – there was a window behind me – as if she was watching down the road. By this time, I had forgotten all about nature calling. I darted back inside my bedroom. I must have been breathing pretty hard or making some noise as I woke my wife up. When she asked me what was wrong, I could hardly say anything. That's when my wife said, 'You saw her, too, didn't you?

"In all of my days, I have never had an experience like that one. If my wife hadn't witnessed the identical sighting I had of the young lady or ghost or whatever she was, I might have been convinced I was dreaming that night. But seeing that woman standing with no feet will stay with me for the rest of my life."

(There is one piece of information in this ghost tale that makes it instantly credible. It is not generally known, but spirits oftentimes materialize with a part of their anatomy missing – very often it is the head or the feet. Sometimes just a set of hands, as we learned about in the previous chapter.)

The haunted farmhouse in St. Mary's no longer stands but the enigma of who this young woman might have been still remains.

lonely hitchhiker of huntington's fifth street hill

Every region has a story about a stranded, hitchhiking ghost. Huntington is no exception. Traveling spirits are reported all over the globe but a young woman hitchhiking in a rainstorm is the by far the most prevalent way this ghost appears.

More than fifty years ago stories began circulating about a young woman sighted at the stone bridge that runs across the Fourpole Creek standing alone in a downpour. Appearing drenched and rather pale, the woman often flags down motorists and pleads for a ride. But before getting to her destination, she will vanish suddenly leaving the driver alone to question his or her sanity.

Usually the hitchhiker is dressed in a thin party dress. Others claim it is a wedding gown. When the driver asks her why she isn't dressed more appropriately for the weather, the girl answers, "I no longer need a coat." Sometimes she will remark: "I haven't worn a coat in ten years." Often the driver will offer his jacket to the young woman. Sometimes she refuses. At others times she accepts the jacket and it disappears with her.

Over the years many unsuspecting Huntington cab drivers have picked up the hitchhiker. As soon as they reach the hill, the young woman asks to be let off. The driver will then turn around and find that she has vanished.

During one cold, November night, one cab driver noticed a dim yellow light in house near where the girl asked to stop. The one-story white home pushed back against the hill looked like a skull gleaming in the darkness.

The cab driver wondered if somehow the girl had gotten out and ran into the house in order to get out of paying the cab fee. Also, the hitchhiker had taken his jacket.

In the pounding rain, the cab driver made his way to the house and knocked on the door. At first, no one answered. The man pounded harder and was surprised when an older woman finally came to the door. She looked at him curiously. The driver asked the woman if she had a daughter or a granddaughter? The woman shook her head 'No.'

As the cab driver turned to leave, he caught a glance of the mantle inside the home and noticed the graduation picture of a young woman. He was surprised to see that it was, indeed, the young woman who flagged down his cab earlier.

Not wanting to be forward, the cab driver inquired, "If you don't have a daughter or granddaughter, who is that in the picture? That looks like the girl I picked up."

The woman gasped. After taking a few moments to gain her composure, she sobbed, "That's my daughter. She died in a wreck near the stone bridge near Fifth Street Hill ten years ago. Tonight was the anniversary of her death."

Stunned, the cab driver was at a loss for words.

Wiping away tears, the woman then asked, "Did she borrow your jacket as well?"

Shocked, the driver mumbled, "Sorry, Ma'am. Just forget about my jacket. Your loss is more important than an old jacket."

"She did, didn't she?" The woman asked. "I need to know."

The cab driver shook his head. "Yes. Yes, she did."

"Follow me." On that the older woman picked up a flashlight from an inn table and headed outside. Behind the house was a cemetery that had a few small graves. The woman opened the iron-gate and the cab driver followed her in. The hitchhiker's mother stood by a grave with an angel carved on the headstone. She bent over and pulled away some weeds. "This is where my daughter now stays," she said. "I don't want my angel gone from me. I always told her that. Never go away from me, Sweetheart. I need you. That's why she keeps trying to come home." The woman wept softly.

The cab driver stood in a numb silence. It wasn't finding the girl's grave and realizing he had encountered the ghostly hitchhiker of Fifth Street Hill that haunted the driver for many years. On the headstone was his jacket, neatly folded and left for him to find. It was right there on the girl's grave, in plain view.

the empty glass in charleston

The Empty Glass Bar is the main haunting place for a number of spirits in Charleston. One ghost is thought to be that of a former bartender who was killed in an automobile crash. One night some of the employees came to discover loud rock music already blasting in an otherwise empty bar. It was the particular kind of music, with select songs that the bartender loved. Before they could unplug the jukebox, the shadow of a man crossed the wall.

Other spirits came with the building, and are most active on the second floor where employees often take their breaks. Restroom doors tend to get stuck downstairs and objects disappear only to show up later in obvious places.

Many believe the ghost of the bartender misses his job and wants to make sure everyone at the Empty Glass remembers him through his harmless pranks. Humor is every bit a part of the spirit world as it is a part of our own human experience. After all, humor, just like our own unique personalities, never really dies.

ghost afloat in rural wood county

A fellow, who often jogged along the old B & O railroad tracks that are now a walking and bicycling trail in rural Wood County, felt chills rise one day just as he was nearing a bend in the trail. As the man turned, he saw a floating woman behind him with her mouth open as if to scream. The woman floated over the trail at a quickening pace. As the spirit neared the startled man, he made out her words as, "Help, Oh Lord, help me." As soon as the ghost's words were uttered, the distressed spirit instantly vanished.

There are other tales of Walker being haunted. Very near the old railroad tracks a Union soldier was sighted leaning on his musket. Others have seen the apparition of a woman in Civil War period dress with a small child near to what they now call "the Bird Farm" at Walker. The Bird Farm once had peacocks and other exotic birds.

haunts of fayette county

Monsters with red eyes, including a flying beast with the wingspan of a small plane and one other creature that resembles a half-man, half-horse are said to haunt an area near Mount Hope in Fayette County. Near Witchy Hollow, it is reported the apparition of an old-fashioned car speeds toward other cars with its headlights on high beams. As soon as the ghost car is about to crash into the other vehicle, it disappears.

haunted house on mclane avenue in morgantown

A ghost encounter by Teresa O'Cassidy of Charleston:

"When I moved to Morgantown to attend West Virginia University in my sophomore year of college, I got my first apartment in the Sunnyside district of town. I stayed there that first summer to work and go to summer school since "Reaganomics" precluded my being able to find a summer job in Boone County where I am from.

"I had three male friends who also stayed the summer and rented an upstairs apartment to the old house on McLane Avenue. One of them named Joe worked at the Subway sandwich shop with me. Joe had the closing shift that ended around 2:00 a.m. He usually got home by 2:30 in the morning. We all fell into the habit of hanging out at the guys' apartment on McLane once the bars closed and after Joe got off work (we were, after all, young college students and that's what college students do).

"The way the apartment was laid out, there was a door at ground level that led to an enclosed stairway on the inside of the building which led straight into the apartment. The landlady lived in the downstairs. There was only the one apartment upstairs that never stayed rented for very long.

"As time passed, we noticed that almost every night we heard the door open and someone walk up the stairs. The footsteps sounded heavy, like a man's footsteps would sound. Someone would always remark, "That must be Joe was coming in." Always, the footsteps would stop about halfway up the stairs and no one would ever come. Later, Joe would arrive home. We would hear his keys, the door open and close, and his footfalls all the way up the stairs. Joe would normally come in with some outrageous story about his most drunken customer of the evening.

"As time went by, we figured out that the footsteps always came at precisely 2:00 in the morning and so we wondered what the landlady's boyfriend was doing downstairs at that time every night. Maybe he was coming home from work or was a night owl. That's all we thought about it.

"We were all on very good terms with the landlady. She was young to be a landlady, not quite 40. She and her live-in boyfriend had it written right into the lease that the landlord liked to party and if loud music late at night was offensive, it would be advised NOT to rent from her. One evening when a few of us were at her apartment (again, partying) we asked her what her boyfriend did at 2:00 in the morning because it always sounds like someone coming up the stairs.

"The landlady got the brightest sparkle in her eye and said, "I see you've met the ghost." Ghosts hadn't entered our minds! She said the ghost had been there as long as she had (over ten years) and she had no idea where it had come from. The house had been built in the 1860's and she hadn't researched its history. She said that when the apartment upstairs was empty, at the times that it was quiet in her apartment, she could hear sounds coming from up there like furniture moving and people walking. When she'd get the key and go into the apartment, everything would be still and it was obvious that no one had been there and no furniture had been moved.

"I went to visit the guys upstairs one evening. I knocked on the door and heard my friend's voice calling down the steps, "Come in. Door's open." I opened the door and saw what I believed to be my friend Andy (judging by build of the back lit shadow) as he walked away from the door toward the first step. I gasped, "Oh, Andy!" (I was surprised to see him so close to the door.) As soon as I said that, Andy's head popped around the doorway at the top of the stairs. As he answered, "Yes?" and the shadow immediately disappeared! I slammed the door shut and ran all the way to Sunnyside Superette to use the payphone. I called Andy and told him what I'd seen and asked him to come out for a drink because I really didn't feel like going back at that moment. He laughed and said he'd wondered why I turned white as a sheet and took off running.

"I've always thought it was funny how utterly normal seeing the spirit was at the time– Of course 'normal' until I realized it was a ghost.

"Once when the guys were out of town on a holiday break, it was lonely and I was visiting with the landlady and her boyfriend. We didn't have the TV set on and were between albums on the stereo. I suddenly heard noises coming from upstairs: feet scuffing and the muffled sounds that you hear when people are talking in another room but you can't hear what they're saying. We rushed out with the key and went into the apartment. The whole place was still, the kind of still that falls over a room when no one's been around for a while.

"We never learned the reason behind the ghostly footsteps and I lost touch with the landlady. I am willing to bet, though, the house on McLane Street is still haunted."

run like the devil in lincoln county

Lincoln County may be the only spot in West Virginia to claim that the Devil himself appeared there - and fully formed on a footbridge near a place called Dry Branch Hollow. It just so happened that Old Scratch was looking for someone in particular - one Lincoln County resident who had challenged him earlier.

The man's name has since been lost. But the story tells that in Lincoln County in the 1950s one particularly violent and ill-tempered man boasted that he was mean enough to whip the Devil. One night in drunkenness, the man waved his fists to the darkness and challenged Old Scratch to a fight.

It didn't take the Devil long to show up at the end of the footbridge nearing Spry cemetery leading to the man's house. The Devil's hands and face where charred and covered with soot. The air smoked with a smell like rotten eggs. A long, spiky, whip-like tail wagged out from under the Devil's waistcoat as he stood watching the man with arms folded over his chest.

"Whip me?" Old Scratch asked incredulously. His teeth gleamed yellow like winter corn. "And how, pray tell, have you decided to do that?"

"Just like I always do," the man spat. "Come over here and I will fight you."

"You know who I am," sighed the Devil, "Besides, I can't cross running water. You know that. It doesn't look like there's much fight in you anyhow. You're wasting my time." Old Scratch snickered. Sparks flew and then, with a bang like a firecracker, he disappeared in a cloud of sulfurous smoke.

The next day, the man now with a much more moderate temper, brought his son to show him the spot where he had challenged the Devil the day before. To their shock, cloven hooves were branded into the wooden planks of the footbridge. The seared footprints lead into Spry Cemetery…

So how did the braggart and boy react when they found the Devil's tracks on the footbridge? They did what any self-respecting country folk might do when meeting up with Old Scratch— they dropped everything and ran like Hell.

At Spry Cemetery, where the Devil's tracks were said to lead, there is the spirit of a woman who died in childbirth that haunts the graveyard. Her newborn also succumbed during the especially difficult birth. On nights of a full moon, when their names can still be read on their gravestones, the woman is seen rocking her baby in the cemetery. Witnesses say the ghosts are dressed in white frocks and the mother appears weeping.

an incubus & a black dog ~ calhoun county

Haunted tales are just as appropriate nearing Christmas as they are at Halloween. It is believed ghost tales were told by Druids around the fire during the dark night December 21st, when the earth is a far away from the sun as it will be all year. Perhaps spinning dark tales near the darkest day of the year helps alleviate any anxieties we might feel about ghosts, both past and present, and perhaps our own demise. Apparently author Charles Dickens was aware of this when he wrote one of the most famous ghost stories of all, "A Christmas Carol." The following article appeared in The *Charleston Daily Mail* on Dec. 27, 1925, just two days after Christmas.

"NEARLY 40 years ago the Calhoun county correspondent of the Cincinnati Enquirer prepared the following account of Calhoun's most prominent ghost, which the Enquirer printed. Interested persons saved the clippings, with the result that the story has reappeared recently in various weekly papers in north central of the state. It combines all the elements of a good ghost story and contains about every characteristic spirits are known to possess, and reads as follows:

"Grantsville, Calhoun county, W. Va., 1886—The following history of the haunted house, situated on the bank of Little Kanawha river, about three miles from this place, is presented to the scientist for explanation. The skeptical reader is frankly and honestly referred to any one of the persons named herein for verification of their of the history. Although it is one of the strangest and most unaccountable stories written on this subject within a quarter of a century, every detail is well authenticated. A solution of the mysteries connected with this history will be received with gratitude and pleasure by hundreds of the respectable and honest citizens of Calhoun, Ritchie and Wirt Counties. But back to the history...

"About three miles from the county seat of Calhoun County there resided, and still resides, Mr. Collins Betts, a farmer, who is well known throughout this section of the state. His house is a one-story, rambling affair, close to the banks of the stream and but a short distance from the highway. But for the reputation of the house it would be a frequent stopping place for the wayfaring; as it is, there are now but few men, in a country famed for its nervy and physical giants who would dare to stop over night at Bett's house.

"The reputation of the house as being haunted was acquired some years since then. By some – many in fact – it is ascribed to the disappearance of a peddler in the neighborhood and never to be heard of more. It is surmised by the most cautious that the peddler was known to have had over $1,000 in his possession at the time; and was probably murdered in the vicinity. Others say his horse had been left and no one ever came for it. Be this as it may, from that time forward Collins' house has borne the reputation of being haunted.

"Among the first who tested the truth of these rumors was a Methodist minister – Rev. Wayne Kennedy – who was well known throughout the state; a nervy, courageous man, who was never accused of a particle of cowardice. The reverend gentleman stopped at Betts' one night when belated, and willingly took the haunted chamber as his bedroom. About 12 or 1 o'clock the preacher felt something that was heavy bearing down upon his chest. The sensation of smothering awoke him. When he had collected his senses he declared that he saw something like a big black dog sitting upon his body in the bed. He said that it was with the greatest difficulty that he able enough to throw off the incubus and release himself from the deadly pressure.

[Note: Incubus is a spirit that violates sleeping women. Its counterpart, the Succubus applies to sleeping men. We've left the term here it as it was originally written although the real meaning is different than the way it is applied here.]

"In the morning the preacher left, but before doing so he told Betts' that he was not a particle superstitious, but that he would not stay in the house another night for the whole farm. The ghost or phantom appeared in different forms and was not confined to the house, but has been seen as far away as the top of the mountain opposite the house.

"One night James Wolverton and his son, a boy about 18 years of age, were on their way home, driving an ox- team. When almost at the top of the hill Wolverton declared he heard the tramping of hundreds of horses, and the rattling as of so many sabers in their scabbards and upon looking back saw what he thought a troop of cavalry riding at a gallop upon him. His oxen saw them also, and became frightened, and ran off down the mountain. Wolverton said that just as he thought they would rider over him he threw up his hands and exclaimed, "My God, men, don't ride over me!" He declares that the mystic cavalry disappeared instantaneously just as he cried to them to stop. Mr. Wolverton and his boy have always adhered to this story, and as they are men of probity, nobody questions but they saw something.

"Now comes another still stranger story: John Betts, brother of Collins, came to Calhoun from Colorado on a visit to his brother. He was a large muscular, rough-speaking man, and when he heard these stories he laughed at them and sneered at his brother and everybody who had the temerity to tell him of the rumors. He declared his intention of sleeping in the room where the phantom was often seen. One night he went into his room as a hale, hearty man as one would see in a month's travel. In the morning he was found lying upon his back perfectly helpless.

"He said that sometime during the night he felt some heavy weight upon is breast. He undertook to throw it off, but was unable to do so, and suffered torment until daylight, when the oppression ceased but he had lost the use of his limbs. Mr. Betts has never entirely recovered. A man named also Haverest slept there one night. He claims he heard the rattle of chairs upon the floor. Nothing can induce him to try it again!

"A strange feature of most of the cases is that the victims seem, although perfectly conscious but deprived of power to resist the incubus, and will suffer its torment for hours.

"Many people profess to believe that it is the effect of some sort of gas that arises from the earth and is inhaled, but others disbelieve in the gas theory. All would like to have it explained.

"Captain Hayhurst. a visitor also from Calhoun County, stopped along with Betts. What appeared to be a headless man rose up before Hayhurst's vision in the middle of the night and frightened the gallant captain so badly that, as he says, he "wouldn't stay another night in the house for all the gold in the kingdom.

"Henry Elliott met with a fate somewhat similar to John Betts. He slept in this room and was nearly smothered to death by something he took to be a large black animal. Elliott has been an invalid ever since.

"I had a conversation about the haunted house with Mr. Henry Newman, a prominent timber man about 60 years of age. Mr. Newman is not the least superstitious, but he fails to explain the mystery. He said he had heard the stories often, but didn't pay any attention to them. One night, however, he stopped at Betts' and was asked if he objected to sleeping in the haunted chamber. He said he did not. Mr. Newman's story is that he went to bed, but being very wakeful he lay still and mused until about 12 o'clock. About that time something commenced to clawing the bed clothing off his person. He said he threw himself up in the bed, expecting to catch a cat or some such animal, but there was nothing there. A second and third time the act was repeated but he could not see anything. He left the next morning, and says he does not want any more of it.

"Young Hosey a nephew of Betts, who resides on a farm several miles distant, says he had occasion one night to pass the haunted house on his way home. Just about half way up the hill, some strange apparition appeared and frightened the horse so badly that it ran off down the hill through the brush. It could not be found until the next morning. This is another instance when the phantom or whatever it was, was perceptible to both man and animal.

"John Jenkins, a well-known citizen of Ritchie County, was reported stopped one night. What John saw does not clearly appear, but whatever it was it frightened him so badly that he got out of the room as quickly as possible, ran to the stable, saddled his horse and left in a gallop. He never could be induced to go back.

"It is claimed that the sound as of persons whispering can be heard in the room, and also at the windows. A sound as of water dropping into a tin vessel is often heard, though no such article is about.

"The Betts people are as annoyed as are other people. The women say they hear all sorts of odd sounds as of water dropping, whispering and the sound of the fall of some heavy body.

"Two nieces of Betts stopped over night at his residence some time ago. One of them was overcome by the fear of some peculiar shape and ran out of the room followed by the other. Neither can be induced to go into it again. They say they saw horrible phantoms, but could not describe them.

"A sister of Betts, in a conversation about the house, said there was something mysterious connected with the house but she couldn't explain it. According to the lady's story the house has never been haunted or in any way different from others until after the death of an old woman named Riddle. Since then the place seemed the abode of some restless phantom.

"It is no trouble to find people by the dozen in Calhoun who have heard and had some queer experience with the Betts house. Such men as Captain George Downs, whose word cannot be disputed, declare they saw the phantom of a headless man or some other headless sight. To be stripped of bed clothing in the middle of the night, without any tangible means, was not uncommon. In fact, the reputation of the place appears to be widespread, and no one seems to be rash enough, after such experiences as the above cited, to test the matter or find the solution of the mystery.

"Your correspondent had often heard of the haunted house of Collins Betts, and determined finally to learn all he could about the mystery. He has interviewed dozens of respectable people, and all of them, though disclaiming any superstition, seem thoroughly mystified. Everyone who ever stayed there over night has heard or seen something strange or horrible. I have no doubt but that some one will yet be able to explain this mystery, but until then the haunted house of Collins Betts will be the notoriety of Calhoun county, West Virginia."

Over the last 115 years (to our knowledge) the Calhoun county ghost tales have not been added to. However, they are very much in keeping with current stories of ghosts. Many of the above reports seem to parallel the Old Hag paralysis phenomenon that is experienced worldwide throughout the ages. Generally, this is not dangerous but it is extremely frightening. Some of the ghost story does have elements of an actual haunting having taken place.

sawyer-curtis home
little hocking, ohio

Thought to have once been a station on the Underground Railroad, the Sawyer-Curtis home is one the oldest in the Mid-Ohio Valley, and was built by Nathaniel Sawyer in 1798 across the river from then Virginia, now West Virginia.

Above the sloping banks of the Ohio River, this evocative old house has gone through numerous face-lifts and transformations, though its ghosts stay pretty much the same. Owners have talked about an "eerie presence" felt throughout the home often when visiting the cellar where the candles and soap were made.

One former resident reported waking up to see a "beautiful lady" sitting at the foot of her bed. She was playing a music box, sweetly, as if she meant it especially to be heard by the house's surprised owner. Others who have lived in the home have heard their names called when no one else is around. Windows slam themselves shut and candlesticks were known to fly through the air, only to go crashing in the opposite end of the room.

There is a feeling of unrest to the building, and in researching the history of the house, it was discovered that Sawyer was involved in the Blennerhassett conspiracy and was a close friend of Aaron Burr. (Strangely, Burr's ghost haunts a number of places as is mentioned in this book.)

For some reason, Nathaniel Sawyer left the area quickly, perhaps losing his fortune like his friend Harmon Blennerhassett. Others say the place was used later to hide runaway slaves. Up until this very day, the owners talk about a feeling of presences and Santa Claus statues turning up missing. It does seem the Sawyer-Curtis House still holds onto the memories of the people who once lived there.

civil war ghosts of evans

The events in this account took place only a few miles from the peaceful Ohio Valley town of Ripley, West Virginia during the middle of the 1980s. As it was one of the first true hauntings that I (Richard Southall) investigated, it naturally has left a very distinct impression on my views on the paranormal not to mention my firm-held belief in the existence of ghosts.

According to Mrs. Ruby Milan (not her real name) and her family, certain strange and troubling occurrences started very soon after they moved into their farmhouse on Route 87 in the hilly community of Evans, WV. At first, small items would appear to be lost or misplaced then turn up in obvious places a week or so later. During the day, when Mrs. Milan was alone at the house and her sons were away at school, she heard loud, urgent knocks at her front door. She was surprised to learn that when she went to the door, no one was in sight. At first she thought it was a prankster but never found anyone in the area although she searched several times.

On another occasion, Mrs. Milan, while sitting in the living room notice the temperature drop suddenly. She heard then heard noises upstairs, as if someone in heavy boots came down the steps. (Footsteps are very common in manifestations of poltergeists and other associated haunted activity.) The stomping continued and when it got to the bottom of the steps, the stairway door opened, and the sound disappeared. This occurred at the same time each month for nearly eight months. Usually, this took place during the day when her children were at school. She was afraid to mention this to her sons for fear that she might frighten them. Little did she know that they would have their own encounters.

In the early winter of the same year, Mrs. Milan's two sons were at home playing with slot racers. Suddenly, the house grew colder (the house was heavily insulated, there were very few drafts, and it was a relatively mild night), and the stomping started.

The stairway door opened, and again no one was there. Her oldest son took a loaded rifle upstairs to see if anyone had broken into the house, but he found nothing in the otherwise empty rooms.

Later that same month, Mrs. Milan woke up around 3:00 one morning. The bedroom was adjacent to the bathroom, and standing in the bathroom doorway was an ominous looking soldier dressed in a Civil War uniform. At this point, Mrs. Milan describes it best in her own words.

"I could see the brass buttons shining on his uniform. The cap had a bill, but it was not like a baseball cap. I could easily see that it belonged on a uniform, a military uniform from another time. The soldier stared at me. I covered my head, but then I thought that I couldn't do that because he was between my boys and me! Although something told me he was not there to hurt my sons or anyone else for that matter. So I stared at the soldier just as he stared at me. This continued for a few minutes until I finally asked, 'Just who are you looking for?' and that's when the spirit disappeared."

After doing some research, it was discovered that a rag-tag group of weary Confederate soldiers had marched through the area where the house now stands. Many of the men died in route. Now, over the fifteen years after this encounter took place, Mrs. Milan lives in the same house and only encounters paranormal events on an infrequent basis – and as she tells me in a recent, follow-up interview –this suits her just fine.

harpers ferry's haunts

Despite its long, troubled history, Harpers Ferry is a garden spot. It is undeniably one of the most beautiful small towns in the eastern United States. Located along sloping hillsides and divided by the waters of the Potomac River, Harpers Ferry was a pivotal point in both the Revolutionary and Civil Wars... But one would have trouble pinning the loyalties to any particular cause. Like the houses that cling to the hillsides, it is a hardy, adaptable town, clinging to what it needs to go on.

But if travails and troubles bring on ghosts then Harpers Ferry is one intensely haunted town. After all, Harpers Ferry is where abolitionist John Brown was eventually caught and met the hangman's noose. Earlier, Brown's men led slave revolts and were murdered in the streets. Eventually found guilty of murder, treason and inciting slave insurrection, John Brown was imprisoned and hanged in Harpers Ferry on December 2, 1859, ending his dream of freeing the slaves.

John Brown - About 3 years before the events at Harper's Ferry

But many in Harpers Ferry say that was not the end of John Brown. It appears he still walks the streets looking for wrongs to right. Nearing the anniversary of John Brown's execution an older man with shock of snow-white hair and wild eyes is said to wander the streets dressed old-fashioned tattered clothing. Tourists, believing him to be an actor in a local theater presentation, asked to have their pictures taken with the strange little man. Often, without words, he agrees and poses with them for a few moments and leaves without saying anything. When the photographs are developed, there is a blank spot where the man should be.

John Brown is not the only ghost that haunts the cobbled streets of Harpers Ferry. His presence in Harpers Ferry was only a preview of what was about to happen during the Civil War. During the battle years, the town was seized and held by both Union and Southern armies on a number of occasions.

In what is now the Iron Horse Inn housed the superintendent for the Union army as well as other officers. Shortly before the Battle of Gettysburg, a young confederate spy stayed at the Iron Horse Inn to determine the strength of the Union Army. For a while, the spy came and went completely undetected.

One day, the young spy's clandestine efforts were exposed. When he was confronted, the boy raced toward the door frantically, but was shot dead by a Union soldier. The very same door is said to rattle furiously on certain occasions. Many employees at the Iron Horse Inn report they can even hear the young confederate officer taking his last fall.

Another ghost tale that takes place in Harpers Ferry is one about a young woman who catches on fire. As the girl ran from her house screaming in an effort to put out the flames, she was struck and killed by an oncoming train. Some claim you can still see the blazing torch of "Screaming Jenny's flame running down the railroad tracks – but only when the night is especially clear and dark and the spirits are gathering high.

pentagrams, ufos & restless spirits
athens, ohio

Would you believe it if we told you there is an Ohio Valley town where five graveyards create the exact dimensions of a witch's pentagram – an ancient symbol of mysterious powers and magic? There is such a town – it is the quaint and mystical Athens, Ohio.

Located 45 miles west of Parkersburg, hometown of Ohio University and famous for its campus Halloween celebrations, Athens has a plethora of intriguing tales that cannot be explained away easily.

Ancient Adena Indian mounds dot the rolling hills and twisting waterways of Athens County. Various cultures, such as the Shawnee Indians, considered southeastern Ohio, much like West Virginia to be an especially sacred area, filled with wandering spirits.

In the 1840s, a number of spiritualists were drawn to the Athens area, searching for a spiritually receptive spot to communicate easily with their "ghosts" and "guides.' Mount Nebo, the highest peak in Athens, County was where the Spiritualists put down roots. They opened their "sittings" to anyone in the area that might be interested in communicating with "guides." It didn't take long for their séances to develop a large following and to make important spiritual connections in Athens.

In 1852, local farmer Jonathan Koons was instructed by a séance medium to build a specific structure at Mount Nebo in which they could hold their sittings. Koons, as well as all eight of his children, were instructed they had the gift of spirit communication and should continue with it. Such séances in Athens grew wildly famous inspiring the British Psychical Society to state that Athens and Mount Nebo were the most haunted spots on earth. In later years, others would have to agree.

Such a fascination continued well into the late 20th and early 21st centuries when Ohio University students often visited graveyards in which to conduct their own updated version of a séance – albeit in Bell, Book and Candle style. Such impromptu séances may have stirred up a number of ghostly occurrences in local burial grounds, especially those in the Hanning Cemetery where several public executions took place in the 19th century.

Many report gruesome apparitions in Hanning Cemetery, ghosts of dead men with bluish, bloated faces, drifting through the graveyard in the late hours of the night and early morning. Some believe they are spirits of the men who were hanged while others claim one is the ghost of John Simms the guilt-ridden hangman (whose remains are also buried in Hanning) is the one that haunts the graveyard.

Wilson Hall on the campus of Ohio University has a famous haunt in room 428. It is believed the room is haunted by a young woman who became involved in the black arts died or committed suicide in the room in the 1970s. Students who have stayed in the room claimed they heard doors opening and closing, resounding footsteps and have watched objects move on their own. Whether a student unexpectedly died there is up for debate but the room is no longer used – probably to avoid hysteria for new students or to curb any occult activities going on in room 428.

The most interesting part of the story of Wilson Hall is that it lies in the exact center of the pentagram created by the five Athens graveyards. For some reason, the hall seems to be a power point, whether associated with anything truly occult in nature, or just something that is merely a coincidence – it grabbed enough attention for the TV show to tape a segment of "Scariest Places on Earth" that aired in 2001.

Athens has its share of railroad tunnel ghost tales along the once-traveled Cincinnati & Marietta railroad. One story involves a headless conductor who swings his lantern in attempt to get motorists to stop.

UFOs are not missing from Athens' mixed bag of paranormal events either. On March 29th, 1966 several Ohio State policemen and about a dozen Athens County residents reported a bright, whirling object flying in the sky.

A highway patrolman was the first to report the unexplained object at around 5:15 a.m. Others said the object moved for a while in a "slow drifting motion" until it disappeared from sight. Many believed later that the UFO was simply the planet Venus since it often appears as a bright object in the morning hours. The patrolman disagreed saying he knew what Venus looked like, and he was sure what he saw " was not Venus."

ed koons at north bend state park

Some years ago there was a blind man named Ed Koons who lived at what is now the entrance to the North Bend State Park at Cairo, West Virginia. But being blind wasn't the worst thing that Ed Koons had to deal with in his life. He had married a shrewish woman, whom along with her mother, cruelly abused and taunted the sightless man throughout their marriage. So much so, that Ed ended up hanging himself from a large tree that is at the entrance to the park. Many riders that pass by the place in cars claim they sometimes catch sight of Ed's lifeless body swinging from the limbs of the tree in their beams at night. Young couples that parked their cars at a lover's lane in the 1960s reported having their vehicle being soundly whacked and pounded as if by a weighty fist. Often, as the young couples drove away in a fright, they would see a man's handprints smeared in the dust on the windows of the car.

The strangest apparition to appear near the spot where Ed Koons allegedly hanged himself is some spiritual thing that resembles a small metal barrel wobbling on spindly legs through the trees. Those who chose to enter the park at night, claim as they walk over the path near where the park's lodge is, they can still hear the heavy footsteps of Ed Koons crunching the gravel and echoing directly behind them.

mary greene on the delta queen

Some souls love their life's work so much that they don't want to ever leave it – even after they've died. This could be said of Mary Becker Greene whose ghost still haunts the *Delta Queen* riverboat, although quite peacefully, for it appears Mary is a spirit that is mostly content.

Mary Becker was born in Marietta, Ohio in 1869 and married the riverboat Captain Gordon Greene in 1890. The Greene's were a prominent river-boating family in Marietta and so it is no surprise that Mary Greene was the first woman to become river pilot captain along the Mississippi and Ohio rivers, receiving her official license in 1896.

When Mary died at the age on 80 in 1949, after many thrilling and fulfilling years on the river, it seemed perfectly logical for her ghost to turn up in the place that she loved.

It seems Mary Greene was a teetotaler and had no use for alcohol – at least the drinking kind. One night in the lounge of the *Delta Queen* during the 1990s, after an especially tiring day, a few members of the riverboat crew decided to enjoy some relaxing moments with drinks to wind down after an especially difficult day when the room went cold. As they laughed and toasted each other, almost every glass above the bar fell and shattered into smithereens on the counter-top.

Although he has never witnessed the ghost of Mary Greene in any visual way, first mate Mike Williams told of an event that caused him to become a believer.

One night in 1982, Williams felt a cold breath and heard whispering in his ear. As Williams startled awake, doors slammed throughout the boat. He followed the sounds into the engine room and found a broken pipe with water rushing in. As she had done so many times in life, Mary Greene saved the *Delta Queen*, if not from certain ruin, at least from one big headache from Mike William's standpoint.

An elderly woman has been witnessed throughout the *Delta Queen*. When the portrait of Mary Greene is later pointed out to witnesses, they are in complete agreement that this is the older woman they have seen wandering throughout the riverboat lounge.

After all, the *Delta Queen* was Mary Greene's home. It is only fitting that she still wants to stay – if only in spirit.

fantastic phantoms in marietta, ohio

It's easy to step back in time when walking the brick streets of Marietta, Ohio. History abounds in the classic buildings, brick streets, quaint cafes and historical landmarks. It is no wonder Marietta was once considered the most civilized city west of the Alleghenies. All kinds of historical characters have set foot there – usually staying for a while if not permanently – these include Lafayette, Harman and Margaret Blennerhassett, Johnny Appleseed and the early settler of the area, Rufus Putnam.

We associate rich histories with haunts and Marietta has more than a few. In the older Harmar section of the small city, there is a house built in 1859 by Douglas Putnam for his wife Eliza. It is an exact replica of a house Eliza admired on the Hudson River in New York. The Putnams had always been one of the wealthier families in Marietta, but sadly, Eliza Putnam did not get to fully enjoy her handsome house as she sickened soon after it was completed and died there in 1862.

Since then, a "presence" that appears to wait at the bottom of the sweeping staircase has been sensed by many who have stayed at the home. Cold spots are reported throughout the house. A few have actually claimed to see Eliza Putnam at the bottom of the stairs as if she is greeting her guests for a grand party or celebration. When a spirit appears over and over again throughout a number of years, it is usually trying to express its pleasure or displeasure over something.

In Eliza Putnam's case, the pleasure is in the house, but the displeasure is over not being able to fully enjoy her husband's loving gift. Still, she makes her presence known.

In later years, the Putnam house became known as the Anchorage Nursing home. Over the years, employees of the nursing home noticed a number of uncanny things that occurred. For instance, consider the lights. Employees at the Anchorage would notice after they closed up the kitchen at night, turning off all the overhead lights, kitchen help would find the lights back on in time for the early morning shift. One woman even took the time to write down exactly when she turned off the lights in a notebook.

To no avail! The very next morning the lights would glare with no one inside to have turned the lights on. The Putnam House, now known as the Anchorage is an historical building open to the public. Reports of ghosts in the Anchorage have since been far and few. Still, Eliza Putnam's presence remains—while she is not seen, she is certainly felt.

Another important haunted place in downtown Marietta is the historic Lafayette Hotel, named after the French explorer. It appears that former manager and hotel owner S. Durward Hoag still likes to make his presence known. Mr. Hoag often appears as flashes of light –like a light bulb going off on a camera whenever a picture is taken.

It seems that the ghost of Durward Hoag is most active on the 3rd floor of the hotel and many employees are afraid to venture there alone, even though nothing of a malevolent nature has ever happened there. Light bulbs throughout the hotel also tend to flicker and even explode whenever the spirit of Hoag is around.

Sometimes spirits like to show their disapproval by exploding bulbs. But it is just as likely that they are simply trying to get the attention of the living. This tends to work well since exploding lights are just an early, rather easy way for ghosts to announce themselves. Exploding lights aside, there is no reason to fear ghosts.

the ghost of johnny appleseed
dexter city, ohio

Located on an overgrown hilltop, where Ohio's I-77 intersects with old route 821 north of Marietta, is the old Chapman family cemetery – an unimpressive briar patch where less than a dozen modest graves lie in ruins. It is believed the graveyard is haunted by the specter of a gaunt man dressed in rags, with wild, dark hair and hazel eyes ablaze.

The Chapmans were early pioneers in Washington County having arrived in the area in the mid-to late 1700s. They were a simple, hard-working family who settled along Duck Creek between Whipple and Dexter City. But it is the one Chapman who is not buried at the cemetery that causes motorists to stop and historians to gawk, someone who inspires families to pose for pictures in front of the large monument paid for by the pennies of schoolchildren along route 821. These are the graves of the siblings and step-mother of John Chapman otherwise known as "Johnny Appleseed."

Depending upon your outlook, John Chapman was an unsophisticated 19th Century preacher, a neo-pagan hero, a visionary soul, or just a plain old sower of apple seeds. Perhaps Johnny was all of these things. Perhaps he was none of them. After all, rare personalities are faceted and cannot be described in just one way.

Some recent writings claim Johnny was the American Dionysus, Greek God of pleasure, spiritual intoxication and wine. Many point out that when an apple is sliced in half the seeds create a pentagram, a five-pointed-star or a mysterious ancient symbol used to denote occult powers. Even in the "Witches Tarot," a tarot deck for Wiccans the card for 'the Fool,' (representing faith and trust, making a leap or taking a chance, encountering the wilds, or facing the rough magic of the wilderness) corresponds to the "mythic figure" of Johnny Appleseed. Yet Johnny Appleseed was real.

There is no doubt the Shawnee Indians were in awe of John Chapman because he did in fact, have such unusual powers. To harm or dishonor such a great person would certainly bring misfortune on their tribe. They wouldn't dare harm hurt the wild man.

That's why the Indians always allowed Johnny to sleep in their encampments whenever winter closed in. They honored this strange man. After all, Appleseed John was considered by the Indians to be sacred, holy, touched not only by Swedenborg's angels but also by other spirits.

John Chapman cared more for others than he ever did himself. While his outer appearance was craggy and austere, his inner world of God and spirit was rich and varied. John's only wish in life was to spread his vision of heaven, and to love and care for others – this included all sentient beings, not just humans.

Although Johnny Appleseed died in Indiana around the age of 70, it is said his spirit often visits the graves of his relatives on a hilltop quite visible from I-77.

Many say he left the Ohio Valley in bitterness over a broken-love promise. A girl promised to Appleseed John married someone else. Although the young lady's name is no longer remembered, it is said she decided not to marry John thinking him "just too odd." With his lumpy, wounded feet, wild hair, craggy beard and ragged clothes, John Chapman didn't appear to be a very good prospect for a young pioneer woman.

Bitterness followed Johnny, but love never left him. Except for preaching and planting, love was the only thing John knew how to do. That's why his grave in Indiana, is always covered with apples of every variety, thank you notes, and an epitaph that reads John Chapman 1774-1845 'He Lived for Others'

adena mounds & the state penitentiary at moundsville

Anyone who has visited Moundsville, West Virginia knows the Ohio Valley town is famous for two things – it has mysterious Indian burial mounds built by ancient Adena Indians two thousand years ago and a Civil War era prison with an extremely violent history that closed down in 1994. In fact, the Gravecreek Mound is located directly beside the old penitentiary. This conical 69-foot-mound was well within the view of the prisoners who had more than enough time to stare out the window and ponder their fates.

When you put these two factors together – the disturbance or removal of human remains and artifacts in one instant, coupled with a place that has seen much violence, evil and sadness, you have the right ingredients for a haunting... and not one of the pleasant kind.

The electric chair that was used condemned prisoners was once given the name "Sparky." It remains there and is one place that seems to be affected the most by paranormal events. Near the chair, many have reported icy cold spots, iron doors clanging, the shuffling of footsteps, and the disembodied voices of men yelling and screaming.

Recently, there have been tours of the old prison and a number of people have paid fees to actually spend the night to investigate the haunts. On one trip, a group from Parkersburg videotaped one of the guides telling stories from one of the more violent areas of the prison. Slowly, a wailing cry intensified and grew louder as the guide talked. The wailing voices indicated great suffering had occurred there.

There has also been a number of appearances of black mist throughout aged building, strange, ghostly formations of beings without any human features, the sound of footsteps running up stairs that are no longer there and apparitions of men who were once prisoners there ... and no doubt still are.

(Left) A photo taken at the Moundsville Penitentiary by Mark Chambers shows a mysterious & unexplained image near the center of the room.

keith-albee theater in huntington

Built in 1928, the Keith-Albee Theater houses not only popular movies, but is reported to have a number of ghosts and "presences" throughout the building. It is the woman's restroom that is the most active with spirits. The restroom door has been known to swing open some then close all on its own accord. Muffled footsteps are heard regularly outside the projection booth and the sound of human voices echo in the building whenever workers enter in late morning or early afternoon.

dark night of the soul ⟶ darkish knob

The ghost of a young slave woman is said to return to Darkish Knob near Parsons, West Virginia on the eve of the anniversary of her death that occurred more than 140 years ago. She is one of many spirits of runaway slaves that are believed to haunt Darkish Knob since the area was once an important stop on the Underground Railroad as were many places just south of the Mason-Dixon line. The hiding place for the slaves was actually in a house tucked within the dark foliage at the bottom of the mountain, a place not visible from the road.

But on reaching the bottom of Darkish Knob, the beautiful slave lost her direction. She came up on the meeting place in the dark of night but didn't see the house. Instead, she and her horse climbed the steep embankment since she assumed the stop on the Underground Railroad was on the other side of the hill.

Horse and rider went up the path that overlooked the Cheat River. As they started for the summit of Darkish Knob, the horse lost its footing causing them to fall into the river below. The horse swam to safety but the girl was killed.

On the anniversary of the slave girl's death, residents of Parsons claim to hear her moaning cries at twilight. As it grows closer to midnight, the cries turn into ear-splitting screams. Some claim the ghost of the ghost's horse is a white mare. This may be another variation on the Banshee tale – interesting since the woman is not Irish or Scottish. Such tales do get around and thus, this ghost story is an intriguing blend of the varied cultures and influences that continue to exist in Appalachia to this day.

the ghost of mamie thurman

Murders, even in the present day, are rare events in West Virginia. So it is no surprise that one ghost out of small community near Logan is still talked about into the 21st Century. On June 22, 1932 a doe-eyed, dark-haired beauty by the name of Mamie Thurman was found murdered outside of Holden, on what was then Trace Mountain. Her body was recovered from the hillside but no one understood why the young lady was killed. She had neither enemies nor a shady reputation. Later her murder was pinned on a man by the name of Clarence Stephenson – although many in Logan, including prominent citizens, never believed in his guilt.

Sources contradict each other to the manner of the young woman's death. Some say Mamie died of two gunshot wounds to the brain while others claimed her throat was slit from ear to ear. Nothing of any value (other than her life) was missing from Mamie's body. She had eight dollars in her wallet, a gold watch was clasped about her wrist and she wore two diamond rings. These were certainly a small fortune during the depression days and any robber would have taken those immediately from the body.

The reason behind the murder was never solved. We know by the case of the Greenbrier Ghost, that when a person is unjustly murdered and the killer goes free, the spirit cannot rest until he is brought to justice or at least recognized as the murderer.

Some residents of Logan claim Mamie Thurman's ghost still wanders the hills and hollows of Logan, wearing a navy polka dot dress and a finger-wave hairstyle of the 1930s. Mamie's ghost is said to flag down cars on the winding road of 22 Mountain where her body was left lifeless and bloodied many years before. Then she just disappears.

Interestingly, even where Mamie Thurman's body rests is still in dispute. Records show she may have been buried in Kentucky, the state of her birth, while others insist her body was in fact, interred in Logan at the Logan Memorial Park. But Mrs. Thurman's grave is not noted, and it is claimed her ghost continues to haunt the cemetery, seeking justice and pleading for a headstone to mark her life, if not her final resting place.

phantom of tollgate

Early in the evening, during a light, misting rain, a Clarksburg couple drove home after visiting relatives in Parkersburg. They came upon an area called "Tollgate," a place in Ritchie County near the Doddridge County line. There they noticed a man climbing over an embankment, waving his arms wildly as if to flag down a car. Before the couple caught him directly in the beams, his figure had clearly vanished. Yet the man's expression told them something was terribly wrong. Perhaps his car had veered off the highway, they thought, and he was hurt or in serious trouble. The couple finally turned their vehicle around and returned to check on the man but found no living soul in sight.

After arriving in Clarksburg, the couple phoned the state police and asked if there had been an accident or stranded motorist in the Tollgate area? The police seemed puzzled and said no one had reported either. When the couple told a female relative of their strange encounter, she said, "Did you not hear? A man was killed on that lonely stretch of road a few weeks ago. They didn't find his body at first. Emergency workers said he tried to climb up to Route 50, but never made it that far. His dead body lay just a few feet from the road for a couple of days. Good thing it was cold. Sounds to me like you two saw a ghost!"

headless ghost of dorcas hollow

It seems many areas have a bone-chilling tale of a headless ghost such as Washington Irving's classic tale "The Legend of Sleepy Hollow."

One might believe that headless ghost stories are highly embellished folk tales, mostly bogus, based on myth—certainly not true! But when it comes to scaring the bug juice out of fussy little kids, stories of vengeful ghosts searching for their heads somehow manages to do the trick.

The Headless Ghost of Dorcas Hollow, near Petersburg in Grant County, West Virginia seems to be one exception. A man was murdered there. But centuries ago, and he was savagely decapitated.

George Van Meter migrated to Grant County in the mid-1700s from his native land of Germany. He married a local woman who was also of German descent. They soon started a family and homesteaded in Dorcas Hollow about fifteen miles from what is now Petersburg.

The entire area of Grant County was sparsely populated in the late1700s and Dorcas Hollow was isolated. However, George Van Meter eked out a living for himself and his family by toiling the soil and working as a carpenter.

Perhaps, Grant County appeared like a biblical Garden of Eden to the Van Meters. The Van Meter farm was directly situated in the midst of the blue, Allegheny Mountains, and green meadows of the Potomac Highlands. No other place felt as peaceful to George Van Meter, or so removed from the troubles of the world.

Until on July 4th (year unknown), when Van Meters prepared to join their neighbors down the hollow for a much-anticipated Independence Day celebration and picnic. George Van Meter and his son David were working in the fields when they noticed a band of Huron Indians coming out of the woods near the edge of their property. The Indian's faces were painted black. Van Meter saw they were on a war party and not just passing through. He told his son David to retreat back to the house and gather up his mother and the other Van Meter children. George Van Meter then ordered David to take the rest of the family and run away as fast as they could and to not even take the time to look back!

The Van Meter family fled to the closest settlement, where they learned neighbors were massacred by the Hurons around the same time. Understandably, this created bad blood between local Indian nations and settlers, leaving it a tit-for-tat situation. By the early 1800s most Indian groups had been run out of the area, leaving full-blooded natives a thing of the past in most of western Virginia.)

Apparently, after David and the other Van Meters fled, George fought the Hurons valiantly, but alas, not well enough to save his own life. When other settlers returned with David, they found George Van Meter dead – and minus his head. The men searched for George Van Meter's severed head for well until dark, but never found it.

The men returned to the settlement waiting for the Hurons with death painted faces to once again attack. This time, the Indians never showed up. But the next day a cooking pot filled with water was discovered just outside the settlement. When the men opened the lid to the pot, George Van Meter's boiled and grinning skull, with lidless eyes, swam to the surface to meet their horrified gazes. Fearing the Van Meter family would be upset by the appalling sight of the father's head, the men hastily buried it right on the spot.

The body, with full services was buried later. Because the scene of George's murder was too painful for the family to return to, they moved to another part of Grant County. For years, no one would even venture near what was once the Van Meter farm.

Perhaps mere superstition about the murder kept people away. The belief that a soul cannot rest if it is missing a part of its body, or the vessel that contained it in life, is a strongly held belief that goes back to the time of the Ancient Egyptians. According to the Egyptians, if the body is not intact the soul of the deceased simply will not be able to rest or enjoy the afterlife. Therefore, respectful treatment and care of a corpse is essential for the soul finding peace in the afterlife.

Does the apparition of George Van Meter appear at Dorcas Hollow searching for his missing head? Many locals claim he does.

Throughout the years, some who have traveled along Route 220 have reported seeing the shuffling body of a headless man wandering the fields and woods near Dorcas Hollow. Many say George's ghostly body, with broad, level shoulders, is encased in a glowing blue light. The ghost never utters a word. He never approaches anyone. The apparition seemingly wanders, without direction, as if fumbling for something he might have lost... lost long ago in Dorcas Hollow, after dark.

headless ghost at north bend state park

The following tale was given to us by Terry Elliott of Cairo:

Another disturbing headless ghost tale comes from what is now the North Bend State Park Road in Ritchie County. About one hundred years ago, between the small communities of Cairo and Harrisville, the headless ghost of a man was said to haunt an area of Park Road near the Jug Handle Campgrounds. But the ghost did not appear on the paved roadway that exists today. It was then a rough and tumble dirt path, frequented mostly by men who worked on the oil wells that flourished in Ritchie County at the time.

The North Bend State Park did not exist then. Instead, the rolling hills and slopes were dotted by numerous oil drilling sites, with men more than happy to claim their piece of the proverbial oil boom pie, or at least land a job that paid more than a month of work on a West Virginia Farm ever could.

But tragically, one day, a worker was killed in an oil well explosion. This happened not far from Jug Handle Campground where workers would gather to be driven by horse and buggy to the oil well sites. The victim's body parts were gathered up and later buried, but the unfortunate man's head was never found.

A few years after the explosion, a gentleman by the last name of Furr drove a buggy from the camp, taking workers up to their oil well sites in what was basically a taxi service. Furr would pick up men at Cairo's train depot and drive them out to their assigned oil wells.

It was nearing dusk one quiet evening when Mr. Furr preceded down the dirt road past the Jug Handle Campground, along his usual route alone. He came across a low creek that did not have a bridge. It was shallow enough for him to drive his buggy through and allow the horses to drink. Furr let go of the reins so his horses could refresh themselves.

As the horses drank, Furr felt the weight of the back end of the buggy bear down as if someone had just climbed on. He turned to see a man's death-pale hands clasping the back seat. Thinking someone was making a fool of him, Furr raised up to catch sight of whomever it was involved in such foolishness.

But no flesh and blood man was playing with Furr. The figure grasping a hold of the back of the buggy was missing his head. To Furr's horror, he clearly saw it was a headless man! All that lay beneath the shirt collar was a jagged, bloody stump.

Almost immediately, Furr was convinced it was the ghost of the decapitated oil well worker. Terrified, he drove his horses at a break-neck speed back to Cairo but the bloody stump held on fiercely for most of the ride.

By the time Furr got home, the ghost was gone. Where did the headless man go? Mr. Furr wasn't sure. He knew one thing, though. He'd not be driving his buggy past the Jug Handle Campgrounds near dark again. Furr wasn't about to challenge this grisly apparition, especially one that appeared to him in such a violent and disturbing manner.

and yet another headless ghost!

Pax is located only thirty-six miles from the capitol of Charleston but is still an isolated village in Fayette County. Sometimes near dusk, when day is darkening into night, the ghost of a man is glimpsed walking along the railroad tracks into town, toward Pax's city hall. The man is reported to be carrying something, at first believed to be a lantern. On closer inspection by witnesses, it is the ghost's own head that he holds.

Many believe the spirit is the residual energies of a man who was decapitated along the railroad tracks many years before. Ghost experts know, however, that headless ghosts do not always mean decapitations. Typically, when an apparition appears solid enough for witnesses to see him, he is usually minus some body part. The Pax ghost is missing the most important appendage of all – his head.

the witch and the wampus cat

There is a power that witches have called "glamoury" that allows them to transform themselves into any thing that they might choose such as a dog, a cat, a bird or just a more beautiful human being. (This is where our term "glamour" comes from –

Interestingly, though, the root of the word for "glamour" is "grammar," meaning to recite a spell or incantation.) The witch's power of glamoury is shown in the fairy-tale Snow White where the beautiful witch transforms herself into an aged crone in order to win Snow White's trust so she will accept the poison apple.

Among mountain folklore in the hills of West Virginia, there is a story passed down about an unmarried woman who lived in a mountain community who had "special powers." This woman stayed pretty much to herself and she seemed to favor animals over people. It was rumored this isolated woman was in fact a witch endowed with supernatural powers, that she was able to use them for both good and ill.

We know, historically, that any time witch allegations are bantered about, there always seems to be accusations of some type of evil-doings on the part of the witch. After all, the woman was odd and kept to herself. She wasn't as friendly as people thought she ought to be.

Local livestock soon came up missing. The cows dried up and would give no milk. The beginning of growing season suffered a serious drought. This simply had to be the fault of the witch. The people had noticed her sharp and mysterious looks.

Many claimed it was the witch's power of glamoury that enabled her to turn herself into a large, gold-eyed, tuft-eared cat that many referred to as a "Wampus Cat." Now as a cat, whenever doors would open, the witch would sneak into houses of unsuspecting families and wait until they all fell asleep. She would pilfer objects from the family to be used in future spells. The witch would then cast her spell over the family causing them to be unable to wake up during her nighttime roaming.

As the Wampus Cat she would teleport herself through the walls, then out to the barn where she would take the smaller livestock, like lambs and calves. The witch had to go easy at first. She could only handle the smallest animals.

For many years, the witch continued her flagrant stealing by using her glamoury spells. She wasn't stopped until some locals caught on to her stealth-inspired, witch-ways.

One night, some village men decided to wait in their barns for the witch, just as she would be transforming herself into the Wampus Cat. Startled in mid-spell, the witch had only changed herself partly into the cat when the men frightened her. Part of her face and breast was woman but the rest of her was a monstrous cat. The witch yowled, fled the barn and disappeared into the woods.

After that, the witch never returned to her home, but over the years the people in her community have been awakened by a mournful howling in the woods at night.

In Virginia and Tennessee, the Wampus Cat is a Cherokee Indian legend and differs somewhat. In fact, some believe the entire tale of the Wampus Cat originated with the Native Americans. Among the mountain Cherokee Indians in North Carolina, the Wampus Cat is called Ewah. Its story began with a large wild cat that plagued the hunters of the tribe. It killed off all of the game, causing the people to go hungry and had to be destroyed.

One Cherokee woman that did not trust her husband during hunts, put on a mountain lion skin and tracked the group to see what he was doing. When the Cherokee braves caught her in her prowling, she was punished by the truth and was doomed to wear the cat skin until eternity. She is doomed to scavenge the mountains as the dreaded Ewah, ready to gobble up bad people's souls.

Another story tells of another Cherokee woman who wore the mask of the cat to spy on her husband while in the woods. She thought perhaps he was lying to her about going hunting and she wanted to catch him in the act of some infidelity.

Finally, when she happened upon her husband, he was innocently tracking a deer. But when the husband saw the dreadful mask his wife concocted, he was driven insane by fear of it. The Cherokee man ran away never to be seen again. As the woman attempted to pull the mask from her face, she found it was stuck to her skin.

Now the young woman, another Ewah or Wampus Cat must wander the mountain's deep thickets to this day in order to make peace or find resolution with the husband she misjudged and scared to death.

briggs public library & woodlawn cemetery ironton, ohio

South of Gallipolis and Chesapeake along the Ohio River, is Ironton, a modest, quiet city with an immodest, unquiet number of haunts.

For instance, the Briggs Public Library sits on the grounds of the former home of a Doctor Joseph Lowry. His ghost appears, allegedly, because Lowry had a business argument with the local undertaker and thus, his body was made a mess of during the embalming (or lack of) process. It seems that after death, the good doctor simply fell apart. Many claim that during the stillness of evening in the library, the doctor's footsteps are heard dragging and echoing throughout. Many are convinced it is Dr. Lowry searching for his lost body parts in the library's rooms and halls.

But the Briggs Library is not Dr. Lowry's only place to haunt. He also appears to startled visitors in Woodlawn Cemetery where he is buried. The doctor's apparition wanders aimlessly, trying to pull himself back together.

There is also statue in Woodlawn that overlooks the grave of a woman murdered by her husband. A handprint stays on the statue's cheek and many say the statue remains warm to the touch. Some have tried to remove the stain from the statue's cheek but it always reappears. Others claim the cemetery also houses the remains of a ballerina who was interred in a mausoleum. It is said the ballerina dances on the lawn of the graveyard under the moonlight.

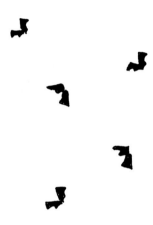

13. how do i know if i am being haunted?

The appearance of ghosts and other types of haunts often start out as very subtle. You may not even notice them in the initial phase of the haunting unless you are a person who is "tuned in" to these spiritual energies. It is only when the haunts become impossible to ignore that we begin to experience the surreal world of haunted houses and ghosts. And this is where the fun begins.

Fun? But, of course! If you find yourself in the midst of a true possession of spirits or haunting count yourself as one of the lucky people who gets a true glimpse of the world of ghosts. Many would love to meet up with a ghost but never do. After all, spirits can be quite unpredictable and generally show up in their own good time and not ours.

Scared? There is no reason to be. The vast majority of apparitions are quite harmless and since ghosts are not really physical, they are usually not able to harm one in any physical way. Oh, there are a few who may trip you or pull your hair. They may break your camera or twist your ear. That's about as bad as it gets although in the case of malevolent spirits there are some psychological dangers that we covered earlier.

How does one know if one is being haunted? There are certain elements of hauntings that are universal when it comes to the matter of ghosts and their manifestations. These happen across the board and occur no matter what country you are born in, what language you speak or even what sex or race you are. The ingredients that indicate ghosts are haunting you are pretty much the same. Although such ghostly occurrences may seem strange or even bizarre to most, they're actually rather ordinary to those of us who study such things.

So – do you think you might have met up with an actual ghost or are you living in a haunted house? Read on and see if the following rings a bell... some delightfully, frightfully, ghostly bell.

➤ You feel as if you are being watched... You know how it happens. The skin on the back of your neck crawls. Hairs lift. Other souls are watching you – you're sure of it. As soon as you turn around no one is there. Did they leave? Do they no longer watch? Of course, not. Your ghosts are still watching, enjoying the show. One thing we have learned from the spirit world, they are just as curious about us as we are curious about them. Maybe more so. And they do like to check in on the living. Those of us who are sensitive enough can feel them watching. As soon as you realize that spirits are really no threat, you can learn to live with your ghost. There is really no reason to run from the room. Such spirits probably haven't been in the world for a while and want to experience it all over again. Ghosts have feelings, too.

➤ The sudden appearance of unusual odors or smells... The presence of odd smells or odors that are otherwise unaccounted for is often the initial phase of a genuine haunting. Smells can be the first (albeit indirect) way that a spirit announces or makes itself (him or herself) known. Usually a scent, such as lingering perfume or cologne, pipe tobacco, gasoline or coffee perking, has some meaning to way the person was in life. If the ghost smoked Cuban cigars – then that's what you will smell. Sweet perfumes and the scent of flowers seem to be a favorite among spirits. That is, was a favorite, before he or she became a ghost! Keep a log of smells turning up in areas of your home or haunted area. This can be a good clue as to who it might be that is actually is haunting your place. Foul odors, on the other hand, are generally not a good sign. Repulsive smells may indicate malevolent ghosts and spirits.

➤ Waking up to a feeling of a presence in your room... Many of you already know the feeling. You startle awake. Your heart pounds. Much to your horror, you realize you are also paralyzed. Can't move a muscle—not a baby finger! You sense someone there... Your eyes can't focus but you feel it. A terrible weight crushes you into the mattress... sits on your chest. Now, whatever it is pulls you by your ankles to the bottom of the bed. In worse case scenarios, there may even be the sensation of a sexual violation. This is no doubt the most terrifying spirit experience of all. Not because the ghostly presence is going to hurt you...it's simply because during such a state, there is very little you can do to stop it. This state of psychic attack is called the "Old Hag" and also "Night Paralysis." Researchers think this has little to do with ghosts but I (Susan Sheppard) am not so sure. I've had attacks of this "Night Paralysis" throughout my life and they always occur in the houses where I've lived that are the most haunted. They also tended to occur whenever I opened up a bit more psychically, as well. I believe this dreaded appearance of the "Old Hag" (fear of it caused me to have insomnia for many years) is both a physical and a psychic attack. Some researchers believe that paralysis happens when we wake up during a period when our muscles have been paralyzed to keep us from thrashing around and hurting ourselves during deeper sleep cycles. During the Middle Ages, the "Old Hag" was associated with demonic attacks such as the Incubus (a spirit that has sex with sleeping women) or a Succubus (a spirit that has sex with sleeping men). If you find yourself the victim of too many "Night Hag" violations (because that's exactly what it feels like,) you may want to bring in a psychic, a healer or some other holy person to try and get rid of it. Prayer often breaks the spell but cursing works almost as well. Recent research shows if you sleep on the left side (and not in a supine position) you will have less of a chance of having an "Old Hag" attack. Why? No one knows for sure. Maybe it is because you are keeping your heart, your vital self, covered and protected.

↩ Drafts and cold spots... Just about anywhere in the world, the presence of ghosts is associated with cold spots, and that means a significant drop in temperature from one room to the next. However, such drafts or frigid areas are not limited to indoors. The next time you visit a cemetery, for instance, you may notice how much cooler the air seems to be inside the gates. Why? Some theorize spirits use natural heat or thermal energies in order to appear or manifest in such way that they can be noticed. In other words, ghosts may use heat to gain energy. The truth of the matter is, no one knows for sure why cold spots are associated with the spirits of the dead. However, cold spots do occur in most cases of haunts whether the spirits turn out to be malevolent or benign. But a briefer, scarier explanation may be, death is cold.

↩ Hearing glass shattering or ice being dropped into sinks, yet when you check out the sounds, nothing is there. This is a familiar story once you start investigating or studying ghosts. More attention getting.

↩ Feeling a weight or seeing an impression at the foot of a bed, seeing the shape of a human body outlined in the sheets, or feeling any kind of weight or impression on a piece of furniture for that matter. Just another unusual, but universal indication of a haunting. Visiting New Orleans a few years ago, we visited the former house of the Voodoo Queen Marie Laveau. Later in the evening, at the Royal Sonesta Hotel, my small daughter gasped and said that there was the shape of a woman's face in her pillowcase. Wanting to reassure her that pillowcases sometimes crease like that, that it is only our minds playing tricks on us, I was shocked to see, indeed, my daughter was right. There was the outline of a very pretty woman's face in the pillowcase.

⊷ Unexplained electrical malfunctions such as problems with television sets, clocks, phones, computers, lighting, etc... Take, for instance, my television set. Since attending a blessing ceremony with Tibetan Lamas a while back, the energies in my house went wild. The night of the blessing, the television set switched itself on after I had walked upstairs and turned off the lights in the house. Unbeknownst to me, I heard the TV blaring then saw a blue light flickering in the hallway leading up the stairs. Absent-minded of me, I thought. But I hadn't been watching TV, had I? So I walked downstairs turned off the television and went back to my room to sleep. The next morning, I awakened to ringing of the telephone. As I sat up, the television set in my bedroom suddenly switched on. So, for this particular week in my life, the TVs have turned themselves on two to three times per day. This has been highly interesting but will soon die down. So, what can this mean? Spirits are electrical in nature and in order to become detectable they will often resort to drawing upon various types of electrical equipment to get their batteries charged. Why is this? Because it is the easiest way. It is so much easier than trying to distract or connect with the mind of a human that is so preoccupied by other things. It takes a bit of a shock. In keeping with this, spirits will also use other electrical items, most especially lights. Flickering lights are the most common for this to take place. If you've ever gone into an old haunted theater or library, you may notice how erratically the lights tend to flicker. No need to worry. It's just the spirits saying, "We are here." You can choose to ignore them for there is no reason for concern. However, when hunting out a haunting, take into consideration any strange electrical occurrences, most especially those having to do with lights. Spirits love fiddling around with the lights. Gets our attention, right?

⊷ Hearing your name called when no one is there... This one is rather fascinating because it usually comes without warning so can be unnerving. Hearing your name being called (or whispered into your ear) may be explained by one of two things. A person close to you may simply have you on his or her mind. This is one form of telepathy (thought transference through psychic means) and is actually pretty common. The other explanation may be that spirits are simply trying to get your attention. This does bring up the question— are the ghostly voices audible to others? In my experience, yes. Other people around usually hear the same spirit voices. This means spirit voices you are hearing as well as other examples of ghosts are not just happening inside your head. Makes one feel a bit less cuckoo, EH?

⊷ Feeling touched, patted or caressed... It must seem odd that a non-physical-being would be capable of human touch, but such is often the case. How this is achieved is a mystery, but allow me to fill you in on the particulars. During our ghost tours each fall, several participants have reported being caressed, fondled and having their hair tugged on around of the Weeping Woman statue. She is the famous statue at Riverview Cemetery. It is her job to watch over the graves of Stonewall Jackson's relatives. But the Weeping Woman seems not to like having her picture taken. This was interesting development since earlier in the tour I dreamed of a woman's icy hand caressing mine. It was not a bad feeling but the hand was eerily cold. By this time this book is out, I am sure there will be even more reports of "touching" around this impressive statuary in seasons to come. What does this all amount to? An awareness of being brushed or touched indicates a pretty intense haunting. It takes a lot of power for a spirit to come across in a physical way. So, if this has happened to you, take your ghost seriously and stay tuned for more developments. However, if ever there is ever a case that you are scratched to the point that blood wells, do be extra careful. This can imply a more negative kind of haunting.

✦ Someone in the home begins drinking heavily. Unfortunately this happens more frequently than most would ever imagine. Many of the most talented mediums throughout the history of Spiritualism ended up alcoholics such as Arthur Ford and both Fox sisters. Never drink alcohol while communicating with the spirit world. This is extremely treacherous. You have our word on it.

✦ Stuff gets lost and then turns up in unlikely places... Missing objects are often the way poltergeists start out. Researchers have found where there are poltergeists there are usually other ghosts. Look for objects of significance getting lost and then turning up in obvious places. The items may be family heirlooms, such as old photographs, or objects that are associated with a family member who has already passed on but now wishes to communicate with the living. This can be true when an item holds meaning to the spirit that haunts your house. The spirit of my maternal grandmother placed one of her hankies on my cousin's pillowcase. My cousin hadn't seen the handkerchief in years... then suddenly there it was on her pillow, unfolded and everything. She couldn't miss it. There was no need for worry. Grandmother was simply making her presence known. There are also nonsensical manifestations of objects, such as finding your hairbrush in the refrigerator or your toothbrush in the toilet. In this instance, it is only your ghost only trying to get your attention... so stay alert. Things are just now getting interesting...

✦ Appearance of poltergeists... If you are interested in the paranormal, you already know what poltergeists are. You've heard it before... "Poltergeist" is a German term which means "noisy spirits" or "to rap or to knock." The word is even older, with Greek origins. (That's how long poltergeists have been around.) The poltergeist attack usually starts out as loud banging noises. Often, there is the sound of footsteps in the upstairs of the house or it sometimes sounds as if someone is walking on the roof. Ordinary objects fly about. Things get broken. Beds begin to shake. Typically, the poltergeist will pester one person in the family more than the others. That person is normally a teenager under stress or with some emotional problems. We know that poltergeists are lumped in with ghosts—

➤ But are poltergeists actually ghosts? Over the last fifty years, appearances of poltergeists are believed to be a latent ability that humans have to move objects with the powers of the mind. Such individuals are thought to have some inner turmoil, which creates the right setting for the poltergeist phenomena to occur, a form of "telekinesis," (moving objects with the powers of the human mind. But you knew that already, didn't you?) Such abilities can appear around adolescents in crisis, usually at the beginning at puberty. Often the poltergeist activity goes away or become buried around the age of twenty. However, the experiences can continue at various times throughout their lives. Only recently, psychic researchers have begun to notice that poltergeists tend to occur simultaneously with other hauntings and these do involve spirits of deceased persons. It could be that spirits also use the magnetic powers of the human mind to appear, especially in the case of psychics who are more in tune with their powers. In this way, the person acts as a portal or doorway for other spirits to arrive on the scene and haunt. Poltergeists fascinate but before you call in some holy person to do an exorcism on your home, keep in mind that poltergeists lose energy and almost always go away on their own.

➤ Certain rooms in a house exhibit dinginess or unexplained shadows no matter how good the lighting is... Houses and rooms absorb all kinds of energies. The minute a person walks into your home, he or she will change the energy in your home. This includes ghostly visitors as well. Usually, if the feeling in the room is bright and expansive, no one really worries about ghosts. On the other hand, if your spirits are earthbound and are of a melancholy nature (as some earthbound spirits tend to be) the room will take on a type of dinginess or shadowy quality. For some unknown reason ghosts thrive best in the shadows. We associate the shadows with evil, because after all darkness is scary since we aren't as able to seen things as well in the dark. They may hang out in sunlight, too, but it is possible more ethereal appearances are not as easy to determine in glaring light as they are in subtle shade. But if you find corners in a house that seem impossible to light well, this is probably the area of the house or area that may be the most haunted.

➤ Dreams that are not typical, involving people you may not know... There are some dreams that are so vivid or real that we wake up worn out by them the next morning. Such dreams tend to have a psychic component, maybe involving people we do not know in our waking world. At times, such dreams can involve the spirits or ghosts that have moved into your life, especially if your dream is recurring and the people you see in your dream are detailed and quite specific. You may want to consider the possibility that your dream characters may be actual people, either living or deceased. The living people may be ones you have a psychic connection to, for some unexplainable reason. If the people turn out to be deceased, well, you guessed it. You may well have a ghost. While on the midst of what you think might be a haunting, pay special attention to your dreams. You very well may solve the identity of your ghost through an especially vivid one. If you get specifics in your dream such as names, locations or events, go to the library or courthouse and see what you can find out about your ghost. You may begin understand why your ghost was initially attracted to you and why they chose to haunt.

➤ Pets or other animals may appear frightened or avoid specific places or rooms in the house... Do you have a room or a corner where pets refuse to go? Are there certain areas in your home that tends to unnerve your cats or places where dogs begin to growl? Since animals rely upon their instincts, they are also able to see and hear things that human beings normally do not. And so, it is not surprising that our pets are able to see and discern spirits even better than we do. After all, animals are very basic. They will behave strangely whenever there are spirits around, oftentimes sensing malevolent ghosts. Many cases of pets discerning spirits have been documented. Pets can be quite psychic, sometimes more than their owners are. Therefore, if you find your life besieged by apparitions and ghostly energies take into consideration the places where your pets act the strangest. These often turn out to be 'hot spots' of ghostly activity when looked into further. In fact, using your pet to find out where your spirits are can work out exceedingly well.

➤ Setting off buzzers and alarms... By this, I mean you and not your ghosts. (Well, maybe it's a little bit of both.) If you are in contact with spirits as well as other types of psychic energies, you may begin to notice that you tend to set off buzzers and other alarms. In my town, this is no problem because everyone knows me. Therefore if I set off the bomb alert at the post office or shoplifting alarms at my local bookstore, no one is too surprised. In fact, when in contact with spirits either intentionally or unintentionally, you may notice all types of instruments will go haywire. You may get a few funny glances as you are walking across a parking lot when the automobile's lights come on and the engine suddenly starts up even though there is no one inside. Just don't chuckle to the stranger beside you and say, "Did you see that? It always does that whenever I come around!" This is just one interesting by-products of dealing with the paranormal. It's fascinating and usually temporary, so enjoy it. If the activity continues, consider calling up the Amazing Randi to take his paranormal test so you can collect your million dollars. But it's doubtful he'd believe you anyway. Oh well, what the hell...

⊷ Unexplained health problems, specifically headaches or feeling drained... There is little doubt that directly communicating with spirits can wear you out. Disembodied entities will draw up on your resources, and this will drain you. There are ways to avoid this such as imagining a white light surrounding you at all times, but most especially when you are in communication with spirits. Also, if your spirit gives you the creeps, you can clap your hands loudly in areas you may feel are spiritually dangerous areas. This may seem ridiculous, but most spirits, like small animals avoid high-pitched noises or ringing sounds. One other problem, which is both a physical and emotional one that is the suffering from depressive episodes that are difficult to shake away. This may indicate spiritual oppression where some negative entity has wormed its way into your life. Using bells, burning sage, creating circles of protection and white-lighting exercises can all work to get rid of any negative spiritual influences in your life.

⊷ Seeing shapes that float, dark spots, small lights or shadows... Perceiving ghosts can sometimes be like staring at a faint star. When looking directly at it, the star seems to fade or disappear. But when adjusting your vision to look at it slightly askew, the faint star comes into focus. The same is true of ghosts, especially if there are several moving about. Sometimes, apparitions are most visible when looking out of the corner of your eye, or in your peripheral vision, as it is called. Pay attention to movements that happen quickly, such as shadows, flying orbs and lights. Ghost orbs, (and other ghost images) can be seen by the human eye but they most often appear lightning quick. If you have recently become aware of such shapes around, you might try to capture them by using a camera of your choice. Prepare to take several pictures before capturing them. As mentioned before, they are as slippery as mercury and just quick! You can train yourself to recognize spirits. All you need is patience.

⊷ Waking up suddenly at the same time each night... This can clue you in on the hour that ghostly powers are most strong in your home. It can be your haunts waking you up in order to convey some message but never manage to make the connection or otherwise appear. Waking at the same hour can also indicate the hour your ghost may have died and this is his way of reminding you that he is not entirely gone. Continuance seems to be the main theme among ghosts. It is just one way of telling us that we never truly die.

➡ Hearing music or singing at odd hours and places when no one else is around... This is a strange one but easy to figure out. Music seems to remain important to those in the spirit world. Many ghosts communicate through music such as disembodied singing eking through when you're on the phone. It's not unusual for radios and tape players to start up in haunted houses when the radios or recorders have not even been turned on. Ghostly voices and choruses layered over the piped in elevator music, the kind played in hotels and Drs. Offices are fairly common. Often, the music has a religious tone, sounding like a Catholic mass or sopranos of angelic choirs. (Apparently there is no rock n' roll music in heaven and for that, we are disappointed.)

➡ When entering a room, you feel a presence as if a crowd has just left it... It is interesting to walk through a house and realize that empty rooms often feel full. The energy is still present, it seems, from all of the people who've lived or even visited there. Rooms that feel "full" are often the most haunted rooms in the houses, no matter if that energy feels light or heavy. This can clue you in to the most haunted areas of a home. If this happens in your search for ghosts a room that feels the most active is the one to pay the attention to.

➡ Last but not least, seeing someone who shouldn't be there... First of all, it's not like in the movies where ghosts appear as filmy, see-through apparitions, with full moon light misting around while some spirituous wind blows. Ghosts and apparitions often appear as solid and look much as they did in life. Sometimes the spirits are missing a head or their feet. This does not mean the ghost died in some violent way. This is because it takes great energy for ghosts to appear so the extremities of heads and feet tend to get left behind. However, because the apparition is mostly solid, we are tricked into thinking it is a living person we see. It is only when the spirit vanishes that we realize we have been in contact with the spirits of the dead. Poltergeists, of course, never look like animals or people since poltergeists are nothing more than unleashed psychic energies. Spirit recordings do appear as people or animals but usually perform the same act over and over again, without any real consciousness behind them. If you think you will die of fright upon seeing one very real apparition, think again. Apparitions disappear quickly, sometimes even before you can get them into full view. You won't have time to have heart failure. Ghosts normally vanish even more quickly than they originally appeared.

what if i want to get rid of my ghosts?

You actually want to get rid of your ghost? Even after we have assured you that probably nothing bad is going to happen? Okay, okay, we do have some techniques to banish spirits. Here is a list of a few things that you can do:

⤙ Smudging. Try burning some sage. This is a familiar Native American method for banishing negative spirits or entities. Buy a wand of sage at your local herb shop. Put some in an ashtray or shell, set it afire and let the smoke roll. Make sure you blow the smoke in the four directions.... This is very important in Native American spirituality. Sage supposedly gets rid of the bad ghosts. Plains Indians believe smoke travels upward into the spirit world. Ghosts will follow wherever the smoke goes. It is interesting to note that Sage is a natural antiseptic. Sage also makes baked turkey taste really good.

⤙ Using Bells or Cymbals. Spirits flee from sudden, high-pitched sounds, especially if the spirits are negative or base, or in other words, the baddies. The ringing sounds of bells or cymbals will shatter such ghosts. They hardly ever come back as strong if you keep this up. Brass bells work well. Cymbals from Tibetans are the finest ones I've ever used. Clapping your hands loudly, especially around the areas of the haunting can also be effective in getting rid of your ghosts. As before, spirits simply don't like shrill or loud clapping noises. Shamans throughout the world often use rattles, bells or clapping in their exorcism or other spiritual rituals.

⤙ Prayer. This can't hurt but it may not help that much either. You can use whatever prayer makes you feel the most comfortable. Admittedly, this is not the best defense against ghosts though. However, prayer does let your ghost know that you are seriously trying to put him out of your house.

⤙ Exorcism. Any number of spiritual leaders or clergy can perform an exorcism such as Catholic priests, fundamentalist preachers, psychics, Native American shamans and even Druids. One fair warning. Exorcism can make matters worse. Why? Many ghosts crave attention. They will gravitate where all of the excitement is. I recommend that you only resort to exorcism if nothing else seems to help. Exorcism can actually pull in other spirits and you'll have quite a ghostly mess on your hands.

➤ White Lighting Exercises. "White lighting" techniques have been popular in New Age circles for years. Each time you feel threatened by your spirits, visualize standing in a lit cocoon of protection symbolized by a brilliant white light. Some see themselves standing inside a white aura. This can help since it keeps you focused. Probably what this exercise actually does is to help center you so you can feel strong and in control of the situation. Ghosts and other spirits can be amazingly obedient to authority. Stay strong.

➤ Tell your ghosts that they are dead. This may sound far-fetched but earthbound spirits sometimes do not realize that they have already died. They will hang around places where they formerly lived or will gravitate toward people that are psychically receptive. In essence, this means your ghosts are just lost. What do you do? Enter the alpha state (in other words, relax and put yourself into a bit of a trance.) As soon as you feel you have made contact tell your ghost has died and that he must turn in the direction of the bright light so he can follow it to meet his relatives there.

➤ Ignore your ghost. Sometimes the simplest methods work the best. Hauntings happen in cycles. You may have a great deal of ghostly activity for a several weeks or months and then it will stop abruptly. The more you worry and panic over your spirits, the stronger they become. This is because the vast majority of spirits thrive on attention and sometimes the emotion fear. For instance, if a house or an area becomes well known for haunting activity, other spirits will be drawn there. This becomes the place where all of the fun is, spiritually speaking. It's like throwing a big party for your ghosts. Ignoring your ghosts, or learning to live with them, is the best approach. They generally just go away on their own.

13 places most likely to be haunted

In reading ghost stories, and listening to tales of the paranormal, it becomes pretty clear that spirits tend to choose to visit some places over others. It is important to point out, that in my opinion, there are spirits around us at any given time, but the energies of certain areas creates the right atmosphere for the ghost to appear. And, in literature and movies, we are probably right to assume ghosts gravitate in old places.

Why? More has happened in older places, and there is a longer history to the haunting, causing the right environment for "energy imprints," or a residual haunting. This doesn't mean the places need to look run down and scary. It just means old houses have more of what is called "place memory." Another interesting feature is, energy imprint ghosts, have no consciousness to them (at least in the current way that we understand) and won't be upset by anyone showing up in their place and snooping around. It is not likely a spirit recording is going to follow you home and annoy you, in the way another haunting might. Plus, these ghost imprints often show up in pictures, such as in the case of Bessie Bartlett, and the ghost hunter and ghost enthusiast is better able to capture the image by camera.

1. Cemeteries. This is a given! But when you really think about it on a deeper level, why would anyone want to go back to the place where her or his remains are buried? Cemeteries are places of high emotion, and ghosts are sensitive to this. This can help attract them. Also, some spirits may not completely accept the fact that they are dead and hang around until the body decays. This, of course, is not the primary reason that ghosts haunt cemeteries. It could also be that although such spirits may only exist in the afterlife, many like to be remembered and have their stories told. If people go to graveyards to remember their dead, the dead will often show up. Cemetery ghosts may learn to like it so well, they stick around to see who else is going to show up and ask about who they were and how they lived.

2. Churches. Another odd choice especially since most of us are stilled influenced by the demonology of the Reformation and Inquisition that evolved during the time. After all, churches are sacred grounds, aren't they? With Protestantism, there was no longer a purgatory –All souls either went to heaven or hell. If a haunting started, it had to originate in hell. That's what many people thought. But the British Isles has a long tradition of Churches being haunted. On the night of April 24th, St. Mark's Eve it was thought to be a time when the wraiths, phantoms and ghosts of those who will die in the coming year are said to wander through churchyards or pass through the front doors of the church. In Britain many believed those who were not baptized could glimpse dead people hoisting their coffins to the graveyard, perhaps with the idea that those not baptized were not able to distinguish good from evil. Many old churches have graveyards, as well, a good place to start a ghost hunt. As always, get permission first.

3. Battlefields. Since Gettysburg, Pennsylvania is perhaps the most haunted town in the United States, this tends to add to the theory that battlefields are notoriously haunted. Many areas of violence or high emotion are. The atmosphere can take only so much. Plus battlefields have the tragedy of lives cut short, creating a situation for many spirit recordings, as well as unsettled business ghosts. But as it is with most hauntings, battlefield ghosts, more often than not, are residual hauntings, meaning that if you are one to witness such a ghostly imprint such as a

Civil War solider sitting on a cannon and smoking a pipe, do not be alarmed because evidence is pretty clear that he can't see you.

4. Hospitals and Nursing Homes. Again, these are areas/buildings where most of us die and families go through grief, setting up a perfect environment for a haunting. Of course, going on a ghost hunt or an investigation in a medical facility is about as tacky as anyone can possibly get, but interviewing people who work in such places, discreetly, and outside of the nursing home or hospital is okay. In fact, I am always hearing from people who work in these places and they have some pretty amazing stories of dead people returning to visit often.

5. Museums. Naturally, museums have lots of old stuff. Old stuff of great historical and emotional value that tends to reign in ghosts, or at least, residual haunts. Objects themselves can be haunted, as there was many famous ghost tales about haunted dolls, haunted boxes and haunted furniture. Some friends and I once went on a ghost hunt in a local historical museum. Interestingly, the only objects that revealed ghost anomalies on our film and camera screens were the Indian artifacts buried away in the basement. Although some objects were said to be close to 12,000 years old, they were still the most spiritually active artifacts in the museum.

7. Any area where an act of violence or tragedy has occurred. In these areas, ghost investigators must use their own discretion. For reasons we do not clearly understand hauntings in such areas can be malevolent ones. It is as if malevolent spirits are attracted to the negativity of the place. However, if the tragedy or event happened long ago, it might not be quite as intense and or as active. Therefore, not as overwhelming to people who are sensitive to such things. Keep in mind many stories about murders or suicides may well be bogus or entirely made up. Check your facts before visiting such a place.

8. Tunnels. Perhaps, these create a vortex effect that pulls in or amplifies ghostly energies. No matter what your take is on haunted tunnels, there are so many haunted tunnel tales that attest to the fact that tunnels must be places that spirits love to lurk. A few of the hauntings may have to do with fatal train wrecks, accidents in caves, people losing their way and end up dying outside in the elements. If you are looking for a place to investigate and your area has a few tunnels that are safe to visit, you might want to ask around about the stories surrounding such tunnels. It is likely that your state or region may have a haunted tunnel, or two. These are often quite spooky to visit after dark. So, you might want to avoid railroad tunnels that are still used, or check the schedule. You don't want to end up as a ghost on your own investigation.

9. Schools. Everyone knows children see and draw spirits better than adults do. For this reason, spirits are wildly attracted to schools as well. I can't begin to tell you how many pictures that hit my email box with ghost anomalies that have been taken at school graduations, and also at children's birthday parties, of all things! There is a lot of evidence that shows that spirits, the kind that need to communicate (and not the spirit recording type) thrive on excitement and children can add energy aplenty to the environment. This doesn't mean we should encourage our children to channel, visit graveyards after dark or play with Ouija boards. It does mean that when children start talking about people or personalities that others cannot see, you should listen to them. Abandoned schools, as long as you can get permission to go in, are a good place to investigate the spirit world, especially schools that once had a religious angle.

10. Crossroads. Of course, universally the crossroads are considered to be a place of spiritual power but also, danger. Usually when something has a long history behind it throughout different cultures, there may be some truth to it. Some of the crossroad's powers might have to do with the Christian cross exerting mystical powers over the area except that a belief in the crossroads pre-dates Christianity by several centuries and the powers believed to be in place at the crossroads are not usually thought of as positive. Abandoned houses at a crossroads in rural areas might be an interesting place to investigate. Of course, get an okay from the owners, if there are any.

11. Hotels. Much like hospitals and schools, hotels have a lot of foot traffic passing through them. Because many different people stay in hotels over a number of years it should come as no surprise, that hotels with some age to them, are likely to be haunted by one type of spirit or another. Some of the older hotels typically have many spirits. Can anyone, for instance, who stays in one of the hotel's "haunted rooms" get to see its ghost? (Pardon me— this always makes us giggle a bit.) Firstly, over time, certain rooms will have "spirit activity" but this almost always changes, just like the spirits who stay in or visit the hotel. It's hard to predict where a spirit will appear. But a good way to start out an investigation is in the area where there was a recent sighting or spirit activity, and also, an area that has a history of sightings and ghostly experiences. Staying in a "haunted room" almost never pans out for your basic ghost hunting hotel guest who does not have any ghost hunting experience. It is only the people who don't expect to see a ghost, are invariably the ones that do.

12. Historical homes or Estates. Now we come to "The Old House on Haunted Hill" part of the book. This is just the fodder some scary movies are made of. Hollywood makes those kinds of movies because there is an element of truth to them. Older homes, as well as family estates, tend to have had a number of owners over the years and sometimes those owners have personalities that attract ghosts, have fooled around with elements of spiritualism, such as playing with Ouija Boards, or basically are the spirits or imprints of the people who formerly lived there who may return for an occasional visit or the house may be in close proximity to an old cemetery or even a Native American burial ground or sacred site. Old houses are also interesting to investigate, especially if the owners are open to such things.

13. Theatres. As any Shakespearean, (or other kind of) actor will tell you "Every theatre has a ghost." Theatres are areas, once again, that bring out strong emotions in the people who visit them. Couple that with tragic or complex emotional tales that may belong to the road shows or vaudeville acts passing through and you set up the atmosphere for a haunting. Like bookstores that have their own resident cat, many theatres, especially the older, historical variety have their own resident ghost.

Encountering ghosts is endlessly fascinating. Their existence indicates that there are things that remain that we don't completely understand about our world, or even the world beyond. Observe your ghosts and be in on the secret of one of life's great mysteries. What the appearance of your ghosts proves is that there is a world beyond and such things are worth looking into.

14. are you ready to meet your ghosts?

Linking up with the spirit world is really not so difficult and there are many methods that can be used to achieve communications with ghosts. Overall, spirits usually have quite a lot to say – that's one reason they turn up and appear!

Psychic mediums have the easiest time of contacting the spirit world through their special talents – abilities, in truth, that many are born with but learn to deny. This form of spirit communication, really, is a most subtle kind. You just have to learn how to recognize the signs and feelings—by seeing the pictures and getting the messages—as many television psychics have done and, we might add, have attracted a great deal of money and fame in doing so.

But let us now look at the more blatant type of way that ghosts can manifest. These are the kinds of spontaneous appearances that lead to the famous ghost tales. This is when you actually see the ghost—no, not as in a dream—as a living, breathing person—right before your very eyes!

This is a type of intrusion from the spirit world. It simply means your ghosts want to get a message across. You don't have to be a psychic to see ghosts this way. In fact, ten percent of the population claims to have seen a ghost.

Incidentally, don't buy into all that touchy-feely-New-Age stuff that states that only psychics can see spirits. We've found that when ghosts appear in an obvious way, the witness seldom considers himself to be psychic and may have only had a few paranormal experiences, if any, throughout his life. Truthfully, getting a ghost account from one of your basic salt-of-the-earth types can have more credibility than from people who consider themselves shamans or psychics or visionaries because pretty much, the last thing Ol' Salt of the Earth was expecting to see is a ghost! That means the spirit has made itself really blatant and very much wanted to make the witness aware of his presence.

With this spontaneous appearance of an apparition, the spirits look very much as they did in life, wearing the clothes that they once wore (ones you may even recognize) and typically appear to be around the age of 30 to 35 years old but also the age the spirit wants to project. Some speculate thirty is an ideal age or perhaps is when the person feels the most vital during physical life.

Of course, small children who have died prematurely will appear as children. This is common. At times the ghost will show up as older though. It is usually if there is something about that particular age the ghost is trying to communicate. Or, possibly, as with the Chancellor ghost at the Blennerhassett Hotel, this gentle spirit was at his peak career-wise around the age of 60 when the hotel was thriving or when he was mayor of Parkersburg.

With such full-bodied apparitions, you may be surprised to learn that most appear for only a minute or seconds—almost like a flicker of lighting. You typically shudder and think, "Did I just see that?" This is why some eyewitnesses are lead to believe that they may have hallucinated until they meet others who have had a similar sighting in the same place.

It is rare to be spoken to by an apparition, but as in the case of Zona Shue, the Greenbrier Ghost, it is possible. Apparitions tend to communicate their feelings or intents through their expressions, such as looking pleased or melancholy. Sometimes the key to their message is in the area where they appear, perhaps near a grave or an old chest, a house, a building, records, or even a piece of furniture.

At times, such apparitions are even photographed as human figures in the windows of haunted houses and also other areas. Not frequent, but it can happen.

Rackets, such as footsteps, voices, thumping noises or even the sounds of water running or ice being dropped into a sink also can also be categorized as a type of apparition. Sounds associated with ghosts are really the way most hauntings start out.

The other way to perceive spirits is through clairvoyance or a type of inner vision. Psychics have honed such talents and can communicate or visualize such energies, receiving messages, symbols or words that are somehow important to the spirit when he or she was alive. This is more like channeling, as the connection is made through psychic's cultivated sense of awareness. However, this can open a doorway for other communications with the spirit world.

Often after visiting a psychic medium, people can actually experience genuine spiritual contact - such as loved ones pictures floating up out of their frames, lights switching off and on, music blasting, or even objects associated with the deceased person will suddenly show up quite mysteriously. Many people miss such attempts to communicate from the spirits because they lack awareness of such ghostly happenings that a psychic has learned to look for in understanding the messages and symbols.

Other than being besieged by pushy ghosts, or visiting a psychic medium, how else can we detect spirits? By conducting your own séance, of course. Does this work? You'd better believe séances work despite all of the chicanery that happened during the Victorian ages to cause people like Harry Houdini to expose numerous frauds. In most instances, if you attempt to contact your spirits, most will respond. So be prepared.

Are séances safe? Yes, as long as you have a group of down to earth people with open minds and sincere hearts. Plus, it's a lot easier (and cleaner) than reading the entrails of gutted sheep the way ancient seers did to communicate with the spirit world in the 'good-old-back-before-the-bible days.'

We will cover all the basics of the séance later on in this chapter. Now you just need to understand the differences in types of spirits, and how and why they choose to haunt.

definitions of ghosts & spirits & other otherworldly things

↪ **Ghost.** We all know this one, now don't we? Ghosts are disembodied spirits of the dead that return to the earth plane to haunt a place, usually to convey a particular meaning to a specific person or to many. Ghosts are typically the ones responsible for most of the hauntings. Ghost can also be a generic term used to describe all manner of spirits, however - such as "the Holy Ghost." You see, what I mean? Very few spirits are malevolent in nature. You meet them occasionally, but not often. Most religions have a concept of evil spirits, and call them demons. Of course, in ancient times, the word that demon came from a word that meant "intelligence." Universally, demons are a part of religious beliefs but at this point have no place in science.

↪ **Spirit.** Another generic term for ghosts, some spirits do not have to have lived as humans, or as animals previously. Spirits can be angels, elemental forces of nature, the Arabic jinn, or fairies or any number of spiritual beings that are thought to have a focus and intelligence. Ghosts, however, are most often believed to be spirits of the dead that are attached to a place. Even so, the words "ghosts" and "spirits" can be interchangeable in their meanings.

↪ **Spirit Recordings.** Also called residual hauntings, ghost sightings, especially those that happen over and over again in the same way, can be a spirit recording that is responsible for the haunting. They are simply a residual energy that survives death, but no longer has a consciousness behind the haunting. In other words, you would not be able to communicate with a spirit recording anymore than you could communicate with a couple dancing on videotape. These are simply "shadows." There is rarely any awareness behind this kind of ghost. Some spirit recordings are psychic formations from the decedents last thoughts, though, shortly before they died. In some cases, though, such as apparitions of beheaded Queens who float about the tower of London— it's as if sad memories are saying, "Look what injustice has been done to me! Be reminded and do not allow this to happen again."

 ᴴ **Poltergeists.** You probably know the answer to this one, too, but if you don't: No, the movie of the same name has little or nothing to do with actual poltergeists! Poltergeists are not spirits of the dead. These rocking, rolling, thumping and banging ghosts are believed to be 'thought forms,' or deeply buried, psychic powers hidden within the human brain that are sporadically released through unconscious psychological tension. Sounds of footsteps, objects moving, missing things, mysterious fires starting as well as odd odors can also be aligned with poltergeist appearances. Poltergeists do hang out around kids – teenagers, to be precise – and while, for many years we believed poltergeists were telekinetic forces brought to the surface by the stress of puberty, recently we have found out that where there are poltergeists, there are usually other ghosts and haunts lurking about.

 ᴴ **Apparition.** Apparitions are usually spirits that clearly visible or palpable in some way that appeals to the five or six senses—meaning: When a spirit is called an apparition this suggests there has been at least one eyewitness to the ghost. However, appearances of apparitions can also be related to divinity, God, Gods, Goddesses (we have to be fair here) and religious figures such as saints. For instance, when visitations of the Virgin Mary are reported at Catholic holy areas, such a sighting is also called an apparition. Spirits appearing as they did in life as real people are also classic apparitions. Appearances of apparitions are usually very short-lived and rarely photographed. Some apparitions look solid. Others come across a blur.

 ᴴ **Entity.** Can describe anything that is not clearly understood – so a haunted house might have an "entity" haunting it, but a four-foot-high, gray creature or a tall dude in a black coat walking out of a spaceship can also be called entities.' When we use the word entity, this means we know it is something– we just don't know exactly what it is in its present form.

⌐ **Phantasm, Phantom, Specter, Spook, Wraith, Haint, Booger, Haunt, Ghoul, Spirit Guide.** These terms all pretty much relate to ghosts, spirits and their related lore. Another odd fact about sightings of apparitions is that many ghosts are missing parts of their bodies once they appear. Sometimes the spirit shows up without feet – sometimes as disembodied hands or a torso. This might imply the person died violently. This is not at all the case. Some say that is takes a great deal of energy for the ghost to appear or look as he did in life. Often, something has to be left behind... sometimes it's the head, at other times the feet or even the body – someone shows up as a floating head and that's it! Such appearances are not only left up to British Tower Queens or people who've had their heads chopped off in some battle or accident – other ghosts do it, too. If you read up on ghosts you'll learn all manner of apparitions drift or walk about without their heads.

Some ghosts just throw in the towel and don't even try to appear as they once did— It's too damned hard! These kind of spirits manifest as ghost orbs, mists, vortexes and other light anomalies. For the same reason as above, it's just a whole lot less hassle for the spirit to appear this way.

conclusion

why we are convinced the spirit world is real and why we believe spirits wish to & do communicate with the living ⌐⌐⌐

In this book, we have covered a number of otherworldly presences that we believe to be spirits of the dead as well as other types of beings we still do not clearly understand. We know them by their names given as the Mothman, the Marrtown and Center Point Banshees, the Flatwoods Monster, and Indrid Cold... But this is just what we call them.

In studying such things, it is clear there is a science of ghosts and the paranormal, but then there is also the "fun stuff." We can give you the science behind the listings above where we speculate (and we hoped we have done that) but heck, that's not as much fun. Truthfully, we can probably only explain such mysterious occurrences only slightly better than ghost experts did in the past. Admittedly, though, we are getting closer to the truth.

We have quickly learned on our journey into the surreal world of the paranormal that there are "presences," and such beings permeate our day-to-day existence. They are not just some rare haunted house incident or reports of ghosts. It is also apparent that many such spirits are still interested in interacting with living persons and remain curious about life on earth. They show us this time and time again through their actions and their interest in communicating with the living.

It really doesn't matter what we call our ghosts. If you call them something, they will come. As we have found, spirits are greatly responsive to human beings.

Many years ago the British Society for Psychical Research attempted a unique experiment. Members made up a name for a spirit guide and began to have séances where they attempted to communicate with this self-created spirit. The unexpected happened. Their ghost began to tip over the furniture, ring bells, make noises and was more active than any true spirit they had a real name for.

Spirits are eager to communicate, and even if you are the least little bit aware, and if you have an interest in their world, they will let you know.

If you are a Scottish Immigrant in the 1800s, and the spirit of a ghostly woman on a pale horse finds you on a lonely trail above some body of water, then she is probably a Banshee whose story was told in ages past. However, if you are near Point Pleasant, West Virginia in 1966 and something large and gray flies over you then tries to outrace your car, you can assume it is the Mothman.

If you are poor, black and living in the Mississippi Delta in the 1920s, that strange man you met at the Crossroads is mostly likely the Devil. But if you are a Black Dutch West Virginian named Woodrow Derenberger, and you encounter a dark-haired, olive-complexioned man at another Crossroads, on I-77 and Route 47 south of Parkersburg in November of 1966, to be exact, it is not the Devil you met it is the alien Indrid Cold.

A few years ago, a paranormal researcher from Virginia named Bo Kitchens drove up to the Parkersburg area with his wife Debbie. We had a splendid time covering haunts and hunting ghosts that afternoon. Bo and Debbie were genuinely enthused when it came to searching out ghosts. Bo, in particular, solved a number of mysteries that had always intrigued us on our ghost tour, things we never understood until he explained them to us.

When Bo and Debbie left, we thought it might be a great idea to put on a ghost conference in the Ohio Valley, an area so obviously rich with haunted activity. But before we were able to finalize plans, a tragedy unfolded. At only thirty-eight-years old, Bo suddenly died.

Although we only spent a few short hours with Bo and Debbie Kitchens in 2001, we were saddened over the loss of such a special person as Bo, a most kind and decent man.

As the ghost tour came on stronger than ever in the fall of 2001, I (Susan Sheppard) led a troupe of schoolchildren from Mannington, West Virginia on the ghost walk. Atypically, the tour took place during a bright and colorful afternoon in mid October.

The air was clear and sunny. I thought it might be nice to take the kids directly in front of the Captain's House on Juliana Street. It had an interesting casement window where Captain's pipe is often seen smoldering with an orange glow. I noticed the house was happily decorated for Halloween, and this always makes tour guides feel good that neighborhoods along the ghost walk seem to have as much fun as the visitors do.

As I told the ghostly tale of the sea captain who allegedly haunts the home, one little girl turned and commented to her friend, "Why, look there. That sign says 'Bo.'"

Shocked, I glanced over my shoulder to look at the Halloween decorations. I, too, recognized what the sign read. One of the 'o's had fallen off of the word "Boo."

The Halloween sign now read "Bo." Beside it was the cartoon of a smiling ghost.

Such mysterious incidents are why we firmly believe in a world of spirits and how many wish to continue communicating with the living. The real fact is no living energy ever ceases to exist. It is only transformed into something different. And despite the human sadness that is often lost in these tales of haunts, as in Bo's very real story, we feel fortunate in the fact that we know clearly that life goes on.

Life is a blessing, so much so, that spirits often have to remind us.

So, have fun while you're here, spirit-seekers. The spirits want you to. Take joy in your meeting up with a few new friends, that others like to call "ghosts."

glossary of terms

anomaly

An event, an image, or a thing, than cannot be explained by the usual means. Most ghost anomalies appear in pictures. In reference to ghosts, anomalies may be a spirit when the image or anomaly cannot be ruled out by ordinary means. The West Virginia Mothman might also be considered an anomaly since there was no sighting of any such creature before or after the years of 1966 and 1967. An anomaly is something we cannot yet explain away by rational or scientific means. Anomalies are things that deviate from the norm.

apparition

An apparition is usually a ghost with an identity or a personality that the living can recognize or see - if only for a few brief seconds. Apparitions usually appear much as the person did in life and often as solid. Typically, the clothing looks touchable as does the rest of the ghost appear- except a few may lack legs, feet, hands or a head. (This is not rare, believe it or not.) Hauntings are not rare but solid apparitions are somewhat. Supposedly, it takes great energy for ghosts to fully materialize and look as they once did. When seeing an apparition, don't blink your eyes. Many apparitions only show themselves for seconds - just enough time to make an impression.

aura

A field, thought to electromagnetic in nature that is said to surround the physical body, appearing as colored lights, bands and energy patterns. Although psychics are usually the only ones who are supposed to see or detect auras, auras can also be glimpsed in shadowy areas such as movie theaters or darkened rooms by ordinary people as well. Health conditions, talents and personality are evident in the human aura.

automatism

Automatism is a practice, a talent or a discipline that allows communications from the spirit world to flow easily to the living by such means as an Ouija board or automatic writing. Psychic Edgar Cayce accomplished automatism by going to sleep and by allowing the spirit messages to be taken down by his secretary. Upon wakening, Cayce had no conscious knowledge of the psychic information that he had been given while in a sleeplike trance.

banshee

An Irish or Scottish attendant death fairy associated with certain Irish and Scottish clans. Banshees appear as women, young and old, ugly or beautiful, but most reports have them with blood red eyes, caused by their endless weeping for the dead of one of the members of their Irish or Scottish clans. Sometimes the Banshee rides a pale horse followed by a hearse. At other times, she hangs out at waterways, wailing over her dead.

Interestingly, three Irish clans that have been associated with Banshees are the O'Kennedys, the O'Lennons and O' Reagans. These names were later shortened to Kennedy, Lennon and Reagan – names of three famous men who were shot by assassins in the 20th Century America. The United States has had more presidents of Irish descent that any other nationality.

banishment

Banishment is a type of ritual, spell or form of magic used to cleanse and chase away negative spirits, emotions and outcomes. Banishment is possibly a Wiccan (the modern religion of Witchcraft) response to the Christian Exorcism. Although the Christian form of banishment has more to do with a belief in devils and driving out diabolical forces, the Wiccan variety emphasizes getting rid of a force that is simply negative, not necessarily evil, or banishing spiritual forces that are not particularly healthy or useful.

black cat

Long thought to be witches familiars (helpers), black cats date back to a time in Ancient Egypt where cats were worshipped, lovingly cared for and deified – after all many cats were entombed with Egyptian royalty. There is no evidence that a black cat is more special than any other feline – other than the effects they have on our imaginations as shadowy forms, forever in tune with the mysterious powers of the night.

black dog

Until recently, pretty much a British phenomena, black dogs have been associated with all type of occult powers and the underworld of darkness, seeming to bridge this world with the world of the dead. The belief in black dogs as harbingers of death and as glowering eyed watcher of graveyards, can be traced in a modern form to Arthur Conan Doyle's "Hounds of the Baskervilles" even though the legend of the Black Dog precedes this Sherlock Holmes classic. The legend of the black dog may even trace to the Greek Goddess Hecate—overseer of witchcraft, the crossroads and night magic—who always traveled with three black hounds at her side and sometimes with a raven perched on her shoulder.

Master occultists say that if you hear more than one hound baying in your neighborhood late at night, you can be sure that Hecate is prowling the streets, working her special brand of witchcraft.

black dutch

A mysterious group of dark-skinned, small, colorfully dressed people who settled among the Pennsylvania Dutch in Pennsylvania with whom they shared a language. Many later settled in West Virginia. Evidence is growing that the Black Dutch were, in fact, partly German Gypsies (or Rom) who lived with the Pennsylvania Dutch and shared with them their unique forms of magic. This includes a belief in the Crossroads, spells, ghosts, powwowing, séances and the practice of witchcraft that most likely dates back to their point of earliest origin, India. Having "Black Dutch," "Black Swiss," or "Dirty Dutch" ancestry in West Virginia is common, especially in the northern part of the state where some descendents of Pennsylvania Dutch. West Virginia's "Black Irish" are thought to be of Welsh ancestry. But the "Black Irish" have a wedding tradition of "Jumping the Broomstick" that was earlier practiced by Romanian Gypsies in the 1400s.

boggart

Related to the Night Hag, a Boggart is a mischievous ghost that crawls into the beds of sleeping people, sometimes pulling the covers off, or placing cold hands on the otherwise unaware. A horseshoe tacked over the door is said to keep Boggarts away.

charged areas

An area or a place that has become psychically charged with unseen energies because of it being a sacred place, an area of religious relevance, or a spot that has experienced high emotion and that can be in a positive or negative way. A charged area might be an Indian burial ground, an abandoned building that may have had lots of parties or festivities, but more typically an area where a suicide, murder or unsolved death has taken place. This probably stems from the fact the hauntings that tend to get our attention are not usually the happiest ones.

corpse candles

Corpse Candles are lights seen over graveyards, churchyards or other haunted areas. In England, they are sometimes called "fetchlights," or "spooklights," and are thought to predict the death of a family member. Corpse Candles come in all sizes and appear in almost any color.

contactee

A person who has one or more direct experiences with alien intelligences connected to UFOs and other type of spacecraft. While some may have a direct, physical encounter with outer-space aliens, such as the claims of Mineral Wells resident Woodrow Derenberger. Other contactees report to connect with or contact such alien intelligences through guided imagery or a type of trance-state where they receive messages from other planets, galaxies and civilizations through telepathy or thought transference.

conjure book

Oddly, the bible was referred to by some Pennsylvania Dutch as "conjure books" by which they used to divine knowledge or to be used in their ritual magic and spells. There is no evidence that this unusual form of magic is being practiced today, but there is no evidence that it is not either! The PA Dutch have been known to be secretive.

crossroads

The Crossroads is a place of spiritual danger, where devils, witches, vampires and ghouls are thought to lurk. Some evidence suggests that the Crossroads as a haven for evil ghosts was brought by the Gypsies to Eastern Europe in their travels – a concept having originated much earlier in India. Legends surrounding the Crossroads have been incorporated into the Hoodoo practices along the Mississippi Delta and also in New Orleans. A book about Pennsylvania Dutch magic entitled "The Long Lost Friend" was written and published in 1820, and later circulated among freed blacks in New Orleans (among them Marie LaVeau, "Queen of Voodoo" from New Orleans –1792-1897) and other towns along the Mississippi. This theory has not been proven, but it remains a compelling argument.

curse

An ill-omen caused by evil words or thoughts – or – a profane proclamation by individuals with special powers to bring about bad luck upon whomever they choose by the chanting of words, uttering threats or by using the evil eye, or sharp glance. Curses were said fueled by vengeance, avarice or jealousy. The ancients feared curses to such an extent that the tradition of wearing a bridal veil in the beginning was a way to cast off any evil eye or jealous looks by envious women or men attending the wedding. Such an act would surely bring ill luck to the marriage. In truth, more evil has been brought on by those who think they are cursed, such as in the Salem Witch Trials than the reality of a life that failed all on its own, which is a lot more true and considerably more dull.

doppelganger

Doppelganger is a German word for a ghostly double that is said to appear to foretell an early death. The poet Shelley spotted his doppelganger outside one of the terraces of his then residence in Northern Italy. Shelley spied his soft profile floating by one of the terrace windows and drowned a few days later. President Lincoln also encountered his doppelganger when he was up late and heard a rapping on the door to his study in the White House. When Lincoln opened the door, he met his own image standing there. The image quickly faded. In a few short months, Lincoln was dead.

earthbound spirit

An Earthbound Spirit ghost that, for whatever reason, cannot move on, as they did in life. Somehow, they are "spiritually stuck." Such spirits are then doomed to return to the places where they lived, or perhaps to the area where their remains have been placed. Many believe the reason is such spirits are confused, or they don't know how to "go into the light" or vanish into the arms of God, or the rewards of heaven. In reality, this is rarely the case as oftentimes spirits stick around to get their message across, or perhaps, they want to return to check on their relatives or to just re-experience the happy times.

Saying ghosts are "angels who have not graduated into heaven," as I have heard TV psychics claim, is simply wrong and very unfair to these ghostly manifestations. Many ghosts lived wonderful, productive lives and sometimes, they simply want to return and listen to stories about their lives on earth, how they are still thought of and wish to visit loved ones. Demonizing ghosts is a destructive force in modern ghost theories.

ectoplasm

A misty yet dense substance that turns up during times of communications with ghosts or spirits or in haunted areas as well as in ghost photography. They tend to look like dense streaks or have appendages. During the 19th and early 20th Century, any medium worth her salt would always produce ectoplasm at séances. This was a crowd-pleaser but usually fake. The bogus ectoplasm had the consistency of a stringy cheese and was usually made from household chemicals or detergent foam whipped up right before the séance. Real ectoplasm is rarely picked up by the naked eye. In ghost photographs the ectoplasm resembles a whitish, misting effect, one that is cloudy and stringy and is denser than what should be present in the atmosphere for the time.

electromagnetic field

Electromagnetic Field is the electrical force field that surrounds or permeates life. Many believe areas that are haunted will show high electromagnetic readings. Scientists dispute this, saying most areas and all living things radiate electromagnetic fields.

entity

The presence of a spirit personality that does not have any human-related physical form and in most instances the entity does not actually have a physical body. The word "entity" is often used to describe a spiritual being when we do not know what it is, defying definition. This can be a generic term used early in ghost investigations – before the ghost hunters come to a decision as to who it is really haunting the place. In many instances, they never clearly know and entity is as good a word as any other while explaining an otherwise, unknown, unseen presence.

evil spirits

A belief in evil spirits has always been with humankind since humans pondered discarnate ghosts and spirits of the dead. However, most spirit appearances have nothing to do with evil. Such forces do exist and there are certain things one can do to protect oneself against spiritual evil.

Although Evil spirits can mask themselves as something else, they often turn up as foul odors, clammy bone-chilling coldness, drug or alcohol abuse, thoughts of suicide or murder, sadistic fantasies or dreams of violence, rage, jealousy, and any number of negative patterns. The way to have power and authority over evil spirits is to not fall prey to such things.

evps

Refers to the tape recording of ghostly voices on a cassette recorder. This can be done with your basic tape recorder and cassette tapes, but often the sound levels have to be adjusted with more sensitive equipment to pick up the subtleties of spirit voices and their messages. It is always best to address to the spirits and communicate with them. This seems to bring about the most successful results.

exorcism

A religious rite sanctioned by the Catholic Church used to drive evil spirits out of victims thought to be suffering from spirit possession associated with the Devil and his battle for control over the earth plane. Exorcisms are still not common, but a few have been practiced by some non-Catholic faiths. A few victims will improve after the exorcism while others may get worse. Full possession by evil spirits, is most likely rare, but being possessed by self-destructive habits and unwholesome impulses may be helped or curtailed by the hope of some higher power or religious authority.

extraterrestrial

Living creatures from other planets or galaxies that are said to visit earth. Also called aliens, most extraterrestrial life appears to have a consciousness that helps them understand the human condition.

fairies

Especially among the Celts, fairies are intelligent beings associated with the earth, astral and supernatural realms. Some fairies have been thought to be expressions of the forces of nature and other elements. The Celts associated fairies as governing the last earth phase before a soul passes over into the astral. In ancient times, some fairies were linked to the spirits of the dead and many were feared. To slide into entropy, depression or hopelessness meant that you had given up and were being "fairy led." In ancient belief, this was not a good thing.

fetch

Fetch is an English word for the ghostly double. The poet Shelley glimpsed his fetch or ghostly double walking the window on a terrace where he was staying only a few short weeks before his death.

ghost

The essence of a living being that is believed to have survived death. Most believe ghosts are personalities of people or animals that continue to live on in the spirit world, but sometimes they will return to people places that were dear to them or somehow connected to them in life. Some view the word "ghost" as something to be feared or as a bad thing. But most hauntings have no evil or diabolical element. Many ghosts will return to visit their earthly remains, making one wonder what happens when bodies are cremated. Are the ghosts upset?

ghostly hitchhiker

Stories of the ghostly hitchhiker are universal and occur in many countries, not just the U.S. Usually the spirit is of a young woman lost in a rainstorm that flags down a ride. During the ride, the young woman says very little, but directs the driver to a specific place – sometimes a house, a cemetery, or a graveyard. As they near the destination, the driver will turn around only to find the girl gone.

As the driver attempts to locate the young woman, he will often find out that a young woman of the exact same description died – either on the spot where she was picked up – or left at the cemetery where she is buried.

ghoul

A ghoul is a type of ghost that haunts graveyards and the crossroads and eats human flesh. Ghouls are really more akin revenants (the re-animated dead,) zombies and vampires, than to spirits or ghosts. A ghoul is considered a type of a ghost. However, one doesn't want to cross paths with a ghoul. They can be evil and capable of murder.

granny witch

A mountain term for a mature woman who practices various mystical arts passed down through her family or community. The Granny Witch is usually consulted for folk remedies, the use of herbs, midwifery, the right times to plant, the best times to get pregnant or contact ghosts. But many times young women will consult the Granny Witch for the reading of tea leaves, divining the future with playing cards, mirrors, tokens as well as suggestions for special love and marriage spells.

haint

A southern mountain term used to describe various types of ghosts that haunt the areas. Much folklore surrounds stories of "haints" in the Appalachia. Most haints are thought to be menacing spirits, much like the 'boogers' that haunt mountain hollows.

haunting

A period of time associated with a place, such as a tavern, home, railroad tunnel and other areas that report ghostly or other unexplained activity.

hexen or hexenmeister

Hexen or Hexenmeister are the German words for witch, male or female. Hexens were the bane for the Pennsylvania Dutch whose ancestors ended up in not only Pennsylvania, but also parts of Appalachia. Although witchcraft was freely practiced by the Pennsylvania Dutch – they remained superstitious over hexing and using hexen "powers"—evidence shows a great deal of spiritual warfare fought between the Hexenmeisters in not only Pennsylvania, but Maryland, Ohio and West Virginia.

hex

A magick spell among German peoples that is meant to stop someone from attaining something you'd rather they not attain – such as something that belongs to you or something you feel you must protect. A hex might be used to protect your livestock and your family from the Evil Eye or some other evil intentions. Hexes also shield you from starvation and poverty. Hexes can also cause negative events to happen. The best person to cast a hex was a Hexenmeister or witch. Although the PA Dutch used Hexenmeisters, they also greatly feared them. Therefore, being a Hexenmeister in the 19th and early 20th Century among the PA Dutch was a pretty lonely profession. A number of Hexenmeisters ended up murdered because of rumors of diabolical hexes or suspicions of evildoing.

incubus

A spirit entity that many believe to be a demon or ghost that has sex with human women while they are sleeping or unable to move, speak or cry out. This phenomenon was reported on widely in the Medieval times and revealed women as witches for having sex with the Devil. In reality, this phenomena is related to the Night Hag experience, a psychological state, and may be caused by brain patterns firing in the temporal lobe area while women are sleeping that leaves them vulnerable to all types of weird, nightmarish sensations. Still women who have had this bizarre, ghostly rape insist the experience was a real attack and not an hallucination.

inter-dimensional being

A being that is capable of passing through dimensions, such as fairies, banshees, aliens, ghosts, Mothman, Men In Black and any number entities that can slip through space and time, without human intervention, detection or even belief.

intuitive

An intuitive is a sensitive person who can "read between the lines." This means, an individual who is able to put two and two together, tally up all of the information and with more than a dash of psychic ability, will come up with the correct answer even while having little information to go on. In most instances, women are more intuitive than men are. This probably stems from the fact the more intuitive one is, the better chance for survival and protecting one's young.

kinetic energy

Thought to be an energy contained within an object that can be released through some psychic means. This is usually associated with poltergeists but sometimes other kinds of haunting. It is likely spirits can tap into the kinetic energy of people and other surrounding objects.

ley lines

Ley Lines are considered to be Earth Energy lines that either cross over or are aligned over several strategic spots in compliance with ancient stone or earth monuments, especially those in the British Isles. But this theory has moved to America. Ley Lines are believed to exude great psychic powers and all types of paranormal activity found along their path and this includes spirit formations, UFOs and ghosts. Parts of the Alleghenies and the Mid-Ohio Valley are situated along Ley Lines formed by ancient Adena and Hopewell Indian burial mounds that surround parts of West Virginia, southern Ohio, Kentucky and Pennsylvania. Many Adena mounds are over two thousand years old.

magick

Magic with a "k" is used to distinguish from stage magic, such as that practiced by Harry Houdini and others. Magick, instead, derives from more ancient form of High Magick related to sorcery and the bringing about of miracles through supernatural means, instead of the usual sleight of hand stage and card tricks. Among the two, "magick" is more difficult to achieve than "magic" but many mediums have resorted to the use of sleight-of-hand variety in faked séances. These were the ones Harry Houdini debunked. magick, on the otherhand, demands endurance and is more difficult, and to many, impossible to achieve.

mediumship

Popularized in the 1980s as channeling, mediumship is a psychic talent where a gifted individual allows certain spirits to take over his or her consciousness, allowing them to dictate messages for the living from other realms or the grave. This can occur at a séance, where people are gathered for the purpose of speaking to the dead and other souls, or through an individual who does not have to go into a trance to receive the messages. Instead, as in the case of psychic medium John Edwards, a calming of the consciousness and voyaging inward is enough to meet up and receive messages from the souls of deceased relatives. It is very possible that we are all capable of spirit communication with dead relatives and other souls, but we don't take the time to quiet our consciousness minds, nor do we have the faith or insight in understanding the information that we are receiving. A good medium can do this.

men-in-black

Linked with the appearance of flying saucers and aliens, Men in Black are just that – two or three men wearing black, usually dressed in suits – but sometimes in pants and shirts – who appear to interrogate and subtly threaten contactees who claim contact with outer space beings or UFOs. Although some have speculated the Men in Black are government agents, their behavior often comes across as downright "alien."

During the Mothman sightings and Woodrow Derenberger's account of meeting Indrid Cold in November of 1966, several Men in Black were later spotted in parts of the Ohio Valley. Most were described as having exotic or "gypsy looks" and dark almond-shaped eyes. They dressed nicely enough and may fit right in with our current age of black clothing. But writer John Keel found the Men in Black to be menacing when he was writing "The Mothman Prophecies" (see below) and although the men dressed in dark clothes seemed pleasant, Keel viewed them as dangerous and not to be trusted.

mothman

A pale, gray (although some have reported him as being flesh-colored) creature with the wingspan of about 20 feet and standing more than six feet was sighted over 100 times in West Virginia and southern Ohio in 1966 leading into 1967. This supernatural being was the subject of several popular books and movies including John Keel's classic 1970s The Mothman Prophecies and later, the movie 2002 of the same name starring actor Richard Gere.

night (old) hag

An extremely disturbing psychological state that occurs during sleep when one wakes up suffocating, crushed, paralyzed and even sexually violated by what seems to be a demon or a ghost. There are many theories surrounding the Night Hag experience. It happens much more frequently to women than to men. One theory has it the Night Hag is caused from firing in the temporal lobe area of the brain while sleeping the part that oversees imagination and sensation, and the victim wakes up hallucinating. Theorists say that the paralysis the victim experiences during the Night Hag assault is caused by a protective mechanism in the brain that keeps people from thrashing around and hurting themselves during nightmare or dreams. Regardless what experts say, the Night Hag does seem to be connected to hauntings and many interpret this bizarre experience as an alien abduction. Since the Night Hag assault often leaves victims exhausted in the morning, there are many who think the phenomenon may have inspired beliefs in energy draining ghosts or vampires in Europe and America.

necromancy

Necromancy is communication, of any kind, with alleged ghosts or spirits of the dead. Although the Christian and Jewish Bibles warn against necromancy numerous times throughout, it is still practiced every day by people who speak to deceased relatives through prayer, use a ouija board, hold séances or attempt to connect with the souls who once lived. And many believe, still live – if only on the other side.

orb

A ball of light that is often luminescent but not usually visible to the naked eye that is associated with all types of spiritual activity, but primarily with ghosts. Usually the orb is first seen when pictures are developed. Orbs are usually completely spherical but the insides may appear different. Some people see faces in them while others see rainbow effects. The orbs may be brighter or more dull, or changing in color. Orbs are the most fascinating areas of the paranormal as it looks as if we may be proving the existence of an energy of some spiritual nature. But a number of orbs can be ruled out as particles of dust enhanced by the flash on the camera. Many effects can cause orbs in pictures and some are not ghosts. However, since many orbs are captured in graveyards, battlefields and haunted areas do show orbs as a worthy area of study for ghost researchers.

orb trail or plasmoid

An orb trail is a ghost orb traveling at a high rate of speed that is faster than the camera can catch it, leaving a comet like tail sometimes appearing as a rod or rope.

ouija board

The Ouija is board game made fashionable in the early 20th Century, published by Parker Brothers that was devised specifically to communicate with spirits. Ouija boards emerged out of the popularity of the Spiritualist movement. They can be effective tools in contacting spirits, but can be spiritually treacherous and should never be used while alone nor allow children to play with them unsupervised –if at all.

paranormal

The science that goes beyond the normal and more appropriately, beyond what we can currently understand or evaluate through accepted scientific means. Therefore, because such things have not yet been proven as a normal part of life that we can adequately understand, nearly all of the subjects in this book fall under the topic of the "paranormal."

pentagram

The mystical five-pointed star that is usually connected with the religion of Wicca, although it's origins is considerably older. In fact, the pentagram can be found in most world religions – to Christians, the pentagram represented the five wounds of Christ on the cross. In Freemasonry it is called the "Seal of Solomon."

The five points of the star are associated with the five elements of fire, water, earth, air and ether – the Far East called it "Akasha" or void –the western world saw the fifth element as "Spirit." The pentagram during the Middle Ages was sometimes referred to as the Goblin Cross or a Witch's Foot.

phantom

A phantom is a mysterious ghost or presence that hides and shows no distinct personality or appearance. Phantoms are often associated with grand old homes and historical theaters, remaining cloaked in the shadows.

phouka

A Phouka is a type of Irish fairy that kidnaps people out of their beds at night to take them on a ride across the countryside. A Phouka often appears as a pale, gray hairy beast. Sometimes the Phouka appears as a big dog or a goat or a horse. The concept of the nightmare is very much related to the Irish Phouka Victims are usually tucked safely back inside their beds at dawn, in many ways similar to reports of alien abductions.

poltergeist

German for "noisy ghost" or "knocking spirit," poltergeists are fairly common in households but maybe are so subtle not all victims recognize them as so. Poltergeists are not actually a spirit of the dead or even a ghost, but they are often in the same area other types of hauntings are being reported. For the past 40 years or so, poltergeists have been linked to latent telekinetic abilities that some trouble teenagers have but go unrecognized. Poltergeists are usually sporadic and no special interference is needed since they usually go away on their own. Some poltergeists have been said to bring on slapping or punching, but it is doubtful this is truly a poltergeist. A poltergeist is fascinating to witness, albeit troubling, but is not usually harmful in any permanent way.

portal

A portal is an opening that somehow bridges the physical world with other dimensions such as the realm of ghosts, aliens and anything supernatural. Some believe portals are really "tears or rips" in our dimension giving us a clear spot to see through to alternate realities. Others believe a portal is a place where the atmosphere is ripe for spiritual forces to come together bridging the gap between the physical and spiritual realms.

place haunting

This is how most ghosts appear, through place hauntings. Spirits can attach themselves to anything, however, and this includes pieces of furniture or human beings. Generally, if you are called in on a haunting, you can almost be assured it is a place haunting or sometimes when a person is haunted, carrying parts of the spirit with him or herm usually attached to the human aura.

residual energy

Energy left over after as person has died, sometimes in a home or even on a piece of furniture associated with the deceased. This appears to be the kind of ghostly energies that manifest in spirit recordings where ghosts are seen to be doing the same task over and over again. What brings this about is not entirely understood, except perhaps some spirits have a greater focus in life that sticks to a spot, or something traumatic in life, such as a war or a battle has something to do with why these energies remain.

sacred site

An area that becomes spiritually powerful because of religious activity or for being located along Ley lines or vortexes as well as certain rites or rituals that brings about the appearance of spirits of various kinds.

seance

A séance is a gathering of people coming together with the explicit purpose of contacting spirits and higher beings. The séance room is normally darkened, only lit by candlelight, members of the séance circle will hold their hands, or place palms flat to the surface of the table in order to detect the energies. Sometimes rapping and knocking sounds will be heard and the candle flame might flicker erratically. One spirit medium is usually present, but the more the mediums, the more the merrier. Séances were practiced in the 19th Century Spiritualist movement and remain popular even to this day.

smudging

Smudging is a Native American ritual and rite where sage or cedar is burned, allowing smoke to rise in order to get rid or banish negative spirits and energies. There is no evidence that smudging helps that much in places fully in the throes of an intense haunting, but it smells nice and balances the energies in a room.

specter

A ghost that is typically transparent or ethereal or appears as veiled wisps. Most apparitions appear much as they did in life – often around age thirty or thirty-five – wearing clothing or having expressions by which they can be recognized. Specters have a more shadowy quality, lacking specificity.

spells

A spell is a ritual that is used to bring about a certain result that the spell-caster has in mind. Sometimes this is done through incantations, poems, magic herb bundles, potions and other ritual effects. Spells are a very ancient way of practicing magic by bringing about what you wish for through imagery, words and intent. Some witches write down their spells in a book that is called a "Grimoire."

spirit

The spiritual energies linked to a personality that survives death. When we consider spirits, we usually think of people but there are many types of spirits such as animals, elemental spirits of nature, guides, and angels. Spirit is a more generalized term for ghost. The word ghost is usually associated with a personality. A spirit is too, but not so clearly defined. For instance, if objects in the house start to move on their own accord, we might say our house has spirits. If we see an apparition that looks to be a person, we'll mostly likely say we saw a ghost.

spirit guide

A spirit guide is a spiritual being that watches over us in a loving and protective manner, sometimes since birth. Everyone has a spiritual guide. Some have several.

spirit recording

A spirit recording is an apparition that appears over and over again, repeating the same task, in the same mode of dress as if locked in time. Spirit Recordings are imprint ghosts without any consciousness to them. In other words, spirit recordings are not souls, and they are not even earthbound spirits. Spirit recordings do not inter-act with the living any more than a person would interact with a taped television show. Such spirit essences are somehow imprinted on space and time, usually through some feeling of tragedy or loss, but not always. Many spirit recordings are sounds, such as people talking, walking or women screaming. It is usually some high, emotive event that causes these residual energies to linger.

spiritualism

The religion based on the communications with spirits founded by the Fox sisters, in upstate New York in the 1840s. The teens claimed there was a ghost in their house after hearing a series of rapping and banging sounds in their bedroom. They soon began to communicate with the ghost by rapping on the walls themselves and were surprised that the spirit immediately knocked back. Through a code, they communicated with the ghost and found that it was a man murdered in the home and buried under the house. An investigation did yield the jawbone of a human beneath the foundation of the home.

The Fox sisters then traveled the world conducting séances and performing as famous mediums. The religion of Spiritualism soon began.

succubus

As a female counterpoint to the Incubus the Succubus attacks unsuspecting men while they sleep often by raping them. Often when the man opens his eyes, he sees a decrepit hag with stringy white hair and boils all over her body. This may well be the male version of the Night Hag, involving a mysterious function of the dreaming brain that causes a person to hallucinate the sexual assault by what, in essence, seems like a female demon.

talisman

A talisman is a charm used to ward off ghosts, bad luck and evil spirits. Most cultures have talismans and many people throughout the world would not leave their homes without their talismans. Gems and crystals are the most popular types of charms.

telekinesis

Telekinesis is an ability to move objects with the unconscious powers of the human mind. Poltergeists, for instance, are thought to be a form of telekinesis. Other evidence points to actual ghosts involved. We really don't understand any of these things completely. Any real evidence of telekinetic powers is rare because no one - including the one causing it - knows exactly when it is going to occur. For this reason, it will remain a mystery for most- left up to the very few who have the ability.

telepathy

Thought transference through psychic means, telepathy is possibly the most universal psychic talent of all. Many have picked up the phone to call a person only to get a busy signal and find out the friend has been on the phone attempting to call them at the same time. Others have had the experience of thinking about someone from the past all day long, only to encounter him or her on the street or meet the person in a store hours later. These are all forms of telepathy. Telepathy tends to be most strong among relatives and close friends.

trance

Sometimes referred to as the "alpha state," trances are a shift in consciousness that allows individuals to enter into and experience spiritual realms and other realities that are normally not achievable in a normal state. Such reveries are places where artists and poets receive inspiration and where spiritualists and psychics make connections with the spirit world. Trances are not as dramatic as they are portrayed in movies, books or television shows. In fact, watching television is just another form of a trance – it's just most of the time a television trance is not usually a very productive one.

ufo

A UFO is an unidentified flying object that is not necessarily a spacecraft from another world. Anything that flies through the air, and is witnessed then reported upon, without being explained away as something else, is referred to as a UFO.

ufology

Ufology is the study of UFOs and extraterrestrial life. Contactees, spacecraft, Men in Black, flying saucers, aliens and even crop circles (until we know otherwise) all fall under the category of Ufology.

unfinished business

Also called unsettled business, is a primary reason some ghosts appear. Something has been left over from, or not realized for them in life and needs to be completed. At times spirits with unfinished business appear sad or melancholy if the message is not received, or the living do not understand the message that the spirit attempts to convey. Often, when the message is received or understood, or the goal is realized, a ghost with unsettled business will not make any more appearances.

urban legend

The urban legend is a mysterious or shocking story that is told over and over again, is embellished, until it creates a reality all of its own. Although urban legends are typically bogus sometimes the spirit world responds to the telling of the tale and molds reality accordingly. In other words, if one tells that a house is haunted long enough, the attention will most likely attract a spirit looking for a home. Some spirits remain social and are lonely for human contact.

vortex or vortices

Like orbs, these are seen mostly in ghost photographs rather than by the naked eye. Vortices appear as tornado-like funnels in photographs and are usually are whitish in color, but pictures of them at the DeSales Heights nunnery came out as dark red. Many believe vortices are orbs in motion while others thing they may imply portals into other dimensions. No matter what the theory is— orbs, vortices and ectoplasm are the most common ways ghosts show up in photographs.

There are pictures of apparitions, the ghost as he appeared in life, but these are less common. It is much easier for a spirit to form of a ball of energy or tube.

wampus cat

A Wampus Cat is a type of Appalachian werecat, believed by locals to be part wildcat and part woman. The Wampus Cat has been associated with the power of witches in some parts, stemming from the beliefs of Irish-Scottish settlers in the Appalachian Mountains, while other sources trace the legend of the Wampus Cat to native Cherokee Indians.

wicca

A 20th and 21st religion of Witchcraft, it has older beginnings in the ancient Celts and other magical or earth-centered beliefs throughout the world. Wicca merges ancient pagan festivals and ideas with 19th, 20th, 21st Century occultism. Currently, Wicca is pretty much a nature religion. It is made up primarily of individuals who believe in and want to develop their psychic powers, they hold the changes of the seasons and the earth in reverence, wear capes, pentacles and other emblems, give psychic readings and advice, heal the sick with spells and herbs, etc. Wiccans give special meaning to places like Stonehenge and other sacred earth sites. One of the most famous witches of the later 20th Century was the English witch Sybil Leek, a talented ghost hunter and expert astrologer.

witch

An individual who has certain mystical powers that reaches beyond the usual psychic ability. Witches have the power to influence events or outcomes or affect changes outside of them themselves. This can be achieved through spells. At other times, witches achieve their desires just by concentrating on them.

A witch can be a man or a woman or a follower of Wicca, the pagan-based religion of Witchcraft. But one does not have to be a Wiccan to be a witch. Some modern witches believe they are born witches and that is the spiritual path intended for them to follow.

witching

Also called "water witching," this is a form of dowsing where metal rods are taken (or the forked branch of a certain tree) to divine the areas of not only water, gas, even telephone lines but also graves. In older cemeteries, areas of earlier graves may have been obfuscated, covered up or lost. A "witch" (someone talented in dowsing, often a senior citizen with the knowledge having been passed down) is contacted in order to check areas where houses are being built or new roads are planned to go through in order not to disturb older graves, perhaps long forgotten. Certain spirits are funny about such things, and do not want roads or houses disturbing their burial places. Others don't seem to care.

women-in-white

Women-In-White ghosts are believed to be grieving spirits tied here by a tragic event they have trouble letting go of. It is theorized that such unhappy forces are put into place after a murder, sudden death or a suicide has occurred, but Women-In-White ghosts can also be linked to the death of a child, an unhappy love affair and any number of events that would bring about extreme sadness or depression. These types of apparitions are reported on all over the world, but seem to be most common in the southern United States.

sources & suggested reading

Barker, Gray, They Knew Too Much About Flying Saucers (1956)
Barker, Gray, Silver Bridge (1970)
Cartrell, Connie, The Ghosts Of Marietta (1996)
Deitz, Dennis, The Greenbrier Ghost (1990)
Dougherty, Shirley, A Ghostly Tour of Harpers Ferry (publication date unknown)
Eno, Paul, A Face At the Window (1998)
Eno, Paul, Footsteps in the Attic (2002)
Frost, Gavin & Yvonne, Witch's Grimoire of Ancient Omens,
Portents, Talismans, Amulets and Charms (2002)
Guiley, Rosemary Ellen, Encyclopedia of Ghosts & Spirits (2000)
Sheppard, Susan & Roger, editors, The Derenberger Tapes, (2002)
Swick, Ray, An Island Called Eden: An Historical Sketch of Blennerhassett Island (1996)
Kaczmarek, Dale, Field Guide to Spirit Photography (2002)
Taylor, Troy, The Ghost Hunter's Guidebook: The Essential Guide
To Investigating Reports of Ghosts and Hauntings (2001)
Taylor, Troy, No Rest For The Wicked (2001)
Taylor, Troy, Field Guide to Haunted Graveyards (2003)
Keel, John, Haunted Planet (1999)
Keel, John, The Mothman Prophecies (1995)
Wamsley, Jeff & Sergent, Donnie, Jr., Mothman, The Facts Behind the Legend (2001)
Yeats, W.B., editor, Fairy and Folktales of Ireland (1888-1892)

websites of interest

Haunted Parkersburg Ghost Tours – www.hauntedparkersburg.com
West Virginia Hauntings – http://www.callwva.com/hauntings/calendar.cfm
Ghosts of the Prairie – http://www.prairieghosts.com/
Mothman Lives! – http://www.mothmanlives.com
New England Ghosts.com & Good Spirits Newsletter— http://www.newenglandghosts.com/
Parkersburg West Virginia, A Vintage Portrait—http://www.electricearl.com/parkersburg/
National Trust for Historic Places— www.nationaltrust.org/
Blennerhassett Hotel – www.blennerhassetthotel.com
Blennerhassett Island Historical State Park: http://www.blennerhassettislandstatepark.com/
Parkersburg/Wood County CVB – http://www.parkersburgcvb.org/
Haunted Parkersburg Ghost Hunters – http://www.zzzip.net/hpgh/
Mid-Ohio Valley Ghost Hunters
http://www.geocities.com/midohiovalleyghosthunters/movgh.html
MAJDA Paranormal Research Group – http://www.majda.net/index2.html
West Virginia Ghosts.com – http://www.wvaghosts.com/
West Virginia Penitentiary Online -- http://www.shadowsofmoundsville.com/

acknowledgements

Grateful acknowledgement is made to the following individuals and organizations that have assisted us in our quest of writing this book of West Virginia and Ohio Valley ghost and paranormal tales, as well as contributors to the Haunted Parkersburg Ghost Tours. Without your help, we could not have done this so easily. Thank you for your stories, your leads, and your help!

Doni and Robert Enoch, Ray Swick, Henry Burke, Simone Chiodini, Gary Wolfe, Danette Lemley, Peter Poulos, the Blennerhassett Hotel, Donna Smith, the Blennerhassett State Park, Chris Friend, Gwen Friend, Nellie Ruby and Marilyn, Mark and Kristall Chambers and their friend Wes, Lea Wilson, Virginia Lyons, Terry Headley, Chris Stirewalt, The Charleston Daily Mail, Bonita Nichols, Becky Johnson, Bonnie and Craig Wix, Lisa Collins, Ruby Ruppel, Abby Hayhurst, Artsbridge, United Bank, Jim Chapman, Mr. And Mrs. W.P. Chapman, Jr., Doug Posey and the Grind, Randall Hupp II, Jay Harmon, Brian Kesterson, Brent and Rae Ann Kesterson, Terry McVey, Betty Stewart, Terry Elliott, Greg Leatherman, Jeff Wamsley, Donnie Sergent, Jr., Sam Gault, Glenn Wilson, Regina Metzger, Barbara Orr, Sandra Moats-Burke, Jeanie Cochran, Norma Hartness, Becky Sheehy, Jean Grapes, Shelley Rusen, Walt Auvil, Kirk Auvil, Czar Bailey, Wendy Bailey Sims, John Sims, Gennie Sims, Rochelle Lynn Holt, the Dils Center, Dave Ruble, Millie and Forrest McNemar, Chanda Wright, Connie Richards, Kevin Moorehead, Scarlet Sheppard, Roger Sheppard, Betty Sheppard, Serenity Bookstore, TransAllegheny Books, Paul Eno, Tom Moore, Joyce Ancrile, Eleanor Lowe, Teresa O'Cassidy, Marsha Raiguel, West Virginia Public Radio, Paul LePann, the Parkersburg News & Sentinel, Don Staats, WTAP-TV, WCHS-TV, Goldenseal Magazine, West Virginia Writers Inc. Pearl Ward, Kevin Moorehead, Matthew Devore, Troy Taylor, Jim Dawson, Josh Danko, Yancy Roush, Jack See, John Frick, Jeff Stoll, Carla, David, Jimmy, Janet, Tyler, Ryan, Amanda, Ethan, and the woman who emailed us the wonderful ghost story from the Parkersburg Elks Club.

about the authors

Susan Sheppard is a native West Virginia and grew up just a few hills away from the first Mothman sighting. She is a writer and artist and the founder of the acclaimed Haunted Parkersburg Tours, as well as the annual Haunted West Virginia Conference. Her poetry and art have won numerous award and she also a popular television host in the area. She is the author of *The Phoenix Cards, A Witch's Runes, The Astrological Guide to Seduction & Romance* and now, *Cry of the Banshee.* Sheppard is the founder and remains the main tour guide for the popular Haunted Parkersburg Tours that take place each fall. She currently resides in Parkersburg with her family.

Richard Southall grew up in Ripley, West Virginia and has had articles featured in a number of magazines, such as Fate. Southall is the author of *How To Be A Ghost Hunter,* published by Llewellyn Publications. With Susan Sheppard, he is one of the early founders of the Haunted Parkersburg Tours. Richard Southall now lives in Charleston where he is pursung a degree.

about whitechapel productions press

Whitechapel Productions Press is a small press publisher, specializing in books about ghosts and hauntings. Since 1993, the company has been one of America's leading publishers of supernatural books. Located in Alton, Illinois, they also produce the "Ghosts of the Prairie" Internet web page and "Ghosts of the Prairie", a print magazine that is dedicated to American hauntings and unsolved mysteries. Whitechapel Press also owns and distributes the Haunted America Catalog, which features over 650 different books about ghosts and hauntings from authors all over the United States. Visit Whitechapel Productions Press online and browse through our selection of ghostly titles, plus get information on ghosts and hauntings, haunted history, spirit photographs, information on ghost hunting and much more. Visit the Internet web page at:

www.historyandhauntings.com

Or visit the Haunted Book Co. in Person at:

515 East Third Street
Alton, Illinois 62002
(618)-456-1086

Printed in the United States
34533LVS00013B/120